The Potioner

ISBN

The Potioner

Tommy L Barton

Thanks Lane

Table of Contents

Prologue

Two bald, muscular men in loose black tunics and billowing red pants stood at attention outside the ornately carved doors leading to the throne room. As Soles approached, they each opened one of the double doors and stood stiffly, one might even say nervously, as Soles entered the room. Stepping over the threshold, Soles's fear almost overwhelmed him when he saw Rex Almanon sitting on a plain, silver throne. The man wore a gold crown with silver horns jutting forward. The tips of the horns glowed like embers in a fire. Rex Almanon's countenance was completely hairless and strangely waxlike, forming a grotesque mask. A black silk robe with silver threads forming swirls, circles, and loops hung loosely on the small man's frame. The garment foiled any attempt to see Rex Almanon's posture. The last time they had met, Soles had been horribly disfigured.

Rex Almanon spoke to Soles in a clear bass voice. "You will lead a contingent of my men over the mountains. Once you have conquered the upstart kingdom, you will slay every male over the age of twelve. The women and children are then to farm food in our fields for Viridian."

Rex Almanon thought again of what would result from his carefully wrought plan. *Let the farmers' guild choke on it. I will bring monetary pressure to break the guild's back. It was easier in the old days to quell any dissention by ripping someone's spine out of their fleshy back. Now I must rely on pandering fools like this one. Look how stupefied and groveling this so-called villainous man standing before me is. At least I have taught him the price of defiance.*

"As you wish, Master," Soles said, looking at his feet. "I will start the process of gathering the weapons and transport."

"Idiot," Almanon said vehemently. He almost pointed out the fact that the people beyond the mountain could reverse engineer Viridian weaponry and technology if Soles failed. Thinking quickly, he said instead, "Viridian technology cannot take the cold of the mountains. The steam ignition chambers would contract and swell, making it too fragile for pressure." Soles nodded at this, apparently not noticing the slight hesitation in Almanon's response. Almanon continued, "I have acquired a traitor to lend you help in conquest. The Erimos people are barbaric, agricultural. Intelligence reports a mineral-starved kingdom. They use glass as weapons, no match for iron. The people are pathetic vermin, and you will make them slaves again." Though the Erimos people were like slugs, mindless and slow, Rex Almanon thought, they were at least tasty.

"As you wish, Master," whispered Soles. A slight tremor ran like a current over his entire body. Sweat pooled under his armpits. His eyebrows felt like sponges full of water. He waited for the order to be dismissed.

Rex Almanon said nothing, pleasantly pleased by the salty smell of the frightened man. The smell, an aphrodisiac in essence, tickled the olfactory cells in his nose. Rex Almanon's instincts screamed for a kill. Instead, he at last dismissed Soles with a curt nod.

Part One: The Soldier
Chapter One

The small armored herbivore's eyelid popped open, and the eye whirled in the socket before focusing on the huge horse. The minmi decided to move, since horse's hooves are hard, and anyway she felt hungry for a radish. Propping up her longer back legs first, she stood on all fours barely taller than a man. The protruding armor on the dinosaur could probably withstand the hooves of the horse, but the minmi, with its upper blunt beak and toothless lower jaw, usually ran from predators. Besides, the minmi had sunned enough in the open road. She swished her tail before wandering into a cornfield.

The covered wagon, wheels running in ruts, plowed down the road. The wagon was an assorted fair of brightly colored blue cloth stretching over the framework. A monstrous stallion, head held forlornly, pulled the wagon at a slow, methodical pace. Muscled, sleek, and seventeen hands high, he remembered being a war horse, not a draft horse. Perched on the buckboard, a man as round as he was tall sat dozing in the late summer sun. The reins were wound around his hands, and a large-brimmed straw hat covered his head. He wore a loose-fitting blue shirt with ruffles in the front and a pair of bright-green pants that clung to his thighs. He considered himself fashionable, but actually he could not color coordinate. A wagon wheel ran over a large rock, jolting the entire wagon and almost toppling the fat man. He woke with a start from whatever he had been dreaming about in his lazy doze.

"Ah, Cow. I told you to watch out for stones," he complained. He had nicknamed the horse Cow since any sincere war horse would hate the name, and this particular war horse never listened anyway.

Cow just shook his head and snorted in response.

The man peered around, looking for a landmark. All he could see was sunburnt corn. The fields stretched out over acres of flat land. In the distance to the right, a large barn poked out of the fields.

"Finally, a homestead. I hope they have something to eat other than corn," he said. He flicked the reins, thinking about roast goose, and headed in that direction.

The wagon shambled into the yard of the homestead. It was typical of every other farm in the Meadow Province; a house built like a shed, a silo to house the corn, and a barn to house the farm animals. A waif of a child ran into the house.

"Hello there! I have coins or potions for a little bit of hospitality!" the man called to the house as he clambered down from his perch and landed, a bit ungainly, to the earth.

A woman came out of the doorway with the child wrapped around her legs. "Potioner?" she asked.

"Why yes, healing potions, strength potions, and others," he said.

"I don't like Stem," she said, thinking about her lazy brother-in-law who was addicted to the substance. He always had to borrow coin.

"I do not traffic in Stem. My potions are for people who claim the bounty of the earth. For people who get kicked by horses or have a running fever."

She looked him over one more time. "My husband is in the field. You can unhitch your horse and stay in the barn until he returns. Supper will be in a couple of hours."

"Thank you," he said. He shook the reins and shuttled off towards the barn with the woman staring holes in his back.

A couple of hours seemed like an eternity for a man with such a large girth. He tried to keep his mind preoccupied by doing busywork. Feeding, watering, brushing, and checking the horse's hooves, all time told, took an hour. Cow acted like a prince during the manhandling, stoic and not taking notice of the man. Next, he decided to organize his potion case, deeming which would be likely to appeal to hardy folks. It didn't take him long. His potions were the one area of his life he kept in strict order. After organizing his potions, he still had almost an hour to wait. He decided to clean the wagon. He peered into the wagon at the clutter in every corner and decided to take a nap.

He dozed for the allotted time. Years of practice at the king's court had made the man an expert at dozing. Galas, speeches, and royal court drama were not times to be paying attention after years of doldrums. When he thought the time was just about right, he worked himself out of a pile of hay and steered himself towards the house.

A table made of plank wood with four chairs sat in front of the house. The Potioner thought to himself that he was definitely in the backwoods today and wondered if he should be worried. Commoners thought that Potioners were not to be trusted. It was reasonable, he supposed; any man that could drink a potion and tear down a house with his bare hands would be someone to be wary of. At the moment, the fellow could not quite recall anyone actually doing this, but people imagine a lot of things. The truth was a Potioner could do a lot worse. If common people really knew what a Potioner was capable of, they would be scared horribly.

A burly man not apparently frightened at the sight of him stepped out onto the porch. His clothes were ragged but well mended. "My name is Frank," he said. He made no move towards the table.

The rotund man replied, "Pleased to meet you, Frank. My name is Zen. I have wares you may be interested in, but I always pay coin for my suppers." Zen weighed his purse with his hand.

"And charge us an arm and a leg for potions," Frank said with suspicion.

"Some do, but my potions are the best—and free," Zen said to quell the uneasiness of the man.

"Why would a peddler not charge for potions?"

"The ingredients are free, so why shouldn't the potions be the same?"

"Then how do you make a living?" Frank believed in a hard day's work for pay.

"I only sell to the merchants in towns who meddle in potions," said Zen with patience.

"Hmph." Frank accepted this answer. "I hope you like catfish stew. That is all we have. I caught them in a pond nearby. We did season the stew with potatoes and carrots. You are more than welcome to join Susan and I." Frank said this a bit stiffly, but he gestured towards the chair nearest Zen, and his face showed that the welcome was genuine.

4

"The stew sounds delicious," replied Zen. "I would also be thankful of any words about these parts. I have not traveled this far south in years."

"We can talk over supper."

Frank insisted on describing the drought over the past couple of years. Farmers are always afraid of droughts. He said this was the worst drought he could remember. The crops were drying in the field. He planned on looking for work in town because his crop was a bust this year and last. Frank described a small town north of his homestead, a simple place called Durns. It was the usual backwoods town trying to hang onto civilization, but crime had escalated due to the corn dying in the fields. Frank said softly, "People do funny things when they can't feed their children."

Zen listened with half an ear but relished the catfish stew. Food was very important to Zen. A catfish stew was basic fare in any farming community, but Zen enjoyed every mouthful. The one thing in life that made Zen happy was food. Of course, he missed the extravagant dinners at the castle, but even catfish stew had a place in Zen's heart. All food had a place in Zen's heart. And gullet.

Frank asked an important question: "Dessert?"

"My, I cannot remember the last time I had dessert. So, yes please," said Zen.

"Normally we do not have dessert, but my wife picked up some bread from Stephen."

Zen was crestfallen. He had imagined a huge cake with frosting or an apple pie—anything but bread.

"We only get one slice apiece. Stephen sells the bread for a penny a loaf, but we don't buy it often," Frank said.

Frank's wife plopped a slice of bread on the table in front of Zen. The first thing Zen noticed was the golden-red color of the bread. He picked the bread up and smelled it. The bread smelled like cinnamon. Zen thought, *Why does the bread smell like cinnamon? Are these people trying to poison me?* Zen could think of half a dozen deadly potions made from cinnamon. He noticed the family ate the bread in small bites, savoring each one. Zen nibbled on the crust of the bread. The crunchy slice was delightful.

"This is incredible. Where did you get this?" asked Zen.

"Stephen makes it. No one knows how he makes it, but everyone buys his bread," said Frank.

"He cooks better than a woman," said Frank's wife with a sideways look at her husband, obviously thinking how nice it would be to have more help in the kitchen.

"Does he make other things this unique?" asked Zen.

"No, but all his food is good. He makes the best suppers anywhere," said Susan with a fond tone.

Frank answered part of Zen's question. "Stephen invites families over for supper every night." He obviously liked the boy. "He cooks the meal and does not ask anyone for coin in return. People bring the meat, and he prepares vegetables from his garden. It will be our turn in a couple days. I can't wait. No matter what he cooks, it is good. He doesn't show off; I think he is just lonely since his mother left."

"Did his mother teach him how to cook?" asked Zen.

"No," answered Frank shaking his head, "there is a story of Stephen's grandmother catching him frying an egg when he was four. They say she beat him silly because she thought he would catch the homestead on fire. Stephen told her he knew how to fry an egg because he had done it before. She told him to show her. Ever since that day, Stephen cooked the meals for the family with his grandmother. A pity really; Stephen is a strapping young man doing woman's work." Frank spoke with a hard conviction from a farmer's view of the world.

Susan rolled her eyes but said nothing.

"You know the king's head cook is a man," said Zen.

"Really? Well, Stephen could cook for the king. Anyway, you can sleep in the barn tonight. If you want some more of Stephen's bread, he lives outside of town. Ask anyone, and they can point it out to you." Frank waved his hand in the direction of the town.

"Well, thank you for dinner. I will see you in the morning then." Zen pushed his girth away from the table.

Zen left in the morning. He paid the family a five-ounce silver coin for dinner. Frank was not interested in potions but thanked him repeatedly for the coin. Just that one coin would be enough to pay for supplies for a year.

Zen decided he would like to meet this young prodigy, Stephen. Zen had no illusions; commoners had bland taste buds when it came to preparing food. Zen was more interested in how the young man managed to use a cinnamon concoction without poisoning the bread.

Chapter Two

Stephen's house was more like a shack built of old timber, but everyone in town knew exactly where to find it. As Cow pulled the wagon down a dusty, cobblestoned lane, the first thing Zen noticed was the garden that completely surrounded the log cabin. Vegetables abounded with a number of different herbs in neat little plots. A pump well on the side of the abode looked out of place in the green leafy garden. Zen noticed he could distill at least three different healing potions from the herbs in the garden.

A young man walked around the back corner of the home. He was shirtless, and dirt covered his chest; the teenager had obviously been working in the garden. He had a small frame for a young man, but every muscle seemed to have been chiseled out of stone. He smiled and waved at Zen as if every stranger was welcome.

Zen pulled on the reins to stop the wagon. "Hello, Stephen," he called.

"I am sorry, but I do not have a place for your horse," said Stephen, wiping his dirty hands on his pants.

"I came for a visit, not a prolonged stay. Cow here is likely to be happy standing still rather than pulling the wagon. I came to ask if I could join you for supper this evening. Everyone says you are the best cook in town."

The young man smiled, obviously proud of his skills at cooking, but cast his eyes down, not wanting to accept the compliment. "You are in luck. The Thomas family killed a deer this morning. I am sure they would not mind sharing their fortune with you this evening. Come back at dusk, and we will have a fine supper."

"I would appreciate that," Zen said. He flipped the reins and continued down the lane.

Zen was perturbed. Two of the herbs he had spotted were not used in any cooking recipe he could think of even with his considerable knowledge of food. The cinnamon bread itself was not poisonous, but cinnamon was a catalyst for various poisons. He had spotted oregano in the garden. Oregano was the hardest damn thing to keep alive, much less have a whole plot of the stuff. This young man was turning out to be a mystery. *I hate mysteries,* he thought, but he knew he would have to unravel it.

After pulling the wagon into Durns square, Zen procured a hayloft in the smith's barn for a room in town. The town was so small, it did not even have an inn for sleeping overnight. Zen was not happy about leaving his horse and goods in the smith's barn. The smith had the bloodshot eyes associated with using too much Stem. Zen considered that a smith would need a lot of stamina to stay in business, but Stem always caught up with you in the end. Zen decided he needed to conduct a little business. If this small town had a merchant who dabbled in potions, he could make his living.

He found a small shop in town that could buy some of his potions. The place was well stocked with things a farmer needed on a daily basis. Tackle, farm implements, and seed were in neat berths. The shop even had a small grocery store for staples such as honey, sugar, and flour. The proprietor of the store sized Zen up before he had taken two steps inside the door.

"Selling, not buying," the proprietor said.

"Is it that obvious?" replied Zen with a smile.

"No, but strangers in town can be easily spotted. And you do not look like a farmer."

"Well, I am a salesman. I have several potions you may be interested in."

"Really? I cannot remember the last time a Potioner made it this far south. Listen, I need things for fevers, cuts, and, if you have it, broken bones. I cannot sell anything else to these farmers. Do you also have Stem?" he asked cryptically. Most men who sold Stem were nefarious characters.

Why do they always want Stem? Zen shouted in his head. *Because it sells, dolt.* He lied and said, "I am currently without any Stem, but the rest is not a problem."

"Even the broken bones potion?" asked the proprietor anxiously. The potion was expensive and hard for some Potioners to make.

"Yes, even that potion. But it is not cheap."

Zen's haggling powers lacked skill. He felt the proprietor made the best deal for himself, but at least now Zen had some extra coin. He decided to visit a tavern. Zen thought, *even farmers drink, right?*

Zen walked into the tavern, and conversation stopped. He fingered the potion in his pocket. Everyone turned back to their friends, and Zen continued to walk toward the bar. Shabby little place. Cheap tables and chairs. The only thing worth coin was the large oak bar against the back wall. Oak was expensive, even in the city.

"Honey beer and some fresh bread if you have any." Zen never missed a chance to eat.

"The bread was baked this morning. With the beer, it will be two pennies." The barkeeper did not move until Zen paid him.

Zen stayed at the bar and sat on a stool. Eating the bread with swigs of beer, he listened halfheartedly to the conversations nearby. Most were about the drought, men complaining about their livelihood. Crime also seemed to be a topic. Several individuals spoke about needing a sheriff for the town. Their counterparts all complained it would raise taxes. After finishing the beer and bread, Zen decided a nap in the hayloft would be more interesting than listening to the farmers.

"You're a big boy," said a sneering voice.

Zen slipped a potion out of his pocket.

"I bet you need a lot of money to be so fat," the man said directly behind Zen.

Zen tipped the small vial to his lips. Zen hated that he was going to feel drowsy and foggy-headed later.

"How about you buy us all a beer and bread," said the man as he laid his hand on Zen's shoulder.

Zen reached up and grabbed the man's hand, crushing it with his own. The man screamed in a high pitch and fell to his knees. Tears started cascading down his face while he blubbered. Zen stood over him, broke two fingers in the robber's hand, and then let go.

As he strode to the door, Zen said, "If someone wants to buy a potion to heal his hand, I will be at the smith's."

The man screamed, "Damn Potioners!" He continued to cry while holding his broken hand.

Zen exited the tavern rather quickly before someone decided they wanted retribution. He slowed his walk to the smith's. He knew a nap was out of the question now until the potion lost some of its potency. Zen had used a potion meant for quick strength, which meant it also burned out quick. He just hoped when he did sleep, he did not sleep past dusk. He was looking forward to a nice meal. Zen did not worry about someone bothering him while he slept this afternoon. Cow could handle any farmer.

* * *

The sun had just set when Zen walked up to Stephen's home. Zen could hear laughter emanating from the house; the high-pitched squeals of children and the deep, rolling laughs of adults. Zen could only smile as he knocked on

9

the door. It opened and bright light poured into the yard, temporarily blinding Zen.

"Oh, hi Zen," said Stephen. Zen's name had already circulated through the village gossips. "Come in, come in. The party has already started." He opened the door wide and beckoned Zen into the house. "This is the Thomas family. The big man there is Barny, his wife Melinda, and their kids Jack, Carl, and Sarah. This is Zen, everyone."

Zen grinned and walked into the light. There was a table in the middle of the room heaped with food. Roasted deer on a wooden platter, a bowl of mashed potatoes, steamed broccoli and carrots, and a platter of sliced tomatoes, all surrounded by the farmer's family sitting at the table. Tucked in the corner was a single cot, and one wall was devoted to the kitchen. Sparse, but the room was clean.

"Pull up a chair and dive in. Sorry we did not wait, but we really have not even started," Stephen said.

The children chattered, obviously enraptured by so much food. The adults just smiled and savored the flavors. Zen piled a plate high with goodies, nodded all around, and started eating. The roasted deer was seasoned with rosemary leaves. The potatoes were mashed with bits of garlic. The broccoli and carrots were flavored with parsley. The tomatoes were slightly salted. Zen could not remember such a fine dinner in a long time. Commoners did not season their food. They thought the herbs used in potions would somehow make them sick. Only the very best cooks in the capitol painfully experimented to find the right flavors.

"Stephen, I must admit this is delicious," said Zen.

"Thank you. You should also thank Barny. He killed the deer. It has been hard to find deer since the drought," said Stephen.

"Barny, only the best hunters can kill a deer without tarnishing the meat with adrenaline," said Zen.

"It was actually a stroke of luck. I was hunting rabbits at the time, and there it was," said Barny. "I hate to ask, but one of my little ones has been running a fever the past couple of days. Do you have anything that can help?"

"Yes, as a matter of fact I do. Come by the smithy's tomorrow if the fever has not broken. After tonight, I would not dream of charging you for the potion."

"I will send my oldest one in the morning," said Barny.

"Not too early. After this meal, I plan on sleeping like a babe myself," said Zen.

They laughed and continued eating. The night was wholesome, the food was good, the conversations light and friendly. Zen particularly liked Stephen. He had a quality of sharing everything, even conversations with the children. He cleaned up after dinner, talking the whole time like a barkeep, always injecting a good point in the conversation.

As they were all leaving, it started to rain. Everyone stood in the cool rain, thinking that maybe this was the end of a two-year drought. Zen and the Thomas family said their goodbyes and left with a sense of better times to come.

***

Zen missed the hailstorm that came in the darkest hour of the night. Keeping to his word, he slept like a baby. Thunder did awaken him in the earliest part of dawn. He stood at the barn door looking out at the torrential downpour. He noticed the dawn grew in a greenish tinge of light. He thought in alarm, *Not that.* He knew a green dawn signified a tornado.

The air became perfectly still. The rain abruptly stopped. He could hear a fly buzzing in the back of the barn. Motes in the irregular sunbeam that came through the crack between the slats of the barn floated gently. Zen's sphincter tightened. He knew everything became perfectly still and deadly quiet before a tornado. The winds picked up speed and slammed the barn door shut. He retreated to the back of the barn and held onto the horse, placing his hand on Cow's brow. The horse trembled in anticipation. The wind screamed through cracks in the barn, stirring dust into a heavy cloud. If the horse had not been trained well, it would have bolted out of the barn. The wind howled in a concerto. Zen imagined a fabled dragon bugling. The sound grew enormous, then it was gone.

Zen could not see. Dust covered his countenance. He stumbled over to the trough and splashed dirty water on his face. He sagged against the trough, coughing up clumps of dirt. Finally, he sipped some of the tepid water to clear his throat. He sat up, considering what to do next. He did not want to look out the barn door. He knew the tornado had barely missed him.

It had wreaked havoc on the western part of town. As Zen walked outside, he could see the path of the tornado had dismantled several homes. The general store and tavern were demolished. Winds had damaged most of the remaining buildings. Twelve people had been killed in the tornado, including the Thomas family. Several people were injured with minor contusions. Either victims were in the path of the storm and died, or their homes held together in the peripheral winds. Stephen's house was a pile of sticks.

Zen followed the path of destruction carrying his potion case. He wanted to help if at all possible. Buildings and homes were ripped from the foundations. Trees were felled. Broken pottery, toys, furniture, and all manner of things littered the ground. He was overwhelmed by the destruction. The tornado seemed to have gouged the earth. The cobblestone lane was mostly obliterated, with only scattered stones remaining. As Zen followed the path, he could only think of a young man who was so generous and who did not own anything of monetary value. Zen saw men picking through the debris of Stephen's house.

"What are you doing?" shouted Zen. "The boy was a pauper."

"Charles said he heard something," the man shouted back. "What are you doing here? What do you want?"

"I just want to help," answered Zen sheepishly.

"Well come help, but I just don't know what to expect." The man turned over the front door atop the pile.

"He's here," shouted a man. He threw a board aside while uncovering Stephen's body.

Zen rushed over. The boy was in bad shape. Zen could see that his leg was broken. His breathing was ragged. His face was bruised purple. Shrapnel had lacerated the side of his body.

"You," said Zen, pointing at a man. "Hold him still. I have to set his leg."

"What good is setting his leg? He is bleeding all over the place."

"Just hold him. I can't give him a strong potion without setting his leg. The leg will mend poorly if not set."

Zen wrenched the leg. Stephen only gasped, too weak to even move. Zen turned over his potion case. On the bottom was a hidden latch. Zen pressed it, and a hidden compartment was revealed. In the cache, a dozen vials were attached to the bottom of the case. He carefully chose a vial.

He held the back of Stephen's head in his hand. "Come on, boy. You must swallow the potion. You hear me? Swallow the potion."

Zen parted Stephen's lips with the rim of the vial then poured the contents into his mouth. Stephen swallowed once automatically as something blocked his airway. Zen sat back and smiled. The potion took immediate effect. Bloody holes closed. His breathing evened out. The bruises cleared. Stephen thrashed for a moment as if he feared being caught in the tornado.

"Calm down now, son," said Zen. "You are all right. You are going to sleep now. And when you wake up, I promise you a bit of pie."

Stephen turned his head and said, "Mama, it was so loud." He went immediately to sleep.

"Hey, you didn't sell me any of that stuff," said the shopkeeper.

"Yeah," answered Zen with confidence, "and you won't get any either. Just feel lucky you were not in your shop when the tornado hit. Now give me a hand. Let's carry him to the smithy's hayloft."

The shopkeeper and Zen carried Stephen to the barn. After the shopkeeper left, Zen stashed his case in the wagon. He knew it would only be a matter of time before someone tried to steal it.

"Well, it was a nice town while it lasted," Zen said to Cow. He knew he could not stay now, but he wanted to at least wait until the boy woke up. It should only take a couple of hours.

Zen paid the smith his rent for the past couple of days. In town, he was able to scrounge up supplies for his expedition. The prices were high for the goods since the tornado had devasted the town, which needed time to heal. Already men had removed the wreckage on the west side of Durns. The men salvaged boards from the buildings and stacked them neatly next to the carnage of houses. Excess timber, shards really, burned in bonfires. The town would rebuild, but the loss of so many close friends seemed overwhelming for this sleepy burg.

Zen walked into the barn. Stephen was brushing Cow's hide. He turned to Zen and smiled.

"Cow does not trust most men," said Zen.

"Lucky for me, I am not yet a man. He is a beautiful horse," said Stephen cheerfully.

"Yes. Have a seat. I need to check you over. The potion I gave you should have completely healed you, but you never know."

"I feel fine. My leg's a little sore, but other than that I feel like I slept for days." Stephen sat on the edge of the water trough.

"Well, what are your plans?" asked Zen as he peered into Stephen's eyes.

"Plans? What do you mean?"

"There is nothing left of your home. The garden was destroyed, the house a pile of dead wood after the storm hit. The vandals have probably toted everything of value off." Zen patted Stephen on the cheek as if to say everything was going to be all right.

"I was thinking about going with you," said Stephen quietly.

"Me? I—"

"Listen," interrupted Stephen, "I am not stupid. That potion you gave me was powerful." Stephen looked at his toes. "I just want to learn. I want to be able to help people, like you have done." Stephen looked up. "You are not a charlatan. The potion proved it."

"Well, most potion makers are not charlatans. But it is true; the recipes I have are unique. My family has been making potions for a long time in the company of the most powerful."

Zen sat down on a milking stool. He confessed his past to Stephen with a slight bend, erring on the side of caution. He told Stephen about being the king's personal potion maker. For generations, Zen's family had been the Potioners for the royal family. Each generation passed down the recipes they discovered over time. Father to son, the secrets were passed. Zen had no children though; he preferred the company of a roasted duck to a comely maiden.

More than two years before, Zen had passed his position as the king's Potioner over to a family equally worthy of the king. Zen did not pass on the secrets of his personal family potions, but Zacadam Maximum's family history went back almost as many generations as Zen's lineage in making potions. Zacadam had an infant son, an heir in line to be the king's next generation of Potioner, unlike Zen, who had no children.

Zen told Stephen that he had wanted to increase the recipes of his family's potions. So, he traveled to try to find something new and worthy of a new potion. Zen did not reveal to Stephen his own, personal family tree. The news would surface later and be less overwhelming for the boy.

"What is your surname?" asked Stephen.

"Zenith Alexander. What is yours, boy?" reaching out to shake Stephen's hand.

Stephen grasped his hand and said, "Stephen Bishop."

"Bishop, huh? I won't hold that against you if you don't hold drinking against me."

"So, can I come?" asked Stephen.

"Harness the horse," said Zen, thinking *What am I getting into?* He decided to wait and see.

Stephen harnessed Cow. He spoke softly to the huge horse, rubbing his flanks as he hitched him to the wagon.

The wagon emerged from the barn and headed out of town. A fat man steered while a young man waved at the townspeople. The wagon pulled onto the dirt road headed north.

"Where are we going next?" asked Stephen excitedly.

"I have some questions for some old tutors. We are going to Stone University." Zen smiled and slapped the reins. Cow only flinched without picking up the pace. Cow would decide if they needed to go faster.

Chapter Three

Zacadam Maximum stared at the crystal growing on a string which dangled in a beaker full of a deadly viscous solution. Though the crystal took a week to form on the surface of the string in the solution, it took less than ten minutes to mix the inert ingredients in a glass graduated cylinder. White and crystalline, the gob had to be crushed into smaller pieces to work. Ground down, the crystal looked and tasted like table salt. The mixture of certain fungi made the "salt" deadly over time. *Too slow,* thought Zacadam. *I want the crown now.*

"Tilly!" he shouted.

"Yes, sir," the page said, entering the room.

"Here, take the salt, pepper, and basil leaf to the king's chef. And tell him take it easy on the seasoning. I am tired of supplying him with ingredients." He handed the spices to Tilly. *It is too easy,* he thought. *The fools trust me to supply seasoning for the king's supper. If they only knew, they would cut my head off. But I still have my head.*

Zacadam sat at his cluttered desk in his laboratory. The room was filled with glass jars of mushrooms growing at different stages. The room was chaotic, with paper strewn upon the floor and chairs haphazardly placed. The room was the reflection of a sick mind.

He felt impatient. The king's health declined every day, but not fast enough for Zacadam. "I should murder him in his sleep," said Zacadam softly. He took a deep breath and thought about the plan. It always made him feel better.

His cohorts had promised him the crown when the kingdom disintegrated into chaos. Already the kingdom was at a breaking point. His collaborator, Rex

Almanon from Viridian, for two years had been changing the weather patterns of the kingdom. The Meadow Province was dry now, not producing any crops. Famine would sweep the kingdom. Refugees were driving inland, as Rex Almanon had sent hurricanes blasting the coast for the past two seasons. People could not afford to rebuild even if they wanted to. It was enough to send the kingdom into disarray. The dukes were clamoring for more support from the king just to feed their populace. Men, women, and children were becoming beggars, thieves, and outlaw highwaymen. The kingdom was ripe for the picking.

When the king died, Zacadam would step into his place and prophesize help from beyond the Barrier Mountains. Then Rex Almanon would send supplies over the mountains, which Zacadam would use to rebuild the kingdom. Finally, Zacadam would be all powerful, his allegiance to the king over the mountain slowly dissipating over time. Almanon was not the only one who could be devious.

Rex Almanon had sent an emissary to Zacadam a couple of years ago, outlining the plan. Zacadam had known nothing about Rex Almanon or his man. No one had ever crossed the Barrier Mountains and come back to talk about the kingdom beyond. Everyone in Erimos thought the world ended at the Barrier Mountains. Only a few men alive knew what was past the mountains, and Zacadam was not one of them. Proof of the kingdom over the mountains was a bar of gold given to him. No one in the Erimos kingdom would have wasted the fortune in gold.

"I will be king someday," said Zacadam under his breath. He relished the idea.

"Sir," said Tilly, quietly knocking on the door.

"What?"

"There is someone hear to see you."

"Fine, send them in," said Zacadam. He pushed his chair back and tried to look nonchalant. He wore a wrinkled and dirty black robe. The cloth clung to his skinny frame. His pale face was all angles. Even his mother would not have called him handsome.

A man walked through the door dressed in black leather with red emblems emblazoned upon the chest. His shins and forearms were protected by steel plates. The hobnail heels of his black, knee-high boots were clacking on the stone with every step. A mask of leather, completely hiding his face, molded

16

to the contours and planes to easily facilitate sight. A long sword was belted to his hip.

"Are you insane?" whispered Zacadam, looking over the man's shoulder and out into the hall.

"Yes, but that is really not the question," answered the man.

"You cannot sport a sword within this kingdom. There are only six iron swords in the entire kingdom: five for the dukes and one for the king. Already you have marked yourself as an outsider. The scullions in the kitchen are probably gossiping about you right now," moaned Zacadam as he ran to close the door.

"It does not matter; the time has come. The plan must be accelerated today. I am here to advise you and protect you. Kill King Norman Alexander of Erimos, Zacadam."

"Now?" he blanched and asked. "But what about the plan? The kingdom is in turmoil but not at its knees. How can I be its savior?" His voice wavered. The thought of actually killing the king made his chest tremble with nervous energy.

"Not savior, usurper. I will help, and no one will harm you."

"Usurper?" The coward in him cringed, but his power-hungry ego screamed in joy. "When?" asked Zacadam under his breath as he sat back down in his chair.

"Tonight. My troops are massing at present. You will murder him in his sleep before the assault."

"Me? Why can't you do it?" asked the cowardly man in a high-pitched voice.

"There is always a price for power—either him or you." The man in the mask waited for an answer with a hand on his hilt.

Zacadam slumped in his seat. "I will do it tonight. I will use some pretense of a healing potion. It will work. The king's health has deteriorated, so they will let me see him. I will just use a poison instead. He will never wake up in the morning."

"Then the assault will begin in the morning. I would find a place to hide until it is all over." The black-leather-faced man turned and strode out the door.

"Tonight, one moment of bravery for a lifetime of power. I can do it," whispered Zacadam while staring at the closed door. His hands shook.

Chapter Four

Zen stirred the vegetables in the clay pot over a fire. He stood upright, stretching the cramp in his lower back. The sun was setting, and long shadows lay over the campsite. The fire cheerfully heated the stew. Next to the fire were a couple of stools, so Zen sat down. He reached behind him and picked up a sword lying on the ground. He set it on his knees and waited for Stephen to return.

Stephen clamored out of the woods. He must have stomped on every twig or branch on his way out. A sack in one hand and a staff in the other, Stephen stepped into the circle of firelight. He sat down next to the old man.

"I could only find one of the mushrooms you described to me, and I also found some mold growing on a tree," said Stephen.

"Well, that is a start," said Zen. "Let me see the mold."

Stephen handed Zen the bag and leaned over to stir the pot. Zen reached into the bag and produced the mold. Stephen had cut the bark from the tree, leaving the mold intact. White and powdery, it glistened in the firelight.

"Why did you collect the mold when you were supposed to be looking for mushrooms?" asked Zen.

"The mold looked important and unnatural," said Stephen.

"Good instinct. This particular mold is hard to find. Mixed correctly, it will make hyper-thinking last for hours."

"Hyper-thinking?"

"Hyper-thinking can find solutions to any problem, with inherent knowledge of a subject. The clues seem to fall into place. Not many people use the potion for hyper-thinking, but it does have its place. One reason is that it induces vomiting almost immediately."

"Do all potions have side effects?"

"Yes, in some varying degree. The better potions have fewer side effects. The talent of a Potioner can be attributed to how few side effects are produced by his potions. Enough about potions; we have talked enough during the wagon ride. Have you seen one of these before?" asked Zen, holding up the sheathed sword.

"Only at a distance," answered Stephen, looking intently at the scabbard.

"Well, here, unsheathe the sword carefully. The edge is very sharp."

Stephen stood and did as Zen asked. The sword seemed to glow white hot in the firelight.

"Why is it glowing?" asked Stephen fearfully.

"The light from the fire reflects off the glass."

"Are all swords milky-white glass?" Stephen experimentally waved the sword over the fire.

"Again, in varying degrees. The better the sword, the whiter the color within it. It is extremely sharp and very durable. That sword was given to me by a duke. His smith was renowned for making extremely fine swords."

"I have seen our smith make things out of glass to use on the farms, but not swords." Stephen stared at the blade, which was three feet long and three inches wide. A crossbar at the hilt was tubular, with twisted glass ends protruding outward to protect the hand. The leather wrapped around the hilt felt supple. He ran his thumb over the edge, slicing a sliver of his skin off.

"Smiths have been working with glass for centuries. In fact, fifty years ago a smith made five swords for the king. They call them the Diamond Swords. Unlike the white swords made today, the five swords were almost completely transparent. The man died before telling anyone his incredible secret for making the nearly invisible swords."

"Will you teach me how to use a sword as well as how to make potions?" asked Stephen, looking over the edge of the sword at Zen.

"No, I do not know how to wield a sword. It is more a status symbol than anything else. Very few men know how to use a sword, and they are either employed by the king or his dukes." Zen stirred the pot of vegetables.

"Is it true the king and his dukes all have swords made of iron?"

"Yes. Those swords are more decorative than functional. They displayed wealth for the rulers."

Stephen handed the sword back to Zen and sat down on the stool. "I can't imagine that much iron."

"The greedy fools have more than iron. They also have coffers of gold and silver."

"Why is that?"

"A long time ago, the king decided commoners were only allowed iron as currency. The aristocrats stockpiled gold and silver. Gold is a shiny yellow metal, and silver is a shiny grey metal. Silver is still mined today, but very little is found. No gold has been found in years. The ruling class jockeys for position depending on their wealth of gold and silver. Political intrigue harkens the growth of wealth. I believe it to be a silly game, something to keep them busy instead of fighting for land."

"The stew is ready," said Stephen. As they sat in silence enjoying the vegetable stew, he tried to imagine wealth. He could not wrap his mind around the idea of hoarding gold or silver. He decided to turn his mind to more practical thoughts about potions. "Why can't you mix potions like speed with strength?"

"Potioners have tried but failed. If a Potioner can improve on one recipe in his repertoire, he has succeeded for his generation. The book of recipes is then passed on to his son." Zen slurped broth off a wooden spoon.

"Can I see the book?" asked Stephen while cradling his bowl in his hand.

"Later, when you have learned the necessary ingredients to make potions. Besides, you could not read the book even if I showed it to you. Each book is ciphered. Petty jealously between Potioners keeps each family's book a secret. Enough questions for the day; I am turning in. Please clean up and turn in yourself, because we leave at daybreak. I want to arrive at Stone University in a couple of days." Zen handed his empty bowl to Stephen then climbed into the back of the wagon to sleep.

Stephen carried the dishes and spoons to a small stream just off their campsite for rinsing. After shaking them dry, he repacked the dishes. He picked up around the campsite and then turned to his bedroll. He could not believe the things he had learned in the past couple of days. It daunted him how little he knew about the world. The conversations with Zen had opened his mind to so many possibilities. The talks about ingredients for potions came easy to him, as he was already familiar with so many different ingredients. Things like mushrooms, herbs, and molds were all part of his past. Berries, bark, flowers and rocks were a mystery, but he decided he would learn as much as possible. He fantasized about inventing something totally new while he fell asleep.

***

The next morning, Cow pulled the wagon down the dusty trail. Zen described rock strata to Stephen, and they discussed different types of rocks and their properties. Zen taught him the scratch method: harder rocks, such as granite, cannot be scratched by shale, and shale cannot be scratched by limestone. To determine the type of rock, color and weight can also be a clue. As for potions, the most difficult rocks to ground into dust determined the power of a potion. Potioners typically knew a few rock potion recipes, but most were the result of generations of specialization in the field. Family history was important in establishing a talent for rock potions. The Gregorous family was well thought of for making the best strength potions, which they made with crystals found in deep, extremely hot caves.

"Crystals? How do you crush a crystal?" asked Stephen.

"I wish I knew. The Gregorous family cornered the market on strength potions. They mine crystals and produce hundreds of potions a day. But don't be put out—they found their niche. I would never drink a Gregorous healing potion, because they lost the art of the other disciplines. Hey, are those bluebells?" Zen pulled on the reins to stop the wagon. "Jump down and retrieve the blue flowers on the side of the road."

Stephen dismounted the wagon. "What is so special about bluebells?"

"Well—"

"Don't move!" shouted a man stepping from behind a tree. "And you—off the wagon!"

"Sir, we don't have anything," said Stephen as he slowly backed away.

"I said don't move!" The man shook a knife in Stephen's direction. "Get off the wagon, fat man."

Zen wrapped the reins around the brake clutch. "I am coming down. You do not need to do this. If you are looking for money, I have some here." He produced a pouch as he climbed off the wagon.

"Throw the pouch on the bench, and both of you slowly back away from the wagon." Dressed in rags, the man looked desperate, which made him more intimidating.

Stephen darted a look at Zen. Zen shook his head slightly. Both of them stepped away from the wagon. The man hastily clambered up the side of the wagon and grabbed the reins. He shouted at the horse, but the horse did not move.

"What the hell is wrong with the horse? Is this a trick?" asked the man stabbing the knife in their direction.

"He will not move without permission," said Zen.

"Well, give him permission!" shouted the man.

"You have to do it," said Zen calmly. "You have to talk to the horse."

"I did!"

"No, you have to talk to the horse calmly."

The man jumped down from the wagon. "You do not know how to treat a horse." The man walked to the front of the wagon and roughly grabbed the horse's bit, jerking it to the side.

Zen quickly shouted, "Strike!"

Cow reared and struck with his hooves. One crushed the man's head, and the other struck his chest, flinging him down the road.

"Is he dead?" asked Stephen, holding his stomach and feeling a little sick. The man's head had spouted blood.

"Yes. Cow is a war horse. He was trained to kill infantry. Here, help me drag the man to the side of the road." Zen picked the man up under the shoulders.

"Shouldn't we bury him?" asked Stephen as he grabbed the man's feet.

"No. He would not have buried us," answered Zen as they threw him into the bushes.

They climbed back aboard the wagon and rode in silence down the wide trail. Stephen had never seen a dead man, much less touched one. He could not control his breathing; he was panting like a dog.

"Stephen, think about the rock strata."

Stephen's breathing slowly returned to normal. "Have you ever killed a man?"

"No, but it is a long walk to Stone University. Without supplies, we would not have made it. The kingdom is becoming desperate. I must know why. Hopefully, the university will have answers. Listen, I will tell you what is so important about bluebells."

Zen started a lesson about the properties of flowers. Stephen only half listened, not being able to concentrate. All he could see was the man's face exploding. He was only able to focus when Zen finally told him the property of flowers was pyrokinesis; the power to control fire.

They made camp at dusk. Zen brought out the cook pot and motioned for Stephen to go into the woods. His duty was to find three types of flowers that grew in this part of the country. Stephen did not want to go out alone, but he grabbed his staff and stepped off the trail. After an hour, the tranquility of the woods finally soothed Stephen's mind. He could no longer picture the man's horrific face. He returned to camp only to find Zen snoozing, the pot bubbling, and the horse munching on tall green grass. Stephen let Zen sleep.

Stephen wandered around the camp as Zen slept soundly. A pterodactyl perched on the top of a tree above the camp contemplated swooping down and grabbing the tasteful morsel of human flesh. Lucky for the humans, the pterodactyl had just finished its dinner. Its claws still dripped fresh blood from its latest kill. The predatory dinosaur decided instead to glide on the upper currents of the wind. With one beat of its leathery wings, the pterodactyl launched itself into the sky.

***

Zen woke Stephen before dawn with the smell of porridge. Zen wanted to be on the trail as early as possible. He had decided that if he pushed Cow hard on flat stretches of the dirt road, they might reach Stone University by nightfall.

Zen spent the day reminiscing about Stone University; his favorite professors, the hard lessons, and the great food. Stephen's mood slowly lightened with the telling of practical jokes, fond memories, and descriptions of delightful meals at Stone University.

In between stories of food and fun as described by Zen, Stephen could see the antics of boys at Stone University: a university dedicated to enriching the lives of the privileged. Classes in mathematics, scholastic reading, history, and Zen's favorite, food preparation, were lovingly taught by old, wise gentlemen. War history, a thing of the distant past, was considered extracurricular, as were the arts, such as poetry, music, and painting.

The campus itself sprawled over the countryside. Dormitories were called Wagon Wheels, each housing forty students. A circular building with a courtyard in the middle, the dormitory was broken into rooms shared by four students. A common area, small library, and laundry room were housed in each dormitory, and five dormitories were grouped together. The buildings for classrooms surrounded the dormitories, and on the outskirts of the campus, the staff and professors lived in small houses. Dotted amongst the buildings, small structures were full of support staff, as well as food, medical, and open range markets for the students. A place to grow and entertain the minds of young adults, the university was considered a rite of passage for some few lucky men and women.

As the day progressed, Zen's face sported a boyish grin. He spoke in a loud, high voice and gestured wildly as he remembered good times and told tall tales. The wagon pulled around a bend, and Zen stood looking for his boyhood dreams, only to find a field full of horses and men shouting commands.

Chapter Five

The captain of Rex Almanon's brigade zigzagged through the tents pitched outside of the capital city of the kingdom Erimos. The campaign was not going well. The traitor had reported that the capital, Sires, held only five hundred decorative soldiers. Rex Almanon's brigade outnumbered them three to one. Captain Steg expected a rout with so few men guarding the only real fortification of a proper castle. The damn Erimos men were fighting with glass swords. How could glass swords stand up to steel?

The castle was a formidable structure built as a foothold for a new kingdom. The castle, four stories tall with a fifty-foot turret built on the corner of the square fortress, was fashioned from stone and wood. The only entrance to the walls of the castle was a great gate made of hard wood and bound in iron. When the settlers first arrived in Erimos, the wilderness was overrun with man-eating dinosaurs. The settlers pooled all the iron from things like pots, belt buckles, and any other miscellaneous items they possessed to create a wooden, iron-bound gate to keep the forces of nature from destroying the fledgling kingdom. The landscape around the castle had been cleared of any obstructions for security. Now, the mile-wide perimeter was a unique garden of flowers, paths, water fountains, and small fruit trees. The citizens of Sires had used the garden as a place for meditating and as an escape from the city streets that had grown around the castle.

The Viridian army had trampled and practically destroyed the once beautiful grounds surrounding the castle, but had mostly left the city intact. The commander of the army had ordered his men to loot the city, and the citizens of Sires had abandoned their homes as the army marched in. Some escaped to the castle, while others ran for the hills seeking shelter in the nearby towns or the forest. For those who stayed, the army had been merciless.

The campaign was already in its third day, and Captain Steg had lost over two hundred men. The men, mostly garbed in leather tunics and cotton pants, were easy targets for the powerful longbows. Normally, the tunics were sufficient armor for arrows, but the men that wielded the bows seemed to have super human strength. The glass arrow tips would punch a hole right through a man. The Viridian men returned fire with iron crossbows, but that had little effect against the fortified walls of the castle. Now he had to report to Commander Soles another botched attempt at pushing tall towers against the walls. The towers were wrapped in fresh, uncured cow hides, which made them very difficult to burn, but the flames shooting from the walls of the castle were nothing the captain had ever seen before; a continuous torrent of fire. The jets reminded him of pressurized water hoses, but instead of hoses shooting water, the flames came from the hands of the "decorative" soldiers. It was unnatural to see men shooting flames from their hands. Some of the Erimos men had sent down fireballs upon the head of the attacking troops, while others managed to expel torrents of flame like water. Obviously, the fire was some type of magic unheard of in Viridian. The men from Sires had held the invaders off from thirty yards away inside the walls of the castle. Flames shot from the top of the walls, burning men and towers before they were in position to strike. The captain did not relish the idea of reporting another failure to Commander Soles. The captain reached the command center, and the two guards waved him inside the pavilion tent.

"Well?" said Soles, noticeably grimacing even with the black leather mask hiding his face. He stood over a table with a scale model of the castle.

The mask reminded the captain of a faceless nightmare. "The siege towers never made it to the wall. Jets of fire erupted from the castle, burning the men and structures."

"So, building a wooden ram is out of the question to breach the main gate." Soles asked, "What about the scaling ropes weighted with lead?"

"They have flung the grappling ropes away from the wall while at least ten men were climbing up. The Erimos bowmen just drop their bows and grab the ropes. We lost another twelve men from falls, and a few others have broken bones. The strength of the Erimos men is uncanny if not bewitched." The captain felt pressure building inside of him.

"Potions. The traitor warned us about the potions. Who could believe that men could harness fire or have such strength? We have underestimated the people of Erimos. Glass swords, superstitious concoctions, and limited manpower favored our victory. The truth is, they match, if not exceed, our own troops. Feint meets with feint, as if Queen Clarissa is in my command center. We should have killed the bitch instead of the bastard. Stand down for the day; we will count our casualties and regroup. I need time to think of something." Commander Soles turned and walked to the back of the tent as the captain exited.

"Sapping," muttered Soles. "It will take weeks to sap the walls." Soles ground his teeth. "We will have to feint every day, losing more men, but it will work."

Chapter Six

The meadow surrounding Stone University had been churned under by horses and men. It seemed to scream for relief, as did the overworked men. Zen navigated through the field and headed towards the university. Chaos ruled the campus as running men intertwined with buildings. Zen drove to the stables.

"Master Alexander," cried a stableboy. "Can you please park behind the stable? I will find a berth for Cow."

"Damn it, Ruport. I told you to call me Zen. Sorry, yes, I will park behind the stables. Where is Master Salender?"

"He is quite agitated. He has not left his bungalow since he discharged the students."

"I know the place. Stephen, come with me."

They walked past several buildings, away from the chaotic meadow. The further they traversed, the less crowded the pathways became on the campus. After winding around the campus, Zen found the bungalow. The red door had a Keep Out sign posted haphazardly on a string. Zen knocked and shuffled his feet.

"Go away," said a voice from inside.

"Master Salender, it's Zen."

"Terse. Sue."

"I never did well in that ancient, outdated language," said Zen while entering the domicile.

"You never studied. Welcome to my nightmare," said Salender. He sat in an armchair in a room off the front hall with a glass in one hand and a half-empty bottle of liquor in the other. The room was dark, with only one candle burning on the mantle.

"What is happening?" asked Zen as he entered the room.

"My precious collegiate life is forfeited. Come, I will tell you about the demise of knowledge."

Zen sat down in a matching armchair facing Salender. Stephen stepped up and stood behind him. The man was obviously drunk. He rattled on about his unfortunate topple from academia. How Erimos soldiers had charged into his office and announced that the campus was closed. They were taking the facility. All staff was to report to a sergeant in the army. Capable men at the university were to be drafted, either to fight or lend support. Obviously Salender was too old to do either. Stone University no longer would exist, and Fort Ween was born.

"But why?" asked Zen.

"Because the marauders of the Barrier Mountains are slaughtering our men in Sires," retorted Salender.

"What do you mean?"

Salender sat the bottle down on a side table next to the chair. The bottle almost toppled over, since the table was unbalanced, with one shorter leg than the others. Furniture had never been a priority to Salender, so everything looked cheap in the room. The only exceptions were the expensive bookshelves with pristine books carefully stacked and cataloged by Salender.

"We have tried to convince people for years that land existed past the mountains. Now fruition has come tenfold. The dukes amassed this army as a counterpoint to the enemy. Training will involve two weeks. If—if—Sires can hold firm, then the new army will strike. Now leave an old man to reminisce about the glory days of civilization." Salender promptly passed out, snoring with one hand clutching the glass to his chest.

"What do we do now?" asked Stephen.

"We ask how we may be of service," said Zen stoically.

Stephen stared at the back of Zen's head. *What can I do? Zen at least has a talent. I know nothing.* Stephen wrestled with ideas of servitude in the army. He realized a call to arms was everyone's duty to defend the kingdom, even a small-town boy like himself. He decided no matter what happened, he would do his best, because his willingness was his only talent.

"I am joining the army," stated Stephen with determination.

"No, Stephen. You can be my assistant," replied Zen.

"You don't need an assistant. I must do my best for the welfare of the kingdom, even if it is only one more person upon the funeral pyre."

"Depressing thought, but I think you will do much better than that. This does not mean you can shirk your duty to me. You are still my apprentice, so sleep will be a luxury."

"Thank you. I will see you soon," said Stephen as he walked for the door.

"Aye, soon." *The boy will survive. I hope,* thought Zen. He reached for the bottle that had slipped from Master Salender's fingers.

***

After wandering around the camp for an hour, someone had finally pointed out the recruiter's tent. Stephen lied to the recruiter, professing to be eighteen. The recruiter had to draft Stephen as a soldier since Stephen was a land owner, even if it was a piece of land with no house. As a landowner under the feudal system, Stephen was responsible for owning a sword. His tenure in the army would amount to two months, as litigated by the feudal system. After a brief talk on the conduct of any soldier, Stephen was assigned to Vector Platoon. The army of cavalry had the auspicious name of Queen's Salvation. The first three hours of Stephen's military career consisted of running around the camp to be equipped.

Later, Stephen sat on his bunk and looked at the pile of military props. The platoon was in the field, so Stephen had time to think about the danger of being a soldier before they returned. He was scared but resigned to do his duty. He did not have long to think; an officer put him to work cleaning the barracks. As he scrubbed the floor, he listed in his mind the various berries needed in a potion to make one swift of arm and foot.

Chapter Seven

Zacadam had found an abandoned storage room deep underground. Two levels of storage rooms of the castle were above him. He was completely isolated but free, and the only thing else in the room was a door at the top of a flight of stairs leading to the cells of the castle's dungeon. The room had no natural light, and only one candle placed by Zacadam burned in the center of the room. Zacadam had managed to collect a box of candles and trail rations from the upper storage area. He slept in a fetal position on the rough, stone tiled floor. He had lost all sense of time, since his cowardly flight from the castle proper. A loud snort caused by dust in his nose woke him. He sat upright. Poorly ventilated, the room smelled of tallow and piss.

"Tilly! Wine!" he shouted at the walls before realizing he was alone.

Oh, yes, thought Zacadam. *I am alone in a prison fashioned by my own failure; prison today, tomorrow king.* He laid back down.

"King Zacadam, the brave, intelligent, and the gracious," announced Zacadam to the shadows. Turning over, he thought, *Hide, Soles said. I should be ruling these ungrateful louts. I killed a king. What frivolous reason does anyone have to be named his successor? I killed a king. No civil war, no revolution, just murder to succeed where others have no stomach to rule. I killed a king. Even regicide does not compete with murder from a trusted man. I killed a king.*

Zacadam turned back over and lit another candle. He started to daydream. The power to control all human life was at the whim of a king. Women, truly beautiful women, could be made into slaves to indulge his every erotic desire—except for his nagging wife, whom he would hang by the neck at his leisure. A fat rope for a fat neck. His wife would never badger him again. She called him opportunistic, weak, and boring. He would wear the crown; she would wear a rope. His infant son would be heir to the throne. He would take no other wife; wives were for a weak man. Lush women were for a king.

Oblivious to having already murdered his wife, Zacadam's insanity comforted him. His mind was splintering. Fantasy and reality intermingled.

His mind racing, he thought, *I will be a tyrant, a king to be feared. My inner circle shall prosper, while common men will bow. Everyone will respect me. I killed a king. Every man will wonder if he is safe. Every woman will wonder if I will bed them. I killed a king.*

He mumbled, "Every king needs a statue. I will erect one in my honor in the center of every town in the kingdom so people can worship my visage. People will come from the countryside just to see their adored king." He ranted like a mad man.

Zacadam stood in the musty room trying different poses for the statue: hand over breast, saluting, praying. Finally, he decided his hands needed to be on his hips. He lifted his chin and grinned. He announced, "I am king."

Saluting imaginary soldiers, he said, "Bow to the king. Pay tribute to your king. I killed a king."

He decided he was hungry. He rooted around his rations and found some dried deer meat. The salt made him thirsty. He tipped a flagon to his lips, drinking the water; it was almost empty. He looked around the room realizing this was the last of the water. He had to have more water to survive.

"I don't want to go up there," he whined.

Chapter Eight

The man in the black mask grimaced as he thought about Queen Clarissa's men. Last night, ten Sires men had come over the castle walls at different locations. The men were as swift as horses. Three men were brought down with arrows; the other seven were able to escape back into the castle. Unbelievably fast, the men did precise circuits around the castle, expanding their search almost to a quarter mile from the walls. The queen knew about the tunnels, but now she was becoming predictable. Her seeming clairvoyance regarding Soles's plans was working in his favor. At least now, Soles could contain her people within the castle. No more charades—he could not afford to lose any more men in mock assaults. The two tunnels were half a mile out from the castle. Positioning the tunnels entrances far back from the castle meant Soles had succeeded in the cat and mouse game he and the queen were playing. One shallow and one deep tunnel led towards the castle. Her men had not discovered them.

Failure was not an option. He reached up and stroked the side of the mask. His master had sent a bolt of lightning directly at his face. Great control of natural energy had scarred him permanently. If his master had been more displeased with Soles's last debacle, Rex Almanon could have incinerated Soles on the spot. Black oily spots on the stone floor were Soles's predecessors who had failed in their past missions. His master killed men like men killed gnats. Failure could lead to war at home. Other kingdoms would circle the failure like vultures.

Viridian, his kingdom, would suffer. The last time there was a show of weakness, the three kingdoms had warred against each other for a decade. Soles's world consisted of three kingdoms in a large geographic area. Viridian, his home, lay against the mountains. On either side, Callisto and Himalia shared a border with Viridian. Viridian was landlocked, but Callisto and Himalia had coasts on opposite sides of the continent. Rex Aristarchus controlled Callisto, and Rex Ptolemaeus controlled Himalia. The three tyrants' war decimated the population. The collision of armies thinned the general countryside as they marched over crops, orchards, and fields. The issuing lack of food brought mass starvation to the population of all three lands. The three tyrants only saw people as lowly servants; they did not care about women, men, or children. The people were only there for servitude. People were only pawns of the rulers' sick games.

To have a decent life, you had to twist your human nature into a vile substitute. Soles did not recognize the boy in his past. He had killed, butchered, and murdered men to succeed in his master's ranks. The boy was lost; the man was a villain. His conscience only felt the fear of who would be next to attempt to kill him. Men in Viridian were animals, and these so-called barbarians in Erimos seemed soft. Soles wanted to feel soft.

"Issue an order: set perimeter guards out of bow range. Now it is truly a siege," he said to a runner of Rex Almanon's brigade who was waiting nearby. Soles sat down at a table to write administrative missives to the hierarchy of the brigade to maintain a siege. Maybe the damn Sires people would starve to death.

Chapter Nine

Stephen emptied the contents of the wash bucket outside the barracks. An officer approached, and Stephen hurriedly saluted.

"Awful salute, boy. Fenton is your squad leader. Join her and your squad for sup. You will find them in the mess hall." He turned and strode away.

Stephen visualized the camp. He remembered one of the class buildings, where lecturers taught in a large hall, had been turned into a mess hall, its only designation being a sign hastily driven into the dirt outside the doors. He considered changing his wet clothes but decided the other men were probably as filthy as him. He meandered through the buildings in the general direction of the mess hall.

A platoon stood at ease in front of the building, the men chattering like school boys. Stephen approached the platoon leader.

"I am to report to Fenton," said Stephen.

"Third squad, fall in," said the platoon leader.

The platoon consisted of four squads. Each squad of men lined up in a row like a field of corn which formed a square. The men were at ease except for the squad leaders who stood at full attention. Stephen stepped up to the third row, and hoped it was his squad leader.

"Fenton, Stephen Bishop reporting for duty."

"Don't call me Fenton. That is my father's name. Call me Kira, and you're just in time to report for dinner. What have you been doing in the meantime?" asked Kira Fenton.

"I gathered my equipment and scrubbed the barracks floor."

"They send me a maid instead of a soldier. Fall in at the back of the squad, and no talking. We are going to be the best squad in the battalion, so be mindful."

Stephen saluted and walked to the back of the squad. He peered around the platoon and noticed Kira was the only woman. He brought his attention back to her. Her white tunic hugged her frame, close cropped to be effective in battle. Her silky, black hair was in a long, loose braid down her back. She wore riding leathers, the supple black leather conforming to her body. He averted his eyes away from her derriere. His neck flushed. He had never seen a woman look so athletic. He could not look at her directly. After a couple of minutes, to Stephen's relief, the squad was ordered to march into the building for supper. The men found a table already laden with food, and each man had a plate. Kira ate with the other squad leaders.

"So, you met the bitch. What did you think?" asked a middle-aged man around mouthfuls of food.

"I don't know; I just met her," said Stephen.

Another man with broken teeth said, "Well, don't think about it too much, Maid."

The other men laughed and continued eating. Stephen had a sinking feeling. He knew being the youngest man on the squad would be tough. Now the men had nicknamed him Maid. Stephen concentrated on his food.

After dinner, the men of the third squad formed up in a rank outside of the mess hall. Kira gave the order to march. Stephen started out with his right foot, stepping on the heel of the man in from of him.

"Watch it, dumbass," the man growled.

Stephen did a stutter step to get in sync with the others. He concentrated on the man's feet ahead of him, not seeing his surroundings. The squad marched around the camp and headed towards the sword practice arena. Large torches were set around the perimeter of a fenced corral. After halting, Kira passed out wooden swords wrapped in padding.

"Bishop, you are a couple days behind in instruction, so you will spar with me. As for the rest of you men, pair off, and remember the drill you have been taught," ordered Kira.

The men paired up and started hacking at each other like woodsmen. Stephen noticed that no one seemed to have much ability with the swords. Then he faced Kira, trying not to blush.

"First, reflexes are the key to being a good swordsman. Second, do not grip the sword hard; it interferes with the swing. Third, keep your arms relaxed, only tightening the sword arm when the weapon strikes. Now hit me," said Kira.

Stephen swung the sword at Kira's waist. She parried easily.

"Faster. You won't hit me."

Stephen thrust at her stomach. She parried and stepped to the left. Stephen felt more confident that he was not going to land a blow, so he started attacking in earnest. After a couple of minutes, he became irritated. No matter where he struck, Kira was able to turn the blade. Sweat rolled down his face. He would strike, and miss.

"Watch your feet. Balance is necessary for striking and parrying," said Kira. "OK, rest a moment." She turned and started berating a man for sloppy overhead swings.

Stephen was tired. His sword arm ached, even though it had only been a couple of minutes. He watched Kira instruct another man. Grabbing the man's wrist, she told him to relax his grip. Stephen admired her; she knew how to handle a sword—and men.

Stephen and Kira sparred intermittently for an hour. She would only stop when she saw someone else make a colossal mistake. She would correct them and then continue to spar with Stephen. Stephen could not figure out how she could spar with him and keep an eye on the men. He felt inadequate at swordplay.

"Stop. Stack the swords over there, and form in a line. We are done for the day," ordered Kira.

The men smiled and formed a line. Stephen remembered to start out with his left foot as they marched back to the barracks. Kira dismissed the men outside of the barracks, warning them to sleep.

"Bishop," called Kira.

"Yes, ma'am," replied Stephen.

Kira looked at him sideways for calling her ma'am again. "Listen, you have some talent with a sword. At least more than these farmers do, so keep at it. Now get some sleep. And don't call me ma'am. Either call me sir or Squad Leader Kira."

"Yes, sir," said Stephen as he saluted. He felt some sort of elation from the compliment. He turned and followed the men into the barracks.

The men were not bunking down for the night. The two squads sharing the barracks were playing cards or rolling dice. The place was loud. A man in the corner beat upon a small drum. Stephen sat on his cot. He felt weary but knew he could not sleep.

He thought about what the man had asked earlier about Kira. He felt he knew now how to answer. He liked her. Of course, he could never mention it to the other men. Already the men thought of him as a child. He could not completely sort out his feelings for Kira.

"Hey boy, come here a minute," said the rude man from earlier.

Stephen walked to the back of the barracks. Four men sat facing a wall, and the rude man gestured for Stephen to join them. He towered over the four men, standing next to the rude man.

"Do you have any money?" asked the rude man.

"A little, but I am saving it for something," said Stephen.

"Who needs to save today? Tomorrow we could all be dead. Now listen, come join our game. It only cost a penny. You could lose a penny, now, couldn't you? Or do you want to make a penny scrubbing floors, Maid?"

Stephen stared directly into the rude man's eyes. "What's the game?"

"Listen, it is simple. You roll the two six-sided dice. From the seating positions left to right, the men have declared their winning numbers of the total of the two six-sided die. Each person has two chances of winning with a pair of different numbers. The two and three are assigned to the person sitting on the far left and four and five to the next in line, and six and seven follow, and eight and nine are near the end of the seating order, and ten and eleven on the far right, and your number is twelve on the dice. Everyone puts a penny in the pot."

"But everyone else has a better chance of winning," said Stephen.

"True, but the thrower wins double the pot," retorted the man.

Stephen flipped a penny into the pile of coins. He held out his hand for the dice. The rude man's grin widened as he gave him the two bones. Stephen stared at the rectangular boxes for a moment, and then threw them against the wall. They landed sixes up.

"I won!"

"No, you didn't throw them right," said the rude man.

"Now their Hank, the boy won fair and square. Pay the boy," said a rather large man sitting on the nearest bunk. He had sandy blonde hair that stood out against the dark red of his skin. Not quite handsome, but something about him appealed to men and women. His green eyes could flash anger or mirth just as easily.

"Damn it, Sam. It is only beginners' luck," said Hank. "Throw the dice again, boy. Double or nothing."

"No thanks. I will take my winnings now," said Stephen.

Hank stood up from a crouch to intimidate Stephen. Sam stood up as well, and Hank glanced over at him. "When Papa's not watching, boy," whispered Hank. Hank reached down for the pot and handed Stephen his winnings. Stephen walked over to Sam's bunk.

"You were right the first time. The thrower usually loses. That is why people pick pigeons or hardcore gamblers to be the thrower. Have a seat," said Sam, gesturing to Stephen. "You are going to have a problem with Hank now," said Sam in a loud voice, looking directly at Hank, the threat veiled without being completely belligerent.

Stephen did not miss the exchange of hard looks. "Thanks," he said.

"No problem. What are you doing here, boy?" asked Sam.

"What do you mean?"

"I mean, I get why we are all here. Every one of us is a farmer who has lost crops the past two seasons. You don't look like someone who needs the king's money or owns land."

"No, I did not lose any crops. I did lose my home to a tornado. I thought it was the right thing to do when I heard about the invaders. Also, I follow the king's law concerning the feudal system," answered Stephen.

"Right thing to do," mused Sam. "Well, try to keep out of Hank's reach." Sam reached for a shoe then started wiping grime off the heel with a rag.

Stephen wanted to talk more, but obviously the conversation was over. He walked back to his bunk to count his earnings; he had made ten extra pennies for his savings. The plan to rebuild his home seemed far away at the moment, if not entirely out of the question. Stephen was rethinking the plan. He thought about what a squad leader might like as a present. He had to learn more about her. What pretense could he use to find time alone with her? He decided to go ask her for a sword lesson. His stomach rolled over when he thought about seeing her. He did not have a lot of time left before the march to Sires, so he decided to go see her now. He tucked his money away in his boot and left the noisy barracks behind.

Stephen wandered around the camp for half an hour. He really did not know where to look for Kira. The camp was winding down for the night, so the paths were deserted. He thought he might find someone who could lead him to Kira, but everyone was behind locked doors. He could not necessarily start knocking on doors like a lovestruck puppy. He was thinking of giving up when he decided to take a look at the corral. Maybe he could find a sword and practice—anything to impress Kira.

There was a full moon out. It cast a long shadow of Stephen as he wound his way towards the corral. He spotted a baby camarasaurus munching on a shrub in the middle of the camp. If you could call it a baby—it was already bigger than a large dog. With its blunt snout and long neck, it could easily reach into the bush to get to the greener branches. Its long tail swished happily as it ate. Stephen did not worry about the dinosaur. Even the adult camarasaurus were harmless.

As he came closer to his destination, he heard grunts coming from the enclosed circle. He stopped and leaned on the fence railing. Kira was in the circle. She danced in the moonlight with a sword. Her black hair in a ponytail swayed back and forth as she did intricate steps. Stephen could not imagine anything so erotic. He did not know if he should say something, anything, but he was entranced by the whirl of the sword and her lithe body exploiting the moonlight. He decided to back away quietly and leave her alone. It was foolish to think someone with so many calibers would be interested in him. He took a step back and rolled his ankle on a stone, grabbing the fencepost for support.

"What are you doing out of bed?" demanded Kira.

"I, uh, couldn't sleep."

"The men carousing again? I need to work them harder. How long were you watching me?" asked Kira with deceptively smiling eyes.

"Just a couple of minutes. What are you doing?"

"It is called a kata. It incorporates exercise and practice with a sword." She looked at him sideways. "Would you like to learn a simple kata?"

"Yes, please," answered Stephen. The remark reminded him of answering to his mother. He shrugged off the thought and said, "Yes, I would like to learn."

"Grab a practice sword off the stack and come here."

Stephen obtained one of the practice swords and walked through the gate. She told him to stand still and watch her for a moment. She then performed again. The steps were simpler, but he could not take his eyes off her. She moved so gracefully. The moon reflecting off her glass sword and her movements were in tempo with his heart. She stopped and gestured Stephen over.

"Now stand to the right and behind me. Copy the movements I make. Relax and breathe at the same time. Breathing is important," she said over her shoulder.

Stephen moved with her. His heart clamored in his chest. It seemed as if they were dancing together. He concentrated because he did not want to stop. Each cycle of the busy footwork, Stephen improved until he felt comfortable with the movements. Beads of sweat felt cool in the night air. He felt the elation of simple sword movements for the first time in his life.

"Great, now try it by yourself, and don't feel awkward. I am only half watching," she said teasingly.

Stephen took a couple of deep breaths. He was determined to show what he had learned. At first his movements were choppy. His nerves were wrangled. He closed his eyes and thought of the dance they had performed together. The second cycle of movements was more fluid.

"Wow, you are a quick learner," said Kira. "Meet me here tomorrow night, and I will teach you a more complicated kata."

"Yes, ma'am."

"Has anyone ever told you that you are too polite?" she said with a smile. "Get some sleep. I will see you in the morning."

Stephen grinned widely at her then turned and put the sword away. He started back to the barracks. He was going to see her again tomorrow night. He wondered if a scribbler was a good idea. The ring cost dearly. He had the money, but did not know if it would be appropriate. In fact, he did not know what to do about Kira. He really just wanted to talk to her. *Back down to earth,* he thought. *Do not expect her to treat you any differently in front of the men tomorrow.* Stephen had no illusions, but he was getting private lessons. He grinned at the private thoughts.

The door to the barracks was ajar, noise and light streaming out. Stephen opened the door and saw men fighting.

The barracks was torn apart. Beds were in disarray. Men were clubbing each other with bed rails. Men shouted and cried out in pain. The fight seemed to be heating up instead of cooling down. Someone could get seriously hurt. Stephen ran down the steps, hoping to find Kira. She could stop them. He found her walking back from the corral.

"Kira!" he shouted. "They're fighting in the barracks."

Kira ran towards the building. She swung the door wide and pressed a whistle to her lips. Blowing hard in short retorts, she gained the men's attention.

"Stop fighting," she shouted. "I said, everyone stops fighting!" She blew on the whistle. The men separated into two groups. Kira's squad was on one side, and the other squad stood against the opposite wall.

"I see. Who started this?" she asked.

All the men started shouting at once and pointing fingers across the space. Kira blew the whistle.

"All right, stop. It seems everyone is to blame. Lucky for you, we need a new ditch latrine."

"I am not digging a ditch in the middle of the night," retorted Hank.

Kira strode up to Hank and grabbed the pommel of her sword. The sword leaped halfway out of the scabbard, the pommel thrusting hard into Hank's stomach. He fell to the floor and writhed in pain.

"Now, anyone else want to abstain from ditchdigging?" she asked. All the men shook their heads. "Good, now line up outside." The men exited the building. "Bishop, pick someone to help you straighten up the barracks."

Stephen waved Sam inside. They started righting beds and placing mattresses on the frames. Some of the beds had sustained only minor damage. They piled sheets on top and picked up miscellaneous debris. After cleaning up, Stephen sat on his bunk. Sam sat down on the edge of the bed next to him.

"Where did you disappear to?" asked Sam.

"I was practicing swordplay with Kira," said Stephen. "What happened here?"

Sam glanced at Stephen knowingly. "Hank. He started mouthing off about how our squad was better than theirs. Stupid, he riled everyone up. So, what did you do to get extra lessons on the side?"

Stephen became uncomfortable. "I just asked, that's all."

Sam laughed. "Just asked, huh? She is pretty. A little young for my tastes."

"Young? How old is she?" asked Stephen hoping for the best.

"You really don't know." Sam smiled and shook his head. "That young lady is a Lady. She is Duke Kedwin's daughter."

"A duchess." Stephen hung his head.

"Now, don't get all sad on me. It would not be the first time the low consorted with the high. Look at it this way—she is only nineteen."

"If she is only nineteen, then why is her father letting her go off to war?"

"Look, I am from her province. It is a well-known fact that Duke Kedwin wanted a son. She started to play the part at a young age. She is a good sort, though. Everyone in the province likes the duchess for trying to be a man to please her father. I have heard stories of her kindness and her noble temper. Keep your head up, boy," he said slapping Stephen's knee. "Funny things can always happen." Sam stood and walked back to his bunk.

Stephen wrestled with the idea that Kira was a lady. It must chap her backside to be a squad leader. She could probably run a platoon. It had to be her age; he could identify with that aspect. Even though he had been alone since he had turned seventeen, people coddled him. He could take care of himself, but people still did not trust him with responsibility. Damn, a lady. What could he offer a lady? She seemed to like him though. She had taught him a kata, but he wondered if it was special treatment because she liked him or because it was her duty to train him. What scribbler could he buy her with ten iron pennies? She probably had necklaces made of pearls. Should he give up? No, he would be the best he could be for her. Funny things do happen. He decided to sleep. He was bone weary. Stephen undressed and stowed his clothes under the bunk. As he lay on the bunk, he daydreamed about saving Kira from a hoard of invaders until he finally fell asleep.

Sam lay in his bed but did not sleep. *I like that young man,* he thought. *He seems levelheaded. She could do worse. I am trained to protect her from an enemy, not from her heart.* Stephen had guessed right though; the duke did not send his only child into the wild alone. *I will protect her, even if she does not know that I am here for her defense. Damn, it's boring to be a farmer.* Sam rolled over and immediately slept.

Chapter Ten

The steps led from the door to the bottom of the empty storeroom. Zacadam perched on the top step of the staircase. He held his left hand next to his head, palm facing upward. He proceeded down the staircase like a matron on her wedding day, one step at a time. He held his chin up, trying to look regal. On the last step, he turned and mounted them again. *No, no, no,* he thought. *I must be grand to receive the crown.* For the fifth time, Zacadam proceeded down the staircase prancing slowly. At the bottom, he turned to go up, and his stomach growled. He grimaced and thought, *The king is hungry. I killed the king.* He sauntered over to the candle in the middle of the room and rummaged through a burlap sack.

Speaking to the shadows, Zacadam said, "Apples, corn, and beef jerky—not a meal for a king." Pausing, he thought, *When will my knights rescue me from imprisonment? I killed the king.* Turning in place, he said, "What rewards shall the people bestow upon me? Fresh young women, boys to do my bidding, and mountains of gold from the dukes will be my reward." A racing thought fired through his brain: *I killed the king.* Zacadam munched on an apple, the juice creating a rivulet of filth as it dripped down his hairy chin and onto his neck. After he finished, Zacadam stared at the core in his hand and said, "I shall never eat an apple again, decrees the king." Zacadam danced around the candle singing in a high-pitched voice, "Apples to oranges, the king will eat meat." A burning thought: *I killed the king.* Imagining a steward next to a table, he said, "What's that you say? Yes, I will have another slice of pork." He bit into the apple core and spat the seeds out. He screamed at the apple core, "Thou shall not take root in my gut. I killed the king," then threw it into a dark corner. Zacadam slumped onto the floor.

"I killed the king," he whispered. He threw his arms straight up, tilted his head back to look up at the ceiling, and shouted, "Give me the patience to receive my just reward."

Zacadam flopped down on the stone floor. He pissed himself in his sleep. He did not awaken. He tossed and turned, grinding his knees into the stone and bloodying them. Muttering and shrieking in his sleep, he dreamed of pouring the poison into a goblet and handing the cup to a skeleton wearing a crown. The bones ashen white, the nightmare drank from the golden chalice. The skull smiled with broken teeth and said, "I killed the king."

Chapter Eleven

Captain Steg hurried through the Viridian encampment. For once, he had good news for the commander. Ten soldiers clamored down the wall of the castle, again swift as horses. The Erimos soldiers searched for the tunnels. The extra sentries proved beneficial for the Viridians. Nine out of ten had been killed with bow shots; one stepped in a hole in the dark and broke his leg. The captain figured the commander would want to interrogate the prisoner personally.

As the captain fast stepped through the camp, a man being whipped against a pole caught his eye. It was becoming a common sight. The men were restless, brawling with each other. Discipline was failing. The men were here to fight, not wait on tunnels to be dug. Harsh punishment was not a long-term solution for the failing discipline of the men. The captain thought another assault would relieve the men of their anxiety, but they needed every man for the final assault. The tunnels were taking too long. He hoped they would catch a break with the tunnels, which were proving to be difficult.

Besides, the captain was losing men, a couple every night. At first, he had thought the men were deserting. He'd posted guards around camp to stop the desertion. By the second night, it all became clear. The men were not deserting. They were dying. Captain Steg shook his head and thought, *Damn backwoods.*

Whenever a Viridian soldier went to the latrine at night, a pack of dromaeosaurus would swiftly rip out his throat and drag their victim into the woods. The captain figured the smell of the latrine brought the pack out at night—easy hunting for the medium-sized dinosaur with sharp talons and quick bipedal feet. The captain shivered as he thought about being eaten alive. After setting up torches and guards, the killings had stopped, but the dromaeosaurus pack now knew about the easy pickings of the large army of men. Captain Steg thought, *They will be back. Next, the damn beasts will probably drag men out of their bedrolls.* He shrugged and thought, *I will just have to deal with it later. Damn animals, you don't get them in the city. Every child's nightmare, mothers talk about dinosaurs. The only dinosaurs I have seen were in traveling shows, housed in cages.*

"Reporting to the commander," said Captain Steg to the pavilion tent guards. They waved him in with sharp eyes on his person.

"Sir, we have a prisoner," said the captain. "He is being brought here for interrogation."

Soles appeared out of the gloom at the back of the tent. He stood transfixed next to the model of the castle. He did not say a word. He wanted the young captain to sweat. Captain Steg was proving to be a capable man. Capable men needed to know their place.

Two men carried a third into the tent. The commander pointed to a chair, and they placed him in it. The young man looked haggard and obviously in pain, his left leg hanging at an awkward angle. Breathing in ragged gasps, the man stared at the floor.

"You already know your fate. Your answers will determine how your fate will be played out: a quick death or a painful existence until death. Do you understand?" asked the commander.

"Yes," sobbed the young man.

Soles walked behind the chair and gripped the man's shoulder. "How many fighting men are left to defend the castle?"

"Over four hundred," he said with tears running down his face.

"How many potions do they have for individual men?" demanded Soles.

"I don't know."

The commander nodded to the captain. Steg kicked the broken leg, making the young man scream.

"I said, how many potions do the men have at their disposal?" growled Soles.

The man wailed, "I don't know. Each man stocks his own."

"Now, now," said Soles, patting the man's shoulder. "One last question: who is leading the defense of the castle?"

"Queen Clarissa, my honorable lady," said the young man with respect and homage in his voice.

Soles strolled from behind the chair and turned to face the young man. The man's face was white, bruised, and scraped from being beaten. His feminine face reminded Soles of his dead mother.

"Hang him by his feet close to the castle. His screams will remind the Erimos men we are not here to play." Soles sauntered into the gloom of his personal space at the back of the tent.

The man screamed, "Kill me! Please just kill me." He was dragged out of the tent.

The man's beaten countenance haunted Soles, dredging up long-forgotten memories of his mother's death.

She had left Soles in an alley, promising him a sweet cake if he remained quiet and did not wander off. He was ten years old. His mother was the only family he had in the world. He adored her. He promised not to wander off, having been left in alleys before. At the time, he did not know his mother was a whore. He thought she was a grand lady to be let in the back door of grandiose houses. He waited like he always had before. An hour later, the door opened. A man dragged his dead mother into the alley. She had been beaten to death. Her face was mash, and her neck was unnaturally crooked.

Soles's young face turned red. The man had killed her and was going to leave her for garbagemen to throw away along with the other trash in the alley. Soles did not realize he gripped a brick in his hand. As the man stooped over the body and searched for valuables, Soles ran up behind him and smashed the brick into the back of his head. The man crumpled over his mother. Screaming, Soles drove the brick over and over again into his head until he sat down, exhausted. He looked at the brick covered in hair, blood, and skin. He dropped it and grasped his mother's hand.

The people in the house found Soles crying over his dead mother. The steward of the household staff had rooted out what had happened. The dead man had killed the whore over payment, actually pocketing the money for himself. The lord of the house decided Soles would replace the deceased man as reparation for the greedy man's death. Soles became a slave at the tender age of ten.

The household servants treated him with disdain because he had killed one of their own. The first time one of the children called him a bastard son of a whore, he broke the boy's nose. Soles had to endure a terrible punishment for the offense, but the children never taunted him again. As for the adults, they made his life unbearable. Soles was completely miserable, but even at a young age, he knew he could not run away. The street would kill him in a matter of days. Finally, an old retired soldier employed as a house guard took pity on him. He taught Soles the only thing he knew: how to fight. By the time Soles turned eighteen, he was a competent soldier. The old man had taught him military tactics, code of conduct, and how to handle military weapons. Soles partitioned for his release from slavery with a veiled threat to his master. After being released, Soles joined Almanon's army.

Two years later, the day after his mentor died, Soles burned the lord's house down in the middle of the night as everyone slept.

Soles had advanced rather swiftly through the ranks. His mentor would have been proud. Soles lived and breathed being a soldier. He had no family, only the men in the field. Honor was the only true virtue one could aspire to in a military career. Soles considered himself to be an honorable man, but not just.

Soles now sat on the edge of his bunk at the back of the tent. A small candle burned on the nightstand. A worn, beaten journal rested next to the candle. Soles picked it up and flipped to the beginning. The entries heralded Soles' early accomplishments in the military. As he moved steadily up in rank, the book described a younger man. Towards the end, the entries became darker and more sublime. One page in particular, earmarked, described Almanon's temper. That day Soles's life changed abruptly— the day when the mask became a part of him. Soles's mind took him to that time.

The offense to Almanon, a little more than casual, had marked Soles for the rest of his life. Almanon had given him a mission. A merchant in town was actually a spy for Aristarchus of Gosh. He had been caught in the act. Chained and whipped in Almanon's palace courtyard, the merchant professed his innocence. After days of torture, the man finally divulged the secrets he had learned. The merchant spy was near death. Hanging from the crucifix, the man could only see what lay at his feet. Soles' mission was to slay the merchant's daughter and dump the body at the base of the crucifix, thus breaking the man completely. Other spies would hear and take it as a warning that Almanon was not a merciful king.

Soles located the daughter at the merchant's home. The slaves had tended to her needs while her father had been tortured. Soles had never failed in a mission. The tactics he employed to succeed were becoming legend. Murder, deceit, and trickery were his tools for success. No one bothered Soles as he entered the house. His reputation preceded him.

Soles found the girl sleeping in her room. She was a child, no more than eight years old. As she slept, a small smile suggested the contentment of a child's innocence. Soles hovered over the bed; one hand grasping leather bonds, the other a small knife. A tear fell from above onto the girl's soft eyelid, rolling out of the corner of her eye. Soles was not aware of crying.

He imagined the torture and pain of her tears would burn his soul. Soles gasped and turned from the child. He walked calmly out of the room, thinking he would take the lashing for failing at his task.

Later that night, a slave would break the girl's neck and deliver her to Almanon. For the deed, the slave was rewarded the right to bear a child. Funny that.

The day of hearing about the girl's death, Soles reported to his superior for his punishment for failing the mission. His superior laughed, telling Soles he had an audience with Almanon. Soles's heart quaked. He had never been brought to Almanon's attention. Even this mission had come through military channels. Soles had only seen the king twice in the distance over Almanon's long military career. An audience with Almanon meant a horrible death. Soles was shackled and imprisoned until the date.

Soles was brought before Almanon in the throne room. Chained and gagged, Soles stood before the throne. His face was haggard, but even the bruises could not hide his good looks. Men seemed to respect him for his noble appearance. Women were tantalized by his chaste countenance. His long blonde hair was twisted and matted from being held captive. The monstrous Almanon only peered at him for a second and then said, "Potential." The word burned in Soles' brain. Then the king flicked his wrist, and a bolt of lightning spewed from Almanon's hand, burning the flesh of Soles' face. His long tresses flared like a torch. Soles screamed into the gag as he felt his face char. Men rushed forward and pulled Soles from the king's sight. From that day on, Soles wore the black mask.

In his tent on the battlefield outside the walls of Sires, Soles peered at the diary entry with only one word on the page: "Potential." Soles harbored the word. His world had changed dramatically after hearing that one word. Soles considered that the people of Viridian needed potential. Slaves should not murder children. Men should not have slaves. Soles wanted potential for the Viridian people. He did not know how to complete the task; he only waited for an opportunity to arise. Soles wanted to murder Rex Almanon; a thought considered blasphemy by the people of Viridian.

Soles had positioned himself to be the commander of the troops detailed to conquer the barbarians. His plan was to be a hero. A hero would be awarded the highest honor of seeing the king for a brief moment. Soles wanted to die by driving a sword into Rex Almanon's chest. Soles had no qualms; he knew the king would kill him in the attempt. But maybe Soles would persevere. Soles would be a martyr for the people with potential.

Soles turned his mind to the task at hand. He was no fool. Time was his enemy. The tunnels were proving to be challenge for his engineers. Queen Clarissa had an advantage. He knew she was fielding an army somewhere. Intelligence said the dukes only had personal guards of twenty seasoned soldiers per duke. It was only a matter of time for the guards to train and outfit an army. The timetable swung on a pendulum. Would the army arrive while Soles' troops were with their backs against the walls of the castle, or would Soles's troops be defending a castle against the dukes' army? Soles's men would be crushed if he did not topple Queen Clarissa.

Soles stretched out on his bunk trying to clear his mind of a gory daydream. He had been watching these Erimos people. Of course, he had burned down the town surrounding the castle. The people fled into the countryside. It was the local people that intrigued Soles. Even fleeing, the people had stopped to help the less fortunate. Later, Soles had used field glasses to watch heroic events on the castle walls: men sacrificing themselves to help their comrades, women ripping the wounded from the walls to attend to them, all of them sharing courage in the face of the enemy. Soles' men lacked courage. They were brutes. Most of them only enlisted because Viridian was not kind to free men.

Viridian people were in two classes. You were either in good graces with the king, leading to wealth and prosperity, or you were a slave. Even the prosperous people felt a fear of slavery. To fall from grace could lead to the slave block. The king of Viridian supported infighting among his wealthy citizens. Soles preferred to think of the games the wealthy played as a method for Almanon to control the populace. The fear of losing to another family kept the rivalries going for generations. The king's support of families fluctuated only with his own designs.

The slave proportion of the population of Viridian led a miserable existence. The threats of violence were a constant reminder to the slave, as they were not seen as people. Free men could not identify with a slave, because their lives were just as precarious as the slaves'. Slaves had no echelon of freedom. The free families delegated family members to oversee the slaves, so cousins lacking the intelligence or drive to succeed in life controlled the family slaves. These people were mean-spirited. They were shells of human decency, playing for favor by manipulating the only resource available to them—slaves. They curried favors amongst the families using slaves as bartering chips. Soles's mother had been a chip. She had been too beautiful to be wasted on scrubbing floors, growing food, or being a steward. Soles wondered how the freemen of Erimos spent their energy.

One of the guards pushed open the tent flap, and said, "You have a messenger here."

Soles stopped musing about the fate of mankind in Viridian, and replied, "Send him in."

"Sir, reporting the progress of the shallow tunnel," said a messenger.

Soles rolled out of the cot and walked to the center of the tent. "Report."

"The shallow tunnel has reached its objective. They believe they're under the flagstones of the courtyard outside of the portcullis. Captain Steg wants to attack."

"Figures. He was always shortsighted. Tell him no. How far is the deep tunnel?"

"The engineers are still experiencing trouble with large stones set in the ground. They gave no timetable."

"Dismissed," said Soles.

The messenger covered his heart as a salute and left. Soles imagined this traditional salute meant, "You could stab me in the back, but not in my heart."

Soles gnawed on the idea of sending troops into the castle. Queen Clarissa was expecting a tunnel. He must wait until the deep tunnel was finished. It must be a three-pronged attack: men in the courtyard, men rising from the bowels of the castle, and his secret weapon. His engineers had built him a siege weapon. Now covered by a tent, it had been rolled into position last night. Ten men slept in the tent so it would look like a barrack. The weapon would rain down stones upon the walls of the castle. Four hundred men could not defend against three different strikes at the same time. The damn deep tunnel was the problem. The engineers were moving at a snail's pace. The attack would be successful without a doubt; the only gamble was time. Queen Clarissa could field her coming army before Soles struck. He decided to put runner stations outside of camp. The army would not be a surprise. If he had to, he would attack early as soon as he detected an army at his back.

Soles stared at the model castle. "I have to win."

Chapter Twelve

"Wake up, you louts," yelled Kira as she walked through the barracks. The men groaned and complained, but they slowly rolled out of bed for another day of training.

"Hank, what are you chewing?" asked Kira testily.

"Nothing," said Hank, swallowing quickly. He coughed up spittle.

"Let me see your teeth," said Kira. She peered at yellow-stained teeth with bits of Stem jammed in the crevices. She turned and said, "I do not condone chewing Stem, and neither should you. Five laps around the practice field before breakfast. Fall in!"

The men grumbled and shot Hank hard looks as they amassed outside. Kira marched the squad to the practice field and counted the laps as the men ran. After five laps, the men lined up to go for breakfast.

"Sam, take the men to the mess hall. Stephen, we are getting you a horse today. Move out," said Kira. Stephen separated from the group and stood beside Kira. The dawn air was a little chilly on his face, but the sun shone brightly.

Kira and Stephen started walking towards the corrals. They dodged other soldiers walking in formation throughout the camp as well as men with errands who were always in a hurry to get nowhere. The camp was busy all the time, with no space for the mass of personnel and animals occupying the grounds of the old university.

Stephen said, "Kira, do you think you can give me another lesson tonight?"

Kira smiled slightly and said, "Yes, when the men are put to bed. Now let's see about us getting you a horse."

Kira found the wrangler outside a corral. "I need to procure a horse for a recruit."

"Sorry, ma'am, we are a bit shy on horses. I might have something in a couple days," said the wrangler.

"The recruit has already missed a couple training exercises. He will fall woefully behind the others if we do not have a horse today," said Kira.

"I am sorry, ma'am," he said, turning his head to watch the horses in the corral.

"I might have an idea," said Stephen. "Zen has a horse I might borrow."

"What kind of horse?" asked Kira.

"A stallion. He is grand." Stephen's chest swelled.

"Well, OK. Meet us on the practice field and try to get something to eat. It is going to be a long day." Kira turned and walked towards the mess hall.

I hope I can get a horse. Zen will lend me his horse, won't he? thought Stephen worriedly.

Stephen searched the empty houses left by the scholars. He found Zen camped out behind a large house, blissfully snoring away this early morning.

"Zen,' said Stephen shaking his shoulder. "Wake up."

"What? What time is it?" asked Zen.

"It's sunrise."

Zen rolled over and said, "Wake me up when it's breakfast."

Stephen thought about shaking him again but came up with a better idea. He headed to the mess hall for leftover breakfast. The hall was deserted. Stephen found some leftovers and stacked a tray with anything sweet. He gobbled down some eggs and bacon for himself. Stephen headed back to where Zen was sleeping.

"Zen? Don't you want some sweet cakes?" he asked, holding the tray under Zen's nose.

Zen's nose wrinkled up. His eyes became slits. "Well, at least now you're being polite." He sat up and reached for a sweet roll. "What are you doing here anyway? Shouldn't you be practicing?" he asked around a mouthful of food.

"I've hit a snag. They're out of horses," explained Stephen.

"So, you want to rob me of my horse in trade for the sweets." Zen stared at the boy for a moment. "I have made less. I guess you want my sword too."

"No. I mean, yes. Well, it would make practicing with Kira more interesting."

"Getting private lessons, huh?" He smiled at the young man who was obviously nervous about the subject. He decided to change the conversation. "What makes you think you can handle Cow?"

"I've barrel raced horses in the annual rodeo since I was twelve. And I actually won first prize when I was fifteen. I gave old man Jackson half the prize, since he always lent me a horse," Stephen explained hurriedly.

"Stole horses from other people too, I see," said Zen with a slight smile.

"I didn't steal a horse, he lent me one every year," said Stephen, chagrined.

"Now, now don't get upset. I'm just teasing. I would think Cow would be much happier as a warhorse again. As for the sword, it's more decoration to me than anything else. Fine, a trade: sweet cakes for the goods."

"Thank you, Zen," said Stephen happily.

"All right, now go gather up the war toys while I have breakfast. By the way, you need to ask your superior for time at night. I need a hand in making potions for the army."

"No problem. Kira will let me."

"I bet she will. Now go and let me enjoy myself." Zen reached for another pastry, smiling to himself. *To be young again. For one thing, food tasted better*, he thought.

Zen finished breakfast and decided to go talk to Master Salender. Maybe the old scholar could answer some questions. Where did these villains come from? Could they make a truce without fighting? Could they be bought? Zen had more questions, but did Master Salender have the answers? Master Salender had lived in an academic world his entire life. He had to have learned something, right? Zen tottered off towards Master Salender's bungalow.

The sign hanging on the door had an additional message scrawled at the bottom: No Trespassing. Zen ignored the sign and knocked on the door. He heard a sharp retort, "Go away." Zen knocked again, calling out his master's name. The door flung wide open.

"I thought you had better manners," said Salender. "It's barely past sunrise."

"And I thought all scholars worked from sunrise to sunset. So, you going to let me in?" asked Zen.

"Only if you have wine."

"How about a couple fresh pastries?"

"That will go well with my morning fortitude of port. All right, you can come in," said Salender, moving down the hallway. "Lock the door behind you."

Zen watched Master Salender plop down into his comfy chair. The only difference between now and the previous visit was that more empty bottles of wine surrounded the chair. Also, Master Salender had managed to pull every single book off the shelves, and he had dumped them in the middle of the living room floor. Master Salender had a glass of port in one hand, and he reached for the pastries with the other hand.

"Have you been doing nothing but getting drunk?" asked Zen as he sat down in the opposite chair.

"Libations cajole the heart."

"I am not here for a vocabulary lesson. What do you know?"

Salender yelled, "Know? Know? I know we are slaves. Our father's father was a slave, and we in return will become slaves."

"Calm down, old friend, and explain to your old student a lesson in history."

Salender smacked his lips and took a sip of wine. "I checked my books, and I found the prestigious first king's diary. We all were born from slaves." Salender leaned forward in the chair. "You see, fourteen generations ago, we escaped from Viridian. The Masters of Viridian were playing with weather patterns. The mountain passes were favorable for climbing. A young slave, our first king, tested the conditions for passing over the mountains. When he returned, the slaves made a pact: either all of them would journey over the mountain, or none of them would leave that particular part of Viridian. The entire town of slaves stole away in the night; taking no personal belongings, only tools and food they stole from their masters. They blooded the sills of the master's doors, kitchen floors, and parlors. The idea was to make the exit look like a supernatural event. It worked; no one came over the mountains to enslave us. After a couple of seasons, the mountains clogged again with snow and became a natural defense. We are doomed to forget our resourceful past and again become slaves of the tyrannical masters." Salender slumped down in the chair. "The resources the Viridians can wield far outweigh our own. The siege over the castle, more like a skirmish to the Viridians, has prophesied the doom of Erimos. We are ill equipped to defeat the Viridians if the masters determine us as a threat."

"What can we do to save ourselves?"

"The only resourceful thing: return the weather patterns to normal so the mountains become a natural barrier. Or kill the reigning king over the mountain."

"How?"

"Don't ask me; I read books. Someone will have to sacrifice themselves for the greater good. In the meantime, we will have to fight." Salender took a sip out of the glass.

Zen sat back in the chair, going down depressing avenues of thoughts. It would take a sacrifice and a resourceful fellow to pull it off. No one in Erimos had the espionage training to be successful in a foreign country. The circles turned in Zen's head. "Hand me a glass of port."

The two old fellows sat brooding, each of them trying to imagine a solution. After a bottle of the port, Zen asked, "Who are the kings?"

"The diary was cryptic regarding the masters. More like demigods than rulers of three great nations. The slave hinted that the kings controlled the heavens. From what I could discern, the heavens control the three kings. A monarch's power cycles with the stars—one grows more powerful than the other two. A tripod of power and political circumstance. The kings wait their turn to rule supreme. The one in power against the others, the three never truly compromise for fear of death."

"You act as if they live forever."

"Perhaps a spring of immortality was tapped by the damn monarchs. Maybe they train secret successors. From what I read, Viridian, Callisto, and the Himalia people do not know a time without being ruled by three single men."

"What does a man want when he is immortal?" asked Zen wistfully.

"Power. The Viridian, Callisto, and Himalia people—even free people—are only pawns in the sovereign games. Food, wine, and women or anything else like human trappings have been sampled and then discarded by the kings as time wanes."

"You paint a bleak picture."

"The bleak landscapes of the three kingdoms' lives are horrific. To fall from grace means eternal servitude for your family. History has shown that when the powerless outnumber the ones in power, revolution sparks to sway the balance. Our agent of espionage must bring a revolution to fruition."

"Why not assassinate one man instead of committing a genocide of the people? I mean if they are so powerful."

"What, do you not think people have tried assassination? Even a monster can be killed if you imagine hard enough, but the kings seem indestructible. The diary of a slave recounts an assassination attempt made by a young officer. The man hacked at Almanon, prone on the floor, with a sword. The monarch laughed the whole time, and then lightning engulfed the young officer, burning him to a cinder. The creation of an imaginary monster can be slain, but a demigod must be dethroned."

"A champion?" questioned Zen.

"Yes, a champion could sow the seeds of a revolution."

"The champion would have to be seemingly as powerful as the three kings," replied Zen skeptically.

"Potions, my friend. The Viridian people have no knowledge of potions, nor does Callisto or Himalia," said Salender, perching on the edge of the seat in his bathrobe. Zen seemed overly dressed to him, in his homespun pants and blue tunic.

Zen sat back in the chair, thinking of the implications. To a world without potions, a man with potions would seem extremely powerful. Able to heal the wounded, have immense strength and control the natural element of fire, be as fast as a wraith, and kill with a few poisonous drops. These were supernatural powers a champion could wield. The Viridian people would be enthralled. The only hitch was that the source of power would have to be a secret.

Zen said, "We are conniving old men. We would conquer a kingdom with the help of the young."

"A young man of extraordinary honesty could be the one. A false pretense would be easily unveiled. A weapon forged to strike at inhumanity. One willing to bear the repercussions of mass genocide by the hand of a demigod to free the Viridian people from the bonds of the king is an unlikely hero, but a hero nevertheless," said Salender with anger in his bloodshot eyes.

"Damn, I need a drink!" exclaimed Zen.

"As have I over the past couple of days," said Salender as he uncorked a fresh bottle of wine and then poured the white wine into both glasses.

Chapter Thirteen

Stephen rode the powerful horse to the training ground. Cow came alive with a skilled rider at the reins. The once docile horse ran with energy. Its muscles were taut; it held its head high. Stephen was thrilled with controlling a highly trained horse. Stephen reined the horse in as they approached the squad, the horse rearing at the last moment.

"What's that?" asked Kira.

Stephen patted Cow's neck and said, "My horse."

"Not that," she said. She leaned over and patted the sword on Stephen's hip. "This."

"Oh, Zen also gave me a sword."

Kira looked askance at Stephen's name dropping. "Well, keep it in the scabbard. The squad has not graduated to real swords. Grab a wooden sword and run your horse through the obstacle course." She motioned towards the field.

Stephen wheeled away with the squad watching his every move. He grabbed a practice sword held out by a soldier and turned Cow to the obstacle course. Nudging the horse into a canter, Stephen swung at the scarecrow men lined up between tents. Zigzagging through the course, Stephen hit his marks. As he approached the last dummy, he kicked Cow's flank, urging the horse to go faster. He chopped down on the helm of the last dummy. The blow sent shockwaves up his arm, causing him to drop his sword. He glanced back, embarrassed.

"That is why you strike the neck and shoulder, and not the helm," pointed out Kira to the other recruits. "It's your turn, Hank."

As Hank clumsily rode through the obstacle course, Stephen dismounted and picked up his sword. At the last dummy, Hank veered wide left, startling Cow and almost trampling Stephen. Stephen managed to jump back against Cow's flank.

Kira kicked her horse into action and rode up to Hank. "What is your problem? Can't you control the horse?"

"Sorry, ma'am, she spooked to the left at the last minute," said Hank, looking directly at Stephen.

"Yeah, well, try it again," said Kira wearily.

Hank saluted and trotted off to the beginning of the course.

"Are you OK, Stephen?" asked Kira softly.

"Yeah, I'm fine. What did you think of the run?" asked Stephen hopefully.

"You can handle a horse, but try not to lose your sword next time," said Kira with a crooked smile. "Fall to the back of the line."

The day progressed with the squad practicing their swordsmanship on horseback. Kira yelling encouragement or a scathing retort at the troops as they rode around the course. The men showed increments of improvement throughout the day as Kira instructed them on proper handling of the sword and horse. As the sun was setting, the men were soaked with sweat and could barely raise their sword arms. Kira called a halt to the relentless racing. Groomsmen handled the horses as the men dismounted, some falling to the ground. Smelling of salt and grime, they lined up to march in step to the mess hall after a long day.

The men said little as they ate dinner. Some ate with their left hand, the right arm dangling at their sides. The only one in good spirits was Sam. He seemed fit and ready for another hard day's work.

Sam said around a mouthful of food, "I'm impressed, Stephen. You can handle a horse."

"Thanks, but I keep dropping the damn sword," said Stephen, angrily shaking his right arm that carried the sword.

"It's your swing. You come overhanded at the targets. You need to slash instead of chop," explained Sam.

"Thank you. I noticed you did well today," said Stephen, looking directly into Sam's eyes.

"Ahh, I wrangled horses on the farm," said Sam, diving again into his meal.

After dinner, the men marched to the barracks. Each man sat on their bunks; Kira had pushed them hard today. The men started chatting with each other, not having any energy left to burn. The other squad in the barracks seemed just as ill feeling. While the two squads complained about their tyrannical squad leaders, Stephen slipped out of the barracks with his sword.

Stephen found the practice circle lit with torches and Kira leaning against the railing. She said, "I didn't think you would show."

"I wasn't sure I would either," said Stephen with a sheepish smile.

"Well, you will be glad to know that you will be practicing a kata with your left arm," said Kira with a slight smile.

Stephen unsheathed the glass sword and stepped into the circle. Kira taught him a small intricate dance with the sword, laughing at his small mistakes, her small hands touching him to improve his stance. Stephen felt electricity run through his limbs each time Kira touched him. He could only smile, thinking about her hands running over his entire body.

Kira said after a couple of hours, "That's enough for now. You should really get some rest."

"Kira, I, uh, need a favor. Zen wants me to make potions for the troops. He asked me to assist him at night. Could I be released from duty to help?" asked Stephen sheepishly.

Kira put her hands on her hips, "If I see one iota of exhaustion, you will be dropped from the squad. But yes, you may help your friend."

"Thank you. Can we still dance at night?" asked Stephen hopefully.

Kira laughed heartily. "Yes, we can still dance." She slapped him on the shoulder. "Go help your friend, and we will continue to dance tomorrow." Kira shook her head, smiling to herself as she thought about a real dance with Stephen. She sauntered out of the firelight, looking one time over her shoulder at the farm boy.

Stephen stepped to the middle of the circle; he practiced two turns of the kata. He sheathed the sword. He figured Zen would find him when the time was right for making potions. Stephen snuffed the torches and meandered back to the barracks.

Sam watched Stephen fall into his bunk. *The boy has spirit, and all the energy of youth,* he thought. Sam turned his thinking to the problem developing. Kira was the daughter of a duke. Duke Kedwin would not be happy to learn a farm boy was courting his daughter. Sam liked Stephen; the boy had an honest charisma.

Sam thought about his orders. The duke had assigned him to protect Kira from harm, and Kira did not know he was her bodyguard. She had fought relentlessly with her father to be a part of the army. The duke had raised a girl with a man's ideals. It was the duke's fault; Kira could only be what an old man's wishes were for her. One day, she would be a duchess. Sam thought she would excel at the task. She was what every father could expect from their children to be in a time of crisis. Sam had come to respect her and knew he would die for her. Hard men like Sam looked to find someone to lead graciously. She had qualities found in only the best of men, but she was still a child.

A child blossoming into a woman. The suitors knew only the duchess. She called them pompous and said they sought only a trophy. She had forced the suitors out of her life, claiming the role of a woman to choose her man. The men had called her treacherous and boyish. Sam believed the young woman only sought love, something men of power disdained as they were only seeking the seat of government. Sam decided he was here to guard her life, not her heart. He only hoped the boy would also be a man to be reckoned with by men. The boy would need power and popularity to succeed in convincing the father. He thought the boy had already wooed the daughter.

Just then, someone with a candle stole into the barracks. Sam coolly turned over in his bunk away from the light when he recognized who it was coming in the door.

Zen held the candle to light his way to Stephen's bunk. He grabbed Stephen's big toe and squeezed. The boy rolled over in bed. Zen whispered in his ear, "Time to wake up."

"Is it breakfast time?" asked Stephen sleepily.

"It's always breakfast time," chuckled Zen.

Stephen sat up in bed. "What time is it?"

"Four in the morning, plenty enough time to distill a potion before sunrise. Get up," said Zen, tossing Stephen's hair.

Stephen swung his feet over the side of the bunk. Rubbing his face, he stood up and dressed. He followed Zen outside. "Do you always make potions in the middle of the night?"

"No, but I figured you needed the sleep. I will have you back before morning call," answered Zen.

They walked the camp, the candle throwing long shadows in their wake. Zen led Stephen to an abandoned building. Taking out a key tied to a red ribbon, he unlocked the door. Stephen followed him upstairs to another locked door. The same key unlocked the door to a laboratory. Zen touched the lamps in the room with his candle to brighten up the place.

"Now there are certain principles in making a potion: heat, exact measurement, timing, and order of ingredients. Duke Kedwin asked for a batch of healing potions first. Easy to make, even in a large quantity. Healing potions were first invented by a Marcus Feeling. Marcus was the first male acolyte to the three sisters. The three sisters were the first Potioners. I will tell you about them at another time. Some other Potioners, male and female, followed suit down the ages, improving on his mixture. Grab the glass kettle from that shelf," said Zen, waving his hand in its general direction.

"It has hashmarks down the side," said Stephen, staring at the glass kettle.

"Yes, I told you exact measuring is important. Fill the kettle with water from that barrel to the top hashmark. We are distilling enough healing potions in one sitting for an army. Normally I could not make such a large portion, but this laboratory is well stocked. Bring the kettle and place it on top of the burner. All the glass in the room is tempered to handle heat," said Zen while lighting a round pot with a flute full of coal.

"What makes the burner heat up?"

"A wire is embedded in coal and conducts the heat to the burner. It takes time to heat up, but the temperature stays stable. Now, while that is warming up, hand me the items out of the cabinet marked 'healing potions.'"

"I thought all potions were secret," said Stephen as he looked at the different labels on the jars.

"Rudimentary potions are not secret. The secret is how well the potions perform. My family makes some of the best potions in the kingdom. Remember the Gregorous family potion for strength?"

Stephen nodded.

"Well, I am quite envious of their strength potion, but my family has made potions for generations. I am proud to say that my family's potions are the best in general. We did not specialize in one potion, but my strength potion is very close to being a Gregorous potion."

"If all potions are pretty much the same, then why guard the secrets?" Stephen dumped some jars on the table.

"Does a master chef tell you his secret ingredient? No, because that ingredient makes his living. Same with potions. We all have to make a living."

"You must improve the potions all the time."

"Sadly, no. It is each generation's responsibility to improve at least one potion. Sometimes it skips a generation, but I managed to improve a potion for my generation. It will be your responsibility to improve a potion for your generation."

"Why can't you mix potions?" asked Stephen as he looked at the contents of a jar. He rotated the jar in the light.

"It's not enough that a man can control fire; you want him to have incredible strength also. I must admit Potioners have tried to mix potions but always met failure. The kettle is bubbling. It is time to begin. For tonight, all I want you to do is watch. Tomorrow you will be mixing the strength potions, so be diligent."

Stephen watched Zen closely. He recognized some of the herbs used to make the healing potion. Zen measured each ingredient first. Then he set out varying sizes of hourglasses. As he dropped an herb in the kettle, he turned over an hourglass with one fluid motion. Stephen counted while the sand fell. The first glass was a minute. The second glass used lasted exactly ten minutes. Zen used the hourglasses to time each drop of the herbs into the potion's kettle, never stirring the pot once. Back and forth, a fluid motion of hourglasses with a drop of an herb. The procedure lasted for exactly forty minutes. The main ingredients Stephen recognized as sassafras roots and willow bark. Zen lifted the glass kettle off the burner and wiped his brow.

"What if you don't have large amounts of ingredients?"

Zen sat down on a stool and breathed heavily. "It's all proportions. Can you cook a dinner for two with the same ingredients for eight people?"

"I get it. What about chanting a dead language or piercing your hand for blood to make the potion?" said Stephen with a grin.

Zen laughed "That's just crap to scare folks. There are three principles that are needed to concoct a potion. The bloodletting just scares folks for the Potioner's entertainment—and to keep the secrets."

"The color just turned purple," said Stephen, staring in amazement.

"That means it worked. The glass kettle can hold up to five hundred potions, enough that I could retire. Unfortunately, I will not see a penny. Not my ingredients, and the duke is adamant about me supporting the cause of war. Be a good lad and spoon the liquid into those small vials. By the time you're done, your squad will be waking up for morning duty. I will come and get you tomorrow night." Zen walked out of the room.

Stephen carefully spooned out portions of the potion. The kettle made exactly five hundred potions. Stephen cleaned up quickly and left the potions on the table behind the locked door. He walked down the stairs in the predawn light. Stephen loved cooking, and the potions seemed like cooking. He hoped one day he would make a contribution to Zen's family history of potions. *Family, Zen is becoming family,* thought Stephen. Stephen deliberated on that fact as he walked back to the barracks.

Stephen's family had broken up a long time ago. His father left his mother when he was born. His mother remarried when he was fifteen and she and her husband moved to another town. The only family Stephen had was the friends he cultivated by cooking. He could not remember a time where someone wanted to be his friend for the sake of friendship. Zen had adopted him and entrusted him with family secrets. Stephen decided that the military would be a temporary thing for him, only to repel the invaders. He wanted to make Zen proud of him. He must learn as much as he could about making potions so he could contribute to Zen's family recipes. Stephen considered Zen a father—a father he could love and cherish. A father that one day would be proud of him.

Chapter Fourteen

Zacadam sat hunched over the burning candle, his mind reeling with possibilities. Had Soles conquered the Erimos people? Had the Erimos people routed Soles's army? Was he king, or had Soles claimed the throne? Would the Erimos people torture and kill him for his transgressions? What day was it? Soles had told him to hide; had he hidden too well? Could Soles not find him? Or had he not hidden well enough, and would he be discovered by Queen Clarissa? Should he venture out to find news? Zacadam sobbed and lay down on the floor, curving his body around the warmth of the candle. He closed his eyes and thought about what had gone wrong with the murder.

Zacadam thought of himself as being a brave man. He had acted the part of a concerned subject to the king. He had walked bravely into the king's bedroom. Smiling at the queen, he reassured her that the potion he had concocted would cure the king. Being brave, he poured the potion into a golden goblet while speaking about the vitality the king would obtain. Smiling the false smile of a jackal, Zacadam told the king to drink the potion for his health. He patted the queen's hand and told her that the king would be well. He had left the room with a twinkle in his eye that the queen had misinterpreted as faith.

The plan was perfect. The potion was not perfect. He had dallied too long in the castle. The potion was supposed to kill the king in his sleep around dawn. Instead, the king died violently an hour after Zacadam's visit. Zacadam had not taken into account the king's frailty when choosing a poison. The queen had ordered the lockdown of the castle. She turned out her men to guard the castle, believing Zacadam would have accomplices. Zacadam had barely found this hiding place in the bowels of the castle in time. The room was forgotten, an abandoned storage room below the dungeons sheltered the murderer. The walls were bare earth with a stone tile floor. A few brick steps led to the only exit. A tomb really, but Zacadam dared not think of that idea. As for the attack of Soles' troops, Zacadam had inadvertently alerted the queen's troops to the imminent assault.

"I killed the king," moaned Zacadam. "Riches and glory should be my prize. Soles has won, and I am his benefactor." He stood and raced up the stairs then planted his ear against the only door in the room. He crouched, listening. His hand shaking, he reached for the doorknob. As his hand touched it, he screamed and jerked his hand away. "I have the will to embrace my destiny." He reached for the handle again. His hand shook violently, the will being sapped from his arm. He dropped it to his thigh and rubbed his face on the panel of the door.

"Please rescue me, Soles. The murderous bastards will torture me for days if they find me. Am I not benevolent, a man worth being rescued? A man destined to lead; a man deserving the adoration of his subjects? Soles, I vow on my family's souls that if I am not king, I will kill you in your sleep." Zacadam wept at the top of the stairs thinking about how much courage it would take to murder Soles. He snuffled and wiped the snot from his nose. *I killed the king,* again the litany of thought.

He plodded down the stairway. At the bottom, he rummaged through a box full of candles. He lit the new wick with the old. As the new candle sputtered, the shadows danced in the room. Zacadam imagined a ballroom full of guests praising him for his act of valor. He bowed and waved at the four corners of the room. Kissing his hand profusely, he smiled and accepted the ghostly praise.

Chapter Fifteen

Soles paced the tent. The damn engineers were not working fast enough. They whined about delays and having unearthed huge stones. The tunnel was supposed to be as wide as two men. After digging out stones, the tunnel in places was as wide as four men abreast. Soles would use the stones for his siege engine, hurling them as ammunition. The delay cost him time for the attack. The three-prong assault would only work if he did not have an army at his rear. How long would it take to field an effective Erimos army against him? Soles felt time slipping past at a terribly fast rate. He decided to burn some energy by walking around the encampment. The sun stood low in the heavens, barely past dawn.

As Soles left the tent, his bodyguards followed a couple paces behind. Men huddled around campfires for breakfast. Some stood and saluted. Soles ignored the salutes and walked towards the castle. Near the castle walls, a dead man strung up by his ankles hung from a pole while a crow breakfasted on his tongue. The bird pecked and ripped at the soft tissue. An arrow protruded from the dead man's chest. Soles recalled the report of the man screaming in pain, pleading for mercy for hours. Soles had given the order to hang the Erimos prisoner with the broken leg a few days ago. A fellow Erimos soldier had shot the man from the walls of the castle, silencing him forever. Soles hoped the man's screams harbored doom for the besieged. The Erimos troops' morale must be fading, but each day brought hope of reprisal from an as yet non-existent army. When would the new army come over the horizon to free the trapped men in the castle? Soles knew time was not on his side.

He surveyed the land surrounding the castle. His army had razed the houses surrounding the castle proper. Soles had personally given the order to torch the town. He had to give his men a victory. When Soles's army had arrived, the castle portcullis had been lowered as if expecting an attack. His men needed encouragement, so he turned them onto the town. The men looted it, burning down homes, raping women, and killing men on sight. The men had expected riches; instead, they only found iron coins. Soles had not known the Erimos kingdom to be starved for precious metals. The Erimos people had adapted by inventing glass rudiments—glass as tough as steel. Soles envied the unique weapons made by Erimos smiths. Soles' order to loot the town only delayed the apathy of his army.

Soles's men were becoming impatient. Fighting, drinking, and gambling instead of making war became the army's bailiwick. The army had a cancer gnawing at its heart. Captain Steg had suggested attacking nearby towns to quench the men's violent behavior. Soles contemplated the idea. The strict codes of soldier behavior were breaking down. He stared at the castle wall, inviting an arrow.

Soles turned to his bodyguards. "You—tell the captains to report to my tent in one hour."

One of the bodyguards saluted and hurried of to complete the command. Soles turned back to the walls. *I hate the idea of harming civilians, but discipline is failing,* he thought. Soles did an about-face and marched with his head held high towards his command tent. The men in the camp stared at the back of his head.

An hour later, plans were drawn to attack a small town ten miles south of the capital. Soles decided to leave an auxiliary attachment to guard the castle as the main force marched to the town. Soles watched the men depart, feeling his guts twist in a knot.

He returned to the isolation of his tent. It would take the army two and a half hours to reach the outskirts of the town. Soles would join them by riding a horse in a quarter of the time; meanwhile, he waited, staring at the paper model of the Erimos castle. He cursed it and its inhabitants. He was a man of war, not a maniacal monster preying on civilians—at least, not before today. He touched the side of the mask, thinking how much it had changed him. No longer a man of justice, he had become a wraith. His soul battled against the will of Rex Almanon. He would do his duty for one chance in a million. The Viridian people deserved to have "potential." He called for his horse; the self-loathing thoughts had taken up the time needed for the army to reach the other town.

He caught up with the army on his stolen horse. Only a couple of horses had managed to be captured by his men during the first raid of Sires. The horse was cantering at an abnormal gate after thirty minutes of hard riding. Soles had taken out his frustration on the horse, pushing it beyond its limits. He was lucky it had not come up lame. The captains had their orders; Soles was only there for any intendancy. He rode up his horse onto a small hillock outside of town and scanned down. His stomach twisted again. The townspeople had not abandoned the small enclave. Soles had picked the nearest township thinking it would be mostly abandoned. He had expected some holdouts, but the town's population had decided to fight if invaded. Rude fences and earthen works surrounded the town. People defended the makeshift barricades.

The army ran over them like a line of ants. The screams and curses of the dying men drifted up to Soles. Women were being raped on the streets by at least two men at a time. Houses burned and buildings collapsed. The scene was chaotic as his men ran in packs of three or more. No one was spared, not even the children. Soles's men were murderous bastards. He knew the carnage would be intense. No mercy or quarter was given to the people of the small town. It was a sacrificial lamb for the bloodlust of his men as it folded upon itself. Soles passed a signal to mop up and return to base then turned the horse towards his camp.

As he rode, the mountains grew taller. His only wish was to continue riding over the mountains. He kicked the horse into a canter headed back to base camp.

As Soles rode alone, a stone clipped his temple, tumbling him from his horse. As he fell, he went limp to soften the impact. He found himself on his back, staring into the sky. After taking stock, Soles rolled onto his feet and drew his sword in a swift motion. Another stone pummeled his forehead. His head rocked back; his vision blurry. He swung the sword at an imaginary target. Another stone clipped his chin.

He somersaulted towards a tree, putting his back against the bark and facing away from the attacker. He shook his head to clear his vision and peered around the trunk of the tree. A small boy stood in the shrubbery with a sling in his hand, whirling it over the top of his head and taking aim at Soles.

"Boy! A sling against a sword. What do you think of the odds?" shouted Soles around the trunk of the tree.

The boy's face twisted in confusion, the straps still whirling over his head. "What do you want?"

"Not you," said Soles. "Run for the hills, boy. Maybe you can find survivors."

The boy's face crinkled as he started to cry. "They would think me a coward."

"A brave man knows when to run. A coward only knows how to run," said Soles, leaning against the tree staring into space. In the corner of his eye, he spotted an Othnielia, a small bipedal dinosaur that only grew to about five feet

63

long. The tail, held off the ground, was for balance; making it fast and agile. Lucky for Soles it preferred eating plants with its beaklike snout instead of humans. He murmured, "Damn, I hate the country."

A moment later, he heard the boy crashing through underbrush away from his position. Soles sighed and felt the lump on his forehead. He wanted to kill a powerful man, and he was almost killed by a boy. Soles shook his head and thought, *Potential.* Sitting on the ground, he whistled for his horse. The horse meandered through the trees. Soles mounted and started again for the encampment.

He chuckled, relief spreading through his body. He knew he was meant to survive. Only he could bring potential to the Viridians. He thought to himself in a lilting voice, *A small hand almost killed a man—the man trying to kill a demigod with his fist.*

Soles rode into camp. The auxiliary guard reported no trouble from the queen. Soles thought about her. She was not omniscient. If she were, she would have attacked the vanguard left behind. She was a mystery. Her men fought like a pack of Coelophysis, the bipedal dinosaurs that acted as one unit taking care of the pack. Soles liked to think he would get the chance to talk to her. As it went, the outcome would be simple: he would topple the castle. But time was not on his side. He left orders for the army that had destroyed the town to stand down when they returned.

Soles walked into his tent. The stones had given him a headache. The boy reminded him of the futility of his desire. The course was set. The Erimos people would be conquered. He would be a hero. He would reap the awards of victory. But right now, all he wanted was pain relief.

Soles called to the guard outside his tent, "Ask Captain Steg to report to me." Soles did not expect an answer from the guard, only the order to be forwarded. He rubbed his forehead and could feel a small lump under the mask. Funny how the mask, which instilled fear in his troops, probably saved his life.

"Captain Steg reporting, sir," he said, saluting over his heart.

Soles peered at the man through the slits of the mask. "Captain, I want more intelligence. The castle is going to be a maze of rooms. I need someone who has been in the inside. Find me that someone. Dismissed."

As the man saluted and left, Soles checked his jaw. Grabbing the tip of his chin, he worked the jaw muscles. The damn boy had also almost broken his jaw. It felt stiff, and it clicked as he swiveled it. Soles snorted. Deadly men had tried to kill him, and a small boy almost succeeded.

Chapter Sixteen

Zen stood outside the command center located in the middle of the campus. The guards ignored him as he waited for his audience with Duke Kedwin. Zen carried a leather case in one hand with the potions he and Stephen had made the previous night. The sun was sweltering. His brown britches were hot, and the blue tunic he normally wore was soaked with sweat. He was going to have to change tunics after this meeting.

"How much longer do I have to wait?" asked Zen. The slack-jawed guard only nodded. Zen said sarcastically, "You must be the brains of this operation."

The guard stepped forward in agitation when the door slammed open.

A man richly dressed said, "Duke Kedwin will see you now, Zenith Alexander."

Zen smiled at the guard as he passed into the building Rich tapestries hung from the ceiling to the floor. All intricately woven, the cost of each merely the annual salary of an average soldier. Zen ignored the wall hangings. He mounted stairs to reach the corridors of the upper level. At the top, Zen sucked in a lungful of air. He proceeded down the hall to a large set of double doors at the end. Previously the room had housed the state room of the college professors, and it was large enough for meetings to be held. As Zen approached the doors, they swung open on well-oiled hinges.

Duke Kedwin stood up behind the desk and motioned Zen inside. "The great Zenith Alexander here to see me." Even Zen could register the false smile as the pale skin twisted around it. Kedwin's dark hair added shadows to his face. The tall lean man had a pooch of a stomach.

"Duke Kedwin, I am here to deliver the first batch of healing potions for your review." Zen put the case on the desk and opened the latches, spinning the case to reveal the contents.

Duke Kedwin leaned over and peeked at the potions. "My! They are purple. Are they supposed to be purple?"

"Only the very best is purple, sir. The potions can heal fractures in moments, close wounds, and heal internal damage. These particular potions are not your garden variety. A fortune rests on your desk, sir." Zen sat down in the chair facing the duke. "May I ask, why only five hundred? The army is close to seven hundred strong."

"I know, but the farmers are not going to receive one drop of these potions." Duke Kedwin sat back into his chair. "I am not here to coral cattle, Zenith Alexander."

"But what of these men who are putting their lives in your hands?" asked Zen heatedly.

"You don't get it. The tactics we are teaching the farmers are simple. Ride into camp on a horse and kill as many men as you can before being killed. You can't expect me to train an army in two weeks. The farmers are a large club. My experienced men are the surgical tool. Pockets of resistance will sprout up after the initial charge of the farmers. With the men from the castle—experienced men—we will wipe out the resistance of the invaders who will regroup. The potions are for them."

"You would sacrifice five hundred men," said Zen, his brow wrinkling with disgust.

"I will sacrifice them all to rid our kingdom of invaders." Duke Kedwin leaned over the desk. "Listen, King Norman Alexander is dead."

"My brother is dead? Why haven't you told me this?" sputtered Zen. His face drained of color. His eyes lost focus.

"The timing was not right, Zenith. The dukes decided that an electoral king needed to rule. Since tradition dictates the second son may not rule, the decision has been made: the Alexander line ends today. My line will rule." Kedwin leaned back in the chair with a smug face.

"You're a pompous ass, Kedwin. Queen Clarissa has a son. He shall continue the line. The queen can be an interim," said Zen pointing at him for emphasis.

The newly crowned King Kedwin shifted some paper on the desk. "The decision has been made."

"By who, you backstabbing son of a bitch?" yelled Zen.

Papers crinkled in the false king's hands. He shook them violently. "You will not call your king a son of a bitch." Kedwin screamed, "Guards! Take this man to the center of town and let the people see my first proclamation: ten lashes of the cat-o'-nine-tails."

As the men dragged Zen from the room, he yelled, "Your first decree is soaked in blood."

***

66

During the time of Zenith's betrayal, Kira walked into the barracks yelling, "Wake up, you louts! Another day's hard work ahead." The men moaned and slowly rose from their beds. "Nice to see you dressed Stephen. Now strip to your skivvies."

Stephen had not bothered to undress after meeting with Zen.

The men whistled and catcalls permeated the room. Kira endured the calls and said, "All of you will dress only in your undergarments today. Outside is a wagon filled with leather armor. Find the set that is comfortable for you to wear."

The men cheered and talked excitedly as they exited the barracks. They felt like army regulars finally. The gear was piled on the flat bed of a wagon. Discarded pieces from the dukes of the realm storerooms, the pieces were ragged and barely serviceable. Individual men mauled the stack looking for something that would loosely fit.

After Stephen undressed, he started for the door.

"Not you, Stephen," said Kira. "You will not find armor that will fit your small frame." She reached down by the front door, where she had dropped a sack when entering. "I hope it fits. It was my first real set of armor." She reached into the bag and placed the armor on Stephen's cot. "It is a little beat up and not as heavy as the men's armor, but it should protect you."

"Thank you, Kira." Stephen reached for the armor. "It's black instead of army brown."

"Yeah, well, let's hope it doesn't make you a target. Get dressed and join us outside," said Kira as she exited.

Stephen donned the armor. The leather was stiff in places and suppler in others to give full range of movement. Stephen checked the armor after dressing. The chest plate in the shirt was uncomfortable and heavy. Stephen beat his chest with a fist and felt a hard substance sewn into the lining. The leather in the arms was soft but durable. The pantlegs felt heavy. On the outside, the same hard material was sewn into the lining. Looking down at his feet, the brown leather boots looked out of place. Stephen decided the armor felt good and rejoined his comrades outside.

"Well, look at the pretty boy. He's too good for army brown," said Hank. The men turned and stared at Stephen.

Kira interrupted, "With your fat ass, Hank, we may need a sling." The men laughed and turned back to dressing.

Sam walked up to Stephen and commented, "Looks good on you. Don't let the boys tease you too much."

"The only one teasing is Hank," said Stephen. "Why do you think we are getting armor?"

"Can't ride a horse with your ass hanging out. It might get hit. The men like it now, but later it is going to feel as heavy as glass."

"What do you know about wearing armor?"

"Nothing, but it feels heavy," countered Sam while blanching. Stephen just could not put a finger on Sam. He was getting more and more mysterious.

Kira called the men to order. They marched to the mess hall where the men eagerly stood at attention in their new armor. The men felt proud, and it showed on their faces. They felt special. Discipline and order were easy to maintain. At last, the farmers felt the power associated with being in the army. All the men, as little boys do, had once dreamed of being a knight for the king.

Later at the practice field, things did not go as well. As the men rode their horses in their new armor, mistakes abounded. Some actually toppled off their horses while swinging too widely at the practice dummies. Kira shouted instructions. She did not slander the men, only gave them encouragement. After an hour, she called a water break. As the men drank, Kira walked around and gave pointers to the men. Never pointing out specific failures of the men, she lifted the men's spirits. After the break, the men lined up again on their horses. Kira sounded the charge. The men had listened to Kira. Not one man fell off his horse, and the targets took hits. The men felt emboldened. They shouted at each other to improve individual strikes on the dummies. They worked hard until midday.

A messenger delivered a packet to Kira. She tore the top off and read the letter. She called for the men to muster around her. Grooms took the horses. As the men gathered, she read the letter one more time. "Men, we are ordered to march into the center of the campus. By King Kedwin's order," her voice shook, "we are to witness a punishment for insubordination. King Alexander's brother will receive ten lashes for the crime.

Sam said, "But public lashings are outlawed. The kingdom has never endorsed public humiliation."

"I know, Sam," said Kira sadly. "My father has gone too far."

Hank spoke up. "So, what do we do?"

Kira slapped the sheet of paper on her thigh. "Nothing. We are only there to witness the punishment. Don't worry; I will file formal charges with the remaining dukes for this unlawful act. May God help the soul being punished. As for now, we must report to the square, so line up and move out."

The men grumbled as they marched. No form of public humiliation had ever been carried out in the kingdom of Erimos. Some crimes were punishable by death, such as rape and murder, but punishment had always been a private affair carried out by a duke's henchman. Only recently had crime become a problem, since the weather affected the livelihood of men. Bandits had sprung up, but the dukes had dealt with them civilly. Men had been jailed. Bandits had been killed in the struggle of lawful men trying to bring order. Public humiliation was not an option. Public floggings bordered on barbarism in the minds of the freemen of Erimos. Public displays of torture were unlawful. In the men's minds, a sour chord rung.

Kira's eight-man squad formed up with the rest of Vector Platoon. As the platoons marched into the square, the support staff and miscellaneous people followed the army. Each platoon of the army quartered off the middle square of a field. The field had been a wide-open space in the middle of the campus used by students to play games or relax on the green grass. Stephen was at the back of the platoon and could not see very well. He craned his neck, but all he could see was the fat, broad back of a man lashed to a pole.

A trumpet blared, and a herald starting reading the charges out loud to the large audience gathered around the square. Most of the crowd was civilians. "It is decreed that Zenith Alexander receive ten lashes for insubordination to the new king of Erimos. King Kedwin…"

Stephen did not hear the herald. He was making a beeline towards Zen. An arm grabbed him.

"Where you going, son?" asked Sam, stopping him.

"To help Zen. Let me go," said Stephen, struggling in Sam's grip.

Kira broke ranks and grabbed Stephen's thrashing head. "You can't do anything, Stephen."

"He's been a father to me, Kira. He's old; he will not survive the lashings."

Kira held his head. "A father, huh? Are you willing to take his place?"

Stephen sobbed with tears forming in his eyes. "Yes, anything to help him."

Sam said solemnly, "You can invoke 'adam vo,' the sins of the father carried by the son."

"How?" asked Stephen, his face clearing.

"Walk up to Zenith and place your hand on his head and shout 'adam vo,'" answered Kira.

"OK, let me go, Sam." Sam released him, and Stephen trotted into the square.

Sam asked, "Will it work?"

Kira responded, "I don't know, but he has to try. The old man will not survive ten lashes of the cat-o'-nine-tails. Stephen is going to be hard pressed not to be crippled by the lash if accepted as a replacement."

Stephen walked steadily out of the crowd towards Zen. No one stopped him. The crowd seemed mesmerized by the public display. The herald had finished reciting the charges against Zen. Stephen placed his hand on Zen's head and yelled, "*Adam vo!*"

Zen turned his head up to Stephen, "No. Please, son, no."

"You are right. I am your son. Let me take this burden," replied Stephen with tears in his eyes.

King Kedwin sat in a high-back chair on a building's porch. "Who invokes 'adam vo'?"

Stephen turned to the usurping king. "I do. Stephen Bishop Alexander."

"Zenith Alexander has no children," scowled King Kedwin.

"I am the adopted son of Zenith Alexander," replied Stephen, holding his head up and looking around at the crowd.

"Are you wearing my daughter's old armor?" asked King Kedwin angrily.

"Are you sitting in my cousin's seat?" spat Stephen.

King Kedwin peered gravely at Stephen. The punishment was meant to kill the only real threat to the crown. He gauged the crowd's reaction. The crowd expected him to comply. Some people actually started chanting "adam vo." He scowled and said, "Take the man's place. It will amuse me to watch him squirm while each lash tears your skin."

Stephen leaned over and whispered in Zen's ear, "Find me a potion. I will need it." Stephen unbound Zen's wrists from the post.

Zen rubbed his wrists methodically. He caught Kira's eye. "I will find you a potion." He crab-walked over to Kira, his knees shaking. He whispered something to her. Kira waved Sam over. The platoon leader was annoyed by people breaking rank. Kira pierced the platoon leader with a venomous glare, daring him to say something. She spoke to Sam, and then Sam ran towards the old university library.

Stephen took off the armored shirt and threw it onto the ground. He thought about needling King Kedwin again but decided against it. He knelt and grasped the pole above his head. A lackey from King Kedwin's upstart party bound his wrists to the pole.

King Kedwin shouted, "Begin!"

A large man approached Stephen. The tormenter wore a loose-fitting white robe that hung down to his knees. The robe had sleeves that seemed to hang from the man's arms. The wretch's orange hair sprang from the top of the robe, making him look like a live candle. The tortuous cat-o'-nine-tails hung loosely from his right hand.

The torturer pressed his lips together and whirled the cat-o'-nine-tails above his head. He flung his arm forward. The first strike cracked on Stephen's naked back. Stephen screamed, as did the crowd in chorus. A fine mist of blood spotted the torturer's white uniform. The red-haired man struck again. As one, Stephen and the support staff and miscellaneous people who had gathered for the excitement screamed out loud. The men in formation grumbled under their breath. Officers tried to quieten them with stern stares.

Stephen's first and then only thought was to not beg for mercy. His mind seemed to have cracked. A voice in his head repeated over and over again, "No mercy." His back felt like someone had poured boiling oil down the center. Another lash, and Stephen's back sprayed more blood onto the tormenter's white robe. Stephen had lost count of the number of lashes. He could not focus on anything other than the open wounds, cascading blood, and what felt like fire erupting from the jagged pieces of flesh hanging carelessly from his backbone.

As Stephen was flogged, the crowd became restless. Some shouted for the man to stop. As the flogging continued, the crowd started booing. Angry shouts were directed at King Kedwin. The red-haired man was covered in crimson blood. Stephen's blood had splattered the white robe. Men and women pointed and shouted at the caricature of a red demon with one arm like a striking viper.

The last strike snaked across Stephen's torso as he lay motionless at the base of the pole. Stephen's back bled profusely, with torn skin dangling from the nape of his neck to the lower spine.

First one, then two stones were thrown by someone in the crowd—aimed at King Kedwin. More people started throwing stones. Guards shielded their king from a shower of rocks. King Kedwin ducked around the corner of the building, stones following him. The king's men started breaking up the angry mob, threatening them with swords. The mob slowly broke up; the quarry of their wrathful desire had escaped. Even the army men standing in formation muttered under their breath.

Kira ran to Stephen. She tried to mold the torn skin to his back with her hands. The blood made her hands slip. Zen sat down next to her and asked, "Is he dead?" His heart raced.

"No, I do not think so, but he is in shock. Where is Sam?" asked Kira, looking around.

"I'm here," said Sam, dropping down next to Stephen. "Zen, untie his hands and help me lay him on his stomach."

Kira grabbed Sam's arm and said, "Do you have the potion?"

"Yes, but he is unconscious. He can't drink it. I brought some catgut. I am going to sew his flesh together," said Sam hurriedly.

Sam started sewing the jigsaw pieces of Stephen's skin. Someone brought water and a towel to sop the blood off Stephen's body as Sam sutured the flaps of skin. After the last stitch, all three of those who had nursed him were covered in Stephen's blood.

Kira sat back and looked around. The courtyard was empty, as if people wanted to forget the horrible thing they had witnessed. She checked Stephen's ragged breath and sighed in hope. If the boy would only wake up for one moment, the potion would heal him. She decided that a fresh cot would benefit the healing process. She told her companions her plan, and the three of them carried Stephen to the bunk house.

Three hours passed as they stood vigil over Stephen's cot, each of them entertaining dark thoughts. Sam thought about the country he loved colliding with death. Zen thought about his brother's death. Kira thought of her father's ambition and her mother's death. All of them kept their eyes directed at Stephen's broken body, hoping for a moment of consciousness.

Chapter Seventeen

The room, pitch black, echoed with the sound of Zacadam's snores. Every couple of minutes, he growled under his breath, followed by a whimper. His unconscious mind cycled with contempt and then guilt. He rolled onto his back and started dreaming.

Hearing a fanfare, Zacadam rolled down the street in a horse-drawn buggy. Open to the air, he sat in the carriage with a golden crown upon his brow, waving and smiling at the people lining the streets. His brain felt contentment; his stomach rolled with horror. The people cheered his name, danced and played merry tunes on instruments. All of them wore bright festival clothes. All of them leered with empty sockets in their skulls. Each figure, the rotting remains of skeletons. Not even children throwing flowers escaped the plague of rotten flesh. Zacadam realized he was the last living soul in Erimos.

He woke up screaming. He stopped after the breath left his lungs. He peered around and thought he was in a mausoleum. He screamed again. Only after his throat clenched to stop the screaming did he realize he was not encased in an abysmal sarcophagus. His trembling hand reached for the box of candles. After setting up a candle, he pulled out a match. He moaned, not wanting to light the match, scared the darkness covered something even more terrifying. He struck the match against the stone. He concentrated on the candle, blinding his peripheral vision to ward off the creeping shadows. The candle burned brightly, temporarily blinding him with lances of light. He sat back on his haunches.

Zacadam peered into the gloom. His eyes dilated, seeing in the corner a pile of feces from nature's call. Apple cores strewn over the floor and half-eaten potatoes littered the room. He fantasized about a slab of meat. He tried to recall the last time meat touched his tongue. He poked his tongue out of his mouth, willing it to taste meat. The tongue picked up the aromas of the pile of shit. He slapped his jaws together, nipping the tip of the tongue.

He stared at the door at the top of the stairs. The door blended in with the shadows. He was uncertain if he would laugh or cry if someone opened the door. His mind reeled, and he thought *Someone please release me from this pit of hell.* His throat croaked while thinking about freedom. He felt the pressure in his bladder. He shifted his clothes and pissed on his bare belly. The urine felt warm and somehow comforting. After relieving himself, he reached for another apple.

The apple was bright red, promising to be juicy and sweet. He bit into the apple, his throat constricting, not allowing the pulp or juices to reach his stomach. He wretched as the juicy pulp hit the floor. He knew right then that he was dying. A whole castle above his head contained food for hundreds. He only wanted one meal. Starving to death seemed trifle to him. Hung, quartered, or burned were his choices if discovered. He stared at the door again.

Could he afford to be caught if someone found him lifting food? The choice was obvious. Stay here and die from starvation, or climb the stairs in search of food. *I can hold for one more day,* he thought. *Surely Soles will be victorious.* His stomach clenched into a small ball, reminding him of his own cowardly constitution. He made his hand into a fist and slammed it into his stomach, trying to loosen the constriction. He stopped after three blows and stared at the door. An hour passed, drool escaping the corner of his mouth, as he willed Soles to open the door. His blank stare at the door continued for an uncountable amount of time.

Chapter Eighteen

After three hours, Sam made eye contact with Kira. He darted his eyes to the left. Kira nodded and excused herself to Zen. She and Sam walked just outside the open barracks doors.

Holding her head down, Kira said, "He's running a fever."

Sam grabbed her hand. "I know. It doesn't look good, but I have to tell you something."

Kira lifted her head and stared into his eyes. "What?"

"Your father was planning on murdering Zen."

Kira shook her head. "No. No. Anyone would have trouble with the flogging."

"When I was cleaning Stephen's wounds, bits of glass washed out of his skin. The flail had been dipped in glass," said Sam, lightly trying to soften the blow of her father's treachery.

"Glass? I see." In shock, Kira turned to the double doors. Pain swelled in her breast. "The wounds were horrendous. Do you think he will survive?"

"He is a strong young man. Only one moment of clarity, and Zen will give him the potion. We will just have to wait and see," said Sam, staring in the boy's direction.

"Sam," she cornered him and looked directly into his eyes, "you are not a farmer."

Sam considered telling her the truth but restrained himself. "Let's just say I'm well rounded."

"Well, when you are ready, I would like to hear your story." She dropped Sam's hand and returned inside.

Sam stood at the door. He considered everything he knew about wounds. Stephen's back was nasty. The flesh had been ripped from the frame. He judged that Stephen had a small chance to be coherent enough to take the potion. The old man would not have survived. He took a deep breath and headed for the door.

The squad returned after supper; each man gave condolences to Zen. Hank even gave a gruff apology. He figured the boy was going to die. The men settled down. No one spoke; all felt the death watch. Eventually day turned into night. The men slept, and Zen held Stephen's hand.

The warmth and love the old man felt could not be contained in his heart. After midnight, Zen wept quietly. His head bowed; the old man squeezed Stephen's hand as tight as he could.

"Zen, you are hurting my hand," said Stephen in a raspy voice.

"Don't talk, just drink this." Zen poured the contents of the vial into Stephen's mouth.

"Will it make me feel better?" asked Stephen childishly.

"Yes, yes," Zen said patting his shoulder. Zen grinned like a schoolboy on his first date. "Sleep now. In the morning you will feel right as rain."

Stephen nodded sleepily. He turned over on his side and promptly fell asleep.

Zen leaned over and started undressing the wound. The skin was crisscrossed with pink, jagged scars. Stephen would wear the scars the rest of his life. King Kedwin had given him a badge of honor that would rock the kingdom of Erimos.

Zen slept in the chair next to Stephen's cot. In the morning, Kira shook the old man awake, asking, "How is he?"

Yawning, Zen said, "He will be fine. He awoke in the middle of the night, and I gave him the potion. He will bear the marks of King Kedwin's disgrace for the rest of his life."

Kira looked melancholy. "Are they bad?"

"It could be worse, but yes, the scars are bad. The body closed the wounds before taking the potion. The knitting process had begun, so the potion speeded up the process. He will be fine. I recommend he stay in bed today. He will probably fight my order, since he'll feel better, but the potion needs time to be fully effective."

"What are you going to do?" asked Kira thoughtfully.

"I have something I need to pick up. I will be back in a few minutes. Stay here, and make sure he stays in bed." Zen kissed Kira softly on the forehead, passing on a feeling of relief.

Kira's morbid curiosity wanted to see the scars, but Stephen lay on his back. She sat in the chair, her feelings like a winter storm. Her attraction for him had grown in a short period of time.

Stephen did not open his eyes but said, "Shouldn't you be with the men?"

Kira smiled and said, "All my men are my responsibility. The other men are being looked after by another."

Stephen opened his eyes and grinned. "And I was hoping for special treatment." He sat up in bed. "Where's Zen?"

"Zen said he had to get something. He will be back in a couple of minutes. You have to stay in bed." She felt a warm glow in the pit of her stomach.

"I feel fine," said Stephen, reaching for his clothes.

"Zen's orders: stay in bed for the day." She thought hastily *What has this boy done to me?* "Are you hungry?"

"Ravenous."

"When Zen returns, I will round you something up."

The door creaked open, and Zen ducked his head in. For some reason, Kira felt relief at the thought of escaping the moment. She could not pin her feelings down. She stood up as if to leave.

Zen said, "Stay a moment, Kira. I need to talk to you both."

Stephen remarked, "I feel fine."

"I know you do, son." Zen gripped a belt in his hands. "I am leaving the camp."

Kira and Stephen started to protest.

"Hush, hush," said Zen softly. "I need to talk to Queen Clarissa. After yesterday's fiasco, reports of violence and protesting have reached King Kedwin's ears. I do not know his play, but someone has to stop him."

"Zen, why did you not tell me you were the king's brother?" asked Stephen softly.

"I'm sorry, Stephen. I renounced any intentions to the throne when I was a young man. It was understood that I would be a Potioner, and my twin brother would be king. Believe me—I do not want to be king. My nephew is the rightful heir to the throne, and I will see to it he has a chance. I did not mean to deceive you, Stephen," pleaded Zen. "You are the son I never had."

"And you are the father I never had," said Stephen with his face screwed up tight.

Kira nodded and turned away for a moment.

"Well, son, I have a gift for you before I leave," Zen said, handing the belt over to Stephen.

Stephen turned it over in his hands. A small, hard pouch was attached to the belt. He popped the latch.

"There are ten potions in the pouch, two of each for healing, fire, strength, swiftness, and poison for you to use in an emergency. As you know, one potion is good for only twenty-four hours, so choose well. As for the poison, do not let it touch your skin. It is highly corrosive and deadly, a secret recipe of my family to be used only in a life-or-death situation. This is all I can give you in these troubled times to remain safe. I hope it is enough." Zen turned to Kira. "Please look after him in Kedwin's suicidal attempt to kill the invaders. You do know its suicide?"

"I have always known, but I will look after my men. I hope the training I give them will be enough. I cannot abandon them. Some will survive." Kira planted a kiss on Zen's cheek.

Stephen was confused about what they were talking about but decided to have faith in Kira.

"Well, I must be going. I have a long journey ahead. Keep safe, Stephen, and I will see you at the capital." Zen bent down and kissed the top of Stephen's head. Zen turned and thought, *He is resourceful. He will survive.*

"I'll go find something for you to eat," said Kira.

"Kira," said Stephen. "Thank you."

"Not a problem," she said. "You just rest." Kira thought to herself she needed time to sort out her feelings.

Zen was waiting for her outside. "Can I speak to you for a moment, Kira?"

"Anything, Zen. You have been my friend for a long time. Remember when you found me in the castle eating the king's breakfast pastries?"

"I remember. You were a small girl then; now you're a young woman. Be careful, Kira. Your feelings for Stephen may get you in trouble with your father. Believe me, I am happy for both of you, but just be careful."

"I don't know what you're talking about," said Kira shyly.

"Well, this old man thinks it is wonderful. You will figure it out. Now excuse me, I have to talk to an old friend before I leave. I love you both. Goodbye."

Kira watched him leave. She was slightly confused. She knew she had feelings for Stephen, but could she call it love? Kira decided to ponder her feelings later; right now, Stephen needed hot food.

***

Zen sat in the armchair looking at a dead man. Master Salender had wasted away in the past couple of days. He had decided to drink himself to death.

Zen leaned forward. "Master, you need to eat something. In these unruly times, we will need every wise man."

"Wise," said Salender shaking a bottle. "We will need a surgeon to cut away the putrefactive boil our country will become."

"All the more reason wise men need to help our people in this time of crisis, a crisis of nationalism."

Master Salender leaned forward and conspiratorially whispered, "He tried to kill you."

"Will he kill the boy?" asked Zen quietly.

"He may not have to. King Kedwin and his men could be slightly late in their attack. The castle seized by the invaders, the queen and her son dead; then the heroic new king taking vengeance and garnering the people's support." Salender spit on the floor in contempt.

"You really don't think it will come to that. The loss of lives would be too great." Zen sat back in his chair, anguish outlining his face.

"If someone had told me yesterday a member of the royal family was to be flogged in public, I would have called him a buffoon. Kedwin has his sights on the throne." Master Salender sighed. "The man is a lecherous bastard. He only wants power."

"What can I do?" asked Zen thoughtfully.

"Protect your nephew and his mother if you can. You will have to come up with a strategic plan." The boldness in Salender's voice petered out. "I don't know how."

"For one thing," said Zen loudly, "stop drinking. We will need you in the future." In a kinder voice he said, "I will need your guidance, old friend."

Master Salender stared at the bottle for a long time, then he murmured, "That's the easy way out. I will not take that road." He dropped the bottle to the floor. "I can't come with you, but I will sow seeds of dissension if Kedwin uses unscrupulous methods to seize the throne."

Zen nodded. He had a mission but not a plan.

Chapter Nineteen

The dust clogged Zen's nostrils. After buying a donkey to replace Cow, Zen started his journey north at midday. The heat of a summer day bore down upon him. Shrubs and small trees lined the road, affording no shade. The road was a main artery to the castle proper. Zen expected the journey to take a couple of days if the donkey could sustain a decent speed.

His thoughts scattered in his head. First, how to sneak past enemy lines to the castle; second, how to gain entrance into the castle. No easy feat to overcome these. He angrily shook the reins. He needed a plan.

He considered deception. Should he play the sleazy type looking to make coin from the invaders selling his wares to the enemy? No, he could not rationalize selling potions to the enemy. He thought about sneaking through camp after dark—Not easy for a large man. Could he disguise himself as a refugee? Lost, disoriented, a person who was not threatening. They would kill him on the spot.

Zen had to think of something to make him personally valuable to the insurgents. Eureka! He had it. An ambassador for surrendering the castle. A man looking for concessions. A false pretense, of course, but an ambassador would need to return the response from the invaders to Queen Clarissa. Zen's mind heated up.

An ambassador under a flag of parlay would be welcome to the invaders. A truce called for the surrender of the castle. He would devise concessions for the people of the castle. A plan, but a dangerous one. He could be held for a political hostage. Zen's mind turned, weighing the options. He decided to take a chance. Maybe a political figure would be invited to dinner. He could not remember the last time a feast was prepared in his honor. His stomach growled just thinking about it. Out of a bend in the road, a man appeared.

"Hey, you're going the wrong way," shouted a man.

The shout startled Zen. "What?"

A man wearing leather clothes and carrying a gunnysack over his back replied, "You can't go that way. Everyone is dead that way."

Zen stopped the donkey. "What happened?"

The scruffy man leaned against the wagon and said, "The invaders attacked Simone. They wiped us out. A few of the less hardy folks hid outside of town. The rest are gone. They burned everything, killed everyone, and marched out of town like a parade." The man spat. "They even killed the women after they raped them."

"How many people survived?" asked Zen mournfully.

"Just the ones hidden outside of town deemed unfit to man the barricades. Some women, children, and older men are the only survivors." The man hung his head and said, "I ran away as soon as I saw them coming." He looked up. "I pulled ahead of the crowd, maybe to get help for the refugees from someone at Stone University."

"You're not too far away. How far back is the rest of the group?"

"About half a day's travel behind me. The group moves slow."

Zen shook the reins. "You will find help up ahead." As Zen pulled away, the man turned his back and trudged down the road. Zen thought about the ramifications of the army attacking the small town. Did they need resources, or was it just for sport? If it was for sport, he thought his plan may be too perilous, but he could not think of a better way.

After several hours, Zen caught up with the refugees. He pulled the wagon to the side of the road. He passed out food and water to the people. Some were hurt, not used to walking a long distance. Older folks and children were crippled by the long walk. Zen gave them cheap healing potions from his stash, ample enough help for the ill-gotten. He spent the rest of the day encouraging people with the knowledge that relief was up ahead at the university. After the last trailing body passed Zen, he decided to camp there for the night. He had lost time, but he had to help the unfortunate.

As the campfire burned low, Zen reached within his tunic and pulled an iron chain over his head. He unclasped the chain and extended it above his right hand. A silver ring slid down the chain and landed in his palm. He turned the ring over, peering at the design in the fading light. The ring, stamped with the royal seal, glittered in the dying light. He placed it on his ring finger. It was too small and slid only to the first knuckle. He chuckled silently and placed the ring on his pinky finger. He remembered a time when the ring fit properly. He mused about too many sweet cakes. He closed his fist and stared at the ring.

Chapter Twenty

Kira hurried through the camp in the predawn light. The refugees had trickled in during the night. The soldiers on watch shooed them past the base camp until they milled around at the perimeter. Women, children, and old men collapsed into a makeshift camp. The soldiers kept watch over them, warning them not to enter the base camp. The people were too tired to argue. Kira was going to speak to her father.

Kira brushed passed the guards outside of her father's office. She flung the door wide and demanded, "What are you doing?"

King Kedwin looked up from his desk at the back of the room. "My dear daughter, what do you mean? I am quite a busy man." He shuffled a pile of papers. "Come see me at a more appropriate time, say, dinner."

Kira stood in the middle of the room, glaring at him. "I am talking about the refugees from Simone."

King Kedwin stood up and walked around the large oak desk. He placed his hands on Kira's shoulders and looked down into her eyes. "Those people are the collateral damage of war." He turned briskly and said, "They are not my problem."

Kira screamed, "Not your problem! You profess to be the king, and your people are not your problem?"

"Kira," shouted Kedwin, "take hold of yourself, or I will have you whipped."

"Like you did Stephen?" Kira shouted in retort.

Kedwin rubbed his face. "What do you propose?"

"Food, blankets, and coin for the people," answered Kira.

Kedwin waved his hand, half turning. "I cannot give them coin."

"These people have lost their homes. They will need to build a new life to survive," pleaded Kira.

Kedwin looked askance at her. "You never look at the big picture. Peasants will always need coin. I will service their needs but expect something in return. They will work for the support of the soldiers."

"What about the children?" asked Kira.

"They're peasants. They know how to work. Now leave me. I will delegate the task to someone appropriate. Do not take actions on your own. Already people are saying you're not adequately training your men, being inappropriate while coddling Stephen." Kedwin turned his back, dismissing his daughter.

Kira stared daggers into his back before leaving.

***

Kira slammed the barracks door open wide, "Get up. Put your gear on. We are running before breakfast."

Stephen hopped up from his cot. "Is everything OK, Kira?"

"Everything's fine, soldier. Get dressed." Kira walked around the barracks, slapping men on the back and telling them to hurry.

In full battle gear, the men ran laps around the practice field. Kira leading the way, she pushed the men hard. After five laps, she stopped the men while her breath rang in her ears. She thought, *I am not my father.* She felt a pang of anxiety for taking it out on her men. She looked around, thinking these men would likely die, but she would die with them. She dismissed them for breakfast.

The men returned to the practice field after breakfast. Kira stood next to the pile of wooden swords. "Men, while others believe you will not fall from your horse in battle, I think of it as inevitable. Stephen, do you remember the first kata I taught you?"

Stephen stepped forward. "Yes, ma'am."

"All right, men, form a line facing me spaced apart. Stephen, please perform the kata for the men," she said, handing Stephen a sword.

Stephen gracefully danced with the sword. Kira felt proud of him for remembering the moves so flawlessly.

"I'm not doing that. It's silly," said Hank.

Kira stared into Hank's eyes. "Really. Why don't you and Stephen spar?"

Hank grinned and flexed his muscles. "I would be glad to hurt the whelp."

Hank and Stephen faced each other. Hank held his sword in his right hand, legs spread, his weight resting on his toes. Stephen faced him like a fencer, right leg in front. Hank swung wide at Stephen's midsection. Stephen danced back. Hank tried an overhead chop at Stephen's head. Stephen parried and kicked Hank in the chest. Hank fell on his back. Hank rolled to his feet; he was angry. He charged Stephen; sword held low in front of him. Stephen whirled around and smacked Hank's buttocks as he passed. Hank came up limping, grabbing his left butt cheek. He turned and faced Stephen again, murder in his eyes. Hank grabbed the sword with two hands, slashing the air right and left, charging at Stephen. Stephen parried the sword strokes with one arm while stepping back, and then pivoted to the right, slapping his sword down onto

Hank's wrist. A loud crack issued. Hank dropped the sword, his wrist broken. Hank's face a mask of pain, he yelped.

Kira strode up to Hank. She grabbed his arm and examined the wrist. "It's broken. Stephen, take him to the medic."

Stephen felt giddy. During the fight, Stephen had remembered Kira's advice to breathe. Now his legs felt like noodles. He had not been in a fight since he was a child, and he felt sorry for breaking Hank's wrist. He dropped the sword and hurried to Hank's side.

"I am sorry, Hank. I didn't mean to break your wrist," apologized Stephen.

Hank shrugged. "I was trying to break your head open." Hank thought for a moment. "I'm sorry too. I am not the easiest man to get along with." Hank looked at his feet. "The men think I'm a boob."

Sam clapped Hank's shoulder. "I wouldn't mind playing with you for a while."

The other men laughed and gathered around Hank. They knew the score; every man was needed for the upcoming fight. The men patted Hank's back as Stephen led him away to the medic. Hank's smile could be seen a hundred yards away.

Stephen returned half an hour later, reporting that Hank had bed rest today to heal. Kira asked Stephen to lead the kata, and she walked around encouraging the men. After a couple of hours, she called for a break. The men sat down in a loose semicircle to chat about the experience. They all agreed the extra training would be worth it.

Stephen approached Kira and shyly asked, "Does this mean we will not be meeting tonight?"

Kira thoughtfully smiled and replied, "I will see you tonight."

Sam did not miss the exchange. He thought the young man was drawing a lot of attention from very powerful people.

A wrangler drove the horses they needed to continue the training into the field for the men. Cow had dominated the herd. The black stallion trembled beneath Stephen's hand, anticipating the action.

The men applauded the performances of the individuals riding through the maze. The squad started behaving like a cohesive group. Under Kira's tutelage, the men were instructed to attack the maze as a squad instead of individuals meandering in the maze. As Kira expected, the men fouled up their comrades. Some horses stopped completely, others were shunted from the maze, and men collided, falling from their horses. After the fiasco, Kira reprimanded the men. For the rest of the day, the squad walked the horses into the maze of dummies to learn how to control the horses' movements and anticipate the movements of comrades. The sunset found the men dirty and emotionally exhausted, the toll of today's events written in their faces. Kira felt that the men's spirits were low from exhaustion. Kira engaged each man in the squad, lifting their spirits with praise for a hard day's work. After a long, hot day, the men proceeded to the mess hall.

Later in the night, Kira leaned on the post of the corral looking up at the stars. She imagined each twinkle was dedicated to the fallen soldiers of the millennia. The thought depressed her, because the stars were a vast number. She tried to pick her own star from the constellations. The one dedicated to her death.

Stephen walked up slowly and said, "The stars are beautiful, each one representing the birth of life."

Kira frowned. "I was thinking they represented death."

Stephen looked up into the night sky. "How could something so pristine represent death? The blackness between could be death, each star struggling to hold back death while lighting the night sky. Why would you be fixated on death?"

Kira sighed. "My life has always been about death. How to gut a man with a knife, run him over with a horse, and swing a sword are the lessons of my childhood."

Stephen laid a hand on her shoulder. "What about music, cooking, and funny stories told by elders?"

Kira placed her hand over his. "My father wanted a boy. Now that he is king, he may yet still have a boy when he remarries. I will be lost in the maelstrom. Not knowing how to be a woman." Tears formed in her eyes.

Stephen took a chance and hugged her. "You are a woman—a strong, competent woman who will make a man very happy. The guiles employed by women to seduce a man are only entrapments of our time. You will be the next generation of strong, fearless women. I would not change anything about you."

Kira stepped away from Stephen's embrace. "Why do you call the katas a dance?"

Stephen felt her need to change the subject, so he replied, "They remind me of the festival dances of home."

"Do you wish to return home?" asked Kira.

Stephen stared up into the sky. "At first, I did, but things have changed. I planned to go back home after Zen taught me how to be a Potioner. Now the town seems small and insignificant in the world. You see that star up there?" He pointed at a constellation. "I can see that star from my home, but I want to see that star from other vantage points. I guess what I am saying is, I want to travel the world."

Kira slid back into Stephen's embrace and looked skyward. "I wouldn't mind seeing that star with you."

Stephen peered at Kira, grinning. "Let's dance under the stars."

Kira seemed concerned. "I never learned how to dance."

"It's easy. I will teach you the box step first." Stephen dragged Kira into the corral. "Trust me, it is easy to learn."

The couple danced into the late night, laughing and enjoying the moment. For a while, they enjoyed each other's company without thinking about tomorrow. They did not think about the upcoming battle. They were in the moment—the moment when life was outside of the circle and they were on the inside, alone together.

Chapter Twenty-One

Zacadam's spasming stomach woke him from a dreamless sleep. The candle still burned behind him. He had curled up on the floor at the bottom of the stairs. He laid his hand on the first step and pushed himself up into a sitting position. His stomach clenched, forcing a sob from Zacadam. He knew he was dying. He stared at the closed door.

He stood and peered around the dimly lit room. His eyes saw nothing. He turned his attention to the door at the top of the stairs. He thought pitifully, *I have to go up there.* He tried to remember the layout past the door. At the time of his escape, he had run into the bowels of the castle. Past the servant's quarters and into the storerooms before discovering the dungeon, and finally through to the lowest storage room that serviced the dungeon. The place he hid was the deepest room in the castle. He recalled that there was no one beyond the storage rooms. He could creep past the dungeon and find food in the lower storage. He decided to leave the relative safety of the room.

He climbed the stairs. At the top he felt swimmy-headed. Placing his hand firmly on the doorknob, he twisted it open. A row of torches lit the passageway. It did not occur to Zacadam that someone had lit them. On either side, jail cells lined the wall. At the end of the passage, a door led to the storage rooms. He placed his foot firmly on the floor of the dungeon. He half expected a firm shout of "Stop, murderer!" When his senses dispelled the expectation, he took another step into the dungeon.

He could see into the first cell outside his door. Manacles dangled from its ceiling and straw littered the floor. He imagined the straw soaked up the blood from the torture of a criminal. The torchlight flickered from the draft of his room. He saw himself hanging from the manacles. He jumped back against the other cell, facing his ghostly appearance. He was too scared to scream. The vision slowly dissipated. Zacadam sobbed with guilt.

Staring at the floor, he dashed down the corridor. He slammed into the closed door and fell down onto the flagstones. He lay prostrate for a moment, expecting the sound to draw attention. After a couple of minutes, Zacadam pulled himself up using the doorhandle. Quaking, he willed there to be no one behind the door.

Zacadam cracked the door and squinted through the fine line. He saw no one. He opened the door into a guard station. The room was lit, a small table with two chairs the only occupants. Zacadam passed quickly across the room. He knew food was on the other side of the door. He flung the door wide, startling a servant.

"Zacadam, your murderous bastard!" screamed the servant.

Zacadam reacted without thinking. He reached into his torn robe and found a potion. He flipped the top with his thumb and flung the potion into the servant's face. Its acidic properties started melting the servant's countenance. The man grabbed his face and tried to scream. The potion had already taken his throat. He fell down, kicking like a dying fish. Zacadam waited for the potion to do its work. The skull collapsed into itself in a gelatinous mass. The man died painfully.

Zacadam fell onto his butt, laughing hysterically. After a minute, he grabbed the dead man by his feet. Sliding the body over the stones, Zacadam dumped the body down the stairs into his safe room. Running back to the storage door, he shut the door promptly. He closed all the doors after him until he reached the top of his stairs. The body lay at the bottom of the stairs, twisted in an awkward heap. He thought happily, *Finally, some meat.*

Chapter Twenty-Two

Soles sat at a table, staring at the model castle. His plans were disintegrating with every passing moment. The engineers had promised the completion of the tunnel in a couple of days. Soles felt the death watch, the time ticking away slowly and culminating in an army at his back. His men, anxious and surly, also knew the clock was ticking on their fate. Soles tipped a set of scales that rested on the desktop with his finger. At rest, the scales were in perfect balance. The pressure of his finger tipped the scales in his imaginary opponent's favor. It represented everything wrong with this endeavor. He had assumed at the start that the scales' perfect balance was not an issue for the battle. He had assumed outnumbering the enemy three to one would be enough for conquest. The Erimos people were showing tenacity beyond his imagination. His military career stood in balance—success versus failure. One failure resulted in cruelty; a second failure would mean death.

"Sir," said a man outside of the tent, "we have a man who claims to be an emissary from the castle. He walked right into camp."

Soles stood up. "Send him in."

The first thing Soles noticed was a portly man of median height with eyes that spoke of intelligence. He was dressed in a yellow tunic embroidered with white stitching, which matched his white pants. The man neither smiled nor frowned when he entered the tent.

"Greetings. My name is Zenith Alexander," he said, holding out his hand.

Soles ignored the outstretched hand. "I am Commander Soles. What would an emissary want from me?" *Balance*, he thought. *Always keep your enemy on their heels.*

"Why, concessions for the surrender of the castle," Zen said, smiling.

Now he felt out of balance. "What concessions?" He had to reel his emotions in tight. The man was obviously politically savvy. Soles sat down in the chair to hide his surprise.

"Being the brother of the late king, I am authorized to surrender the castle if our terms are beneficial for the Erimos people," he said, smiling indifferently.

"What would be your terms?" asked Soles.

"As the conquering people, what terms will you offer?" countered Zen.

Soles felt out of his depth. The man fenced with words like a master. If he proposed terms, his successions would be political fodder for the emissary. If he did not, he would appear weak. The man had backed him into a corner in less than a minute. Soles needed a distraction.

"Have you caught Zacadam?" asked Soles wistfully.

Zen's cheek twitched. "I assumed he was here in your camp."

Soles grabbed the chip. "Zacadam will be king."

Zen did not blanch. "His price for murder, a puppet on strings for Rex Almanon."

Again, Soles had to control his emotions. The man knew about his monarch. He felt off balance; the man had an intelligencer, whereas Soles did not. Soles decided to be the military man and lie to gain ground. "Even a puppet can dance for the people."

"Anyone can pull strings, but what about the people in the castle?" asked Zen.

"The seat of the government will not change. Only the pivotal point at the top will change. Zacadam will be king." Soles noticed that when he said Zacadam's name, Zen's cheek invariably twitched.

"What of Queen Clarissa?" asked Zen quietly.

Soles smiled. The man had a crutch after all. Now what to play? A lie seemed best. "She shall marry Zacadam." Soles looked for the twitch. He was disappointed. The man was obviously gaining control.

"I shall bring the terms to Queen Clarissa personally. Good day, Commander Soles." Again, Zen offered his hand.

Soles shook Zen's hand, gripping it tightly. "I expect an answer before sunset." Zen nodded and loosened his grip. Soles pulled the man forward over the table. "I expect full cooperation."

"As do I, Commander Soles," said Zen, leaning against the table.

Soles let go of Zen's hand and watched the man wrestle his girth off the table. Soles watched him depart the tent then considered the situation. *Queen Clarissa must be buying time. Which means the army she fields is not quite ready?* Soles decided to strike tomorrow, even if the second tunnel was not finished. He expected the queen would try to delay him by asking for more negotiations. A surprise attack during parlay—Rex Almanon would be amused. Soles tipped the scales on the table in his favor.

Zen walked directly to the castle gate. His mind was unsettled by the commander of the invaders. The brief insight into the man and the implications he implied scared Zen. He decided the best course of action would be to speak directly with Queen Clarissa. Close to the main gate, a rope was lowered over the side.

Zen shouted to the men on the ramparts, "Can't you open the gates?"

A man shouted back, "Sorry, Master Potioner, we cannot breach security with the enemy so close."

Zen grumbled under his breath and donned a harness to be lifted over the wall. The harness chafed under his arms. He signaled to the men that he was ready. As the men pulled on the rope, he rotated in a clockwise direction. He bumped against the wall several times, scratching his left arm. At the top, men grabbed the harness and lifted him over the lip of the wall. Zen sat down with his back against the wall.

He looked at the nearest soldier and said, "Inform Queen Clarissa I am here, and tell her to meet me in the kitchens alone."

The man saluted and answered, "Yes sir, Master Potioner." The soldier hurried down the line.

Zen took a couple deep breaths, and a man lent a hand for him to stand. Zen passed down the line of defenders, taking a moment to slap them on the back and add praise for the defense of the castle. Zen found the steep stone stairs leading down from the wall. Taking them gingerly, Zen eventually found himself at the bottom. He crossed the courtyard and set his feet towards the kitchen.

As Zen passed down a hallway, the smells of the kitchen reached his nostrils. He could discern roasted duck, collards, sweet meat pies, and baking bread. He groaned at the thought of all the good food. He opened the door and was assaulted by the smells clinging to the room. He hurried to a small table set in the corner. A kitchen staff member dropped off a meat pie saying, "Nice to see you, Zen."

"Oh John, my good man, it is nice to be back. Nice of you to keep my table in my absence," said Zen around mouthfuls. "I missed the food."

"Figures. You miss the food but not the people who prepare it," said John jokingly.

Zen settled in. Courses of food were served to him: after the pie, a steaming roast duck. Zen's mouth watered at the sight. After picking the bones clean, a soup of collards and small boiled potatoes was dropped off by another staff member. For dessert, a fresh loaf of bread smeared with jam. Zen ate every crumb. Zen leaned back in the chair, his stomach content. He really savored the food. His eyes closed; he breathed the aromas of the kitchen.

"A fine meeting place for warfare," said Queen Clarissa. As a child, she had been called "horseface," due to a long narrow nose on an elongated face. The face had caught up with her height. Tall but not curvaceous, the queen was a model of regality. Her brown hair hung loosely around her shoulders. She wore a simple white gown stitched at the waist with a wide, blue belt, and sandals on her feet.

"Oh Zenith, you are wasting away," she said with a smile.

Zen replied, "The road is a foul place to eat."

Queen Clarissa laughed and hugged Zen in his chair. "I've missed you. I wish we were in a simpler time." She sat on the edge of the table like a friend truly comfortable with being herself.

"I need to speak to you alone, Queen Clarissa," said Zen, looking about the place.

"Well, it wouldn't be prudent to stop the gears of the kitchen. Let us adjourn to a quieter place," she said, leading Zen through a door.

They both were silent while walking down the hall, being old friends who did not need to fill the empty space. They seated themselves in Queen Clarissa's tearoom, a place of fond conversations in the past.

Queen Clarissa sipped her tea and asked, "How bad is it?"

Zen answered with a question: "What do you know?"

"I have an army at my doorstep. The missives I receive from the army at Stone University are guarded, all of them saying 'be patient,'" she replied with bitterness.

"How are you communicating with Stone University?" asked Zen.

"Master Salender and I have always kept in touch. I have not heard from him recently, but we use carrier pigeons," answered the queen.

Zen leaned back in his chair and sighed. "Duke Kedwin has committed treason."

"I was afraid of that; he has the dukes in his pocket." Queen Clarissa gestured around the room hastily. "My son will rule here."

"Without a doubt, but first the invaders, then a civil war." Zen leaned forward. "There could be another option."

"Pray tell," exclaimed the queen.

"Clarissa, I know you do not want bloodshed to be your son's inheritance." Zen grasped her hand. "Call for reinforcements now."

"They are not trained. The loss of life would be great." Queen Clarissa sat back in her chair. Her eyes squinted in deep thought. "I see your solution."

Zen explained, "Death of men now, or in the near future, is still death for our countrymen."

Queen Clarissa stood up and turned from Zen. "I am ashamed of what Kedwin has wrought." She turned back. "I will not see that leach on the throne. His people suffer under his ruling as a duke. Norman and I spoke of his people's plight often. Kira shall take his dukedom. I will cede it to her after this is over."

Zen leaned on the table. "Master Salender and I have spoken. The invaders are only a small vanguard. When we defeat them, our troubles will have only begun."

"Does Master Salender have a solution?" asked Clarissa.

"Maybe, but the details are fuzzy."

"Well, one step at a time. First the invaders, second securing the kingdom, and then we will worry about the repercussions from over the mountain." Queen Clarissa sat back down in her chair. She painfully stared into Zen's eyes and said, "Zacadam?"

Zen answered in a dead voice, "He is mine."

Queen Clarissa nodded in understanding. "I will send for the reinforcements. Tomorrow will be decisive." She leaned forward earnestly. "My friend, will you protect my son?"

"From all things, my queen," answered Zen. He thought painfully, *Running and hiding with my nephew maybe my only option if Kedwin wins.*

Chapter Twenty-Three

The order to march came down the pipeline. The recruits were to move out at midday. The logistics of an early march on short notice sent the camp into frenzy. King Kedwin had decided the cavalry would precede the wagon train of supplies needed in the campaign. Orders were given, and the men were excited. The army would proceed to a new base camp. Since the small town of Simone was reported as being deserted, King Kedwin planned to use the town as a launching point against the invaders. The men's excitement waned as they ate dust on the trail north.

The Queen's Salvation battalion rode two by two in a long column. The refugees had waved goodbye as they rode off, giving encouragement to the men. Now the men felt the sun beat down upon their brow and dust clog their noses. The morale of the men slowly dissipated under the conditions of the march.

King Kedwin led the march in a large stage coach. Riding in luxury, he bantered with his aide de camp. He felt in high spirits. The message from the carrier pigeon stated that anonymous intelligence on the invaders had informed Queen Clarissa of an attack in the morning. King Kedwin's plan was to let the invaders do his dirty work. He would wait until the enemy had breached the castle and then swoop in for a victory. If he was lucky, the queen and her son would be killed in the action. If not lucky, he had an assassin in the ranks who would murder the duo in the chaos of battle. He indeed felt lucky. The death of so many men did not register in his plans or ideals.

Kira rode in front of her squad, her feelings in a tight ball in her stomach. She believed the men needed more training. She was uncertain if she had pushed hard enough. Their lives depended on the training she provided. She worried about Stephen. The young man had found a place in her heart. She was still uncertain about her feelings for him, but tomorrow either one of them could lay on the battlefield dead. She could not reconcile her feelings for the boy. She decided that, if given the chance, she would let her heart rule after the battle. Until then she must help the men survive the upcoming fight.

Stephen felt the reality of the situation. He knew the men surrounding him were likely to die, as well as himself. His only regret was that he had wanted to kiss Kira last night. After dancing under the stars, he found himself enamored with Kira. He decided if he survived, he would profess his feelings to Kira. He only hoped she would not reject him.

Sam rode in silence. He struggled with his duty to kingdom. He would protect Kira at all costs. He would gladly lay down his life for her to survive. As for murder, he struggled with the idea. Kedwin had given him an order: "Kill them both." Sam had no illusions about the statement. The queen and her son rested on the chopping block. He was Kedwin's man, but the idea of murdering the royal family fouled his mind. He decided he would not commit murder, though his duty to Kedwin meant murder. He knew if Kedwin won, he would be a dead man, but at least his soul would be intact if he did not commit the heinous act. Sam was a man of duty, but sometimes you just had to do the right thing. Right?

Hank laughed at a joke told by a colleague. The laugh sounded nervous even to his own ears. His hands shook while holding the reins. He spoke in a loud voice, trying to drown his fright. As a man, he felt confident. As a soldier, he felt scared. He had a feeling: he would die in the upcoming conflict. He thought about his mother. If he died in the service of King Kedwin, his mother would be allotted a new homestead. He giggled and thought at least his mother would be safe. He adored her. Hank decided he would try to be the man his mother believed in, to be brave and confident.

King Kedwin's stage coach rolled into the center of Simone. Kedwin stepped out and took a large, deep breath, trying to savor victory. He gagged and coughed from the reek of the bloated, dead bodies. He hurriedly backed into the protection of his coach. He told his driver to continue to the outskirts of the town. As the column passed through Simone, the men were silent. Most of them had never seen the atrocity of war. The dead people looked like mangled caricatures of death. Some of the men's dread kept them peering at the massacred town. Others fixed their gaze on the rumps of the horses in front of them. All of them felt the horror of the place.

The army made camp on the outskirts of Simone. Even King Kedwin knew to park the army over a rise so the town could not be seen. The people of Simone were not forgotten, but the men settled down into a routine of pitching camp. The sun was setting, and the men were told not to light fires. Men grumbled, but they ate cold pack rations. Tired and emotionally drained, they spread their bedrolls and tried to rest. Ghosts of the massacred town filled their thoughts.

King Kedwin settled in the only tent in camp. A fire burned in the center, roasting a piece of lamb. He called his platoon leaders to order and outlined his plan of attack. His timing had to be perfect, the treachery of arriving too late not suspect. He counted on the inexperience of his men not to spot the timing of his planned treason. He told his men that he wanted good light for the battle, so they would wait until almost full sunup. He passed out flagons of wine and toasted their coming victory.

As the men left the tent, some staggered, having drunk to much wine. Kedwin grinned as they left. He felt very confident in usurping the throne. As the night progressed, Kedwin drank an enormous amount of wine in celebration. His aide de camp rolled him onto his bed. The bed, a thing of decadence, had been hauled by a wagon Kedwin had designed to keep the elements at bay. Kedwin laughed and snorted, curling up into a ball on the bed and promptly falling asleep.

The camp slept through the night. Guards were only posted a couple hundred yards from the perimeter. No one saw the man crouched in a ditch. He watched from a hidden position. He had already sent word to Commander Soles that the army was so close. He felt disgust for the men sleeping. He believed this army would not determine the fate of the war. He saw only farmers dressed like soldiers. His contempt for the men centered on the obvious inexperienced leadership. If the commander had not ordered the attack on the castle in the morning, the man felt he could wipe out this army with a surprise attack. He thought the auxiliaries left in the commander's camp would slaughter these men. The man crept deeper into the thicket. He would pass the word as the soon as the army marched.

Chapter Twenty-Four

Commander Soles outlined his plan for the captains an hour before dawn: a three-prong attack. First, a rush to the walls. The men would carry ladder poles with sharp hooks on the ends to embed on top of the wall. The hooks would be difficult for the queen's men to unhook. The siege engine would also fling stones over the castle walls. Second, three long notes on the battle horn to signal the combatants in the finally completed deep tunnel to emerge. Reports said the tunnel ended at a wall with low light creeping from the gaps in the stone partition. Third, three minutes after the first signal, the trumpeter would play four short blasts to signal to the men in the courtyard to emerge from the shallow tunnel. Fifty men per tunnel and an army at the walls of the castle would be too difficult to defend. Soles ordered the attack to begin at first light.

The captains acknowledged the simplicity of the plan. A simple plan had less of a chance to disintegrate in battle. If the attackers gained the wall, a gap in the defense would allow men to pour over the wall. If the tunnel rats could make a stand, they could raise the portcullis. Final assignments were passed out, and the officers ordered their combatants to a ready formation.

First light crept over the horizon. A single long note from the battle horn sent the men crashing against the walls of the castle. The defenders on the castle walls blasted the men with fire jetting from fixed positions. Men lit like kindle. The first pole ladders dug into the top of the wall. Men clambered up the poles, wincing as large stones hurdled over their heads. Failing to lift the pole ladders, men at the wall hacked at the wooden shafts. The first pole ladders were crippled; other ladders gained position along the top of the wall.

Three long notes sounded in the heat of the battle. The rat men, as they had been affectionately dubbed, hammered against the stones in the floor. Falling debris shifted inside the tunnel. The first man entering the room thought he heard a woman screaming, "I killed the king." A shadow darted for the stairs. The man raised his crossbow and shot at a billowing gown. The bolt bit into the door casing, missing its intended target. The man stepped aside for others to pass and looked down at a dead body in the middle of the room. Unclothed, the body had teeth marks in deep gashes along the breast. As more men filled the room, they rushed the stairs.

At that moment, Queen Clarissa woke from a dream to a nightmare. A male page rushed into the room and screamed in a high-pitched voice, "They are in the castle!"

Queen Clarissa reached into her nightstand for a potion and drank it. As she stood, still in her nightgown, she calmly asked, "Where are they?"

The page replied, "They are coming from the bowels of the castle, but all the guards are on the wall. There is nobody here to defend us. They must have dug a tunnel into the dungeon. We have only moments before they spread into all parts of the castle."

Queen Clarissa said, "If they came from the dungeon, then they must pass through the dining hall to reach other parts of the castle."

She sprinted from the room. People were running in all directions. No one seemed to be taking a leadership role. It was chaotic. She passed people in the halls. Her only thought was to make it to the dining hall before the invaders.

She burst into the dining hall. It was empty. She thought she was too late. Then several men emerged from the doors opposite. She calmly stood in the doorway. More men filtered into the dining room. They started moving around the large table in the center of the room. All the men had wicked-looking swords pointing at the lone woman. Still, she waited until the room filled up with the invaders. The last man shut the door behind himself while leering at the woman who was blocking the other door.

"Not in my home," she muttered. Then she bathed the room with blankets of fire jetting from her hands. She had chosen the right potion from her nightstand.

Men screamed as they burned. The table collapsed from the heat. Tapestries on the walls lit like candlewicks. The stone walls in the room were scorched by the flames.

She took one last look at the carnage then slowly shut the door at her end of the great hall. The fire was out. There was nothing left in the room to burn.

Then three minutes had passed, four short blasts of a horn resounded against the castle walls. A crater in the middle of the courtyard opened up with dust flying into the air. Out of the dust, the invaders ran for the portcullis. Bow strings twanged from the top of the wall, killing the men emerging from the hole. As the attention of the queen's men centered on the enemy in the courtyard, the enemies at the walls were gaining positions atop providing cover for more combatants to surge against the queen's defenders.

Chaos ruled the castle. Men struggled in the heat of the battle. Death prevailed on both sides.

Chapter Twenty-Five

Kedwin sat astride his war horse surrounded by twenty of his professional guardsmen. On a rise, he watched the invaders attack the castle. He slapped his thigh and grinned. His plan was working. A force of auxiliaries held the enemy camp. He believed they would be an easy target. After destroying the enemy camp, he would wait until the last minute to lend support to the castle. After the battle, he would have the only army in the kingdom. No one could deny his kingship. He had an army to quell any doubts. He ordered the attack on the camp.

Five hundred horses came over the rise towards the enemy camp. The men on the horses screamed and waved glass swords above their heads. The Viridians formed into a wedge of steel swords and shields, prepared to take the brunt of the attack.

As the men rode headlong into battle, the tight formations spread out across the field. A hundred yards from the camp, the first horsemen found Soles' trap. The earth buckled under the weight. Horses screamed as they impaled themselves on sharp stakes. The weight of the charge forced more horses into the holes surrounding the camp.

The charge stopped; horses snorted from the strain, dancing in small circles. Crossbow bolts dropped from the sky, impaling horses and men. Kira formed up her squad and started navigating between the holes in the ground. Others followed her example, some finding new holes to impale themselves. As the maze became clear to the horsemen, more horses passed and safely charged the enemy.

The wedge held as the horsemen battered at the shields. The horses flowed around the tip of the wedge. An unlucky fellow caught a crossbow bolt to the heart. Grabbing his chest, he pulled the reins tight. The horse responded by rearing up, hooves striking the air. An invader pierced the horse in the chest with a spear. Screaming, the horse fell upon the tip of the enemy's wedge, crushing men beneath its weight. A heroic man took the advantage and jumped his horse into the middle of the steel wedge. Men scattered as the warhorse trampled the bowmen and spearman in the middle of the formation. The formation lost, men scattered and grouped together in threes and fours to fight the horsemen.

The small knots of men bristled like a porcupine, long spears forward and shields held high. The men were able to gain some ground with threes and fours holding steady. The first bow launched decided the men's fate. Men sat on their horses and fired into the enemy ranks. The arrows penetrated arms and legs thanks to the scant cover of the shields. Without the large turtle shell afforded by the shields in the wedge, the invaders died painfully from grievous arrow wounds.

Individual Viridian men scattered among the tents of the camp. Horsemen chased them down. Hank followed one individual snaking among the tents. Hank was sweating profusely; the horse's broad back seemed to jostle him. He floundered in the saddle but kept his seat. Hank swept around the corner of a tent to find the invader positioned with a long spear aimed at his head. Without thinking, Hank swept the spear aside with his sword, and the horse trampled the villainous outsider. Hank sat in the saddle for a moment gasping for breath. Running his hand across his face, the sweat soaked his hand. He turned the horse to find his squad. At the moment, he was just thankful to be alive.

Cow had charged the enemy division as they scattered amongst the tents. Stephen let the horse have his head. Cow followed four men into the enemy camp. As the men twisted and turned amongst the tents, Cow leaped small, pitched tents, collapsing the white hovels in pursuit. Finally, the men turned in a clearing to face the huge war horse. Cow rode among them, gnashing his teeth at the faces of the men. Taken by surprise at the horse's aggression, the invaders could only perform defensive strikes. The momentum and angle of the horse made the strikes ineffective. Stephen leaned down in the saddle and swung his sword, striking at the four-armed men as Cow turned in a tight circle.

Nostrils flaring, the horse stood still as Stephen took stock upon what he had done. Only a moment passed, and Stephen shook his head trying to clear the tunnel vision. Four men lay upon the ground with mortal wounds about their shoulders and heads. Stephen peered across the field of battle to see Kira take a crossbow bolt to the stomach. He spurred the horse in her direction, and Cow launched himself into a full gallop.

Kira had spotted the obvious leader of the hoard of invading men. Leveling a spear, she charged the position, striking the man wearing a funny little metal skullcap. The spear pierced the man through the chest then broke in half from the charge. She unsheathed her sword and struck at a man on her left, slicing his head in half. She turned in the saddle to strike the man on her right, but he had recuperated and slashed at her waist. She parried the blow. Twisting sideways and standing up in the stirrups, she brought her sword down upon the man's up reached arm, severing it. The force of the blow landed a cleaving strike upon the man's shoulder, penetrating below the clavicle into the breast. She ripped the sword free. Kira screamed as a crossbow bolt from thirty yards away penetrated her armor at her stomach. She fell from the horse. The man with the lucky shot dropped the cross bow and ran for cover.

During the charge, Sam had become separated from Kira. Searching the abandoned camp for her, Sam crisscrossed the field, only striking men down if an opportunity yielded a quick kill. He was becoming frantic. The press of people and horses made it almost impossible for him to find her. He rode down fleeing men, striking blows down upon unprotected heads. Always, keeping an eye out for Kira, Sam scanned the enemy camp. Sam spotted Stephen and jerked the reins of the horse to turn a tight circle and spring towards Stephen's position.

Kira lay prone in the middle of the battlefield. Sam and Stephen rode as one to her side. Stephen jumped down from Cow and reached her first. An invader materialized from nowhere, rushing Stephen. Cow kicked his hoof and crushed the invader's head.

Kira breathed raggedly. Stephen broke the wooden bolt in half without removing it. He grabbed her in his arms and shoved her onto the saddle of Sam's horse, then yelled for him to ride to safety. Stephen mounted his horse and paused to look around the battlefield.

Men, horses, glass, and steel were strewn across the battlefield after the wedge had broken, and men died hacking at each other. Stephen leaned over his horse and vomited from the sight of the carnage. Wiping his mouth with his hand, he realized the battle was complete in less than three minutes. The loss of life made him feel sorry for all of the dead men. He noticed the enemy fought until death, asking no quarter. He saw Hank and the men from his squad formed up in Vector Platoon in the middle of the camp. Stephen nudged his horse in line. He realized a quarter of the Erimos men had died on the field. He waited for orders to continue the attack, supporting the defense of the castle.

Kedwin rode into camp surrounded by his bodyguards. "Victory!" he yelled, and the men cheered and hooted still in the embrace of adrenaline. Kedwin scanned the camp. He felt exhilarated by the death of his men, the power he felt by the death of his men. A platoon leader asked him if they were to press on in the attack for the defenders of the castle. Kedwin ignored him. He felt exalted by the cheers of the victorious men. Holding his gloved hand high above his head, he worked the men into a frenzy, relishing every moment. Again, the platoon leader asked for the orders to attack. Again, Kedwin brushed him off.

Stephen enjoyed his scream. The pressure of death slowly eased from his mind. After a couple of moments, he collected himself. Sitting astride Cow, he waited for the orders to attack the invaders harassing the castle. The screams and yells of victory did not taper off. Kedwin pressed the crowd for more adulation. After a couple of minutes, Stephen felt time slipping away for the people in the castle. He formed an idea and started chanting, "Attack." The men followed his lead.

Kedwin motioned for the men to stop. After the men quieted, he started a speech for the new reign stating that he was King Kedwin.

Stephen felt the pressure of time. If their battle lasted only three minutes, how much time did the people in the castle have before being lost? Stephen felt impatient with the new king's speech. When Kedwin suggested they wait until the last moment to attack, Stephen felt angry. Men and women were dying. The cavalry could be a decisive blow to stop the invaders, and Kedwin was letting innocent people die. Before he knew it, Stephen had guided Cow from the ranks.

Screaming "Attack!" and waving his sword above his head in large circles, Stephen raced for the castle. The men, charged up after the battle, followed him.

Kedwin's horse reared, and he lost his seat, falling to the ground. Gaining his feet, he yelled for the men to stop. No one listened as they charged to defend the castle.

As Stephen neared the castle, he saw that the portcullis stood open. Glancing over his shoulder, he realized Cow had outraced the men. Though the men were only ten yards behind him, Stephen could only be the spearhead. Gritting his teeth, Stephen charged into the courtyard of the castle.

The defenders were being pressed against the main double doors of the castle. Outnumbered, they were making their last stand. The men inside the castle had a slight advantage. A dais three steps high in front of the main double doors leading into the castle provided defensive higher ground. The Viridian invaders were two men deep and pressing the attack upon the castle members. The Viridians were using crossbows, and spears to harry the forces on the dais.

The enemy's back was to Stephen. Cow hurdled the crater in the courtyard where the Viridian men had earlier erupted like ants from a hole. Stephen caromed into the Viridian rear ranks. Slashing at men, Stephen felt the impact of his fellow horsemen crashing into the enemy. Cow danced, gnashing his teeth. Stephen felt a hard blow to his shoulder. The crossbow bolt in an instant cartwheeled Stephen off Cow's back, and he struck the flagstones hard, knocking himself unconscious. Cow stood over Stephen's body screaming, the horse kicking and biting anyone coming near the still form under his fiercely bellowing belly. Cow protected his rider from the invaders.

A lone horseman positioned west of the battle watched the cavalry stampede the castle. Turning the horse further westward, the lone horseman rode diagonally towards the mountains. The black mask was a dot receding from the battle.

A disheveled man wearing a black gown raced out of the castle. Loping like an animal, the man ran for freedom.

Part Two: The Potioner
Chapter One

Stephen lay on a cot in a makeshift hospital. The young man slept peaceably. Zen sat on a stool at his side for a second time. The hospital was full of recovering patients. The throne room, the largest room in the castle, had cots in orderly rows running down the middle. Tapestries adorned the walls— pictures of a peaceful kingdom. Four flags hung from sconces along the walls. Each flag represented a province, with Kedwin's noticeably missing. Queen Clarissa sat like a statue on the throne, as if willing her broken men to life. She had sat on the throne as men died in their sleep, unable to drink a healing potion. In the wee hours of the night, Stephen had woken briefly in sharp pain, and Zen had forced him to drink a healing potion.

Zen, his robust frame slumped over, half dozed in a chair. Stephen smiled at the tottering old man and said, "You should get some rest."

Zen snorted and grinned at his protégé. "All you do is sleep."

Stephen sat up and rotated his stiff arm. He looked at the ragged scar on his shoulder. "What got me?"

"A bee sting," Zen said, laughing. He added in a more serious tone, "A crossbow bolt pierced your shoulder. You lay on the ground unconscious while Cow fought like mad over your body. The damn horse would not let anyone near you until I arrived on the scene."

Feeling the ragged pucker of the scar, Stephen asked, "How is Kira?"

"She is fine. She would be here if not for her promotion."

Stephen looked at Zen quizzically. "Promotion?"

Zen looked strained and said, "Kira has been dubbed Duchess Kira Fenton. She is also training the new army of the Queen's Salvation. She was mortified at the prospect of being a duchess, but she understands that her father has been named traitor to the kingdom."

Stephen looked thoughtful for a moment. "I think my career as a soldier has ended."

Zen laughed, holding his belly. After a couple of moments, he replied, "You know, everyone thinks you're a hero."

Stephen's face screwed up. "I didn't do anything."

Zen laughed so hard he almost toppled from the stool. Holding his sides with arms crossed, he replied, "Didn't do anything." He brushed tears from his eyes. "Son, you led the army to a victory over the invaders. If you had not charged down to the castle, Queen Clarissa's men would be dead. The men are already telling tall tales of your attack." Zen shook his head. "Some of the tales are bloody, but the truth is you saved the day. You also saved the new Duchess Kira. I believe Queen Clarissa plans on knighting you."

"Knighthood?" Stephen's eyes stared into space. "I dreamed of being a knight."

"Well, do not worry. The knighthood will be honorific." Zen sobered up and said, "You are going to be the queen's new Master Potioner. I am going to be hunting Zacadam."

"But I am not trained," exclaimed Stephen.

Zen grabbed Stephen's hand and said, "You have been training all your life. Once I impart some special skills, your cooking talents will be your training. I am sorry that I am putting this heavy burden in your lap, but the queen needs a Potioner. I need to find a killer. Now rest." Zen patted Stephen's hand and smiled. "You will need your strength when knighted."

Stephen watched Zen walk towards the throne. He felt rested. he glanced around the room to see that men were sleeping and people were hovering over their beds. He noticed the attendants held potions in their hands, waiting for the unconscious soldiers to wake up for a moment. Stephen's curiosity was piqued, and he decided to slip out of the room. He was dressed in homespun nightclothes, but he thought he could afford the embarrassment.

Stephen walked into the courtyard where the attack had taken place. Chamber maids were washing the blood off the cobblestones. The hole was being filled in with large stones. Everyone was busy picking up the pieces. The mood seemed cheery to Stephen, yet all he could feel about the place was death.

"Sir, can I help you?" asked a rather large soldier.

"No, I am fine," replied Stephen. He felt sheepish in the vicinity of a professional soldier. "Maybe you can tell me where to find some food."

"Yes, sir," replied the soldier. "I will take you. I must say, I am envious."

"Envious about what?" said Stephen, feeling even smaller.

"Your horse. I never seen horses behave like that," answered the soldier. The man stared directly in Stephen's eyes. "You saved my life."

Now Stephen felt very small in a grown-up world. "OK."

"No, you do not understand," explained the soldier. "Our men were at their limits. In another couple of moments, we would have folded. I was on the line and saw you charge the invaders. Your thrust startled the invaders and set them on their heels, giving our men an advantage. The fight was still bloody, but the help of your men saved us."

"I'm sorry, they are not my men. I was just glad I could help," said Stephen, hanging his head.

"Here is the kitchen." The soldier held out his hand. "If you ever need anything, ask for Parson." Stephen gripped his hand and shook it. The soldier hurried away.

The smell of the food drove Stephen mad. It took only a moment to realize his hunger. Besides, he was looking forward to trying iced tea. Zen had described the concoction to him.

Chapter Two

Zacadam slopped soup over the side of the bowl. He savored every mouthful. The good people of the homestead had welcomed the stranger. Zacadam murdered each of them in turn. Now they all sat around the table: the husband with a broken neck sat at the head of the table; the wife, next to her husband, with knife wounds in her stomach. The teenage daughter sat across from her mother with a slit throat. Zacadam glanced around the table and smiled. He felt perfectly at home.

Zacadam shoved the large bowl out in front of him and burped. He passed on a small apology for his transgression to the dead people. He sat with his hands on either side of the bowl and thought clearly for a moment. *I am being hunted.*

He laughed out loud then fell into giggles thinking about his predicament. He had no place to go. Every man, woman, and child would be hunting him. The bounty on his life must be enormous. His high giggle settled for a moment. He wondered, would Soles protect him? Soles had failed. Soles was on the run like him. *No, he cannot protect me.*

Zacadam panicked. He stood up and ran around the table twice before accidentally tipping over the daughter. He stopped to catch her and took a deep breath. He breathed onto her face. He cradled the dead girl's head in his hands. He brushed a small kiss on her lips and felt energized.

He decided to retreat over the mountain. Soles could be his benefactor if found. Zacadam sat back down in his chair and thought of the journey ahead.

Autumn was already breathing on him. The night's temperatures were dipping well below comfort. If he did not make it to the mountain before first snowfall, he would not survive. He needed a horse, and these poor bastards had none. He would have to walk.

Chapter Three

The turnout for the ceremony was considerably larger than what Stephen expected. The queen sat on her throne with Zenith standing on her left. The nobles of the provinces sat in high-backed chairs facing the queen's dais. A large crowd of soldiers stood at attention behind the chairs. Servants and people thronged outside the entrance. Stephen had found a place near the back wall. He waited for Kira Fenton to be crowned duchess of the Coal Province. The new shirt he wore for the ceremony itched at the scar on his shoulder, but he had never worn a shirt that fit so perfectly.

Kira entered through a door at the edge of the dais. A pipe played a lament. She slowly climbed the stairs to stand at attention in front of Queen Clarissa. The queen, smiling, lifted a small circlet of gold and placed it on Kira's brow. Stephen had never seen gold. He thought the circlet looked regal on Kira.

She turned and faced the crowd, and Queen Clarissa, following tradition, introduced the new duchess to the kingdom by announcing Kira by her new title, "Duchess Kira Fenton." The room broke out in applause, and some of the soldiers hooted. After a couple of minutes, Queen Clarissa motioned for the crowd to stop. She peered into the crowd, and Stephen swore she looked directly at him.

Queen Clarissa held out her hands and said, "Many showed courage in repelling the invaders. It has been brought to my attention the actions of one particular person, a young man willing to sacrifice his life at the whipping post and in battle, a young man who saved the life of Duchess Kira Fenton in battle. Please, Stephen Bishop Alexander, approach the throne."

The sea of people surrounding Stephen parted to create a clear path to the dais. Stephen gulped and stepped forward. As he went, people patted him on the back, with some soldiers thanking him personally for his timely attack. Hank actually grabbed his hand and shook it, grinning. Stephen could not understand why he felt totally alone in a room full of people. He stopped at the bottom of the dais and bowed from the waist. The intent of his fidelity was not lost on the crowd.

Zenith passed a black leather scabbard to Queen Clarissa. She unsheathed a falchion from it. The crowd gasped as the sword shined in the low light. The sword sparkled like a huge diamond, throwing light from its blade. It was one of the five fabled Diamond Swords. Though rumored to be invisible, the sword shined like a torch in the room. A kaleidoscope of colors like a prism escaped from the falchion. Queen Clarissa motioned with the sword for Stephen to mount the steps.

Taking a knee in front of the queen, Stephen bowed his head and waited for her proclamation. Queen Clarissa held the sword aloft and then gently touched both of Stephen's shoulders, proclaiming him to be the first and only knight of the kingdom of Erimos. Sheathing the blade, Queen Clarissa held the sword in outstretched arms, palms up. Head still bowed; Stephen reached forward to take the diamond falchion in his own upturned palms. As Queen Clarissa stepped back, Stephen still bowed with his shoulders shaking from crying.

Kira came to his side and helped him to his feet. She turned him towards the crowd and shouted, "Sir Stephen Bishop Alexander, the adopted son of the royal house of Zenith Alexander." The crowd cheered. One of their own had been lifted up into the echelon of nobility. Kira led Stephen to the door on the side of the hall. Stephen felt better after escaping the loud praise and adoration from the people.

Kira laughed and said, "You really didn't think I would not want to share the glory."

Stephen grinned back at her and replied, "I was not expecting that to happen. Why didn't you warn me?" He shook his head, wiping sweat from the back of his neck.

Kira laughed louder and between breaths said, "Zen wouldn't let me."

"He knew I would have run for the hills," laughed Stephen. They strolled down the hallway, sharing a long moment.

Kira led Stephen to a bench in a private garden near the walls of the castle. Sitting down, she patted the seat next to her. Stephen sat down with a thud.

Kira took his hand in hers and said, "What were you thinking about on the road to Simone?"

"This," he said, leaning forward to lightly kiss Kira's lips. Kira did not flinch. Her soft lips slightly parted. Stephen finished the kiss and looked directly into Kira's eyes, expecting something or nothing.

Kira smiled and said, "Normally you would have to ask my father to court me, but I asked yours instead. Zen sends his blessings."

Stephen chuckled. He unsheathed the sword in his lap. In the sunny courtyard, it shone a rainbow of colors from the deepest violet to the lightest red. The sword acted like a prism; the spectrum of colors shone brightly. Stephen waved the sword in a small circle and said, "You will have to teach me how to use this."

Kira slipped her arm into his and replied, "It's true. A knight must know how to use his sword."

Stephen sheathed the sword. "Zen has asked me to be the queen's Potioner."

"Funny, the queen asked me to be her new commander of her army." Kira leaned in close. "I guess we will see a lot of each other." She darted in for a kiss, one more savage than his. A minute passed by breathlessly.

"Leave it to the kids to find a make-out spot," said Zen loudly. The couple broke their embrace, both smiling sheepishly. "I have been looking for you, Stephen."

Stephen stood, obviously embarrassed in front of his mentor. "How can I help?"

"Well, first, make sure you kiss that young woman every day," said Zen with a twinkle in his eyes. "And second, we start your training today to be a Potioner." This time Zen looked embarrassed. "I know you want to celebrate your new fortune, but time is running out for me to find Zacadam. I think I can teach you the skills needed in a couple days' time."

"I know how important finding Zacadam is to you. We will work around the clock," said Stephen.

"Good. As I said before, the cooking skills you have learned in the past couple of years will benefit this process. Really, a couple of sleights of hand skills is all you need to be a Potioner with my book."

Stephen looked surprised. "You are giving me your book?"

"All things pass to the next generation. Stephen, I may not return. Zacadam is dangerous," replied Zen thoughtfully. "Besides, you are my adopted heir. I love you like no other." Zen hugged Stephen.

Stephen replied, returning the hug, "I will try to make you proud."

"Son, you have already," said Zen. "Sir Stephen Bishop Alexander. You make us all proud." He looked over Stephen's shoulder at Kira. She nodded.

The sun had set over a festival where the people of the Erimos kingdom celebrated their victory over the invaders. Queen Clarissa had presided over contests, games, and musical festivities. Always smiling, the queen let her people celebrate. The furrow of her brow never hinted at her anxiety. A rogue duke in her kingdom, an army over the mountains, and the death of her beloved husband crinkled between her eyes. She managed to escape the festivities after the sun set. She searched for her only confidant—Zen. She found him with the newest member of her court. She did not know what to expect from Stephen.

Queen Clarissa walked into Zen's laboratory and remarked, "Zen, after your meeting with Stephen, I would like to speak to you."

"Yes, my queen. I believe Stephen should be present at our meeting," answered Zen.

The queen looked thoughtful for a moment and then nodded her assent. She turned from the doorway and proceeded to her study.

"You want me to talk to the queen?" asked Stephen nervously.

"When I leave, she must have someone to speak too. She is more alone than anyone you know," answered Zen. "I am confident you will do the right thing. Don't worry; a listener is more important than an advice giver. Now hand me my Potioner's tome."

Stephen slid the book across the table, and Zen motioned for him to open it. Staring at it critically, Stephen saw a jumble of letters and numbers. He could not discern a pattern. He looked at Zen questioningly.

"It is simple, really. A cipher for the letters and numbers to emulate for the twenty-six letters of our alphabet. Substitute the number one for letter F. Wrap the numbers around until twenty-six is the letter E. As for the numbers, substitute D for number one until you reach the end of the alphabet at C, which is the number twenty-six. As you can see, DD is actually the number twenty-seven. Simple really. Now copy a recipe on scratch paper to practice. Always burn the scratch copies after making a potion. After a while, the cipher will look normal, and you will not have to make a copy to read the recipe." Zen watched Stephen transcribe a recipe on paper. "List the ingredients as if making a baking recipe. The order of the ingredients is important, as well as the timing."

As Stephen practiced transcribing potions, Zen perused the ingredients Zacadam had stocked in the laboratory. He noticed a trend in the exotic ingredients. He realized Zacadam's family had developed a number of poisons, though some of the ingredients Zen only recognized as a fungus. If Zen had realized the mettle of Zacadam's family of Potioners, then he would not have trusted the man to be the king's Potioner. He realized hindsight could have saved the king if only he had paid more attention to Zacadam's family potions. He sighed and returned to Stephen's side to examine his work.

"Good, I think you understand how to transcribe. Do you have any questions?" asked Zen.

"If making potions is a matter of mixing the right ingredients, why has no one mixed talents such as fire with healing?" asked Stephen.

"Some have tried mixing talents but met failure. The potion needs a catalyst, and the different talents require different catalysts." Zen looked perplexed. "Be careful experimenting. People have died drinking an untried potion."

Stephen nodded and returned to transcribing. He noticed a formula in writing the potions' recipes. Much like the recipes Stephen had used for cooking, they followed a simple pattern. After transcribing four of them from different parts of the tome, Stephen felt certain he could make the potions.

"Are we going to make a potion today?" asked Stephen.

"No, I think you have had enough for today. I plan on leaving the day after tomorrow, so we have plenty of time for you to practice. We will be making batches of potions for Queen Clarissa. She requested a large number. I believe she sees more danger ahead. Listen, I need to speak to you."

"About what?" asked Stephen. He felt the change in Zen's mood.

Zen sat down on a chair next to the table. "I may not return from my mission."

"No, you will be fine," proclaimed Stephen.

"Listen, Zacadam is more dangerous than I realized. I do not think him to be a sane man," replied Zen earnestly.

"Why would you think that?" Stephen pulled up a chair.

"We found the place where he had been hiding. I will not tell you the details, because I can barely handle them. Let's just say Zacadam is beyond any help. And what I can infer from the ingredients stocked in the lab is that he will not be easy to kill." Zen choked on the word *kill*. "It is going to be hard."

"Then I must go with you," stated Stephen.

"No, you will be needed here. Queen Clarissa will need a strong Potioner. Also, she needs a friend." Zen watched Stephen carefully. "I believe you could be that friend."

"She is the queen," said Stephen loudly.

Zen laughed, holding his sides, and said, "She is not a monster."

"I know that," replied Stephen. "I just mean," Stephen squirmed and said quietly, "she is the queen."

Zen dropped a hand on Stephen's shoulder, squeezing it. "She is human."

Stephen got the point. After his own family had left, he was alone. He could understand the queen was alone. "I will try my best."

"Another thing," said Zen. "What are your intentions with Kira?"

Stephen squirmed again and replied, "I don't know. She seems more advanced than me with relationships."

Again, Zen boomed with laughter. After a couple of moments, he replied, "All women are more advanced than men. Do not think about it too much. She likes you, and that is enough." Zen chuckled and said, "I wish I could see."

"See what?" asked Stephen.

"No, never mind." Zen stood up from his chair. "It is not polite to keep the queen waiting."

Stephen followed Zen out the door. His mind in a fit of turmoil, he thought about his relationship with Kira. He felt confident in that respect. As for the queen, how do you become friends with the queen of a kingdom? Stephen decided he would just try to be himself. *She is human, right?* Stephen felt his nerves jangle as he approached the queen's study.

Chapter Four

The formerly traitorous King Kedwin, now only Duke Kedwin threw his gloves onto the bedroom floor. He flopped down across his large bed. He didn't want to see the day. He closed his eyes and tried to dream of a much happier alternative to his dilemma. He felt restless and turned over onto his back. Looking at the unlit chandler made with sconces which held candles above his bed, he imagined dark shapes in the rafters. Assassins ready to spring on him as soon as he closed his eyes. He sat up and started undressing. Pulling at his clothes, he felt wickedly tired. Lying completely naked, he decided he needed a plan.

Duke Kedwin closed his eyes. The starbursts in the black behind his eyelids circled in his vision. He concentrated on the bursts of light, trying to fathom his inner soul. He realized the pettiness and failure of trying to grasp the crown. He had lost the allegiance of the other dukes. They had pledged their fidelity to Queen Clarissa. Her survival had ruined Kedwin's plan to usurp the throne.

Now, he was a traitor to the kingdom. His own halls rang with men deciding his fate. He could either give in by accepting the headman's block or start a civil war within the kingdom. The stress in the small of his back told him to complete the task of civil war. He was a dead man if he did not assert control over his people. He needed a rallying point for his people to concentrate their efforts of war. He did not believe his personal predicament would be enough.

Sighing, he tried to think of subterfuge. He needed to trick his own people. How could he forge an alliance of people to do his dirty work? The other dukes had sworn fidelity to him, but he imagined they had given up on him and returned the throne to the queen. He had them in his pocket only if they saw a resolution engineered by him. Could he shut down the coal mines, causing unrest in the kingdom? His own people would be unemployed and hungry. They would not be happy. They could turn on him. The answer lurked at the forefront of his brain.

Duke Kedwin swore out loud. He was a dead man. His own people could be plotting his demise. His people would be awarded for killing the traitor. Kedwin rolled around in the bed. Striking the side of his head with the palm of his hand, he begged for an answer. The clock was ticking on his demise.

He sat up in bed and laughed. He would be the people's voice. How long had it been since people were relatively wealthy? The nobles were wealthy, trading in silver and gold, never allowing the populace anything but iron nickels. An influx of wealth to certain families could sway their support. Give them gold, and expect fidelity. The families would have to be fairly well connected to the general populace. The families would have to communicate the desire of more than being poor. The families would have to be extremely connected to each other for support. They would have to be able to communicate to the people that being wealthy was as easy as being poor. They would have to sway the people to realize the nobility were keeping them poor. After a couple of months, the economy of the kingdom would crash.

The economy of the kingdom depended on the poor using iron as currency. A sudden influx of silver and gold would make iron worthless. Trade would become stale, as it depended on a strong currency, mainly in iron. Deflation would spin the kingdom into chaos. The other dukes would not allow gold and silver to be traded in default of iron. If they did, gold and silver would deflate in value. If his people only traded in gold and silver, people would not be able to pay in iron. The tension between the dukes' provinces would escalate. Could he send the kingdom into a recession to save his own life?

Duke Kedwin sat back, disgusted. He could send the economy of the kingdom in a downward spiral, but then he would have to pick up the pieces if he became king. He needed to think of something else. Not because he felt any relationship with the poor, but because he knew the poor would place someone else on the throne.

He rolled the covers around him into a cocoon. He realized the only thing he had to thwart the queen was his title. In his province, he could build an army. He would have to cut all communication with the rest of the kingdom. He was no fool. The queen had probably already named a successor to his province. She had probably already denounced him as not being the rightful ruler of his own people. He realized he needed truly greedy men.

Greedy men could be bought. He could promise them titles after he became king. The whole political structure of the kingdom would be decimated. People would be haunted by the genocide of the nobility. The only thing in his favor was greedy people who would reign with an iron fist. Was his life worth changing the very core of the Erimos kingdom?

Duke Kedwin closed his eyes and sighed. He knew his destiny was to change the Erimos kingdom. He felt no scruples about heaving the kingdom into death's embrace. He felt the warmth of the blanket soothe his aching body. He imagined the people would embrace a new way of life to soothe themselves. He remembered reading about a leader loved by his people. He thought the people would love him. He would be their salvation against the monotony of life. Who wants to work in a field anyway? Who wants to serve guests food and wine? Who wants to sell grocery items? The people would feel the change in their lives. The fear of death has a way of changing attitudes.

Chapter Five

Stephen followed Zen down the hall to Queen Clarissa's study. The first thing Stephen noticed about the room was the entire wall that overflowed with books on evenly spaced shelves. Stephen saw the queen behind stacks of books on her desk. He never imagined this many books in the entire world. Queen Clarissa peeked over the stacks and motioned the men towards chairs in front of the fireplace. She joined them in a rather large chair obviously placed there to read in. It looked very relaxing.

Queen Clarissa started speaking. "I have a mission for our new Master Potioner."

Stephen leaned forward. "Yes, your majesty."

"Kira will be returning to her new province. I do not expect her to be treated kindly. I am afraid for you, young man; you will learn the dark side of being a royal Potioner."

Zen spoke up. "It's a little early for that, don't you think?"

The queen glared at him. "He is a traitor."

Zen only nodded assent. He shifted in his chair and stared at the fire.

Stephen looked at both of them and asked, "What dark side?"

The queen sighed and said, "It is a little-known fact that the royal Potioner is also a political assassin. Early royals used their Potioners sparingly in this position. I can only think of three incidences when a Potioner assassinated nobles. For every death, only the king knew it was not an accidental death. Only the royals have access to this information, so do not speak of it lightly." The queen's voice wavered. "I do not want Kedwin's death to seem accidental. I want him to suffer." The queen frowned and spoke to Zen. "Do you have such a potion in your arsenal?"

Zen stared into the fire. "Yes, my queen, I have a nasty potion to do the trick." He turned to Stephen and said, "How do you feel about being the harbinger of death?"

Stephen stared at the books on the shelves, thinking they contained history no sane man would read. He was becoming part of that history. Would his name be added to the list of death dealers to nobles? He thought about Kira. She would need his protection, but would she understand him killing her father? His small town felt a long way from here. He did not like the idea of killing a man with poison, but he understood the necessity. One death to save the lives of others. Stephen spoke to the queen, "I understand."

The queen nodded and turned to Zen. "What of Zacadam?"

Zen twisted in the chair and replied, "He will have no place to hide in the kingdom. I believe he will make for the mountains. Intelligence reported the pass used by the invaders. It is a three-day ride on horseback. I am leaving in the morning. I believe Zacadam to be on foot, so I will be waiting at the pass. Have you spoken to Master Salender?"

The queen lifted her chin and replied, "He gave me the distressing news."

Stephen asked, "What news?"

The queen straightened her skirt and answered, "In the spring, we expect an army from over the mountains to crush our people. They will not make the same mistake. They expected an easy victory with three-to-one odds. In the spring, we expect an army larger than the invaders wielded this summer. Master Salender and I are working on a plan to circumvent the spring invasion."

"Circumvent how?" asked Stephen.

"Master Salender and Zenith fortuitously stumbled upon the answer. I am working with Master Salender to see the fruition of the plan. After your return from the Coal Province, Stephen, we will speak more about it," answered the queen.

Zen stared at the queen quizzically. She did not comment. Zen felt sourness in his stomach. She was using Stephen as a pawn. He understood the welfare of the kingdom stood in the balance; he just wished she could see Stephen as more than a weapon.

"Please be excused," said the queen.

Zen and Stephen left the room. Walking down the hallway, Zen asked Stephen, "How do you really feel about going to the Coal Province?"

"It tires my mind thinking about the responsibility the queen and Kira have for the people of our kingdom. I understand I am a small cog in a much larger wheel, but I want to protect Kira."

"The act in itself seems easy, but Kedwin is not the trusting sort," replied Zen. "You are the honest sort, but sneaking in a poison is going to be hard. I know Queen Clarissa wants Kedwin to suffer, but I think for Kira's sake it should look like an accident. Can you live with such a burden of a lie?"

"You think it would eventually destroy my relationship with Kira. I would like to think it wouldn't. Listen, Zen: to protect her from her father, I will do what is necessary. You may think I am honest, but even an honest man has his secrets." Stephen opened the door to the laboratory, and Zen walked in first.

"Well, the good news is Zacadam had a rich stock of poisonous fungi," said Zen. "The potion will be easy to make. I do not like making poisons, but the method of mixing is the same for most potions, so I will watch you mix the ingredients." Zen chose several mushrooms from Zacadam's stock. He ground them separately with a mortar and pestle. He explained to Stephen never to touch the ground kernels. Most mushrooms would not kill him, but the fine powder can get on the fingers and be easily swallowed through carelessness. Zen told Stephen to find the recipe in the tome labeled Night's Star.

Stephen followed the directions in the recipe to produce the poison. Zen watched him carefully. Not once did he offer advice in making the potion; he realized Stephen had talent. After completing the task, Stephen moved away from the counter. Zen stepped up and peered at the potion.

Stephen asked, "Do all poisons look like clear water?"

"No, this particular poison is used because it can be easily mixed into any food or drink. Also, if you notice, it does not have an odor." Holding up the vial, he said, "Here, smell."

Stephen took a tentative whiff. He asked, "How does it kill?"

"It acts like a flu virus, but the poison slowly drains the body of vital fluids. After four days, the man dies of dehydration." Zen stoppers the vial. "Be careful when you pour it into his food or drink. A small backsplash on your fingers will make you sick if you ingest it by accidentally touching your fingers to your mouth. Best thing to do is wash your hands before partaking of a meal." Zen handed the vial to Stephen. "You may have to use guile."

Stephen fingered the potion. "I believe in justice, but cruelty is a mistress of justice. Do you really think I can do it?"

Zen placed his hand on Stephen's shoulder, and said, "I think you can do anything you have a mind to. Just be careful. I don't want to lose another family member."

***

Stephen gazed at the constellation Sagittarius. Craning his neck back, he followed the star pattern with his eyes. He sat alone on the bench in the private garden where he first kissed Kira. He tried to make out other constellations. He shook his head when he thought about how small the world actually seemed in the face of so many stars.

"They are beautiful," said Kira softly walking into the garden.

Stephen jolted out of his longing and said, "Makes you wonder if other people are not looking at our sun in their night sky."

"So, you believe in people on other planets?" asked Kira.

"How can you not? Look at how many stars we can see," replied Stephen, staring at the sky.

Kira laughed. "I guess you are right." She sat next to Stephen. "The queen has informed me you are to be my personal bodyguard."

"Really," said Stephen. "I guess a knight must protect someone." He leaned in to kiss her. The kiss was soft and lasted for an achingly long time.

Kira broke the kiss and said, "I did not come here to kiss you. I need to talk to you about what is going on. But the kiss was nice." She entangled their arms together.

"What's going on?" asked Stephen playing with the strands of her hair.

"The queen has ordered me to put my father under house arrest," said Kira. "She expects me to be Duchess Kira, and I don't think I am ready."

Stephen stopped playing with her hair and softly cradled her face. "Kira, you will make a fine duchess. I believe in you." He kissed her on the cheek. "I believe you can do anything."

Kira smiled and laid her head on Stephen's shoulder. "I feel young."

Stephen laughed. "You and me both." He stopped laughing and said, "I guess we must put away childish things."

Kira disengaged their embrace. "What about us? Is this childish?"

Stephen replied, "I sincerely hope not." He put his arm around her shoulder. "It doesn't feel childish."

Kira nodded. She straightened her skirt and obviously changed the subject. "The queen wants to field an army of five thousand by the spring."

"Five thousand?" questioned Stephen. "Where is she going to get five thousand men?"

"She expects each province to produce a thousand men for the army. Each province is to train the men over the winter months."

"That sounds harsh. Training in the winter will not be easy on the men," said Stephen.

Kira nodded. "It can be done. The men will be easy to find. The drought this summer will help the queen's plans. Actually, producing an army this winter will help many people be put to work."

"I understand; the people in my town will be looking for work this winter. We lost everything in a tornado," said Stephen. "Did she say just how badly the kingdom is suffering?"

"She says it's bad. The weather has not been kind to us." Kira shifted her weight and said, "How is Zen doing?"

"He will be leaving in the morning. He figures Zacadam will make for the pass in the mountains. I worry about him. Zacadam is dangerous."

Kira hugged him and said, "Zen is a big boy. He can take care of himself. I am more worried about you."

"About me?" asked Stephen. "What do you mean?"

"I am talking about your place in the royal court. The infighting to gain Queen Clarissa's attention can be brutal."

Stephen chuckled. "I am not worried. If I never see her again, it will be OK with me." Stephen stared out into space, thinking about the conversation with the queen. "I mean, I am not looking for attention."

"But somehow you always manage to attract it." She kissed him. They spent some quiet time together exploring each other. Kira felt on the brink of her emotions. She had known men before Stephen. They had been calloused, either seeking her virginity or making a power play for her office. Kira felt Stephen only wanted her. For the first time in her life, she wanted to give her life to someone. The qualms associated with other men seemed not to develop when she was with Stephen. She trusted him.

Chapter Six

Soles brushed another tree branch out of his way. The underbrush trapped his feet, making it difficult to walk. Sometimes he found animal trails to navigate. The sounds of birds disturbed him. Some cheeped; others made sounds like water dripping into a bucket. Larger animals ran away from his path. Once he saw an iguanodon sleeping. If he did not find water soon, it was going to be a short trip in the woods—even shorter if he stumbled across a carnivore.

The day he rode away from the battle, his horse came up lame. A small stone had worked its way into the hoof. Soles blamed himself. He never should have trusted another man to look after his horse. Now he found himself walking in the woods. He could not trust the roads leading to the mountains. A strange man with a black mask would draw attention. He plodded through the woods, trying to determine his fate.

Rex Almanon would not be pleased with him. For a small transgression, the king had burned away his face. Soles could not think of a resolution to stall his imminent death. The mask marked him. Even in his own city state, he would be easy to find. He had no friends to hide him. The failure of the mission meant sure death.

Soles swatted at a low bush. The Erimos kingdom had seemed too easy to conquer. No standing army, the men farmers, no soldiers—Rex Almanon expected an easy victory. Soles had expected an easy victory. It was the damn potions. The intelligence on the potions seemed obliquely fantastic. Soles believed the potions a myth for the uneducated populace, a ruse to shield the government from transgression. The damn things actually worked. Soles thought about the power he could wield with an army hopped up on potions. He could rule Viridian, Gosh, and Simian.

Soles swatted a bug on his arm, the bug smearing blood. Soles stared at his arm. The king would swat Soles like a bug. He would not consider any excuses. Soles expected groveling would not do the trick. He had no proof about the potions. Any excuse or apology would sound weak to the monarch. Nothing he could say or do would persuade Almanon to spare his life.

Soles sat down with his back against a tree. Soles considered himself to be a brave man, but going home meant suicide. The years of playing political games, the backstabbing, the murder, the lying, the cheating, all of it left no real allies. Soles considered speaking to Rex Aristarchus in Gosh. The secrets he held about his own master Almanon could be useful to another monarch. Soles shook his head. He could bargain with information, but once the information ran out, he would be slain, only a toy to be discarded.

Soles peered into the lower branches of the tree. Already the early autumn had changed some of the leaves. Soles decided to take a nap leaning his head back against the rough bark.

Something tapped Soles's outstretched boot toe. Soles awoke instantly. A man stood several feet away. Dressed in deer skins, the man looked primordial. Soles decided to remain calm and asked, "Do you have water?"

"You are a long way from the road," replied the man.

"I got lost. Can I have some water?" asked Soles, slipping a knife into his hand hidden by his thigh.

"What are you doing out here?" The man made no move towards Soles.

Soles realized the man was uncivilized. He considered that the man preferred being alone in the woods. "Please, some water first."

The man reached for a waterskin at his side, taking his eyes off Soles. Soles threw the small thin dagger at his heart. It skewered the man's chest. The man looked surprised as he toppled to the ground. Soles hurried over to the man's side and turned him over onto his back. Soles had another knife out, but the staring eyes told him the wild man was dead.

Soles first drank from the waterskin. Then he methodically stripped the body, looking for anything useful. The man had a bag of beef jerky and some small iron coins. Soles found a glass skinning knife. He figured the recluse man was a trapper. Soles stood up over the dead, naked body. It reminded him of his own mortality. Soles draped a shirt over the man's bearded face.

He considered his options. He could head for the mountains and his own people, or replace the man in the woods, thus becoming a hermit. The thought of becoming a hermit was a ludicrous idea to Soles. He had been alone his entire life, but the idea of not drinking wine, not having women, and not having power over men was like death.

Soles decided to go home and face the consequences at a later date. He could stay hidden in the city for some time before being caught. As it was, he was the only remaining survivor from the campaign. A deliberate message to Rex Almanon citing his victory over the Erimos kingdom could be arranged. Eventually, the lie would be detected by Rex Almanon.

Soles thought about his contacts in the city. The fear of him could be exploited to intimidate the contacts. Soles figured he could remain anonymous in the city for a couple of weeks before someone ratted him out to Rex Almanon. He knew someone would collect the bounty if Rex Almanon guessed his message to be a fake missive or if he found out Soles was hiding in Viridian. He might even make it until after the winter by sending a missive about the pass being impenetrable for the army to return. Several months of decadence rather than a swift death at the hands of someone appealed to Soles. *As a matter of fact,* thought Soles, *I may find a way to escape death yet.* Soles felt optimistic about his plan to fool Rex Almanon.

Chapter Seven

Zacadam walked down the road lit by the pale moonlight. He was dressed in the farmer's best clothes. He whistled a tune in the night air. He felt in high spirits. He reached in the front pocket of the pants and jangled the coins he had stolen from the farmhouse, the egg money from the wife and the winter store money from the father. The daughter had apparently wanted to escape from the humdrum life with a rather large life savings hidden under her mattress. Zacadam rationalized that the family had no need of money after death. He did not consider it stealing.

Thoughts permeated Zacadam's brain: tossing the house for money, finding clothing, and packaging the food for a long journey. His disguise as a farmer would throw people off his trail. Zacadam plucked a leaf off a low-hanging tree branch and rolled it in his palms. Dropping the leaf, Zacadam sniffed his hands, delighting in the smell. The faint scent of blood on his hands was a loose memory. Zacadam daydreamed as he walked.

A Compsognathus, just over a foot long from head to tail and only eight inches tall, tracked his progress down the dusty lane. The very small dinosaur scented the blood, the sweat, and the piss on Zacadam's unwashed frame. The Compsognathus's lips curled in its small head. It yipped like a small puppy in anticipation. The predator darted forth on two thin legs from the ditch beside the road.

Zacadam spun around in the middle of the road. The carnivore attacked his inner thighs, close to his groin. Zacadam screamed, striking the Compsognathus in the head with an open hand. Zacadam panicked, frozen in place and slapping at the teeth and eyes of the small thing. The pants ripped open. A long furrow dug by the tiny teeth bled on Zacadam's thigh.

The pain sent Zacadam into flight mode. Running down the road with the biped on his heels, he reached for a low-hanging tree branch pulling himself up. The thing jumped, snapping its teeth. It grazed Zacadam's ankle. Zacadam perched on the limb and reached into a bag slung on his shoulder. He drank the potion and threw the empty vial at the sinewy head. The long, slender neck could almost reach Zacadam as it tried to scramble up the tree with its three long fingers on each forelimb. Sitting on the branch, one hand holding on, Zacadam flung his other hand down at the tiny monster, sending a swish of flame onto its head.

The small thing ran for the woods as Zacadam followed the Compsognathus's progress from the tree with the fire. Leaves crackled, small bushes lit the sky, and the woods came to life with searing heat.

Zacadam willed the flames from his hand to stop. He jumped down upon the road and watched the fire in the woods. The flames ate the trees. Smoke billowed in the sky. Zacadam sat down in the middle of the road and laughed. He had sent a beacon to anyone. He considered the power at his disposal. Why should he cower when he was the strongest?

The heat from the fire bathed Zacadam. The smoke rolled onto the lane. Coughing and shielding his face from the flames, Zacadam ran down the road. He sprinted until his lungs tightened in his chest. Wheeling around, Zacadam faced the opposite direction, discerning that he had escaped the fire. Placing his hands on his thighs, he breathed in ragged gasps. His sweating face was a mirror for the forest fire. He chuckled lightly; coughing intermingled with the breathing. He thought, *The trail will be cold.* He laughed at his own observation.

Turning his back on the fire, Zacadam proceeded down the road. As he left the fire behind, the night air felt chilly on his exposed skin. The blood clotted on the ragged gash on his thigh. He stopped and tied a loose cloth around the wound. He donned a poncho to fight off the chilly air. His high spirits had been shattered by the attack of the dinosaur. He sought shelter in a small ditch. Piling up leaves and small sticks, his hand hovering above the mass, he lit the small temple of branches. He threw larger sticks onto the pyre. Sitting with his back against the wall of the ditch, he slept.

Chapter Eight

The darkness before the dawn found a small group of people exchanging goodbyes. Zen rode his horse out of the castle's gates. He felt grim about killing a man. Stephen watched him depart. His mind numbed from thinking about Zen's mission. Kira watched Stephen. She worried about him—and Zen. Master Salender noticed Kira's face and thought about being young again. The group had started to break up when Master Salender stopped Stephen for a moment.

"Sir Alexander, I would be pleased to talk to you," said Master Salender.

"Please, call me Stephen."

Master Salender raised his chin and said, "Time will tell. I have a room near the queen's study. Could you join me, say in an hour?"

"By all means, sir," said Stephen.

Stephen and Kira ate breakfast in silence, each cooped up in their own thoughts. Kira rushed off to do her duty as a commander of her forces. The small kiss she planted on Stephen's cheek lifted his spirits. He decided to find Master Salender but his mind froze. The last time someone powerful wanted to speak to him, it was about murder.

Stephen knocked on the door lightly, calling out, "Master Salender." Behind the closed door a muffled response of "Come in" could be heard. Stephen opened the door. The first thing that drew his attention was the large fireplace centered against the back wall. A roaring fire heated the room. The temperature felt uncomfortable to Stephen. His eyes scanned the living space. A large bed, nightstands, a chandler, and a small table with three chairs surrounding it were the only obvious things in the room. Master Salender sat in one of the chairs. Stephen crossed the room to sit across from him.

Master Salender did not speak for a couple of moments. The man just stared at Stephen and then asked, "What do you know about the man who made your sword?"

Stephen answered quickly. "I don't know anything."

Master Salender nodded. "This is not a test. Relax, have some wine." Master Salender reached for a bottle of wine and then poured two glasses of wine. Master Salender handed one to Stephen and said, "Cheers," and then he took a sip. He looked down into the glass. "Nothing like a good libation." He took his eyes off the glass and said to Stephen, "The story behind your sword is quite interesting. Do you want to hear it?"

Stephen nodded and leaned back in the chair, holding his glass delicately.

Master Salender mused for a moment and then started recounting the history of the five Diamond Swords.

"A smith, his name lost to the annals of history, created the technology of making sand into the strongest glass. He then turned his attention to making swords." He sipped the wine and continued, "One thing he did not pass on to his fellow smiths was the secret for making a sword so strong that it could cut a diamond." Master Salender waved his glass in the air. "Smiths analyzed the five swords, but no one knows the lost smith's technique. Some smiths say that the sword is actually made from diamonds; others just shake their heads in consternation." Master Salender took another sip, gathering his thoughts. "Five swords were manufactured, one for the king and one for each duke at the time. Unfortunately, before the learned smith could pass on his secrets, the man met an untimely death." Leaning forward to impart a small secret, he said, "The smith met his death at his own hands. A sword, a fabulous sword, lies on a block of granite in a secret room in this very castle waiting to be unleashed." Master Salender gulfed down the rest of the wine in the glass and then refilled his glass. Stephen waited on the edge of his seat, not thinking about the glass in his own hand.

Master Salender continued, "After creating the five Diamond Swords, the sword maker decided to make another kind of sword. In the attempt, the sword stayed fired, burning the smithy to the ground, killing the man who struck the sword to the anvil."

"So, the sparks from the sword burned the smithy down?" asked Stephen.

Master Salender swirled the wine in the glass. "No, the sword itself caught fire and burned the building down around the ears of the man who struck it." Master Salender stopped and stared at Stephen. "I see that you are confused. Give me a moment to recount the whole story. You see, the sword never lost its fire. Anything it touched instantly became ablaze." Master Salender wrinkled his nose in mirth as he watched Stephen work out the details.

Stephen nodded. "It will burn anything, so that is why it is on a granite slab," said Stephen while sitting back into the chair.

"Correct," said Master Salender, touching the tip of his nose. "Now, that is a brief history of the five Diamond Swords. Here is another question: Do you know who the first Potioner was?"

Intrigued again, Stephen leaned forward, almost spilling his wine. He caught himself and took a swallow from the glass. "Who?"

"Ahh," said Master Salender with a twinkle in his eye. "It was a trick question, because the first Potioners were fraternal triplet sisters." Master Salender stood up, walked over to a glass shelf storing bottles of wine, and grabbed another bottle. Stephen sat stewing. Master Salender uncorked a bottle with mastery and turned to Stephen while filling his glass. Holding the bottle in his left hand, he pointed with the first finger past the bottleneck and said, "They were beautiful. Even at birth, they were unique: one with hair of honey, one with hair red as fire, and the third sister had hair the color of coal. They were spirited away in the middle of the night to become wives of the three treacherous kings, Reges Almanon, Reges Aristarchus, and Reges Ptolemaeus."

Master Salender walked over to a bookshelf and produced a small wooden box. Digging into the box with the finger he had been pointing with, he stopped and sat the wine bottle on the shelf to fish out a ring. "History recounts Reges Almanon rearing the three girls, keeping them captive in his palace without truly knowing the outside world. He gave them tutors." Master Salender stopped and grinned at Stephen. "His mistake was that he also taught them how to make potions. Now, enough tales. I have something to give you."

"But wouldn't the sisters' potion book be very powerful?" asked Stephen.

Master Salender stopped in his tracks and pursed his lips. "Yes, very powerful, but no one knows the location of the book. Now take this." Master Salender handed Stephen a gold ring engraved ornately with vines. The king's crest was pressed on the top where a gemstone would be held.

Stephen turned the ring in his fingers and said, "I don't deserve this beautiful ring." He started to hand it back.

"You do not understand." Salender paused for a moment and continued, "The ring would have been your birthright if you had been Zenith's son. After the adoption, it is now yours."

Stephen stared at the ring. "I guess it is mine."

Master Salender grunted at the answer. He drank from his glass and then asked, "Could you be a champion of the people?"

"I don't understand the question," replied Stephen.

"Of course, you don't. My apologies. The theoretical tall tales have led me down a different road. Thank you for talking to an old man." Master Salender offered his hand. "I hope we will be able to talk more in the future."

Stephen shook his hand, realizing the dismissal. He said, "Anytime." Stephen walked across the stifling room. He did not understand what had taken place. Master Salender seemed surreal. As Stephen walked down the corridor, he wondered if Stem could be the answer. Obviously, the red blotchy eyes of Master Salender suggested he had been using Stem. The drug affected people differently. Stephen wondered if wine contributed to the conversation. Stephen decided to humor the old man because of his relationship with Zen.

At that moment, Master Salender sat facing the flames of the fire and contemplating whether Stephen could play the part of a champion. He decided against it and tried to think of another course of action.

As Stephen walked down the corridor, Sam called, "Sir Alexander! Wait for a moment." Sam hurried down the hallway.

"Sam," replied Stephen as he hugged the older man. "Where have you been hiding? And please, call me Stephen."

"I'm sorry, sir, but rank dictates I call you Sir Alexander." Sam held Stephen at arm's length. "I knew there was something special about you. Well, are you ready to learn how to use that fancy sword?"

"I don't understand," replied Stephen.

Sam nodded. "I guess an explanation is in order." Sam crookedly smiled in a secretive manner and said, "You really didn't think Duke Kedwin would send his only daughter into battle without help. After the battle, I explained to Duchess Kira that I am a hired sword. After I got a potion in her, of course, you had already charged the castle. We missed the charge. She was more than chagrined about missing the fight at the time. Now she has appointed me her master at arms. My first assignment is to teach you how to use your sword." He poked Stephen in the chest.

"Wow. How good are you really?" asked Stephen.

Sam smiled. "Follow me to the practice arena."

He led Stephen through a maze of hallways to an interior courtyard open to the sky. Men were in the field practicing the art of death. Drills were run with halberds and short swords. Against a far wall, an armory of weapons was stacked neatly. Shields, buckles, spears, halberds, and swords had been churned out by local smiths. The glass from the weapons reflected the light of the sun in a brilliant wash of white. Fifty sweating men shouted in unison as the drill continued under the tutelage of two men.

"Am I to join the men?" asked Stephen.

"No," chuckled Sam, "you are receiving personal tutelage due to your station." Sam walked over to a circle outlined in chalk in the corner of the square. He unsheathed his sword, a short broad blade, and beckoned Stephen to join him. "Duchess Kira said she trained you in the first two basic katas of Hecto. The fighting style of Hecto is perfect for a beginner. After mastering the katas, I will train you in a different style. Attack me. Cycle through the katas you have already been taught."

Stephen stepped into the circle with his blade drawn. Tentatively he started the kata with a naked sword aimed at Sam. Sam swatted Stephen's forearm with the flat of his blade and motioned for Stephen to begin again. The pain in his sword arm fixed Stephen's attention. Starting over, he held nothing back. He performed the katas almost flawlessly, but the fluidity of Sam's motion turning Stephen's blade disheartened Stephen. He realized how inadequate his skills actually were against a trained opponent.

"I see it in your face," said Sam. "Understand, the years of training by my father and grandfather make me an expert. I can teach you the skills to survive." Sam thought, *I have other skills that only Duke Kedwin knows about.*

"Am I a lost cause?" panted Stephen.

"No, you are still young. You have some natural ability. The average man has less than that." Sam beckoned Stephen to continue.

Stephen concentrated on performing each task. As the time passed, his swings became more precise. His speed improved. After an hour, he lost his grip on the sword in an exchange. His hand felt numb. Sam picked up his dropped sword.

"You lasted longer than I thought," replied Sam. "The hand of most men would go numb in a shorter time frame. Do not use a potion for your hand. If it swells, put ice wrapped in cloth on it. Meet me here tomorrow at noon." Sam handed the sword back to Stephen. Sam saluted and walked into the crowd of men.

Stephen sheathed the sword, pleased with the compliment. He flexed his fingers. They felt like large sausages. The back of his hand had a sharp pain radiating from the tendons. The palm felt tight. Stephen decided to take Sam's advice. Besides, he wanted to play with the ice. Ice was a novelty to Stephen. The first time he had seen it in a glass at the castle, he had to restrain himself not to fish it out with his fingers.

Stephen headed for the kitchen. Flexing his hand unconsciously, Stephen thought about Sam. Stephen's world was changing. Men lied, even for a good deed. People pretended to be more or less than they were in public. The nuances associated with castle life wore Stephen's patience. He wished he could have joined Zen in his quest. He felt that Kira had been the only true person he had met. She did not have to pretend. Stephen shook his head thinking about betraying Kira's trust by murdering her father. Stephen thought *No, I do not like castle life.*

Chapter Nine

Zen rode the horse at a trot down a road headed to the mountains. Since leaving in the morning, Zen had made good time on the trail. The horse felt his urgency and so did not complain about the pace. Zen still let the horse walk for long stretches on the rougher path so it could catch its breath. Zen planned the death of Zacadam.

As a fellow Potioner, Zacadam had an equal chance of killing Zen. Zen thought about the fight. Strength could not overcome fire. Speed could not defeat strength. Fire was less likely to defeat speed. Zen worried about the poisons at Zacadam's hand. Some were acidic in nature, so the liquid could be thrown. Others could be gaseous, and close combat could be detrimental. The choice of a potion was like a chess match. One wrong choice in potions would be a defeat.

Terrain could give Zen the advantage. A surprise attack at an advantageous height could kill Zacadam. A flash of fire would do the trick. Cook him in a gorge. Zen considered facing Zacadam on even ground. Seemingly poetic as this may be, Zen had no illusions about murder. Zacadam was a dangerous man. Any opportunity Zen considered an advantage he would take to ensure the death of his enemy. Zen was no coward, but Zacadam had become a nightmare.

Zen turned his thoughts to Stephen. The boy had grown in a short time. The world sliced the boyish exterior off the young man. Zen considered Stephen may not be able to take the pressure of court. The lies, deceit, and backstabbing were rules people played by. Stephen was an innocent. People in the court had learned the rules at an early age. Stephen could only play along, his practical good sense as guidance. Zen determined not to tarnish the boy. Zen promised himself to lead the boy from the mischief of the games at the royal court. He just hoped it was not too late. Queen Clarissa could be conniving.

As the sun set, long shadows enveloped the road. Zen found a clearing off the side of the road to make camp. Pulling a sack from the packhorse, Zen sat down and nibbled on dry bread. Reaching further into the sack, Zen found a neatly folded paper package containing a slice of cherry cobbler. He smirked, knowing the kitchen staff had stashed the cobbler in the sack. He figured he must eat the whole thing as it would not fit back into the sack. Using his fingers, he scooped the pie into his mouth. He washed the cobbler down with lukewarm water. He dozed while waiting for the moon to rise. The horses nibbled on grass not yet burned by the frost that would later come in the winter.

A loud snort escaped Zen's nose. He rolled over in his sleep, and a sharp stone woke him. He had slept longer than he intended. Rising from the ground and brushing leaves off himself, he searched the sky. A large full moon in a cloudless sky spread ghostly light on the ground.

Zen rummaged in his saddlebags. Pulling out a pouch, he leaned against the horse, holding it in his right hand. He stared at the pouch for a moment. The addiction to Stem made his hand sweaty. As an addict, he had beat Stem. For a person not intending on sleeping for the next couple of days, he had to rely on Stem. He pinched the Stem into a wad and put it between his cheek and gum. He closed his eyes as he felt the drug's course through his bloodstream. The stimulant dilated his arteries and veins. Tightening up the pouch, he stored the Stem in the saddlebag. He mounted the horse under the pale moonlight.

Zen rode along in the grip of Stem's stamina. The drug could keep him awake for the next four days. His body would crash and burn after that. First the auditory hallucinations would start. Next his blood pressure would bottom out. If he continued using Stem and not sleep, his heart would stop. Addicts walked a fine line. The enticing effects of Stem had killed more than one man. The positive high of Stem granted the user temporary effects of better concentration, plus feelings of euphoria, stamina, and sexual prowess. As with any drug, the user's addiction culminated in larger amounts to receive the same affect. A true addict felt no benefits; the low-grade high was monotonous but necessary to stop a side effect of migraines.

A Potioner had discovered Stem. The Stem tree is difficult to find because the tree is a fledgling. The Stem tree grows fast, so the leafy tree must be harvested within a couple of years before becoming fully mature. A person would strip the leaves, small branches, and skin off the trunk. Usually, the diameter of the tree is about two inches. Then the man would split the tree trunk in half vertically, making two long strips of wood. The pulp is clearly visible in the core of the two halves and can be easily scooped out by a finger running down the middle of the concave half. The core is a filmy, gelatinous, fibrous pulp that can be cured and stored in special pouches. One tree usually equals one pouch. An addict could use up to two pouches a day. The process is easy, but finding the right tree is difficult.

Zen had ridden the entire night. The horse cantered forward whenever he felt the road unobstructed and level. Most of the night, the horse walked. Zen did not mind, since the Stem's euphoric attributes made the time tolerable. As the moon set, Zen unpacked a breakfast to wait for dawn. After eating, Zen spat out the Stem and refilled his jaw. The rush from the new Stem made Zen sit up straight for a moment. The degradation of Stem use filled Zen, making him angry because Zacadam had managed to rob Zen of sobriety. Zen filled the time with murderous intent.

A large shadow blocked Zen's sight of the stars. In early dawn light, Zen realized the shadow was the mountain. Pushing into the night, Zen had arrived ahead of schedule. After three hours of travel time, Zen found the only crevasse in the mountain leading to the other side. Normally choked with snow and ice, Zen imagined this was where the invaders had crept through and over the mountains unhindered. Zen staked the horse in a copse of trees. He walked the rest of the way into the narrow gorge.

After tromping through the day, he spotted a large ledge overlooking a bottleneck in the gorge. Normally it was a difficult if not impossible climb, but Zen swigged a potion for strength to climb up to the perch. His strength propelled him up the rock face as he found footing and handholds in small apertures in the rock cliff. Only once did Zen loose purchase. The shale rock burst in his hand as he reached for an outcropping. Zen realized his strength almost cost him a fall.

After twenty minutes of climbing, Zen's feet dangled off the shelf. The view from his landing lent Zen a perfect vantage point. No one would be able to pass near without his notice. The Stem would keep him awake and vigilant.

Zen backed away from the cliff edge. He unpacked his supplies and set up a cold camp. The ledge was too narrow for a tent but afforded enough space for a bedroll. The nights would be cold in the mountains. Zen situated the bedroll near the edge. Wrapped up, Zen could still see clearly while he ate a cold midnight lunch of trail jerky.

He imagined the ensuing fight. He would wait until Zacadam was directly beneath him before spraying him with fire. The plan seemed foolproof, but every plan could be contingent. His choice of flame seemed his best option. Zacadam would not be able to harm Zen. Even a fireball could not reach the rear of the shelf, and Zacadam would die trying to climb up to Zen's position. Zacadam's speed could be a factor, but Zen felt his aim was good. Now he only had to wait.

Zen peered over the top of the trees in the forest, noting a small fire a couple mile south. Zen cleared his mind of any thoughts and settled down for the act of retribution.

Zen's mind registered the minutest changes to the countryside. A falcon soared high above. Small animals scurried on the rocks. An orodromeus munched on a fern. Being ten feet long, its duckbill chewed only on plants. It was fast. Lightweight and bipedal, it could outrun other dinosaurs that might try to eat it. Zen could hear minute sounds as insects buzzed and scrambled over rocks. The rocks themselves tumbled down from the gorge's walls. The wind blew in the rocks, and the whistles were a melody of high-pitched sound. The clouds gathered at the top of the mountain, threatening a storm. Zen figured the storm would be here in a couple of days, maybe as early as tomorrow night. Zen focused his mind on the task of watching for Zacadam. The mountain focused on its task of being a mountain.

Chapter Ten

The past couple of days had become routine for Stephen. Mornings involved conversations with Master Salender. The old man tested his resolve about being an adoptee. Stephen found it annoying. After lunch, Sam instructed him.

Sam's skills with a sword impressed Stephen. His skills also made Stephen feel inadequate with a sword. The rest of the day was spent in the laboratory, where Stephen replenished the stock of potions for the queen's troops. He made potions as if he were cooking sauces—like a saucier. Zen was right: potion making was just another form of cooking. The best part of Stephen's day involved waiting for Kira in their secret garden. After dinner every day, Stephen sat on the bench in the garden trying to think of something clever to say to Kira. The moment she walked into the garden; Stephen would forget his clever thought. He was thinking about her right now as he sat on the bench in the garden that had become their meeting place.

"I had an audience with the queen," said Kira, striding into Stephen's sight. She sat down heavily on the bench. "She wants me to take the palace guard into my province. She expects trouble from my father."

"What about going under a flag of truce?" asked Stephen "Would your father respect that?"

Kira sighed. "She thought about it first. I am to fly the royal flag, my flag, and a flag of truce. The flags will symbolize my attachment to the kingdom and also my upward mobility into royalty."

"What can you expect from your father?" asked Stephen while placing a hand in her long tresses.

Kira leaned forward and put her elbows on her knees. "I don't know. I knew my father was ambitious, but he tried to steal the crown. I don't know what to expect from him."

Stephen put his arm around her shoulders and said, "I'm sure he will make the right decision."

Kira turned her head and looked at Stephen. "If he doesn't, we will have to fight. Many men will be killed in the civil war—men we will need to repel the invaders in the spring." Kira shook her head. "I don't know if I can do this." She cuddled into Stephen's side, hiding her face.

Stephen had never seen her so vulnerable. The weight of her position as duchess had taken a toll. Stephen kissed her on top of the head and said, "You will make the right decision—not only for your own people but for the good of the kingdom." He stroked her hair lightly. "I trust you."

Kira leaned back, her face glistening with tears, and slowly moved forward to kiss Stephen. She wanted to feel his warmth. She felt the tenderness in his lips.

The moment was broken by a soldier rushing into the garden. Not bothering to follow the paths, he ran over flower beds to reach the pair. The man stopped short and saluted. "Your grace, the master of arms wishes you to join him in Queen Clarissa's bedroom."

"Sam wants to see us?" asked Stephen perturbed.

"No, sir. The castle's master of arms requests your audience in the queen's chamber." The soldier seemed perturbed and said, "Big Ben."

Kira stood first and pulled Stephen to his feet. "Stephen, it must be really important if Big Ben made the request."

They followed the soldier into the maze of the castle. After taking several turns, Stephen was lost. The soldier kept a steady, fast pace and led them to the queen's bedroom door. He stopped and took a position next to the door with his back against the wall. He reached across the door and opened it, then he gestured for them to enter.

The largest man Stephen had ever seen stood in the middle of the room. Stephen was above average height, but this man stood two feet taller than him. The man's shoulders were the width of Stephen's times two. The man wore a simple tunic and leggings. His muscles rolled when turned as they entered the room. His face was full of wrinkles, but Stephen felt the leashed power of the man. Master Salender stepped around Big Ben.

"Sir, please don't enter further into the room." Master Salender held his hands forward. "We do not know the cause of death just yet."

Big Ben turned and took a couple of steps to the side. Queen Clarissa sat in a chair holding her son in her arms. Her head was contorted back over the top of the chair. Her left arm embraced the child. Her right hand covered the child's mouth and nose. Both bodies seemed frozen in place.

"Obviously poison," said Ben in a deep baritone voice. "I am leery about delivery."

Stephen cast his eyes down, trying not to see the dead figures. He noticed broken shards at the queen's feet. He walked forward and bent down to examine the glass. He picked a larger piece up off the carpet. The top had a circular lip. "It's a potion. The poison was a gas in nature. That is why Queen Clarissa's hand is over her son's mouth." He dropped the shard and turned to Kira. "Who is your father's Potioner?"

Kira answered quickly, "I don't know." She thought for a moment. "Father always kept his identity a secret."

Stephen turned to Big Ben. "Find Sam. He is Kira's master of arms." The huge man strode from the room like a large tiger.

Kira blanched. "You think it is Sam."

Stephen spoke to both Master Salender and Kira. "We know he is Kedwin's man. If he cannot be found, then I believe he is the culprit." Stephen thought, *If the royal Master Potioner was a secret assassin, then it stood to reason that a duke's Potioner would also be an assassin. Sam always seemed to have at least one more secret—the secret being Sam was Duke Fenton's Potioner.*

Master Salender replied, "A snake in the garden. Why now, he could have murdered the queen days ago."

Kira's face drained of color. "It's my fault. I told Sam the queen's plan. He must have thought the timing was right."

Master Salender spoke. "No child, it is not your fault. Sam may have been waiting on opportunity." He gestured at the bodies. "He wanted them both."

Big Ben returned with cords in his neck pulsing like small garter snakes. "He is not in the castle."

Master Salender replied, "We must find him."

Stephen sat on the edge of the bed and said, "No." He ran his hand through his hair. "He is a dangerous man. He will need to feel safe before his guard is down. We wait until he reaches Kedwin."

"But Kedwin will try to protect him," said Master Salender.

"True," replied Stephen. "But Kedwin will have enough problems dealing with Kira. I will kill Sam."

"Sir, you can't," said Ben. "We must protect you. Zenith Alexander is now king, and as his adopted son, you are prince of the realm."

"Fear is weak," shouted Stephen. He took a long breath. "If I let my enemy cause me fear, then he has won. I will personally kill Sam. Kira shall take the province by force if necessary. We will wait for Zen to return before leaving to face Kedwin."

Big Ben's face broke into a large, hungry grin. He could feel the authority in the decree. He liked the young man's courage. Big Ben understood the need to vanquish one's enemies. The royal family up to this point had been spoiled. He relished the idea of new blood. He believed Stephen had led a hard life, and difficult decisions needed hard decisions.

Master Salender left the bedroom. He thought about Queen Clarissa's plan. Stephen had been a large piece in the plan. Could he sacrifice Stephen now that he was next in line to be king? A damn prince held weight, but could Stephen hold up against it? Zenith was young enough to produce another heir. Master Salender thought, *The boy is making things difficult.*

Kira could not believe Stephen was a prince. He was just a small-town boy from nowhere. In less than a summer season, he had become royalty. She was so proud of him. The fierce love radiated from her eyes as she stared at Stephen.

Stephen's thoughts collided with the death of Queen Clarissa. He did feel fear. Would someone come into his room and kill him in his sleep? Stephen decided not to dwell on such thoughts. He made a decision to respect death but not let it rule his life. He thought about Zenith. Zen's entire family had been murdered. Stephen wondered what pressure Zen would feel and how he would cope with it. Stephen made another decision: he would help Zen even if it meant his own death. In his small town, death had been an illusion. Old people died. In this new world Stephen found himself in, death was a reality. He would just have to learn how to cope with death. He feared some men enjoyed death. Sam would be one of those men. Stephen thought, *Death is not my enemy. Only men who wield death are my enemy.*

Chapter Eleven

Soles scanned up the trail to find Zacadam. For the last day, Soles had followed him. He had stumbled across Zacadam's path early in the morning two days ago. Zacadam had been eating mushrooms. As for Soles, he had not eaten after the jerky he had stolen was all consumed. Soles considered finding Zacadam to be a lucky strike. Trailing Zacadam, Soles' bounty of food had improved by emulating what Zacadam foraged.

Soles considered Zacadam to be absolutely insane. He noticed the constant chatter Zacadam produced: talking to himself, animals, plants, trees, and ghosts, Zacadam carried on a constant conversation. From what Soles could gather, Zacadam considered himself to be king. Other times, he acted frightened, calling Soles' name for protection. As for the food, Soles only hoped an insane Zacadam still needed nourishment. Soles monitored his own health after eating Zacadam's picks. So far Zacadam's foraging had caused no ill effects to Soles.

At the rate of constant walking, Zacadam was nearing the mountain pass Soles had previously brought his men through. Soles considered circling around Zacadam to reach the pass first, but Zacadam's picks in food stuff lent Soles' assurance in reaching his goal to cross over the mountain. Even with the constant eating, Soles had trouble keeping up with Zacadam; his insanity lent him stamina. The man hardly rested. He seemed to orient towards a destination, but the process seemed flawed. Only Zacadam's obsession to reach the mountain stayed Soles' intuition from slaying Zacadam.

The trees parted, and open country leading to the slopes of the mountains stopped Soles's pursuit. Zacadam walked on, seeming to garner strength from reaching his goal. Soles hung back, sizing up the distance needed to remain undetected by Zacadam. Some obstacles could be used as hiding places for Soles, but darting from one to the other meant Zacadam might see him. Soles decided to take the chance. He could kill Zacadam if necessary.

Soles's legs burned from the exertion of walking. His left heel was swimming in pus inside his boot. His clothes, torn and frayed at the edges, marked Soles as unseemly. The bags he had stolen from the forester were filled with food picked by Soles' hand. The bags themselves made Soles needy looking. This harrowing sight would be difficult to pass in Viridian. Soles' only chance to pass into Viridian without being molested would be to steal something more dignifying. Once he identified himself at the mountain outpost, his troubles would be over as far as primitive survival.

Soles stooped beside a boulder. Someone was shouting from a ledge down at Zacadam. A torrent of flame descended upon Zacadam barely missing the man. He moved with surprising speed, dodging the flame. Zacadam laughed and taunted the man while skipping in place. Another jet of flame flung in his direction, Zacadam again skipped out of the way. He shouted a child's response of "You can't get me" over and over again. Soles leaned his back against the boulder. He could feel the heat in the air as more flames scattered from overhead.

Soles cursed his bad luck. Someone obviously wanted Zacadam dead, and Soles found himself in the middle. If he scooted back into the rocky pass, he would be seen. Soles could not dodge a fireball. If he stayed, he could be found, again being fried by flame. Soles peered over the boulder's edge, thinking both alternatives were not good. Zacadam was playing a game of cat and mouse. Soles wondered how long the flames would last, beating down upon the ground. Zacadam's insanity lent him fearless aggression, which was useful while dodging gouts of flame. Soles struck his flat hand against the boulder in frustration.

Zacadam danced a jig, taunting his assailant. The man on the ledge stood near the edge throwing flames at him. Soles recognized the man as Zenith. Soles considered his options. If he helped Zen, maybe Zenith would let him pass. If he helped Zacadam, he did not know how Zacadam would respond. The man was clearly insane. If he thought himself to be king, he would attack Soles. Soles considered himself to be a fighter, but Zacadam's speed was unbelievable. Soles considered helping Zenith, since they had parlayed earlier during the invasion.

Soles growled; he was tired of running. He picked up a hefty rock and put his belly on the boulder. Peering around the edge, he waited to see if Zacadam would be in throwing range.

Zen started cursing when the flames started petering out. Taking more deliberate action, Zen watched Zacadam with fascinated horror. Zacadam cackled and taunted Zen. Zen's anger added to the flames, but he knew the time was shortening. Zen stopped. He waited in a defensive stance with his toes hanging over the edge. The flames would last as long as he stayed awake or until the break of the next day. If Zacadam rushed him or made a move for the mountain path, Zen would finish him. It was a standoff.

Zacadam made an obscene gesture at Zen. Leaning against the canyon wall, he watched Zen with murderous glee in his eyes. Zacadam felt boxed in place but intellectually fine.

Zacadam's mind rolled over the possibilities. The rocky walls were too narrow at both ends for him to escape. Luckily the rocky slopes would not catch fire due to any debris. He knew it to be a waiting game. Zacadam's mind felt clear for the first time in weeks. The fear of death has a strange effect on the insane.

A large rock struck Zacadam in the side of the face, stunning him for a moment. He fell to his knees.

The opportunity was not lost on Zen. A billowing cloud of white-hot flame crashed onto Zacadam's kneeling figure. Zacadam screamed as his clothes and flesh produced an acrid black smoke flaring up over the flames and rolling skyward, dissipating in the wind of the mountain. Zen poured the flame onto Zacadam, willing the power of the potion past Zen's endurances. Zacadam's very bones charred and snapped under the pressure and heat of the flame. The rock baked the smoking cinder of a man, becoming black and greasy. Zen collapsed onto his side exhausted and promptly fell unconscious.

***

Before Zen opened his eyes, he could smell the roasting rabbit. His eyelids felt gritty. His body ached from staying awake for so many days. The hard rock pressed into his back. He panicked for a moment before realizing the constriction of his arms was just the blanket from the bedroll. He opened his eyes and stared at the man across from him sitting next to the fire. A roasting conglomeration spitted two rabbits over the fire. Zen's mouth started to water.

"Nice to see you awake," commented Soles. "I was starting to believe you would sleep forever."

Zen rolled over in the bedroll, sat up, and asked, "How long was I out?"

"One full day," answered Soles. "Are you hungry?"

"Starving," replied Zen, rubbing his hands together. He reached for the offered rabbit on a stick. For the next couple of minutes, Zen ravished the food. Juices flowed down his chin and dripped onto his tunic. After eating half the fare, he seemed to remember his manners and started eating slowly, mopping the juice from the corner of his mouth. Savoring the meat, Zen managed to ask, "The rock?"

After studying Zen for a moment, Soles replied, "Yes, I threw the rock. It does not make you feel less victorious?"

Zen laughed, almost dropping the food. The pressure from the past couple of days escaped with Zenith's mirth. He settled down to eating the last little bit. After cleaning the last of the meat off the stick, he replied, "Murder cannot be victorious."

Soles shook his head. "Murder is always victorious."

Zen looked askance at Soles and replied, "Your idea of victory; is it common?"

"Deception is the key to almost all of life's variables." Soles stared over the cliff's edge. "In Viridian, a man is defined on how well he can be deceitful."

"Here, a man is defined by his good intentions." Zen stared at his stomach and replied, "But it seems your world has filtered into mine."

"Zacadam, he was a rat," replied Soles, "a social climber who dreamed of power because he lacked the fortitude to attain power on his own terms."

"Duke Kedwin? He also lacks fortitude and insight?" asked Zen.

"Oh, a civil war has sprung from an invasion." Soles shook his head knowingly. "Some men thrive on conflict; others seek to use conflict as a reason to attain power." He stared at Zen. "The latter men are usually cowards waiting for opportunity."

Zen flung the stick over the edge of the shelf. "Do they stop after they get started?"

Soles thought for a second. "No, the fear of reprisal keeps the coward going."

Zen changed the subject. "What do you want?"

Soles gathered his limbs to himself. "I seek asylum. If I return home failing in the invasion, Rex Almanon will kill me. I could not hide in my own country for very long," said Soles, patting the black mask in explanation. "I would swear fidelity to you."

"You've admitted the art of deception," said Zen gruffly.

"Fear of Rex Almanon keeps the art alive," replied Soles. "I no longer wish to feel fear."

Zen thought for a minute and replied, "I can offer you hope."

Soles grinned. "My people do not know the definition of hope. The king squashes hope and men." A single tear escaped from beneath the mask as he replied, "I wish for hope." The tear striking the back of his hand as it fell into his lap startled Soles. The kink of knots in Soles' gut loosened as he silently cried. He had not known how intense the oppression of life was under Almanon's tyrannical rule before this moment.

Chapter Twelve

Stephen brushed Cow's left flank in the stall of the castle's barn. With the long steady strokes, Stephen let his mind drift. Not quite connecting the dots, he thought about the past couple of days. His mind flitted with half-given orders, consoling Kira, listening to Master Salender, and planning the invasion of Kira's province with Big Ben. The largest single desire Stephen felt was for Zen to come home. The responsibilities of being a prince had taken its toll.

Everyone expected Stephen to have the answers to problems he could not understand. Kira helped by giving him advice for delegating most problems to other people. He told Master Salender to plan the funeral and make the appropriate requests for the dukes and duchess to be at the funeral. Only three out of five of the aristocracy honored the request to attend. Stephen had expected Kedwin not to show, but now one of the other dukes had taken the opportunity to back Kedwin in his claim to the crown. Only Zen's reappearance would calm the other aristocrats. If he did not return, Stephen would be ostracized from the throne—or maybe even killed.

Big Ben had become a problem entirely made by Stephen's lack of experience at being a prince. Only after hearing rumors of guards planning an attack on Kedwin had Stephen reined in Big Ben. Big Ben wanted to hurt Kedwin and his people. After a long conversation with a lot of shouting, Stephen decreed there would be no military recourse until Queen Clarissa's original plan failed. Big Ben acquiesced but he continued to plan an attack, expecting Stephen to fail miserably at secretly murdering Kedwin. Stephen did not countermand the act of forming a much larger army because he believed the invaders would return.

Stephen's mood lightened as he stroked the stallion's iron sides. He turned his thoughts to Kira. She had become a constant source of fresh air. He realized he valued her opinion over more senior staff, but his instincts told him the kingdom was in new territory. Young minds could handle the change. Stephen smiled; Kira was also his first lover. The release of tension experienced through making love lent Stephen new breath for the morning of answers. From the first, Kira taught him new heights. His only regret was his deception concerning Kira's father.

Stephen placed the brush on the hook in the barn. As he exited, Stephen caught a glimpse of a man wearing a black mask headed for a different part of the castle. Stephen followed the queer apparition of the man. The man stopped on the steps of the castle proper leading to the double doors of the main entry and kneeled on one knee with a hand on the ground. Zen stood on a higher step and knighted the man. The sight seemed surreal. There were no people for the ceremony. If Stephen had not followed the man, then no one would have witnessed the indoctrination. After being knighted, the man stood and said nothing. He placed himself on Zen's right side, a solid statue.

"Zen, you're back," stated Stephen, emotionally drained.

"I know the past couple of days must have been difficult for you," said Zen. "I would like to speak to you in private. For now, let me introduce you to Soles. He is going to be one of my advisors during this trying time."

Soles nodded in Stephen's direction without saying anything.

Stephen's face contorted in his concern about the stranger, but he said to Zen, "I feel a little lost."

"I also feel a little lost at times," answered Zen. Zen turned to Soles and said, "I need a couple minutes of free time. Tell anyone not to disturb us." Zen sat on the bottom step and motioned for Stephen to join him. Soles turned and stalked to the top of the steps, out of hearing. From this vantage point, Soles could turn anyone away.

Stephen joined Zen and said, "I have been completely lost without you."

Zen chuckled. "I hear differently. Seems to me you did just fine in my absence."

"I don't know if I can take the pressure of being a prince," stated Stephen.

"I don't know if I will be a good king," said Zen. He patted Stephen's knee. "I never wanted the throne. My brother was raised as a king. I always watched from the side. I just hope I can be an effective king."

"What do we do now?" asked Stephen.

"The same as we have always done. Our station may have changed, but we are still the same people." Zen stared at the walls surrounding the castle. "I expect things will change. Our people are in a crisis. They may not see it, but it exists. Soles has told me some interesting things about Viridian. Rex Almanon will not stop. In the spring, Soles says an army will descend upon us from the mountains. Our only chance will be to change the politics over the mountains before spring."

"How are we going to do that?" asked Stephen.

"Master Salender and I came up with a plan. Do not worry about Viridian at the moment. First, we must deal with Kedwin. Do you remember what Queen Clarissa wanted from you?"

"Yes, but hasn't that changed?" asked Stephen worriedly.

"No, the thought is sound. In politics, you show your right hand but reveal nothing from your left." Zen sighed and said, "Can you handle this new world?"

"Now that you have returned, yes," answered Stephen. "Have you talked to Kira?"

"No, but I must to find out why you're blushing," replied Zen.

Stephen swung his head to the side and said, "She has become important to me."

"Good," replied Zen. "She will become important to me as well." Zen looked Stephen in the eyes and said, "Don't tell her. She cannot understand."

Stephen cast his eyes down. "I understand."

"I would like you to continue your sword lessons with Soles," said Zen. "And you will be joining Duchess Kira as my liaison with Kedwin in a couple of weeks. I believe her men will be ready by that time. Enjoy your time now, Prince Stephen, because time is not our friend." He ruffled Stephen's hair. "I expect Kira and you for dinner tonight." Zen stood up and walked up the stairs towards the castle.

Stephen followed him with his eyes. He knew things were going to change. Just how much, he had no idea. He would like to enjoy the present time with Kira. He thought *Don't tell Kira. How can I not?* Stephen decided he did not like his left hand.

Chapter Thirteen

The turmoil of the past couple of weeks left Stephen tired and disillusioned. Soles turned out to be a unique swordsman. He built upon the base of katas Stephen had learned. As a result of swordplay, Stephen had developed several nicks and bruises. Soles' idea of teaching swordplay left Stephen with light wounds. Once Soles actually cut him deep in the side. An aid rushed to Zen for a potion to heal Stephen. The pain reminded Stephen that swords are dangerous and not something to be taken lightly. Soles never once apologized for wounding Stephen or for giving him a jagged scar.

Big Ben had taken an unhealthy interest in Stephen. After losing almost the entire royal family, Ben's guilt led to overprotectiveness of Stephen. He came to Stephen the day after Zen appeared and announced that he would be in charge of Stephen's training in open hand combat. The huge man, unbelievably nimble, taught Stephen how to defend himself. Big Ben added to the bruises on Stephen's body.

As for Rex Zenith Alexander, his mood had darkened over the past couple of weeks. Zenith never considered he would be king. The responsibility of ruling the kingdom weighed heavily on the once joyful man. He only managed to smile when talking to Stephen at dinner. The office pushed Zenith's limits. The zest for life oozed out of Zenith because of the difficult and rational decisions of the crown. Hard decisions left him depressed. The kitchen staff sent Zenith a fresh pie for breakfast every day. He rarely ate more than half.

What little time Stephen had in the afternoon was taken by Master Salender, who felt his mission in life was to educate Stephen in history, politics, literature, and economics. Stephen's mind swirled with knowledge he considered worthwhile, but the education left Stephen concerned about the welfare of the kingdom. Stephen felt he lacked the education and knowledge to be an effective prince. Master Salender drove Stephen to be a competitive student.

Kira made Stephen feel human. She listened to him gripe about the day's events, adding encouragement. She expected nothing from him. She did not love him because of the man he would be but for the man he was now and before. The time spent with Kira grounded Stephen to life. They spent time together at night lamenting the day's events, each growing with knowledge of their shared love. At times they were against the world. Together, they fought against the injustices of the adult world but always with a pinch of reason. Physically, they shared the abundance of natural energy only youth provide.

Stephen's life felt complicated. At times he felt like the small-town boy. He expected nothing to be given to him. He was his own man. Other times, the pressure of being a prince ground Stephen's nerves. A slight curse could be considered a command from the prince. Any question would be aptly answered by devotion he felt he had not earned. In his heart, Stephen was scared he could not live up to the expectations of so many capable people. He worried about the lives he had sworn to defend—the lives of the people in the kingdom depending on a boy from nothing special.

After weeks of training and dealing with castle life, Stephen's quest for the dead queen's killer began. Stephen rode at the head of over five hundred men on horses in two columns down the road towards the Coal Province. It was an army to bully Duke Kedwin into stepping aside for his daughter to reign. Stephen had to admit, Zen's plan to usurp Duke Kedwin seemed plausible. Duke Kedwin could not field a larger army in the little time he had since announcing his intentions to steal the crown. The army riding at Stephen's back was an amalgamation of the old queen's guard and the survivors of Duke Kedwin's army. The loyalty of the men was not an issue. All the men considered Duke Kedwin to be a coward to murder a woman and her baby. The problem might be to keep the men from tearing the province apart, each seeking their own sort of revenge. The Erimos kingdom was learning about betrayal. Stephen thought about his own future betrayal of the woman he loved.

Stephen looked up at the flags flying high next to him. A rider gripped a pole with three flags flapping in the breeze. The king's standard, a Dimorphodon, a small dinosaur with leathery wings and a large head, and a diamond shaped tail; Kira's standard, a chunk of coal; and a white flag denoting a parlay with Duke Kedwin. Kira's standard was not lost on Stephen. King Zenith Alexander recognized Kira as the rightful duchess of the Coal Province and the city of Gavin. As they journeyed into the kingdom, Kira's flag would lend the people a sort of confidence that the kingdom was healing.

Stephen thought about the changes in the kingdom. Drought had caused famine, and Soles had admitted to Zen that the drought was an artificial environmental change by Rex Almanon in Viridian. Famine influenced the people in the kingdom to find unconventional means of financial support. Gangs roamed the countryside looking for food or coin. The kingdom was flipped on its side and wallowing in pain. Small villages guarded their stores of food from others in the kingdom. Neighbors fought over the rights of pastures for herds. Before the next harvest, people were going to die from starvation. The lack of planning seemed trivial in the reality of the starvation of the people. The only relief was enlisting in the army. The Viridian king unknowingly had supplied the Erimos kingdom with soldiers to fight any future invasion. The Erimos kingdom had been agricultural; now it was developing into a militaristic nation.

The economy of the kingdom of Erimos had been built on agriculture. Bartering, the favorite exchange for the people, was slowly becoming moot. The kingdom had been self-sufficient without trade outside of the kingdom because there was no one to trade with outside of its borders. The mountains had acted as proof against trade. The circulation of coin now swayed the survival of families. The supply and demand tipped towards the use of coin. The aristocrats controlled the exchange with their stockpiles of wealth. People had been more equal under the bartering system. Stephen realized with the drought and loss of goods to trade, the new economics would bring a class differentiation. Even with the little he knew about economics; he was still able to discern that people would be pushed into classes. The burden of self-sufficiency would determine the person's class.

Up to this point, coin had been a tool used along with bartering. An extra mode of wealth, coin had a low place in an individual's life. Now the aristocratic families would use their wealth to influence the use of coin instead of straight bartering. Holding back supplies for coin instead of trading goods for services, the aristocrats would change the entire financial system. Individuals would be more dependent upon coin. The king in Viridian had

141

influenced the very fabric of the Erimos kingdom by involuntarily changing the kingdom to use a monetary system wrought by the death of agriculture.

Kira rode up beside Stephen and asked, "What are you thinking about?"

Stephen blanched, coming out of his reverie, and replied, "I don't know. I feel like an uneducated boar."

Kira smiled and said, "Master Salender is highly educated but physically useless. Try not to think about it. We are still young enough to educate ourselves. For instance, a couple miles down the road, a large ruin is evident. As a child, I played in the ruins, but no one knows who built the large structures. Maybe one day, we can explore the stone pyramids together."

"What do they look like?" asked Stephen. His curiosity burning, he craned his neck to look ahead.

"I don't want to ruin it for you. Just keep your eyes open, and you won't miss it," answered Kira. She turned her horse to ride back down the column, checking on the men.

Stephen kept his eyes forward, searching for the ruins. After a couple of moments, he saw a peak of a pyramid topped over the trees. At this distance, the stones looked small. As he rode closer, the pyramid slowly grew larger. The highest structure Stephen had ever seen, the pyramid stood over the trees. A stone altar lay on the flat top of the structure. As Stephen pulled up to the pyramid, he could see steps leading up to the top. The steps were so steep, they seemed to disappear into the side, like a cliff face. The base of the pyramid was at least four hundred feet across. The sandy-brown stones comprising the structure were cut to fit in large blocks.

Stephen stood up in the stirrups and passed a signal for the column to continue forward. He cantered over to the base of the pyramid. Dismounting from his horse, he stood at the base looking up. It seemed to be a sheer edifice. Stephen stepped onto the lowest tier. He climbed slowly, as the steps were at least a foot deep, and the angle of ascent was almost ninety degrees. A quarter of the way up, Stephen proceeded on his hands and feet. The height made Stephen feel vertigo. Finally reaching the top, Stephen sat on the edge of the platform and looked down. At this angle, the sheer steps blended together to form a smooth side.

Stephen stood up and walked to the other side of the stone altar. The surface was a slab of black obsidian. The bas relief was sandy stone with snake carvings. One of the snake's mouths had a human face peeking out. Stephen shuddered at the thought of being swallowed whole by a snake. Stephen turned his back to the altar and caught his breath.

Two more pyramids were in his field of vision—each as tall as the one he climbed. Leading from the steps on the side of the pyramid where Stephen stood, at the bottom a courtyard surrounded by large structures sat squared. The eye saw an enclosed courtyard backed up to the pyramid. Stone buildings with entrances cut in triangles shored up the courtyard, which was a large field of grass enclosed by the bottom of the steps leading down from each building. The grass field was large enough to race horses. Embossed on the side of each building were carvings of snakes, birds, and ten-foot humans dressed in skirts. To the left, one entrance was round. A tunnel leading from the field cut into the steps at the base to the outside of one of the buildings and courtyard. The buildings were large enough to hold hundreds of people.

Stephen wanted to explore the ruins. He sighed and turned to dismount the top of the pyramid. A shadow caught his eye. Looking back, he saw the shadow of the obsidian altar at the top of a large triangular entrance across the field. It looked like a balancing scale that the sun had tipped down to the right. Stephen knew the shadow was no accident. To climb down the side of the pyramid, Stephen scooted on his butt. He did not want to topple down the steep stairs.

At the bottom, Kira was waiting for him astride her horse. As he stepped onto level ground, he asked, "You climbed these pyramids as a child?"

"Believe it or not, it was an easier climb when I was younger. What did you think about the other side?"

"I have never imagined anything like it. Did you explore the buildings?" asked Stephen as he mounted his horse.

Kira settled her horse by slapping it on the neck. The horse snorted. "Yes. The buildings are all made out of stone. The rooms are a maze. The actual pyramid has no rooms. I have always wondered if the pyramid was hollow with a secret entrance. I never found one though."

Stephen rubbed Cow's neck and said, "I would like to return someday and explore the ruins with you."

Kira grinned at Stephen. "I have often fantasized about lying in the field at night with a lover. The stars are so bright."

Stephen flushed and said, "I would like that." He nudged Cow in the ribs, and he and the horse overtook the column.

Kira rejoined the vanguard. Big Ben noticed the grin on her face and asked, "What's so funny?"

"Nothing," replied Kira, "just thinking about some other time."

"Well, you need to get your head in the moment. We will be reaching your father's stronghold at sundown." Big Ben aimed a disappointed glare at Kira.

Kira ignored him. She felt that small moments were the best. As time passed, she did start to worry. Her father had never been unkind to her. Kira's mother had died in childbirth, so Kedwin often ignored her. She knew he wanted a son to inherit his station, and over time he had treated her more like a son than a daughter. After the riding accident, her father had not been able to produce another child. The fall from the horse had made Kedwin impotent.

Growing up, Kedwin had started training her to become his replacement. She had been educated to rule. It was hard on Kira. Sometimes she just wanted to be treated like a daughter. The first time she cried from being hurt, he told her to man up. Being a woman was difficult enough, and he expected her to act like a man. When she had her first menstrual cycle, a housemaid explained how to take care of herself. No, Kedwin never treated her unkindly, but he did treat her like a son. Her femininity was lost. Men had tried to suppress her to gain the power of her inheritance. She knew that was one of the reasons she loved Stephen. He expected nothing from her but respect for each other. She had used many men to gain respect. Stephen was almost adolescent in his love, which she adored.

***

Stephen stopped on a rise overlooking a valley. He called for the column to halt. Long shadows stretched across the valley floor from the setting sun. Stephen could still see in the failing light a large city sprawled on the valley floor. His first impression was that Gavin was larger than the capital, with its small houses haphazardly spread out over the valley floor. In the center, a large manor was surrounded by gardens, and a low wall separated its grounds from the rest of the city. The roads switch-backed upon themselves at crazy angles surrounded by buildings and homes. Smoke rose from chimneys in the autumn air, draping the city in a slight haze.

Kira rode up to Stephen's side and asked, "What do you think?"

"It's big," replied Stephen. "I take it the manor is your home."

"Yes," said Kira. "Looks as if they are adding to the wall. It only stood four feet high, but I can see where they have raised the level to almost ten feet or so."

"Think your father was expecting company?" asked Stephen nonchalantly.

"Yes, which worries me," answered Kira. "Listen, we can't move the men through the city streets at night. It will cause a panic. We should camp here and wait till morning."

"Won't your father discover we are here?" asked Stephen.

"I wouldn't be surprised if he knew a day's ride out that we were coming." Kira turned her horse. "Besides, I want to visit a family friend tonight to gauge my father's mood. Care to join me?" asked Kira.

Stephen smiled, thinking about prowling the streets at night in a new place. He replied, "Always."

Orders were given to set up camp on the rise over the valley. As the men set up camp, Stephen wondered what the city streets looked like at night.

Chapter Fourteen

The dark streets were lit intermittently by oil lamps. The flames cast eerie shadows on the walls of houses. Kira informed Stephen that this part of town was privileged. The neat rows of houses had brick-and-mortar lanes running between them. The gutters were clean. All the houses are well lighted, with people moving behind the windows. The people were settling down after dinner. The smell of wood smoke hung in the air. Coal smoke burned in other parts of town for the less fortunate. Stephen felt completely safe walking down the lane with Kira.

A figure turned the corner, momentarily bumping into Stephen, and a woman's voice offered a dismissive apology. Stephen's hand brushed his purse strings, and he felt a small prick on his finger. Startled, he reached out for the figure as she ducked around a corner. His purse was gone.

"Stop!" he cried. Stephen turned to Kira and yelled, "My purse!" Without thinking, he bounded around the corner, following the thief. He only caught a shadow running around another corner. Fumbling in his belt pouch, Stephen pulled out a potion as he ran. Swigging the potion, his speed doubled in a moment. Again, he only glimpsed a shadow at the far end of the street. Doubling his efforts, he ran for the woman.

Stephen's speed hampered the chase as well as benefited it. In short bursts, he was able to keep the thief in sight, but the woman knew the territory. She led him outside of the comforting block houses, turning corners at every opportunity. At each corner, Stephen skidded to a stop before pursuing her further. The streets grew dimmer, fewer lamps burned on poles. Some broken, others unlit, the lamps told the story of a worse part of town. Stephen jumped over garbage heaps as he ran down alleys. Twice he had to scramble over low walls in pursuit. The woman slowed after a couple of blocks. She climbed onto a low roof.

Stephen scrambled up the side of the low-hanging roof. Climbing on top of the roof was her mistake. Stephen could see her outlined in the light of the city. Following her path exactly, Stephen avoided drop-offs and dead ends. She was tiring. He was gaining. Ten feet from catching her, the woman dropped over the side of a low building. Stephen jumped blindly. He fell eight feet onto hard, packed earth. The ground felt like iron to his battered knees. He sat down heavily on his rear. The woman stood only a few feet away with her back turned to him.

She slightly turned her head towards Stephen and said, "Now, we're both in trouble."

Stephen jumped up. Two men blocked the alleyway in front of him. Two other men stood behind. Stephen saw the glint of light reflect off the glass knives the men carried. One man moved ahead of his fellow and said, "Dianna, you stepped in shit this time."

"I wouldn't say my name is shit if I were you," replied the woman.

The man coughed, surprised at her reply. "I am going to make this hurt."

Dianna held up her knife. She turned to Stephen and said, "I hope you know how to use that sword."

Stephen unsheathed the sword and faced the men. His sword glowed in the faint light. Tiny reflections of light sent micro bursts down the blade.

He advanced on the men before they could surround him. The potion he had taken earlier still increased his speed. The men only saw a blurring sword. He feinted at the man on his left and drove a swing wide to the man on the right. The sword bit into his upper arm, severing it completely.

Before the man on the left could recover from the feint, Stephen drew the sword up and swung low at the man on the left. The man jumped back and fell against a wall. Stephen managed to impale him. The sword drove completely through the man and the wall behind, with only the hilt thumping hard against the man's chest to stop the blade. The startled look on the dead man's face stopped Stephen for a moment.

A mewling sound cut the moment. Stephen turned, expecting a knife in his back. The other man lay on the ground, barely holding his severed arm to his shoulder. A flap of skin had stopped the arm from completely falling off. The man lay on his side mewling. He had only moments to live.

Stephen allowed his eyes to go up the alley, expecting the woman to be dead. Instead, she was pressed against a wall. Her swings and stabs were calculated to keep the men off her. Stephen stole up behind the men. A loose bottle provided the noise for the men to realize he was behind them. As they both turned towards its tinkling, the woman sliced at one of the men's chest. Taking the hit, the miscreant backed off and ran up the alley. His fellow thug followed him.

Dianna watched the men run. She was tired, not only from running but fighting as well. She faced Stephen and said, "Nice sword." She tossed Stephen's purse to him. "I guess I owe you that."

Stephen fished in the purse and pulled out the signet ring.

The woman looked carefully at him and replied, "You're supposed to wear it."

Stephen laughed and said, "I know, but I hate it." He pulled the drawstrings on the purse, and threw it at Dianna.

She snatched it from the air. "Why?"

"It was never about the money, only the ring," answered Stephen.

Dianna stumbled, favoring her right leg. "At least now I can afford an iron nickel potion."

Stephen stared at her in the low light. She was tall and athletic. Her tunic was green, and she wore black leather pants. Her hair, bound with a black silk scarf in a ponytail, was dark with hints of auburn glowing in the pale light. Stephen felt instantly physically attracted to her, as did most men.

Stephen knelt and tore her pantleg open. A deep cut ran across her upper thigh. He reached in his pouch and produced a healing potion then handed the potion up to her and told her to drink. Squeezing the skin together, Stephen waited for the potion to take effect. The skin knitted, leaving a pink, puckered scar.

Dianna flexed her leg and said, "That cost more than a nickel. Do you always carry a fortune of potions on you?"

Stephen sat down in the dirt. Wiping the blood of his hands onto his pants, he said, "I didn't buy them, if that's what you mean." His hands kept shaking.

Dianna squatted and took his hands in hers. She replied, "First time killing someone?"

Stephen looked up and said, "That obvious? This one seemed personal."

"The thing to remember is to breathe. The rest of your body will follow." Dianna massaged Stephen's hands. "What's your name?"

Stephen felt reluctant to tell her his name. In this city, a price could be on his head. "Just call me the Potioner."

"OK," she said, "the Potioner." She smacked his hands together in a clap. "I think you better find some friends." She turned to leave, but before she did, she said, "If you need something, Potioner," she said his name sarcastically, but her eyes softened, "ask for Dianna Harken at the Waysider Tavern." She trotted down the alley leaving Stephen alone with two dead bodies.

Stephen stood up and walked down the alley away from the dead bodies. He thought about the circular pattern he'd taken as he ran after Dianna earlier. He was lost. He looked up in the sky and could see the stars through the haze. The city lights made the stars appear faint, but he could follow them to the outside of the city in the direction of the camp. He shook his head and hoped he did not run into any more trouble. Hunching his shoulders, he followed the stars.

Kira met Stephen on the edge of the camp. He had gotten lost several times trying to find his way out of the city. It took him two hours to find a way out.

Kira hugged him and then chastised him. "What were you thinking?"

Stephen sighed and said, "I wasn't, but my ring was in the purse."

"You mean the ring you're supposed to be wearing on your finger." Kira stepped back. "Is that your blood?"

Stephen self-consciously rubbed his pants. "No, it's not my blood. Let's just say it's been an interesting night." He walked away from Kira.

Kira watched him leave. She did not press him. He had obviously killed someone, maybe the thief. She shuddered thinking how death seemed to follow her now.

Chapter Fifteen

Stephen, Kira, and Big Ben walked down the lane in the middle of the city. Stephen and Kira wore expensively cut clothes. They were a matching pair to display their allegiance, wearing purple party shirts with black pants. The purple signified royalty to the duke's men. Big Ben was dressed for battle: a scale long shirt made of glass sewn in leather with the arms bare. Leather breeches with glass plates were strategically placed over his thighs and calves. He wore a longsword strapped loosely on his back, and fastened to his chest was a double-bladed battle axe bigger than Stephen's head.

Stephen decided the city looked less pretty in the daylight. Kira had told him her friend had reported that Duke Kedwin had been drunk the past couple of days. She said it probably started when the men were discovered marching towards Gavin. She figured Duke Kedwin had given in to the inevitable. She did not want to spill more blood, so the three of them were going to negotiate with Duke Kedwin. Big Ben's role was not lost on Stephen; if they needed a way out, Big Ben would lead the escape.

They came to the gate of the manor's compound. It was guarded by two men. The gates were new. Heavy wood and bound by glass, they were shored up by the tapering fifteen-foot wall of stone on either side. Men worked on the wall, building upon the four feet to reach a height of about fifteen feet. The two guards bowed and opened the gate without saying a word. The three abreast strode through the gate.

A cobbled lane with low hedges on each side funneled them towards the manor. Again, a guard at the door let them in without saying a word. Stephen could not discern if the men felt defeated or were in on setting a trap.

Stephen and Big Ben followed Kira into the house. Stephen glanced around. On the walls, all manner of beasts was displayed—trophies of kills. The carpets were springy underfoot and richly adorned. Stephen kept his eyes on the carpet. The animals just made him sick to his stomach. Kira stopped at a door and knocked softly. Stephen heard Duke Kedwin utter, "It's open, child."

Duke Kedwin sat on a couch with his feet propped on an ottoman. With a goblet loosely held in his right hand, his left hand beckoned for them to sit. Stephen noticed no trophies hung in this room; only rich tapestries hung from the walls. It was a sitting room with a couch, some chairs, and end tables decorating the floor. The entire back wall was a glass window looking out on the gardens. Sunshine lit the room.

Slurring his words, Kedwin said, "I guess I am to be dethroned."

Kira sat next to him and said, "Oh Father, you have had too much to drink."

Stephen walked over to the end table and picked up a bottle of wine. Holding it up to the light, he read the label out loud, "Swan Hills."

Kedwin replied, "My vineyard, the best in the kingdom. Here, son, please top me off." Kedwin stretched out his hand with the goblet. As Stephen poured the rest of the bottle into the cup, Kedwin chuckled and said, "The prince of the kingdom my wine bitch." Kedwin gulped down the wine. "Am I to be hanged, quartered, or imprisoned for life, my darling daughter?"

Stephen pocketed the empty vial.

Kira replied, "King Zenith has issued an order for your arrest in the conspiracy of killing the queen and her son. Sam is to be killed on sight, and you will be under house arrest."

Kedwin chuckled again. "I guess he is no fool." Kedwin turned his bleary eyes to Kira and said, "Sam is in Gavin. Where, I have no idea." Kedwin sat the empty goblet on the edge of a table. "Will I be afforded the amenities of my station?"

"I said house arrest father, not prison," she said picking him up from the couch. "I will help you to your bed." Kedwin leaned heavily on Kira, and they both swayed out of the room.

Big Ben put his hand on Stephen's shoulder and said, "Gavin. It will be difficult to find Sam."

"Do you think he will hide with cutthroats and robbery men, or hole up in some rich man's house?" asked Stephen.

Big Ben thought for a moment and then said, "Coin goes further with rabble. Anyone else could lose more. Why? What are you thinking?"

"I may have a contact in the city," replied Stephen.

"Really," replied Big Ben. "A kind of mischief."

"Yes," said Stephen, "but I think we will have to wait till dark."

Big Ben nodded. "The kind of person we will need probably doesn't come out until dark. I think I will explore the manor. Duke Kedwin could still change his mind."

Stephen too nodded and then sat down in one of the chairs. He absently stroked the vial in his pocket. Dumping the contents into Kedwin's goblet had been too easy. He thought about his first murder committed in the name of the crown.

***

The sun had set several hours before. Stephen and Big Ben walked down the streets in the not-so-nice part of town. A guard at the manor had given them directions to the Waysider Tavern. Women wearing scanty clothes stood on every corner. After the first time a woman mentioned something absurdly beyond Stephen's sexual experience, he steered clear of them. Men sized him up as he sauntered down the street but quickly found other things to look at once they noticed Big Ben trailing him. Stephen stopped outside of the door to the tavern. The tavern was loud, and light from the windows shone brightly into the street.

Stephen took a breath and pushed the door open. He stepped into bright light. Tables and chairs were strewn across the floor with people astride them. Men and women talked in loud voices. Smoke from the fireplace weighed heavily in the air. A large chandelier hung from the ceiling with gas lamps lighting the place. The eye could see movement, but the mind had trouble organizing so many animated people. Big Ben nudged Stephen to go forward.

Stephen steered around numerous people as he walked to the bar at the back of the tavern. Stools with people leaning against the bar blocked his path. Stephen was daunted by trying to vie for the barkeep's attention. Big Ben barreled up beside him and shook his coin purse. The barkeep meandered his way to them.

"I need to talk to Dianna," said Stephen.

"What did you say?" asked the barkeep, cupping his hand to his ear.

Stephen leaned over and spoke up, "I need to talk to Dianna."

"She should be along shortly," he said. "What do you want to drink?"

Big Ben boomed out, "Ale!"

The bartender nodded and poured ale from a flagon into cups. "Four pennies."

Big Ben gave the man a stern look. "Robbery." He paid the man for the two drinks.

They worked their way over to an upturned table near the edge of the crowd. Big Ben turned it over right side up. They had no chairs to sit on. Stephen sat on the edge of the table, and Big Ben stood next to him. A woman made a beeline for Big Ben, but he waved her off. She gave him the finger and then sat in another man's lap. Stephen could feel everyone's eyes on him, but no one looked directly at them. Both men sipped the ale in the cups.

After half the ale was gone, Dianna made her appearance. Her hair, no longer bound, cascaded around her shoulders. She wore a loose-fitting party dress. The hem above her knees, and the short sleeved green dress was obviously new. She strode up directly to Stephen. "Potioner," she said, "who's your big friend?"

"His name is Ben. Look, I need your help in finding someone," said Stephen.

"Does he want to be found?" asked Dianna. She waved at a friend at another table.

"No," answered Stephen, "as a matter of fact, he is probably well hidden."

"Well, that makes it easier. If he is hiding, then people will know where. I will need some coin to grease some palms," replied Dianna, holding out her hand. "Give me about an hour."

Stephen nodded at Big Ben. Ben reached into his tunic for his change purse. He dug out a couple of iron nickels for himself, and said, "For the wait." He handed over the purse.

Dianna hefted the purse and smiled. "I will see you in an hour." She turned and left the tavern.

"Can you trust her?" asked Big Ben.

"As much as anyone in the city, I guess," answered Stephen.

As they waited for Dianna, the tavern started filling up with more patrons. Stephen and Ben were on their second drinks when a drunken man pushed his way through the crowd and bumped into Ben. Ben smashed his fist into the man's face. The drunk hit the floor hard, knocked out.

"Was that necessary?" asked Stephen.

"Yes," answered Ben. Ben took another sip of ale.

After Ben hit the man, Stephen noticed the feeling of being watched lessened. Stephen relaxed more and scanned the crowd. A man entered and set up a stool in the corner of the tavern. He pulled out a flute and trilled a couple of notes. The people in the bar talked a little less loudly. The flutist played a fast, upbeat song. Some of the patrons banged their cups on tables in time with the beat. A couple of women raised their skirts above their knees and danced a jig. The crowd hooted and hollered at the women. The songster broke into another fast-paced jingle. A couple coins flew in his direction. A man grabbed one of the women's asses; she sat right in the perpetrator's lap.

"Is it always this loud and boisterous?" asked Stephen.

Ben replied, "Yes, at least in the bad part of town. As the night wears on, the ale goes to their heads and fights break out. We will be long gone by then."

Stephen saw movement at the door. Dianna beckoned them to follow her outside. Stephen elbowed Ben and motioned him towards the door. Ben followed Stephen outside.

"Well, that was easy. I didn't use too much coin, but I get a finder's fee," replied Dianna. She walked down the street. Passing by a whore, she slapped him on the ass and grinned. She continued on and said, "Your friend was pretty easy to find. The Serious Men has him."

Stephen asked, "A man has him?"

"No, silly," replied Dianna. "The thief ring called the Serious Men is hiding him. A dangerous gang, mind you. If you want the man, you better see him tonight. He's bought passage out of town in the morning. After tonight, he will probably disappear."

Stephen looked at Big Ben questioningly. Big Ben responded, "If we bring more men, he may be moved to a different location."

Dianna stopped suddenly and put a hand on Stephen's chest. "I take it you want him dead?"

"Yeah, pretty much," answered Stephen.

Dianna swung the coin purse on its strings in front of Stephen's eyes. "I can help, but," her eyes narrowed, "I want more than this."

"I can guarantee ten times that much for your help," replied Stephen.

Dianna looked Big Ben over. She turned her attention back to Stephen and said, "It won't be easy. Do you have more healing potions?"

"Yes," answered Stephen, "and a couple others."

Dianna pursed her lips. "Fire potions?"

"Yes," said Stephen. "Why? Do you have a plan?"

"Maybe," replied Dianna. "Let me think about it on the way."

Dianna prowled the streets. As the lanes became darker, she moved visibly closer to Stephen and Ben. The trio was less likely to draw attention or get mugged by unsavory types. People moved in groups; Stephen never saw anyone alone. Dianna ducked down an alley. The garbage smelled like putrefied fish. She kicked some of the garbage around to make room for them.

"I've been thinking about a plan. The Serious Men's home is in a warehouse a couple more blocks down the road. I can go around back and set the place aflame." Dianna grinned and said, "The rats will abandon ship, and your friend will be out in the open."

"Not very classy," remarked Big Ben.

Dianna's eyes screwed up into slits. "Listen, even you—and especially the boy—would not survive a frontal assault. You would be outnumbered fifty to one, if you catch my drift. Besides, I have to think of my own ass. If I am seen in this caper, I can forget sleeping at night. Got it?"

Stephen grabbed her arm and said, "We will do our part. When this thing's over, you'll get paid. Now relax. We are not the enemy."

Dianna held Big Ben's gaze for one more moment and then turned to Stephen, yanking her arm free. She said, "I want a hundred times what was in the bag."

"She's an extortionist," remarked Big Ben.

Stephen replied, "No, probably just a realist. You will get what you want. You will find us at the duke's manor after this night. Here," Stephen reached into his pouch of potions on his belt, "is the fire potion. What's the signal?"

Dianna turned the potion up to her mouth. She swallowed it in one gulp. She looked at the empty vial in her hand and said, "Nasty." Fire engulfed her hands for a moment, and then she clapped them to put the fire out. She started kicking a path through the refuse and said, "Fire's the signal, smart man." She waded further into the garbage.

"Delightful girl you've found," said Big Ben sarcastically.

"Maybe, but I think her plan will work. Are we going to be able to tell Sam from the others?" asked Stephen.

"I have no doubt," answered Big Ben. "Our hearts will lead us to him." He exited the alley walking towards the warehouse.

Stephen grimaced. He believed Big Ben was right. He wondered if someday a person would hunt him down for his treacherous murder. Stephen smacked his lips and thought about the task at hand then followed Big Ben down the street.

The signal turned out to be billowing smoke. It rose over the building and plummeted to the street. Men and women dashed from the burning building. Some turned around and stared at the building; others ran on, escaping into the crowd. It was Big Ben who spotted Sam as he barreled out of the smoke. The smoke trailed him like a shroud, he was moving so fast. It was their bad luck that Sam chose to turn away from them running at a stupendous speed. Big Ben started after him until Stephen laid a hand on his arm.

"You won't catch him," shouted Stephen over the crowd. Stephen dragged Big Ben into a less crowded lane and said, "I barely caught Dianna when she stole my purse. If I had not had the potion, she would have gotten away. His speed blended with his knowledge of the locale will make catching him impossible. Damn, do you think he will escape in the morning?"

"Maybe," answered Big Ben, "maybe not. If his supporters are the Serious Men, maybe the fire has disorganized them enough for an escape to be impossible. On the other hand, if the plans are laid in place, he will escape. What should we do now?"

"We wait for Dianna to contact us. If Sam stays in the city, she will know where to find him." Stephen looked at the ground, thinking. "Damn it, why didn't we just walk in and demand Sam?"

"Don't second guess the situation," replied Big Ben. "The girl was right. We don't know how deep the convolution between Sam and the Serious Men is. Come, it is time to return." Big Ben led the way through the winding streets to the manor.

Stephen left instructions for the gate guards that a woman would be seeking him. The password would be her reference to him as Potioner. Stephen did not feel well about the sordid events of the night. Sam's easy escape chafed at him. He felt he had let Zen down. His first real mission by himself had been a bust. People's expectations of the new prince seemed diminished by his failure in Stephen's mind. His surly attitude was written on his face, and he felt guilty about destroying the Serious Men's home.

Chapter Sixteen

Stephen slept soundly in the oversized bed. He curled up into a small ball in the middle of the bed with the sheets wrapped securely around him. No creatures stirred in the dead of night. Insects buzzed the room's window. Most of the castle's people slept.

"Prince Stephen," a man shouted as he banged on the closed door. "Prince Stephen, excuse me, but wake up." He shouted a little less. "Sir, please answer the door."

Stephen opened his eyes to a nearly dark room. A sliver of light from the moon slanted through the cracked window. This was the second night he had slept in the bed. He had decided on the first night the bed was a soft cloud. He rolled to its edge, but the covers tangled his lanky body. He shifted and untangled himself. Sitting on the edge of the bed, he took two breaths and launched himself at the door.

Stopping short of opening the door, Stephen asked, "What is it, man? It's late."

"Sir, a woman is hurt. She is the one who calls you Potioner," answered the guard.

Stephen's heart started. He opened the door wide and motioned at the guard carrying her. "Put her on the bed." Stephen rushed over to the closet to retrieve his potions and then stepped up to the edge of the bed.

Dianna's arm was broken. Bruises and contusions seemed to populate most of her body. She breathed in ragged gasps through clenched teeth. Her eyes were open but only stared at the ceiling, her face a black-and-purple swollen mask.

Stephen said quietly, "I have to set the arm."

Dianna's voice wavered. "Have you done it before?"

Stephen replied, "On animals."

"What, like pigs or something?" she yelled.

"Calm down," said Stephen holding her arm. "I can do it. It's just going to hurt for a moment."

Dianna grabbed a bit of the blanket and stuffed it in her mouth. She nodded at Stephen and then stared at her arm. She whimpered as she heard the bones scrape together while he set the broken arm.

"The hard part's over," replied Stephen. "Drink this potion, and you'll sleep. Come on, drink it up," he said, pouring the contents of a vial into her mouth. He dabbed some from the corner of her mouth with the sheet. "Just relax and sleep. I'll talk to you in the morning." Stephen saw her eyes flutter. Her head rolled to the side, and she breathed deeply in a cadence.

Stephen turned to the guard and asked, "When did you find her?"

The guard replied, "Only moments ago." He looked visibly shaken. "Two men dropped her off at the gate, and then turned and ran. She just kept repeating 'Potioner' over and over again. The guard earlier told me to look out for someone using a password. I brought her here as soon as I could understand what she was saying."

Stephen slapped the man on the back and said, "You did good."

"Is she going to be all right? I mean, I never saw anyone beat so badly," said the guard.

"She'll be fine. Return to the gate. You did well," said Stephen. He thought about the young man's innocence. He felt old for a moment. "She'll be just fine," he said as he walked the guard out the door. He closed the door and leaned against it. He decided to sleep in the overstuffed chair in the corner. He pushed himself off the door and walked to the chair.

He could not sleep. Dianna had been dropped off for a message only she knew. The young guard would be typical of the men in this new army. He himself had only experienced one real battle, but he felt experienced in comparison. Kira had been distant all day. Big Ben had kept reassuring Stephen regarding Sam's capture. Stephen's mind muddled through these thoughts as he sought sleep. He dozed until early morning light streamed in through the crack in the window shutters.

Stephen checked on Dianna. She slept soundly. He decided to seek out Kira before breakfast. After exiting his room, he turned down the hall to Kira's room. Knocking lightly on the wood panel of her door, Stephen waited for a response. After a couple minutes, he pushed the door open a crack and looked in the room. The bed was fully made as if no one had slept in it the night before. Stephen opened the door farther and glanced around. He figured she had not been in the room the entire night. A thought came to him.

Stephen walked down the hall to the master bedroom. He knocked on the door lightly. He heard Kira's voice tell him to enter. The first thing he noticed was a stool next to the bed with Kira sitting on it. Duke Kedwin lay in the bed, his face a white pallor. Kira held the duke's hand and looked up at Stephen with red, teary eyes.

"He's dying," she said in a small voice.

Stephen crossed the room and hugged Kira while she sat. Kneeling down on one knee, he asked, "Are you sure?"

"Yes," sobbed Kira. She wiped the tears from her face and said, "Someone poisoned him, and I think I know who."

Stephen's heart jumped, and he hurriedly asked, "Whom do you expect?"

"It can only be one person. Sam poisoned my father. My father told me Sam came to him asking for protection. My father declined his request, saying the civil war was over. My father did not have the resources to fight. Sam got angry. Sam told my father he was his man, and he needed to protect him. My father replied no. Father said he left in the middle of the night before we came. I figure Sam poisoned him out of spite." Kira peered at her father and said, "I will kill Sam for you, Father." She held his hand against her cheek. Tears running down her cheeks, she looked at her father adoringly.

Stephen placed his hand on her shoulder. His emotions cartwheeled in his breast. He thought about telling her the truth. Zen's advice popped in his head. He looked at her and realized she needed someone to blame. Stephen decided a known murderer was the obvious choice. He could not listen to her cry. He whispered, "He's going to a better place now."

"What?" sobbed Kira.

Stephen said slowly, "He's going to a better place."

Kira got angry. "A better place? He is my father. He has been murdered. And all you can say is, 'He's going to a better place'? The man responsible is out there. I will kill anyone who protects him."

"Kill, kill, kill," hollered Stephen. "Why is everyone bent on killing? Regular people don't speak of killing."

Kira stood up and slapped Stephen. Her eyes fierce, she said, "You are only a boy. A boy hides in the garden to kiss his girl. A boy who doesn't understand what justice is for people."

"Justice? How has justice turned to killing? I don't understand," shouted Stephen.

Kira turned and said, "When you become a man, then you will understand. Now leave. I don't want you here. A boy cannot understand the tribulations of an adult." She looked at her father and softly said, "I am no longer a child. I have to put childish ideals to rest. We are done, Stephen." She turned and looked Stephen in the eyes. "Done."

Stephen turned and started out of the room. He glanced over his shoulder for one more glimpse of the woman. She stared back at him with unremorseful eyes. His heart ached.

Kira turned to her father. He lay in the bed wasting away. Kneeling by the bed, Kira said, "Father, you have always been a weak man. Over the years, I tried to please you. I learned to ride a horse when I was eight. I shot my first bow at ten. You never once congratulated me. You never once listened to me cry. But you are my father, and I will avenge you. I believe all men are weak including Sam, Stephen, and Zen. You attempted to take the throne for the glory and power. I will take the throne to honor the people of Erimos. The children and women of this kingdom need a voice. A ruler who will provide not only to those who rule, but for the people. Weak willed men have always trodden down on the less fortunate. I swear to you. No man shall ever rule Erimos. I will be vengeful in my wrath to see the people of Erimos protected from the invaders, and the people will be protected from men like you. Men who only want glory."

After she spoke to her father, something broke in her heart.

***

Stephen watched the sunrise from the window in his room. The weight of emotions bore down upon his heart. He ground his hand into his palm and decided to let his thoughts not rule his emotions. Apparently being a prince was no easy task. The responsibilities, the secrets, and the deaths coincided with being a prince. Stephen felt he would rather have none of it, but he had already dedicated his soul to the state with Kira's father's death. Kira was not being distant; Stephen had enforced the distance. Her father's death would destroy the relationship. His guilt would destroy the relationship. He felt the argument with Kira had made the situation unavoidable. He could not think how to salvage the relationship. Stephen smacked his hand in his palm and thought he would reconcile his guilt by killing Sam for Kira. Stephen's mind muddled through incomplete thoughts trying to save the once-budding romance with Kira.

"Potioner?" queried a voice from the bed.

Stephen turned. He walked to the bed and said, "Stephen. Please call me Stephen."

Dianna sat up in bed and scooted so she could put her back against the headboard. She smiled and said, "You mean Prince Stephen, don't you?"

"No," he growled, "just Stephen Bishop."

"Hmm," Dianna's eyes searched the bedspread. Her eyes locked on his hand. She said, "Prince or not, you have a problem. The Serious Men has decided to ransom your fellow off."

"That's a good thing. We pay the ransom, and we get Sam," replied Stephen.

"You would think that, but they want payback for almost destroying their home." Dianna shook her head. "They will give you Sam—with strings attached."

"What strings?" asked Stephen.

"Coin, and a duel between Sam and your choice," answered Dianna.

"Why the duel?" asked Stephen. "Isn't the coin enough?"

Dianna's eyes hardened. "Blood for blood." She straightened the covers over her legs and then replied, "Not everyone made it out of the burning building."

Stephen's heart shrank. He tallied more deaths to the imaginary scorecard. He wondered how to stay sane in an insane world. He had never had to deal with so much death. Stephen wondered how many ticks on the card it would take for him to lose his sanity or even his life. At least one more tick had a name attached. Sam would die.

***

Kira would not listen to reason. Big Ben and Stephen tried to convince her not to fight Sam. They gave her logical and plausible reasons not to fight. She rejected every argument. Dianna stood in the back of Kedwin's bedroom listening to both sides. In the end, Dianna's suggestion for Kira to fight swayed the argument. Big Ben stated that Dianna had no vote, but it was settled by the women. The men relented only because of the women's pride.

Dianna filled in the details. One thousand nickel coins were to be delivered to the Serious Men. At that time, Sam would be there to defend himself. If he lived, he would be free to leave the city. The interesting sidenote to her story was that no potions would be allowed during the duel. The place to meet was the burned-out warehouse owned by the Serious Men at sunset that day.

Kira's preparation for the duel was simple. She slept most of the day to build her strength, which had been lost during her watch at her father's deathbed. Stephen wandered the halls of the manor trying to reason the insanity of the duel. Big Ben spun his own plans. If Kira did not come out of the warehouse, he would call in reinforcements and arrest anyone in the place. Dianna spent the day eating delicious food. The servants were kept busy by her demands. A bath was drawn. Hair was styled. Her body was pampered by women. Dianna lived like a spoiled duchess for the better part of the day.

The four entities met at the gate leading out of the manor at sunset, each with their own agenda. Walking down the streets, the four prepared for death: the death of Sam, the death of youth, the death of responsibility, and the death of life on the streets were strapped to the hearts and minds of the four people. Dianna led the way to the warren.

Ten men stood outside of the warehouse, each garbed in ratty clothes, with well-worn weapons at their hips. They split into two groups to funnel the party into the warehouse. The place smelled of rat droppings, bird droppings, roach droppings, and burned wood. The floor was an ugly, black, packed earth. Bales of decimated cotton were piled against one wall. The floor was open but crowded with men and women. Children ran in circles among the sullen folk.

Not one man or woman spoke a word. Again, the press of people funneled the foursome into the center. The only light came from the fading sunset through broken windows in the shadowy building and part of the wall that had a hole burned in it. Sam stood in the middle of the throng, sword in one hand, and only wearing a black loincloth. His rigid face spoke of torment. Big Ben dropped the sack of coin onto the ground and stepped back into the crowd that had formed a circle around Kira and Sam. Dianna stood next to Stephen and watched the crowd for treachery. Stephen stood at rigid attention with one hand on the pommel of his sword and the other on the potion case on his belt.

"I didn't expect you, Kira," said Sam. He rolled his shoulders and flexed his entire body.

Kira shouted, "And why not, you murderous bastard?" In an even tone, she said, "You killed the one man who loved me my entire life."

Sam nodded. "I expected a reprisal for my actions."

"Don't you dare try to weasel a nonguilty plea. I expect lies from you," replied Kira. "The point is moot." She drew her father's glass rapier from its sheath. The thin glass blade was almost invisible in the sickly light.

Sam glanced at Stephen and said, "One answers for death." Sam loosened his wrist that held the glass short sword.

Kira swung first. The rapier aimed at Sam's head, but Sam turned the dangerous strike with the glass short sword. Both combatants crouched and circled left. Sam's pirouette ended with a slash to Kira's right shoulder. She skipped from beneath the blow. Both stopped and faced each other. Sam flinched to the right and turned his blade to the left, striking at Kira's sword to disarm her. She caught his blade on the guard and tried to wrench his blade from his hand. Both struggled for a moment, and then backed out and into a crouch. Kira tried a riposte to Sam's chest. He flicked her blade away and returned a strike to her thigh. The sword scored a slash upon the thigh. Wincing, Kira managed to stab his shoulder before the return of his sword to defend. Both backed off to ascertain the damage. Rivulets of blood escaped both wounds. Both knew time was now a factor. Both wounds were lethal, so they could both bleed to death if the fight did not end soon. Sam brought his sword to the en garde position and closed his eyes. Kira's training for an opening registered the moment Sam was blind and with little conscious thought she slashed past his raised blade and to his unprotected throat. Sam opened his eyes and in them Kira saw the dying plea of a man to be found innocent. She did not think Sam was innocent in any sense of the word. Sam crumpled to the floor.

Stephen rushed to Kira's side with an open potion in hand. She sat on the floor and held her wounded thigh while greedily drinking the potion.

A man stepped from the crowd, clapping his hands. His face held no joy. He said, "This is not the end, Duchess." Men around him drew their swords.

Stephen screamed, "You want more death? Then have at it." Stephen dipped into his belt pouch and retrieved a potion.

The move stopped the thieves in their tracks. None knew the nature of the potion. Standing tall, Stephen spread his arms wide. At first nothing happened, but then as if the world's air had become a spigot, wind whistled from the cracks in the building controlled by Stephen's outstretched hands. The wind ruffled everyone's clothing and hair. A dusty vortex appeared in front of Stephen. He released the wind upon the crowd. People tumbled like leaves, flung about, smacked into the ceiling, walls, and floor of the warehouse. Loose objects scattered about the large open area. Oil lamps broke against the cotton stacks, creating a smoky flame. The cotton caught fire, and a red wall of flame licked at the ceiling joists. Big Ben picked up Kira from the floor and ran for an exit. Dianna crept up behind Stephen and whispered in his ear, "Stop." His entire body shaking, Stephen clapped his hands together to stop the wind. Dianna steered him out of the burning building.

As Stephen exited, he saw Big Ben shouting instructions to the fire brigade, his huge form outlined by the raging fire of the building. Kira lay prone at his feet.

Stephen leaned against the adjacent building's wall. He held his hands in front of his face, crying steadily. Dianna hugged him to her breast. Stroking his hair, she cooed at him. He clung to her as racking sobs escaped his lips. Streams of tears washed the ash from his face. After a couple of moments, he said, "I don't like death."

Dianna stroked his hair, placing a cheek on the top of his head. "No one does, dear."

"Then why does it continue to follow me?" he asked pettily.

"It seems to follow all great men," she answered. "Come, I know a place where we can be alone."

They clung to each other as they walked away from the fire, driving back shadows in the night until the dark swallowed them whole.

***

Stephen awoke with light streaming through a window and lighting his face. Dianna lay naked next to him, her head cushioned on his chest. Stephen stroked her hair, thinking about last night. The sex had started as a passionate undertaking by people needing the pure form. As the tension escaped their bodies, the passion turned into indulging the needs of the body. As the sex progressed, Dianna's experience became more relevant. She taught him how to experience the animal side of sex, the brutal side of sexuality. In the end, both exhausted, they experienced trembling muscles strained beyond their limits. They collapsed together, each holding on to still forms for separate reasons, neither really knowing what.

Chapter Seventeen

Stephen's guilty conscious kept him away from Kira. She had spent her time nursing her father until his death. Two days after the fire, her father died in his bed. Kira arranged a state funeral. Zen was expected to make an appearance as well as the other aristocratic family members. Kira locked herself in her room until the funeral. When Stephen finally worked up the courage to visit her, she did not open the door. He left her alone, feeling even guiltier about the situation.

The day of the funeral was dreary and cold. A slight misty rain fell on the processional. A long train of people marched from the manor down to the cemetery outside of town. Zenith and Kira followed behind a carriage carrying Kedwin's corpse. A trail of folk followed in its wake. Kira felt her father should be buried with the common folk of his province. A large, ornate sarcophagus overshadowed the simple graves. Kedwin's casket was lowered into the stone box and closed for an eternity. At the simple affair, Kira spoke of his strengths. The crowd fidgeted in the rain, waiting for Kira's short speech to close. Then people slowly departed the cemetery, leaving Kira and Stephen alone.

Stephen shortened the distance between them. He wrapped his arms around her shoulders and said, "Be as strong as your father."

Kira pushed him away and said, "My father was a weak man." She wiped the tears from her face. "I don't want to see you."

Stephen voice whined, "Kira, why?"

Her face looked cruel as she said, "My life begins here without you. I am no simple girl. I know you slept with that whore from the city." Stephen reached for her. "No, you just leave me be," she said, stepping away from him.

163

"I have to think about the future of my province, and you are not a part of that future. Please leave with Zen in the morning." She turned and walked away from him.

Stephen stood in the rain with his hand unconsciously resting on the sarcophagus.

***

Stephen strode into his room after walking in the rain to find Zen sitting in a chair waiting for him. Not acknowledging Zen, Stephen opened the wardrobe and started packing his clothes. Thrusting shirts and pants into a knapsack, Stephen never once looked in Zen's direction.

Zen calmly said, "There was a girl here before. I sent her to the kitchen for some snacks."

Stephen barked, "Nice."

Zen sipped a glass of water and commented, "She seems a little rough around the edges."

Moving to a chest with underwear stored in it, Stephen remarked, "She's OK."

Zen squinted his eyes. "Will she be coming with us?"

"Are you going to ask her to kill someone?" asked Stephen heatedly.

"Maybe," replied Zen. "She seems like the kind of person that could."

Zen's comment shocked Stephen. Briskly walking up to Zen, he shouted, "Does death follow me?" Turning on a heel and angrily squeezing the knapsack, he said, "I am tired of political intrigue."

Zen's eyes softened. Taking a breath, he said, "Stephen, have I asked too much?"

Stephen eyes became distant. "I don't know."

"As a friend, I feel I have. As your king, I have to ask again," Zen said softly.

"Why me? There are more qualified people who deal in death," cried Stephen.

"Son," said Zen, crossing over to him. He hugged him with arms wrapped around his shoulders and said, "Those kinds of people seek death. The kingdom needs people like you who can solve problems instead of killing." Holding Stephen at arm's length, he went on, "I am not saying death will not follow you, but your compassion will always weigh more heavily than on most people's hearts."

164

Wiping the tears from the corner of his eyes, Stephen asked, "What now?"

"Do you really want to hear about it this moment?" asked Zen quietly.

Stephen sat on the edge of the bed "Yes."

Sitting next to Stephen, Zen answered, "You will lead a team over the mountain to Viridian. Make contact with a local underground thieves' guild Soles told me about and make your way to their capital. Once inside the palace, you must slay Rex Almanon."

Stephen barked out laughter. "Killing seems to be my bailiwick."

"No, son," replied Zen. "Killing is part of being a prince. As a person, you will find your compassion in a time of weakness that will serve you well."

Stephen sighed and asked, "Do you want to be king?"

Zen's persona deflated, and he answered, "I never wanted to be king."

"And I never wanted to be a prince," replied Stephen. "What of the kingdom?"

"The kingdom will always survive with someone leading it—if we can make it through the dark days ahead. I would have happily handed the crown to Duke Kedwin if he had not murdered my family." Zen sighed. "This will be one of the darkest moments in our history. Let the historians piece it together after the fact."

Part Three: Over the Mountain
Chapter One

The snow piled in large drifts permeated everything in Stephen's steps. A field of white broken by slabs of grey glared in his eyes. He had never been so cold in his life. He felt like a sausage wrapped in layers of clothing to beat the cold. His hands tingled in his gloves. His stomach was upset. The Stem always bothered his stomach, but the extra energy had kept him on his feet for ten hours now. The Stem was keeping him alive. Stephen could only watch his feet as he slowly climbed the mountain.

Big Ben led the way. Ropes tied at his waist twisted back to Soles. The rope continued back to Stephen, and pulling up the rear was Dianna. She had not spoken a word in the past couple of hours. None of them had; they all saved their breath for the climb.

Stephen thought about Dianna. She claimed her life was over in Gavin. The Serious Men would seek her out to kill her. Her motives were not clear to

Stephen. She had tagged along when he left Gavin, but she never spoke about sleeping with him. She always seemed to be in the background. She had volunteered to go with Stephen to Viridian. Big Ben had been against it, but Zen persuaded him by informing him of Dianna's Street savvy. She could be an asset. After Big Ben agreed, she became another member of the party in her own right. Stephen felt she wanted something personal from him, but he could not fathom what.

Zen had found Sam's potion book. An encrypted letter folded in half and stuck in the middle of the book spoke about the royal family's death. Sam seemed remorseful for what he had done. Sam had felt the knowledge in the book should not be lost. A key to the cipher, which only another Potioner could understand, was written in the letter. Zen had passed the book to Stephen. At first Stephen declined, but after reading the letter, he held onto the book. Stephen felt the knowledge should not be lost because of foul play. Sam's family had compiled the book over generations, and Stephen felt he would honor the family's secrets.

Zen had warned Stephen to watch Soles. Zen could not discern a real motive for Soles to return to his homeland. Soles' argument was that in defeat he lost his life. King Almanon would not find his excuses adequate enough to spare Soles' life. Soles contended that his allegiance to Zen was ironclad. Stephen confessed to Dianna his own inadequacy of reading people. Dianna agreed to watch Soles closely.

Big Ben was an anomaly. He had volunteered to go on the excursion over the mountain after speaking to Master Salender.

Before leaving the castle, Zen gave Stephen a fortune in gold. To show fidelity to the crown, all five dukes gave Zen a troy ounce of gold. The five pure gold bars the size of a man's thumb was incredibly expensive. Zen cautioned Stephen not to tell anyone about the gold, because it would be beneficial in an emergency.

Stephen bumped into Soles' back. Stephen staggered, almost losing his footing. Soles pointed ahead and waved his hand in the air. A couple of wooly mammoths were rooting around in the snowbank. The mammoths were using their tusks to shovel snow so they could reach the sprouts underneath. Stephen could only see more of the narrow mountain pass, but they could safely get around the furry beasts.

After what seemed like hours of excruciating pain in Stephen's knees, the party stopped to make camp. The group busied themselves with setting up a large communal tent. Blankets and furs were distributed upon its floor. Stephen peeled off the outer layers of his wet clothes and flopped down upon the floor, instantly falling asleep.

The smell of cooking bacon woke Stephen from his dreamless sleep. He felt the body heat of Dianna sleeping soundly next to him. Trying not to disturb her, he roused himself. As he opened the tent flap, a gust of wind awoke her, but she buried herself deeper into the covers. A large fire greeted his stiff limbs.

"Here, eats a piece of bacon," said Big Ben. He grunted, "You slept all night."

"Where's Soles?" asked Stephen.

"He's gathering green firewood," answered Big Ben. "The charcoal keeps them burning."

As Stephen warmed himself next to the fire, Soles returned with branches cut from trees. He sat them on a rock and helped himself to the bacon. Dianna shuffled out of the tent.

Around a mouthful of bacon, Soles said, "We need to talk." He sat his plate down on the snow and rocked on his toes with knees bent. "Slavery is common in Viridian. First, never look a slave directly in the eyes. Second, always keep this clipped to your belt," he said, throwing small leather whips to each party member.

"What is this for?" asked Dianna.

Soles answered, "In case you need to whip a slave."

"Disgusting," replied Dianna.

"Maybe," replied Soles, "but every free man carries one. Also, slaves are easily recognizable. They wear bracelets on their ankles and wrists. Most are cold iron, but they can also wear gold bracelets. Any questions?" asked Soles.

"Why the tutorial about slaves?" asked Big Ben. "Shouldn't you be telling us about the guards or soldiers?"

Soles sighed and said, "The slaves will easily mark you as outsiders before any soldier does. A free man or woman is not bound by too much law, so a soldier would need a great deal of proof before stopping you. A slave chain would be the end of the expedition."

Stephen queried, "Slave chain?"

Soles stood up. "A slave chain is the communication between slaves to other slaves of important people—important people who can administer justice for damaging someone else's property, like slaves. It's the check that keeps free people in line. You can't permanently damage someone's property, hence the whips." Soles gestured at Dianna and said, "Keep your shenanigans in check. If you're caught stealing or whoring, you will be made a slave."

"You can't tell me people do not steal in a big city," laughed Dianna.

"Yes," snorted Soles, "but they don't get caught."

Dianna leered at Soles and said, "Than neither shall I."

Soles frowned. "Don't jeopardize the mission."

Dianna just kept a small smile on her face.

Soles tried to ignore her. He said, "Let me do most of the talking. Outlanders are not all uncommon, but we don't need the attention." He reached over, grabbed some branches, and threw them on the fire, ending the discussion. The fire spit and crackled from the trapped moisture pouring white smoke into the air.

"What about the underground?" asked Big Ben. "Is it to free the slaves?"

Soles laughed so hard he grabbed his belly. After a couple of moments, he answered, "You don't understand. Slaves are part of our culture. The underground is a class of thieves. Thieves don't care about slaves. Slaves are free labor. The division between the poor and rich is a very large gap. The poor have tried to undermine the government to attain prosperity. The underground is nothing but cutthroats pretending to be usurpers. Maybe freeing the slaves would help, but then you would just have more poor folks." Soles shook his head and said, "Listen, there are only three classes of people in Viridian: slaves, soldiers, and the wealthy. Poor people are not counted because the rich pretend, they are not there."

"But you can't ignore them," replied Stephen.

"True," answered Soles, "but you can if they are not organized."

"And you expect us to organize them?" asked Big Ben staunchly.

"Just enough to gain admittance in the palace," answered Soles, "and then we kill Almanon."

"How does killing King Almanon help us?" asked Dianna.

Soles answered, "Because it will bring anarchy. Maybe it will even help the less fortunate. Almanon has an iron grip over the entire kingdom. Once he is dead, then someone will have to stand up in his place. Zen will then be able to negotiate with the new leader."

Dianna grunted, "Sounds flimsy."

"Maybe, but Almanon will never negotiate with the Erimos kingdom," retorted Soles. "He will just try to conquer it. We still have a way to go before getting over the mountain. I don't think such a small party will be seen."

Big Ben said, "You think someone will be watching?"

Soles stirred the fire and said, "If I was Almanon, I would be watching for some reprisal. Look, I should have reported in weeks back. He must know by now I have failed. Rest. We still have a lot of walking to do."

The cold air sapped everyone's strength. The only one hopeful was Stephen. His youthfulness could not see all the possibilities of failure. The other three were lost in their own thoughts, each worrying about the coming days. None could see a clear path.

Two days passed after Soles's lecture. None of the party had talked for any length of time. Everyone was bent on surviving the frigid cold. Soles had said they would reach the summit of the mountain today. The only one who seemed unaffected by the rigorous climb was Big Ben, who led the party. Soles, Dianna, and Stephen could only see their feet treading the snowy mountainside.

Big Ben called a break for midday. Exhausted, the other three went through the motions of making a day camp. Soles searched for green wood. Stephen pitched the tent. The group needed relief from the constant wind blowing down from the peak of the mountain. Dianna unpacked the last of the coals to make a fire for lunch. Big Ben had wondered off alone.

"Wood is getting scarce this far up the mountain. If we don't make it over the peak today, the cold could kill us," said Soles.

Big Ben wandered back into the camp and said, "It may not matter anyway. Look at the storm clouds looming above us."

For the first time today, the other three looked up from the ground towards the sky. Soles swore. Dianna groaned. Stephen just shook his head. The clouds boiled in the sky, threatening to release a heavy blanket of snow and maybe ice. The storm would come quickly and be deadly for the small group. The tent was not adequate enough shelter for such a dreary sky.

"Can we stoke a large enough fire to survive?" asked Dianna.

Soles dropped a smattering of green wood onto the ground and replied, "This is all I could find in the immediate area. It is not enough to weather a storm this close to the peak."

"But can we survive?" asked Dianna in a deflated voice.

"We are too far up the mountain to turn back for shelter and not far enough over to find more," replied Big Ben. "The storm will probably kill us. The ice and snow will likely freeze us to death."

"Is the cold our only real problem for surviving?" asked Stephen.

Soles huffed, "The cold will kill us, kid."

"Maybe not," replied Stephen, hurriedly adding, "Zen said the book of potions could be the key to our survival. He packed me a lot of ingredients to make different kinds of potions. How long do I have to figure something out?"

Big Ben glanced into the sky. "Not long, Stephen, maybe an hour or two."

"Why can't we just drink fire potions?" asked Soles.

"Because the fire depends on the body's inner heat. We would run out of fire before the storm passed over, and our core temperatures would be susceptible to the cold," answered Stephen. "But maybe the fire potion could be the key. I am going to check Sam's potion book. Just give me some space and time to think."

"Space you can have. Time depends on the weather," said Big Ben.

Stephen adjourned to the tent. He opened Sam's book. The cipher was not difficult to understand, and he had been practicing daily on reading the book. Stephen flipped through the pages. Nothing seemed practical for warding off the cold. He closed the book in frustration.

Zen had said creating a potion was dangerous and difficult, but maybe combining a couple of potions while tweaking the ingredients would suffice. Stephen opened the book to the very first pages. The book was chronological in order, and the potions became more intricate as the book progressed. Stephen remembered a potion to improve blood circulation in the beginning of the book. Maybe combining that with a fire potion would keep the frigid temperatures manageable for surviving. Since the circulation potion was more medicinal than magical, then maybe combining the two would work. Stephen set his mind. He decided to try. He let his intuition for cooking guide him while concocting the new potion.

Half an hour later, Stephen emerged from the tent holding four small vials. Three people looked at him, seeming to ask for salvation. Stephen hoped not to disappoint them.

"I don't know if this going to work. In fact, the potions could kill us as easily as the storm. I had to concoct a new type of potion." Stephen held out the potions. Each of them took one.

Dianna said, "I think I should go first. I mean, we can't all die."

"No, I made the potions. I will go first," said Stephen.

"Please. Out of the four of us, you know I am the weakest link." Dianna placed her hand on Stephen's shoulder and said, "I trust you." She tipped the vial to her lips. "Oh, my," she said softly.

"Are you OK?" asked Stephen worriedly.

"I feel wonderful. I can't remember the last time I felt warm," Dianna said happily.

"Give it a minute," said Soles.

"No, I think it is all right," said Stephen before drinking his potion. After a moment, he said, "Wow, you are right. I feel warm."

Big Ben shrugged, looked Soles in the eye, and drank his potion.

"Well," said Soles. "It looks like it was in the nick of time." Soles swallowed his potion and motioned them into the tent. The storm had kickstarted the weather. Snow and ice fell in sheets.

Chapter Two

King Zenith Alexander sat in the plump armchair in Queen Clarissa's former study. He was reminiscing about a state dinner he attended several years past when his brother was the monarch. The table had been laden with roast duck, barbecued pig, and a spit of beef. Side dishes included potatoes, squash, and field peas. The wine had been excellent that night. The camaraderie around the table had been a joyous affair.

Master Salender walked briskly into the room carrying a roll of paper in his left hand. His health had improved after being named chancellor to the king. He only drank occasionally now. He unrolled the parchment and held it out to King Zenith.

"Just read it to me," replied King Zenith.

"It's actually quite formal, Sire. Kira has announced she has raised the thousand men you requested for the new army," said Master Salender.

"And the other nobles?" asked King Zenith.

Master Salender shook his head and said, "All of them continue to decline your request."

King Zenith sighed. "Then make it an order."

"Yes, Sire," said Master Salender. "You still have to oversee the conclave of farmers requesting seed."

"You dispense the seed as necessary," replied King Zenith. "Is there anything else?"

"The local smiths are complaining about the quality of sand shipments from the south," answered Master Salender.

"Have a page look into it," replied King Zenith. He sipped a cup of wine and said, "I will deal with anything new in the morning."

"Yes, Sire," replied Master Salender. He turned on his toes and strode from the room.

King Zenith Alexander stared out the window at the light snow on the branches outside. Kira worried the old man. Her letters sent to the castle the past couple of days had been formal with no friendly gestures. On the one hand, she could be busy. On the other, she could resent him for being tied to her father's death. He took a deep breath and slowly released the air, trying to relax. His paranoia about Kira could be just that—paranoia.

The past couple of months had been shrouded in death. Zen had delayed the party going over the mountain to let Stephen heal. Zen worried about Stephen too. Stephen needed time to reconcile his feelings about Kira. Also, Stephen's moral compass had to be realigned. Killing so many people in such a short time had affected him. With reassurances from Zen and Dianna, Stephen had slowly felt less guilty about the horrendous events of the late summer, but Zen thought Stephen would always carry some type of guilty conscience. Zen carried a heavy burden on his soul, because he felt he had changed the young man forever. Zen only hoped Stephen's young conscience was resilient enough to withstand the irrevocable consequences of his earlier actions.

The land at the moment was gripped in the death of early winter. Zen's mind said, *and such sullen thoughts.* He reached for a deep red apple and bit into it. As the juice touched his tongue, he felt better.

Chapter Three

Several days had passed since the storm. The four wanderers had made it over the mountain with little incident. Now, they stood on a large ridge looking down into a sprawling metropolis, a palace backed up against the mountain. Its walls a hundred feet high, the home of Almanon stood in stark relief to the teeming buildings surrounding the fortress. Large obelisks dotted the city. Each one at the top was scrawled with Almanon's name, a tribute erected by the people for the past six centuries. At the base of the obelisks, chains held the latest political prisoner. They were meant to show Almanon's complete rule of the city.

Stephen's heart ached. The task seemed monstrous. He could not imagine the huge scope of the sprawling city. The city seemed to teem with ants as the Viridians went about their daily tasks. The noise and confusion of the city weighed heavily on Stephen's light soul. He could not imagine a more horrible place.

"What is that sound?" asked Stephen.

"What do you mean?" asked Soles.

"You can't hear it? High-pitched keens, screams, whistles, and chimes," said Stephen, covering his ears.

Soles turned and faced the city. "I guess I am used to the sound of machines."

Dianna leaned against Stephen and asked, "Machines?"

"Constructs, I mean horseless carriages, things on wheels pushed by unseen forces," answered Soles. "All made of iron."

Even Big Ben asked shakily, "Is it magic?"

"No, it is science. Everything down there is powered by steam. A couple of centuries ago, someone found a rock that when put in water makes steam. Steam powers everything." Soles looked at the three and said, "Look, it is no different than Erimos. It is just something new. Our science is more advanced in steam machines, but our society is no more different than yours. We thought you were barbarians, but your society is as rich and diverse as ours. We won't even be in the city." Soles pointed. "See the wave of tents and makeshift structures at the edge of the city? That is where we are going. It is the poorest district. We will be anonymous there."

The three Erimos patriots set their heart for the task to come. Out of the three, Dianna seemed the most nonchalant about the city. The way down the mountain was tame. Over the years, roads had been constructed to access various mines in the side of the mountain. Now that the mines were completely emptied of any mineral or metal, the roads were derelict and deserted. They made for the shantytown on the outskirts of the city.

Stephen drowsed in the warm tent. His mind floating, he thought about Kira. She had resented him for sleeping with Dianna. He had no explanation worthy enough to explain his actions. It just happened. Dianna, on the other hand, had not mentioned the night they slept together. To her, it was the past. To him, it felt awkward. He wanted more than her friendship but could not figure out how to approach the subject with her. His feelings for Dianna had grown. Her sure independence excited him. Her confidence intrigued him. He grimaced and thought about how he had lost one girl, and his shyness was blocking his path to the other girl.

"Stephen," said Big Ben, "it's your turn to watch."

Stephen stepped out of the tent and asked, "Why do we continue to keep watch?"

"Vigilance shows sincerity," answered Big Ben.

Stephen puckered and said, "I would rather go into the city like Dianna and Soles."

"You couldn't keep up, farm boy," said Dianna, walking around the corner. "Your eyes would be glued to the sights." Dianna wore a black leather skirt stopping at the knee. Her blouse, a thin black silky affair, peeked out of her black leather coat with silver studs on the collar and cuffs. Black boots came up to midcalf.

Stephen stared; eyes wide.

Big Ben smiled and asked her, "Where do you keep your knives?"

"Why, right here," answered Dianna, lifting the skirt high on her thigh to show where the knives were strapped.

Stephen gulped.

Big Ben heard him. Turning to Stephen he remarked, "Keep your eyes glued."

Stephen ducked his head, and a crimson wash came over his face.

Dianna pretended not to notice. She said, "Stephen, Soles wants to talk to you."

"Why not here?" asked Stephen.

"Do you want to go into the city or not?" asked Dianna loudly.

The question made Stephen feel like a petulant child. Shaking the feeling, he said, "I'm coming."

As Dianna led the way through the maze of the shantytown, she thought about her remark. It had obviously hurt Stephen's feelings. Dianna had experience with rough men, but Stephen was inherently nice. In the city, she had to portray a confident woman. Men took advantage of less confident women. It didn't hurt to be a smartass. She wanted more from Stephen, but her mouth always seems to get in the way. She vowed to be less antagonistic towards him.

The two travelers stepped from the makeshift shantytown into the city. The streets were lined with people on sidewalks with buildings shunting them like a funnel. Running down the middle of the streets were fitted, well-worn cobblestones, and some were cracked or even broken in two. Stephen gawked like a backwoods boy.

Machines rode on the busy streets. They had no common basic building block other than stacks exuding steam. Stephen stared at a truck that reminded him of a buckboard wagon. Sitting high on the seat, instead of reins, the rider turned a great wheel that controlled the truck. Two large steaming stacks rode as passengers on either side of the man. A tricycle swept by Stephen. The large wheel in the front stood as tall as him, and a man stood on panels in the back with feet braced near the small wheels at its base. The man hugged a stack with steam pouring from the top. The large wheel churned, and the man steered the wheel with deft hands-on handlebars. As they progressed further into the city, Stephen's brain could not fathom the different machines moving swiftly down the streets. The noise of the steam engines hurt his ears so much that it disoriented him. Dianna noticed his distress, so she hooked his arm and bore the brunt of his shuffling walk. She finally pushed him into a doorway. The door closed and silenced the screams of the steam engines.

Stephen blinked, settling his mind and focusing his eyes. He stood in a large common room no different than any tavern Stephen had patronized. In the early hour, Soles seemed to be the only customer. He sat at a table in the far-left corner. The bartender only looked up for a moment, gauging them adequate to visit his bar. They crossed the room to sit at Soles' table.

He studied Stephen's obvious discomfort. Sipping a mug of beer, he waited for Stephen to orient himself. After a couple of moments, Soles asked, "What do you think of my fine city?"

"I hate it," replied Stephen. He motioned to the bartender for a drink.

The bartender dropped off a mug of beer, and Soles paid him. Stephen gulped down a mouthful of grainy beer. Wiping his lips with the back of his sleeve, he finally settled into the chair.

Stephen said, "I don't get it. Why didn't we see machines on our side of the mountain when you invaded?"

Soles looked pitiful for only a blink of an eye. He guffawed and shook the pitiful look from his shoulders. "We really thought we would not need them." Soles sipped his beer and continued, "The intelligence provided by Zacadam stated glass swords and herbal potions."

Dianna interrupted, "Easy pickings for an advanced civilization."

"Exactly," replied Soles. "We had no idea the glass was as hard as steel, nor that the potions would be a factor." Soles shook his head and said, "Look, we have herbal remedies too: green tea to calm the stomach, or a pinch of honey to soothe the throat. Who would dream a man could be near death on the wall of a castle and then the next morning he is right as rain battling our men?"

"There's something you are not telling us." Replied Stephen. "We need to know."

Soles drummed his fingers on the table. After a moment, he replied, "My status as a commander was in question." He slugged a draft of beer. "I failed in a mission early in my career that drew doubt from my superiors. I needed a glorious battle to enhance my career."

Dianna slammed her hand down on the table and said, "You needed coin."

Soles shrugged. "In a matter of speaking, yes. I needed a bargaining chip."

Stephen growled, "You needed to kill my people."

Soles replied, "Don't take it personally." Soles' fingers massaged the top of the table. "My culture is built upon conquest."

Stephen stared at the man in the black mask. Dianna felt the tension, so she placed a hand on Stephen's knee under the table.

"What happens when they find out you failed?" asked Dianna.

"I don't know. Someone else could see this as an opportunity to advance their position. The matter could be dropped due to be being less cost effective." Soles waved his hand and said, "The point is, if they do decide to invade again, they will bring machines over the mountain."

"Could we defeat them?" asked Stephen.

Soles sighed and said quietly, "No."

"Then we must topple a vicious ruler," replied Stephen.

Soles slid his fingers back and forth upon the tabletop, staring at them. "Many have tried."

Stephen said, "Zen would not have sent us on a fool's errand. If he believed we could succeed, then we shall succeed where others have failed."

Dianna looked down at the tabletop and said, "It will take more than men with machines."

Stephen replied, "I don't care if we have to use cobblestones for ammunition, we shall see it through."

***

The chilly night enhanced Stephen's terrible mood. The others slept soundly in the tent. Stephen looked over the shantytown. Grey fog enveloped the haphazard hovels. In the dead of night, people slept in the refuge. Stephen's thoughts turned to the conversation earlier with Soles. *Machines,* thought Stephen. *How can I defeat machines?* The task daunted him. Two days had passed, and the dreaded machines had worked their way into his consciousness. He had asked Soles about the military machines, but Soles had been vague, with descriptions of armored machines rolling across the land. Pressure cannons shooting balls of iron. Fast-moving machines spitting steam that could roast infantry. This world of machines scared Stephen. His home was in real danger. He had to dethrone King Almanon before he turned his evil eyes back on the Erimos kingdom.

A small boy stepped out of the fog near Stephen. The boy held a finger across his lips. He motioned to Stephen to come with him. Stephen stood up from a crouching position and walked into the swirling fog. The boy kept his distance, leading Stephen through the maze of the shantytown. The boy ducked into an actual building, a barn, at the edge of the more industrious city. Stephen only hesitated a moment before following the boy.

The barn opened into a large spacious floor with rafters hanging high in the ceiling. The floor was dirty, and the windows cracked. The barn was obviously abandoned. Stephen could not even smell animal feces from an earlier time in the stalls lining the sides of the barn. Three men stood in the middle of the floor. The only light came from the bank of windows running around the top of the building. The men were just mere shadows. Stephen could not discern a thing about the men's dress or station in society while they were covered in the dark. Stephen noticed the boy was gone.

One of the men spoke. "We have been watching you for the past couple of days. The man in the black mask is the Commander Soles. We are not familiar with the other members of your party. Why are you hiding in Dirt Town?"

Stephen spoke up loudly. "We are looking for the underground."

Another man grunted, "With Commander Soles."

Stephen felt the men slipping from him. He replied, "He is no longer a commander." Stephen thought fast and said, "He is my valet."

"You must be joking," replied the first man.

Stephen replied, "My title is Prince Alexander. We came over the mountains to find help from the underground."

The second man replied, "Why didn't you bring an army?"

"One man can change history," answered Stephen.

A loud grinding noise interrupted Stephen. The back wall of the building collapsed. Several men in leather armor ran past the dust. The three men backed up to Stephen.

Stephen shouted, "Take the exit. I will slow their charge." Stephen sucked down a potion from his pouch. His muscles felt exceptionally stiff. He drew his diamond blade.

As the three men escaped behind Stephen, the soldiers in black leather armor ran at Stephen. Two charged Stephen as the others spread out to flank him. Stephen stepped aside and whirled his blade horizontally. The men brought their blades up to guard against his.

Stephen's enhanced strength sundered their swords. His cut ran deep into their stomachs, and both men dropped to the floor. Stephen backed up to the exit and turned to run. A shot from a steam carbine rifle whizzed by Stephen's head, and one man stood in the doorway, blocking Stephen's exit. The soldier struck an overhand blow, which Stephen swept aside. Reflexively, Stephen stabbed the man in the breast, driving his sword deep. With his potion strength, he slung the limp body against another man running to gain an advantage. As the dead man slammed into the running soldier, Stephen sprinted out of the door. Several shots rang out, slamming slugs into the door casing just barely after Stephen's escape. The fog covered Stephen's escape into Dirt Town.

He ran retracing the twists and turns from earlier. He could hear men shouting in the distance. The fog muffled the sounds. His legs felt like hammers striking the ground. His flight was not fast, but he felt no strain. As he drew near his tent, Stephen whistled a short burst. Big Ben ducked his head out of the flap.

"Ben," stammered Stephen, "grab what you can and wake up the rest. We need to hide." Stephen scanned the fog as Big Ben followed his orders. As the three of them exited the tent, Stephen said, "Soles, lead on to a hiding place."

Soles led the party down the narrow alleys of Dirt Town. The fog kept them hidden. Men shouted orders in the night. Behind them, the soldiers found their tent and ransacked it and neighboring structures. Shots could be heard. In the commotion, the party drew farther away from the shouting soldiers.

Soles led them out of Dirt Town to the narrow streets of the city. Slowing to a walk, Soles led them to a small inn. The proprietor asked no questions as the four of them purchased one large room for the night.

They dropped miscellaneous things on the floor. Soles turned on Stephen and demanded, "What happened?"

Stephen crossed the room and sat on the only bed. He answered, "I met with the underground."

"And the soldiers?" asked Soles heatedly.

Stephen sighed and said, "They interrupted the meeting. I killed three of them."

Soles paced the room. "Great. Now someone knows we are here." He turned on Stephen and asked, "Did you get any names?"

Stephen shook his head. "No, but I think they will contact us again."

"What makes you so certain?" demanded Soles.

Stephen shouted, "Because I killed three men." He crossed his arms and said, "We will hear from them."

Big Ben replied, "We are being hunted."

Stephen turned his head sideways and replied, "I know."

Big Ben turned to Soles and asked, "What were those sounds? It reminded me of bees zooming in on a flower."

Soles answered, "They were shots from a steam carbine rifle. It fires a ball of metal."

Big Ben looked concerned and asked, "How accurate are they?"

"Not very, at a distance, but up close they are deadly. You have to understand that the carbines only have one shot before having to be reloaded with water and a ball." Soles turned in place and motioned towards the city. "It's a deadly place, and we have nothing."

Dianna laughed. Everyone looked at her as she started giggling. After a minute, she looked all three of them in the eyes and said, "You men thought it would be easy." She snorted, pushed Stephen off the bed, and flopped down. As the men sat on the floor with thoughts churning in their heads, Dianna fell soundly asleep.

Chapter Four

Kira sat at her desk in her bedroom perusing a map of Sires. The capitol city offered advantageous insight for an attack. She continued to draw up plans of conquest as her father had in the recent past, except she did not intend to fail. She believed the crown needed to be scourged. The lack of leadership and her father's death enhanced her feelings of animosity. She considered that the crown had become complacent with the dukes due to the prosperity of the past three generations. The kingdom needed a leader born from conflict. The death of her father was an afterthought in her mind, but she considered him a martyr for change in the line of succession of kings. She did not consider herself vengeful as much as practical. The kingdom needed a military mind to survive the coming war. She figured Stephen would fail miserably, opening up a path of destruction led by someone from Viridian.

Kira sat back in her chair, feeling the pangs of loneliness. She considered the emotion as a burden of leadership. King Zenith Alexander had sent a Potioner as an advisor for Kira, but she considered the man to be a spy. She had set the Potioner a task of creating a bounty of potions for the campaign. It kept the Potioner busy and unaware of her plans. She was going to kill the man in his sleep as soon as he finished his task, the murder being only a miniscule part of her plan.

Kira reigned over her men using fear. She drove her officers with an imaginary sword in their bellies. The officers transferred their fear to their men. The violence fed its self. She was creating a cruel army.

She thought about Stephen, his infidelity a twist in her heart. She considered herself lucky. Her father had not treated her kindly, driving her to succeed in every aspect of being a man. Stephen had reminded her that she was a woman. Her ill fortune was having the feelings of a complete person. She did not consider herself a masculine nor feminine personality. She figured her mistress would be the kingdom. She would devote her life to Erimos. Anything else would be considered a failure in her eyes.

Chapter Five

Stephen stood at the open door waiting for Soles to return to the room. He thought about the past three days of boredom. The party had hidden in a room the size of a box, considering that four people shared the space. Dianna mostly slept the day away. Ben and Soles played dice all day. Stephen daydreamed of his house in the country to pass the time. Soles had told the group they needed to hide for a couple of days, but now Stephen felt the time was up. Besides, he was going stir crazy in the small room. He was just waiting for Soles to return. Soles turned the corner, and Stephen wandered down the hall.

"It's time," replied Stephen.

"Time for what?" asked Soles.

Stephen pressed his lips together and then answered, "It is time to leave the nest."

"We'll talk about it in the room," said Soles.

"Fine," replied Stephen backpedaling towards the room. "I'm sure everyone will agree we need to talk." Stephen turned and entered the room. Dianna raised her head, and Big Ben stood up from the floor.

Dianna obviously had nothing to say, and her attitude betrayed her feelings. She was interested in watching Soles and Stephen. The expression on Big Ben's face denoted his absence from the conversation as well.

"What can we really expect from making further contact with the underground?" asked Stephen.

Soles sat on the edge of the bed and replied, "I think they are more rabble than anything else."

"Who do you know would help us?" asked Stephen.

Soles shook his head and looked down. "I can't think of anyone."

"So, you're saying we have lost before we have begun," said Stephen briskly.

"I don't know what I expected," said Soles with his arms outstretched. He dropped them and replied, "You would think someone would want to kill King Almanon."

Ben stirred. "Every dictator has enemies. We just need to find them and convince them we are willing to gamble our lives to kill Almanon."

"We need to prove our sincerity," said Dianna. "Then they will find us."

Soles growled, "And how do we do that?"

Dianna shrugged. "We kill Almanon's allies."

Every person in the room thought for a couple of moments about the implications of Dianna's statement. The silence betrayed their agreement.

"I need to talk to a couple of people, but I may have a man in mind," said Soles. "Give me a couple of days to find where he may be."

Ben looked up and said, "Whom do you have in mind?"

Soles stared into space. "A former colleague before this," he said gesturing at the mask. "He is high on Almanon's ladder."

"That's fine," replied Stephen, "but Dianna and I are going to explore the city."

"To what end?" asked Soles.

"To end our boredom," said Stephen, "and to learn more about the city. You may not always be around."

Ben replied, "Fine, I will go with Soles. We will meet back here in a couple of days." Ben stood. Looking down at Stephen, he replied, "Stay out of trouble, and keep an eye on Dianna."

Dianna breathed, "Keep an eye on yourself, old timer. I plan on enjoying my time perusing the city." She rolled out of bed and grinned at Stephen. She winked at him and said, "Keep your eyes on mine."

Stephen and Dianna explored the streets of the city. At every turn, Stephen managed to see a machine. Being from Erimos, everything was unfamiliar to Stephen. Transports of all different shapes and sizes burped pent-up steam to push them down the street. Bicycles, tricycles, and unicycles transported single men and women. Carriages thundered down the lane with steam screaming from pipes stacked beneath their underbellies. The noise pressed upon Stephen's ears, but he managed to filter out the loud screams of compressed steam escaping from the machines. As they walked down the side of the street, people pressed against them in tighter formations. The people chattered excitedly, funneling them towards an open square.

An enormous crowd was gathered in the square. In the center of the citizens, a large platform was raised with four men sitting side by side at a large table. The men sat in judgment. Five bottles of wine with no labels sat cluttered at the corner of the table, each bottle numbered one through five. The crowd quieted as the first one was uncorked by a man wearing a white suit. He poured each of the men a sliver of wine in a glass. Each man peered at the glass, sniffed the glass, and tilted the glass to his lips, then sloshed the wine in his mouth and spit it upon the ground. Some of the liquid escaped onto the crowd. Stephen was flabbergasted at what the men were doing with the wine.

"Dianna, do you know what is happening?" asked Stephen loudly.

A man next to him gulped and said, "It's the judgment of last year's pressing of wine from the five vineyards."

"So?" remarked Stephen.

"What are you, a dolt?" The man explained to Stephen the routine as if he were a child. "Each bottle is given a number by the judges. The better the number, the better the wine is from the pressing. People buy a number of wines, gambling on which one will win. The higher the number, the more expensive the wine. I myself bought several crates from the Dotter's orchard. I have a strong feeling they will win."

Dianna motioned for Stephen to back out of the crowd. The streets were almost empty outside of the square. Dianna slipped an arm around Stephen's waist and said, "Care to join me for a meal?" Her eyes sparkled with mischief as they walked together down the street.

"But how would we pay?" asked Stephen.

She just smiled as Stephen bumped into a man walking next to them, causing a collision with another man. The last man shuffled his feet, pulled out his lash, and started whaling on the man Stephen bumped into while berating him vocally. The slave cowered as the man lashed him about the face and shoulders. Stephen's jaw clenched as he grabbed the lash from the man and started hitting the citizen in the face. The man screamed and ran down the street.

"Are you OK?" asked Stephen, helping the slave to his feet. "That was entirely my fault," he stuttered.

"Yes, sir," said the man. "Please forgive me."

"There is nothing to forgive," said Stephen.

The slave bowed and hurried down the sidewalk. A moment later, a loud shout of "That's them!" came from around the corner. They turned to find men with batons barreling down upon them.

"Keep up," shouted Dianna as she took off in a full run. Stephen followed in her wake. They ran for several blocks, weaving in and around corners. The men with the batons lost ground at every corner until they finally gave up the chase. Dianna slowed to a fast walk. She smiled at Stephen and said, "City guards are all the same. Mouths full of pies and legs of lead."

"Why did we run?" asked Stephen gasping for air. "We did nothing wrong."

"Maybe, maybe not, but I could not take the chance of them searching me," she said, revealing several coin purses in her bodice. "Still up for a bite to eat?"

Stephen just laughed and nodded. The stolen coin seemed the least of their worries.

Chapter Six

Kira sat astride her horse and looked down the column of men marching in the snow that had coated the land the night before. In lock step, the men trudged down the road. Tree limbs bowed under the weight of the snow, while some had snapped and landed on the road. The column would have to slow and sometimes stop as the dead wood had to be cleared. The snow looked pristine in the woods surrounding the dirty, trodden, muddy road. churned up by supply wagons and the men moving steadily on their horses. In the rear of the vanguard, women and children of the men walked steadily on cloth-wrapped feet that soaked up the cold water on the road. Kira had tried to drive them away, but the people continued to follow their loved ones.

Kira turned her horse, and the horse jumped forward into a trot. She rode up to the front of the column. She thought about the past couple of days. Her bogus letter to King Zenith had declared a marshaling of her troops to be personally inspected by him. She grimaced just thinking about King Zenith inspecting the men. Her fist tightened upon the reins. She felt lightheaded thinking about the wanton destruction of the principality of the kingdom. She would give the kingdom a rallying point to pull it from the brink of chaos brought by the plague of starvation. The other dukes hoarded their stores of food from the general populace trying to gain favors from King Zenith. The very idea of letting people go hungry made Kira's stomach roll.

A haze clouded her thoughts; brought on by grief and Stephen's infidelity, a predatory smile crossed her lips. She would jail the dukes and let them starve for a couple of days before she demanded the release of the food stores. Let them deny her then.

As Kira rode her horse at the top of the column, the men marched proudly. They believed this woman would be the salvation of the kingdom. Her speeches had inspired the men to commit treason. Her very words flowed like honey to sweeten the men's minds with a changed world. Each of them believed she would reward them for their part in the scheme. The men expected to defy death in order to gain rewards from the outstretched hands of Duchess

Kira. She had become a living force to wreak the changes in the kingdom. The women and children who followed the army seemed to have the only clue. They knew death rode on a horse, and Kira's eyes were haunted by the dreams of the self-righteous.

Chapter Seven

Two days of exploring the city had passed for Stephen and Dianna: the warrens with the homes touching each other with cold iron as decorative adorations with fake balconies built over cobblestone streets; lines of restaurants with overhanging tarps clustered on a street with lampposts every hundred feet; the industrial park with tanners, wood smiths, and blacksmiths backed up to the wharfs of a river; the private gardens with statues and fountains in the center of the city, guarded jealously by the nobles. Dianna and Stephen explored with complete abandon. She taught him how to remain unnoticed in crowded areas of the city. He taught her how to dance in the lush gardens. They each taught each other the physical part of love in the middle of the night with stolen money to buy expensive lodging. They played as children would without supervision.

The cold reality of the situation set in their necks as they strode into the common room of the tavern they had shared with Soles and Ben. The two men sat at a table in the corner, waiting for the young people. Stephen and Dianna sat down, waiting to hear the worst from their elders.

"We found the man," said Soles. "He is in the city for the next couple of days."

Stephen leaned forward and asked, "Who is he?"

Soles answered, "A merchant with his hand in politics to make profit."

Stephen frowned. "I don't like being an assassin."

Big Ben grunted, "You won't be." He leaned back in his chair with his arms folded and said, "A prince has no value as a depositor of violence."

"Leave it to Ben and me," said Soles.

"How will the underground know it's us?" asked Stephen.

Big Ben answered shrewdly, "We will leave a witness."

Stephen slumped in his chair. He felt resigned to the murder. He thought to himself that the man profited from politics, so he had to be a rascal, right? Stephen scratched the surface of the table with the tips of his fingers and said, "This better work." He looked up. "We cannot afford to make a mistake."

Big Ben laid a hand on Stephen's shoulder and replied, "This will work. The enemy of my enemy always prospers."

***

The night was cold with sleet and snow swirling down the lanes. Two hooded figures made their way down the street. The men kept to the shadows as a precaution, but the lanes in this part of the warren were unpopulated due to the weather. They stopped half a block from their target and waited next to a window box garden with daffodil sprouts. They both waited for the lights to burn out in the house down the street. As the people of the warren wrapped themselves in heavy blankets to sleep safely in the storm, the two men moved slowly towards the home of a political operator with the intent of harm.

The two men stopped short in front of the shutters of a window on the front of the house. One of the men slipped a stiletto into the crack, forcing the catch to open. The other man kept watch on the lonely street. The first man opened the shutters wide and slipped over the sill. The other man followed.

The house was dark. The little bit of light made the furniture into large humps of shadow. The men carefully picked their way to a bedroom door. Opening it slowly, the men entered the room. As one moved towards the bed, the other grabbed his arm and shook his head no. The first man resisted the grip of the second man. The man held on firmly and nodded towards the sleeping figure. They both backed up into the hallway.

"I can't do it," replied Stephen. "We have to think of something else."

Soles harrumphed and said, "Fine." He walked back into the living room. "We need to leave a message." Soles lit a candle and passed the flame over a large stuffed couch.

"What about the other homes?" asked Stephen.

"They'll survive," said Soles as he climbed out of the window.

Stephen looked down the hallway as the fire engulfed the couch. He ran to the bedroom and shouted "Fire!" then flung the door open. Then he made his way down the hallway full of smoke and jumped out of the window.

"That wasn't smart," replied Soles.

"Maybe," answered Stephen, "but at least he will have a chance to put the fire out."

The two men ran down the lane. Bells and whistles grew steadily louder behind them, warning people about the fire. Stephen looked behind him as they turned the corner. Already men and women were fighting the fire. Smoke poured onto the street, and the home was burning slowly. The crackling heat of the fire was stunted by the ice storm.

Soles pulled up short a couple of blocks from their tavern hideout. He put a hand on Stephen's chest and said, "I don't know what you may think of what we are doing, but you need to grow some balls." He dropped his hand and continued down the block.

Stephen watched him enter the tavern. He thought *What am I doing here?* He felt he needed to be alone to answer the question. He started walking in the sleet and snow, thinking about what was at stake. The entire Erimos kingdom was counting on him to kill a man. In the process, if there was collateral damage, so be it. Stephen hunched his shoulders and continued to walk in thought. The night passed. Small snowflakes alighted upon his shoulders, reminding him he needed to return to the tavern.

He had made a decision. Soles had promised Zenith that King Almanon would not listen to reason. Stephen would just have to take that chance of diplomacy. He would leave the killing to the killers. He just hoped negotiations would not end in a bloodbath. He would go alone to reason with King Almanon.

Stephen walked into the room at the tavern.

"I don't like that look upon your face, Stephen," remarked Dianna. "You look like you have resigned yourself to death."

"Haven't we all?" retorted Stephen. "We sit here in a little room discussing the death of a tyrant like it is child's play. Maybe someone needs to just talk to the man."

"Stephen, when I said to grow some balls, I meant grow up." Soles swept his hands around the room. "It is four against thousands. We just need to be patient."

"I know about patience, Soles. A watched kettle never boils. All I am saying is, we need a plan. We sit here talking about meeting people who we don't even know exist. I say we find them, and if we don't find them, then we take the next step and try to sneak into King Almanon's fortress." Stephen looked at each of the party separately. "Does anyone have a real idea, even if it is just talking to the tyrant?"

Dianna moved closer to Stephen and said, "Give me a couple days. Any underground worth its salt is peppered with rouges, thieves, and killers. I will

187

find them." Dianna moved across the room and paused at the door. "Just don't do anything stupid while I am gone." She closed the door behind her.

"Can we count on her?" asked Big Ben. He didn't think highly of a vagabond from the streets.

Stephen answered, "More than you know."

The task of finding unscrupulous people in a large city took only a couple of minutes for Dianna. She asked a prostitute for directions to the rowdiest tavern in the city. As she entered the Muddy Hole, she felt every eye on her. Of course, no one actually stared at her. Everyone in the place was sizing her up as a potential mark or as someone who was dangerous. Her cool look of someone at home in the tavern led many men to ignore her. She ordered a drink and sat at the bar. She kept her eyes on the crowd, searching for a potential informant.

Three hours passed, and she did not feel a buzz from the four cups of ale. Obviously, the barkeep watered the drinks for strangers. Dianna kept her attention on a small man. He had entered the bar a couple of hours before and seemed to be well thought of by the crowd. He was drunk but kept to his cups. He played a couple rounds of dice in the back of the place. Not being fortunate, he turned his attention upon a prostitute. The talk was not about services, more like friends who were neighbors. The cutthroats and thieves seemed to respect the small man.

In the end, he left alone. Dianna followed closely behind him. She figured the man had contacts. He was obviously well protected, either as a power amongst thieves or by someone with enough power. Dianna's instincts told her the man could be a source in this little caper hatched by Stephen and Soles.

At the first real dirty alley that presented itself, she grabbed his arm, stuck a knife to his ribs, and pushed him into the alley.

"You're making a big mistake, lady," he said with a half-smile. Twisting like a snake, he managed to grip her wrist that held the knife. Stronger than he appeared, he twisted her arm. Dianna painfully dropped the knife and backed up against the wall.

"One moment," Dianna said with hands in front of her. "This is not a robbery, and if I wanted you dead, I wouldn't have dropped the knife."

The man leaned against the opposite wall and said, "It would have been easier to talk in the tavern. I saw you watching me and how you tailed me—both unusually astute, by the way."

"I need information," said Dianna.

"Can you pay for it?" asked the man.

"It's according what you have to sell," answered Dianna. She waited a couple of heartbeats and said, "I need a way into King Almanon's fortress."

The man laughed. He caught his breath and said, "You don't want much." He turned his head and thought for a moment. "Why?"

"To kill him," she whispered.

The man grunted, "I would whisper too." He looked down the alley and around the corner into the street. "Do you have somewhere safe to talk?"

"If you don't mind my compatriots," replied Dianna. She pulled herself off the wall and started a brisk walk back to her friends.

The man followed her from a distance, allowing anyone watching the idea that she was being stalked instead of his being an ally. He walked into the Waysider Tavern and ordered mead while waiting for Dianna to return from upstairs. After a couple of minutes, she motioned to him from the top of the stairs. He looked around the empty room and mounted the stairs, following her to the room.

"Damn, you're a big man," said the man as he walked into the room.

"From what I hear, you may be a big man too," replied Big Ben from the middle of the room. "I am going to stand outside the door to keep any snoops away." As he crossed the room, the small man had to crane his neck to keep eye contact.

"What's your name?" asked Soles.

The man studied the room for a moment and replied, "Just call me 'Mr. Tunnel.'"

"Interesting name for a thief," replied Soles.

"I am not a thief. I am a smuggler," he said. With a twinkle in his eye, he stated, "Your name is Soles."

"If you know who I am, why are you speaking to us?" asked Soles sharply.

"Because of the company you keep," answered the man hotly. After a couple of seconds, he said in a softer voice, "She is a thief. He is a boy. And you are a traitor. I don't know what the hell the big man is."

"Why would you call me a traitor?" asked Soles.

"The word is you went over the mountain but never came back, so traitor," answered Mr. Tunnel.

Soles thought about what the man said. He was lost in the moment.

Stephen asked, "What about you. Why are you helping us?"

"Because lately it does not look good for the bad men," answered Mr. Tunnel. "Look, it has become very dangerous to work in this town. If you're caught by the authorities, you're dead. It makes it difficult to deal with a lot of people because they're either crazy or greedy."

"Which one are you?" asked Stephen.

"I am a little of both, young man," he said. "Now down to business. You need a guide."

"A guide?" said Soles confused. "Why would we need a guide to get into the fortress? Can't you just tell us how?"

"I could tell you, but you would get lost," he said. "Listen, in my business, we have kept a closely guarded secret."

"I'm interested," said Stephen.

"Lava tubes and caves extend under the entire city, including under the fortress," he said. "Some are just narrow tunnels, but others are large caves."

"You mean to tell me smugglers have been digging up the earth under the city," asked Soles skeptically.

"Oh, no," answered Mr. Tunnel, "the city is built from the quarry under the city. Generations have forgotten about the quarry, lava tubes, and caves, except for a few men like myself. The quarry is a couple hundred feet below the entire city." He smiled and said, "Just our little secret."

"I can't believe no one has found the caves," said Soles.

Mr. Tunnel shook his head and waved at Soles. "Oh, no, no, no. People have found the caves in the past, but never found their way out." He smacked his lips against his teeth and said, "And there is the matter of a very large Arthropleura that inhabits the place."

Dianna's eyes widened. "A bug, you say? How big a bug?"

"Big enough to kill a horse," answered Mr. Tunnel. "The problem is Almanon knows about the quarry, so he feeds the Arthropleura to keep it near his fortress."

"What do you want from us?" asked Soles.

"Like I said," replied Mr. Tunnel, "I'm greedy. I will lead you to the fortress, and if you succeed, my price will be very high—high enough that you will need Almanon's coffers. And, I will need a down payment."

"And if we don't succeed?" asked Stephen.

"Well, I am just out on a little walking exercise," he answered. "Like I said, I am just little crazy too."

Soles started pacing the room, thinking about the logistics of the caper. "How much of a down payment?"

"Well, he is interested," smirked Mr. Tunnel. "Let's say midnight two nights from today. Also, the down payment will have to be in gold."

Stephen answered, "We can do that."

Both Dianna and Soles looked puzzled with the answer.

Stephen took off his boot, and reached into the toe. "One troy ounce, and one troy ounce when we get there." He tossed the small gold bar to Mr. Tunnel.

Mr. Tunnel tested the gold bar with his teeth, and just nodded at Stephen.

Dianna said, "We will meet at the Muddy Hole."

"Sounds fine. Now, could you get the big man to stand next to the door instead of in front of it?" asked Mr. Tunnel as he opened the door.

Chapter Eight

Kira's company of a thousand men stood at parade rest outside of Sires. The countryside seemed to be breathing in long sighs. The men were restless. Moving slightly, swords rubbed against armor to create a sound like glass windchimes on a breezy day. Kira and her men had been waiting for an hour for King Zenith to inspect the men. Kira sat on a horse out in front of the armored men, the tension settling in her back.

Kira spotted King Zenith and his entourage approaching the field. She grimaced and thought, *He is not as stupid as I believed.* She was thinking about the thirty soldiers on horseback following the king.

As the group of King Zenith's men rode onto the field, Kira stood up in the stirrups and waved a small red flag over her head. Her men screamed and ran as fast as gazelles. Each of them had partaken from a potion to increase their speed. As the first wave of men crashed over Kira, she kicked the horse in the ribs, advancing with the men.

King Zenith was no fool. As the men advanced upon the king, his own men around him closed ranks with him in the middle and rode for the safety of the castle. Kira's men ran forward and stabbed the riders with long wooden spears tipped with sharp glass. Impaled, Zenith's men fell from their horses.

The king's men surprised their foe. Each of them carried an iron crossbow, a thing not seen in the kingdom in a hundred peaceful years. Thanks to the invaders, the iron crossbows had been taken off dead Viridian bodies. The

Erimos smiths had made glass crossbow bolts, and the king's men had practiced loading the crossbow on horseback. Thirty men had been picked for their newfound skill with the iron crossbow. Each glass bolt pierced the armor of Kira's men, and sometimes wreaked havoc on the man behind the man shot. The men on horseback and the men running simultaneously swept through the streets of Sires, battling for position.

Kira had not let her advance of troops be the only weapon drawn in the scheme. Other men hidden in a couple of aristocrats' houses outside of the walls of the castle advanced upon the portcullis as soon as the king and his men had left the castle. The small contingent of men battled fiercely to hold the position gained at the castle gates.

Kira's knowledge of the castle neutralized the main gate. The castle had been built by the first men to come over the mountains. The counterweight meant to be used to lower the portcullis and move the great ironbound doors was lodged in a structure just inside of the castle walls. Meant to be easily defendable by the castle's men, Kira's men held the structure while waiting for more of Kira's men to arrive.

Time, a definite factor for Kira's men, unraveled slowly. The organization of Zen's men had been at the walls of the castle. Kira's men had only minutes before the castle men regrouped and attacked her contingent of men at the counterweight structure. If Kira's army did not arrive soon, those men would be slaughtered.

Meanwhile, Kira's men harried the group of Zen's protectors. Taking short cuts down side streets, some of Kira's men made it to the castle before Zen's party of horses arrived. As Zen's party broke into the garden surrounding the castle, Zen was trapped between Kira's men at the gate and her men following him.

As he hesitated, one of Kira's men drove a glass-tipped spear into Zen's back. The spearhead sprang out of Zen's chest. A scarlet fountain of blood sprayed out. Zen plummeted to the earth; his crown toppled from his head. Kira watched him fall.

Kira raced over to the fallen king. She turned the king over; the fat man was dead. Kira screamed. It had been a ruse. The crown, made of paper and paint, had been a decoy. The man lying on the ground was a double for the king. Kira motioned for her bodyguards and set off for the castle.

The courtyard became a sea of carnage. Bolts from crossbows rained upon Kira's men from the walls surrounding the castle. Zen's men were shooting inside the castle's defenses. The tide slowed, but Kira's men started gaining the stairs inside the walls of the fortified castle. The long spears worked to push men back upon themselves, creating gaps in the crossbow ranks. Men dropped spears and crossbows alike and drew glass swords for close combat. Zenith's men swept out of the castle proper to engage the enemy in the courtyard. Fewer of Kira's men made it to the walls as the king's men attacked the courtyard. Men screamed, and the high pitch of death ruled the castle. All the men had broken ranks and struggled in individual fights to the death. For the moment, neither side gained an advantage.

Kira strode through the courtyard surrounded by her best three guards. As this small team advanced, they cut down any opposition. One of her bodyguards fell in the close quarter combat. Kira and two of her men made it to the doors of the castle. One of the guards, a raging hulk of a man infused with a strength potion, slammed the doors with a glass war axe. They crumpled inward off the hinges. Kira's two bodyguards fell upon the rear guard inside of the castle.

As Kira's men fought like rabid dogs, Kira gained the stairs to the lone tower of the castle. She zipped up the stairs with enormous speed before anyone could see her. She stopped at the top of the stairs, panting fiercely outside of a door.

Kira flung the door open and advanced into the middle of a corridor. No one was in the hallway. She figured the opposition would want to see the battle. Knowing the castle, she imagined Zen would be watching from the top of the tower which gave a three-hundred-and-sixty-degree view of the countryside. She made her way down the corridor. She had been to the top with Stephen before on a full moon night. She shook her head, dismissing the thought, and the motion flung beads of sweat from her brow.

Kira mounted the last stairs to the top of the tower. The door at the top was half open. She pushed it open with her sword. Craning her neck, she looked at the open sky. No one was guarding the door. She stepped up onto the brick spire.

King Zenith's back was to Kira. He only held one hand up and to the side to stop Kira's rush. "I have been waiting for you," he said. He turned and gazed upon Kira's frame. "You know, you're a bloody mess."

Kira looked down upon her painted-black glass armor. Blood spatters and even chunks of human flesh clung to her. She ignored it and said, "Your time is over."

"My time has just begun," said Zenith. "One question," he said, holding up a finger. "Why?"

Kira answered, "When a party is not responsible for its entire people and only feels responsibility for some in power, then the government fails the kingdom."

Zenith harrumphed and said, "You are going to kill me." It was a statement, not a question.

"Yes, my king," said Kira.

Zenith said, "You know, I feel sorry for you, Kira. Not because you want the kingdom, but because you feel hurt and betrayed by everyone, and especially by your father. Your father never truly saw the woman that you had become."

Zenith palmed a vial and swallowed a potion.

"Even the fastest potion will not save you," said Kira, raising her glass sword to strike.

Zenith held up an empty hand and said, "This particular potion is as old as the beginning of our kingdom. The three sisters that invented potions brewed this one, and the ingredients have been lost to the ages. Sad to say, one of three remaining potions from that time." Zenith turned and leaped from the turret.

Zenith screamed in an unnatural, high-pitched voice. Kira rushed to the edge to watch him fall. Zenith plummeted towards the ground. Fifty feet from the edge of the tower, his clothes burst into the air. A pterodactyl flung its leathery wings wide and swept up and over the wall of the castle.

Kira leaned against the promenade wall. She shook all over knowing today was just the beginning.

The pterodactyl's simple mind screamed one thought: Fly as far south as you can.

Chapter Nine

Stephen sat at a table with Dianna, Big Ben, and Soles in the Muddy Hole. The back of Stephen's neck crawled with all the eyes peering sidelong at him. No one made the mistake of venturing too near the table with Big Ben scowling at the patrons. Soles sat quietly lost in thought. Dianna tapped a glass dagger with leather wrapped around the handle on the tabletop. The look on her face portrayed a question that could not be asked. She was just too professional.

The group was outfitted for battle. Big Ben wore glass plates sewn into black leather covering his chest, thighs, and groin. He had his longsword strapped to his back and the double-bladed hand axe fixed to his chest. Stephen and Soles wore scale mail shirts. The glass on the shirts glistened like fish scales. Both of them had their swords strapped to their waists. Dianna wore leather pants and jacket, having professed that any heavy armor would be detrimental to her speed.

Mr. Tunnel entered the tavern and cast his eyes over to the table where they sat. He wore a brown suit and a white shirt with grease stains on the front. He turned on his heel and walked back out of the door. The three of them stood up and followed him. Mr. Tunnel stood under a lamppost that had been snuffed.

"What do you have in a way of supplies?" asked Mr. Tunnel.

"Just weapons," answered Soles.

"Good. You don't need the extra baggage," said Mr. Tunnel. "The spelunking supplies are near the entrance."

Big Ben said, "Spelunking? What is that?"

"Just think of a rat going through tunnels," said Mr. Tunnel. "You are a big rat, so try not to get stuck. Now follow me, and keep up." He started sauntering down the street.

"Do we trust him?" asked Soles.

"About as much as you trust me," answered Dianna, "and I know you have issues." She grabbed Stephen's arm and walked like a couple on holiday, smiling with her teeth but eyes alert. Stephen just tried to keep the fear off his face.

Mr. Tunnel mounted a small steam truck and gestured for everyone to get in the back. The pressure built, and the truck rolled down the lane. The entire thing vibrated, and Stephen's teeth felt the pressure. He held onto the side, not knowing whether he liked this new experience. When Mr. Tunnel picked up speed outside of the city, Stephen's hair swept back in the breeze. He could only grin at Dianna, because he could not talk over the noise of the machine.

The truck rumbled its way to the outside of the western edge of the city. A large graveyard of a couple acres stood in relief. It was surrounded by a low wall with vines trying to dismember it. Mr. Tunnel parked outside the gate and gestured to everyone to exit the vehicle. Mr. Tunnel pushed open the black iron gate. The moonlight lit the graveyard. At first someone must have portioned out the gravesites, but over the years graves had been inlaid haphazardly with small footpaths running between the tombstones. Graves had plaques, statues, and tombstones marking the dead. Large mausoleums and stone-cut sarcophaguses stood above ground. Mr. Tunnel wound his way past the markers and stopped in front of a large mausoleum.

"The entrance is in the mausoleum?" asked Soles.

"Oh no," replied Mr. Tunnel, "this is just a marker. The entrance is actually behind this monstrosity." He turned and walked around the stone box then over to a grave with a plaque several spaces past the mausoleum. He stopped and waited for everyone to gather round. "The first twenty feet is dark. I mean real dark. Just let your fingers brush the side of the tunnel on the way down a slight slope. At the bottom, I will light a candle. We proceed for another thirty or forty feet and stop to gear up in a small chamber. Ready," he said with a grin, "to be dead?"

The four companions could only nod with each of their own tangential thoughts.

Mr. Tunnel turned around and stooped over to pull a ring hidden in the grass. A door molded and disguised in the earth opened like a coffin lid. They could see a tunnel sloping down into the ground. Mr. Tunnel walked down the slope. Soles followed, with Stephen on his heels. Dianna grabbed Stephen's belt, and Big Ben came last, closing the makeshift lid. When the lid was closed, the party felt the embrace of the earth triggering the cold terror of suffocating. Each of them breathed in labored gasps. A light flared and blinded them for a moment.

"Trust me," said Mr. Tunnel, "that is the worst part, unless you don't like cramped spaces. Follow me," he said, with the candle playing shadows on his thin face.

Stephen expected to see packed-earth walls; instead, the walls were wooden, like a rough hallway built with long planks. His breath eased up a bit.

The tunnel dead-ended at a large door. Mr. Tunnel juggled the candle as he pulled out a key to unlock the door. It opened up into a large room. Shelves had miscellaneous items piled up. Tools, lanterns, masks, and other surplus equipment lined the walls.

"Sorry," said Mr. Tunnel, "I haven't had visitors in a long time. I would have straightened up the place." He lit a large lamp sitting in the middle of the floor and blew out the candle. "Now, things you will need," he said pulling items off shelves. He dumped helmets, lanterns, and gloves onto the floor in a big pile. "Pick whatever fits."

As Big Ben plundered in the pile, he asked, "What do you do if the light goes out?"

"Starve," answered Mr. Tunnel. "If you're in deep, you will never find your way back."

The four tried on different items. After a moment they looked around at each other. Soles, Dianna, and Stephen laughed.

"What?" said Big Ben. "It was the only one that fit." The helmet had three peacock feathers fanned out on the back. Big Ben grabbed the helmet off his head and ripped the feathers out. Placing it back on his head, he said, "Better?"

"Hey," said Mr. Tunnel grabbing the feathers off the floor. "I paid double for the feathers."

"I'll owe you," said Big Ben, grimacing.

"Damn right you will," replied Mr. Tunnel. "Now, one last thing," he said, grabbing harnesses and rope off a shelf. "We all harness ourselves in so no one gets lost or falls down a slippery slope." He held them up, smiling.

"What do we do if attacked?" asked Soles as he slipped into a harness.

"I would think the best thing to do is run like a gallimimus," answered Mr. Tunnel.

"Gallimimus?" asked Big Ben.

"You are just full of questions," said Mr. Tunnel. "Don't you read?"

"Only the grocery list," snickered Dianna.

Stephen hid his grin, not wanting Big Ben to be in a surly mood. He donned the apparel and felt the weight settle on the shoulder straps. The rope in the front and back felt awkward. Each of them carried a small lantern. The order of people was Mr. Tunnel, Soles, Stephen, Dianna, and Big Ben bringing up the rear. Stephen thought, *Good luck trying to run in this mess.*

"By the way," said Mr. Tunnel, "when we are near Almanon's fortress, you're on your own."

"That wasn't the deal," growled Soles.

"Hey, look," said Mr. Tunnel, spreading his hands wide, "I can set you on the right path, but I am not tangling with the arthropleuro. Got it?"

"How close can you get us?" asked Stephen.

"If you're quiet," said Mr. Tunnel, "pretty damn close. Besides, one way or another, I figure you are not returning the way you came."

"Lead the way," gestured Soles.

"By the way," said Mr. Tunnel, "please don't haunt a poor little man." He laughed and snuffed the floor lamp then opened a door on the far wall.

Stephen expected another hallway; instead, a large cavern with a level floor opened up to the light. Square stone pillars were equally spaced every fifty feet. Stephen ran his hand over the corner of a pillar. It felt like hard stone, the edges sharp. He held the small lantern up to look more closely and saw tool marks.

Soles tugged on the rope. "We are not here to sightsee." He turned and followed Mr. Tunnel.

The group continued down into the bowels of the earth. The floor slanted slightly. After three hundred feet, Mr. Tunnel led them into a tunnel about one stretched arm's width wide. Big Ben had enough clearance for his head. The tunnel was hard-packed earth with braces every ten feet holding up the ceiling. The tunnel branched off several times, and Mr. Tunnel made several turns.

The tunnel opened up to a natural cave. Stalactites hung from the ceiling, glittering from a soft sheen of water pushing the light back at the party. They had to circumvent stalagmites on the floor. Sometimes the two formations met, forming a natural pillar for the cave. The sound of dripping water echoed eerily in soft patterns. Stephen stuffed several mushrooms he found on the floor into his bag. Mr. Tunnel found an opening in the cave leading out.

The narrow opening twisted and turned constantly, with water flowing around their feet. Stephen bumped his head several times on outstretched rocks. Big Ben had a difficult time passing through the narrow, natural tunnel. At times, he had to turn sideways, rubbing against the wall. The party sloshed through the shin-deep water. Then the water broke from the narrow tunnel and spread out across another cave. The water here barely covered the tops of their feet. The water escaped by running into a large pool near the center of the cave. There were no stalagmites here, but several stalactites hung from a forty-foot ceiling.

Mr. Tunnel busily unhooked the rope from his harness. He wound the end up to Soles and unhooked the rope from a ring on Soles' harness. He handed the rope to Soles and whispered, "You may need this." He pointed to another tunnel leading from the cave. "You can follow that to a cave that has an opening to Almanon's fortress." He hesitated. "I think."

"What do you mean, 'I think'?" said Soles.

Mr. Tunnel hushed him and said, "Not so loud. The cave is the lair of the arthropleuro, so no one has been there in a long time." Mr. Tunnel glanced at the worried look on Dianna's face. He took a deep breath and said, "I will wait here for an hour. By that time, you will have made it into the fortress, or you are all dead." He held out his hand and said, "Good luck." He went down the line shaking each person's hand. He stopped and grinned when Stephen gave him the second part of the payment in gold.

The party crossed the cave. Soles had to stoop down almost double to enter the tunnel. After a couple feet, he gave up and started crawling on his hands and knees. The tunnel sloped upward out of the water. Big Ben had the worst of it. He had to pick his way carefully on his hands and knees, trying not to get stuck.

The tunnel dumped them into a large opening. They stopped to catch their breath and look around them. The cavern looked like a rock maze. The light of their lamps revealed several openings. The cave looked like a fibrous wheel of Swiss cheese; something had burrowed out the earth, leaving solid rock.

"Don't speak," whispered Dianna. "I hear something awful." It was the plates of the arthropleuro skittering across the rocky floor. The arthropleuro's thirty feet drummed a hollow tune in the small space. In her mind's eye she could see it. It looked like a centipede mixed with a large cockroach. She knew the bug could get as large as ten feet long and three feet across. The mandibles sticking out of the mouth could tear a person's leg off. They were serrated to tear foliage off trees. Notoriously ill tempered, the bug would attack anything moving. She thought, *At least the damn thing will not eat my corpse.*

Soles motioned to everyone to disconnect the harnesses. He picked a large opening that looked more like a crevasse than a tunnel. Almost at once, everyone realized they were not yet armed, so they drew their blades.

Soles picked up his lantern and stepped into the opening. Now everyone could hear the slight noise of the arthropleuro coming from all around them. The place was hot, and they were all sweating, the heat uncomfortable in the tight space. They followed Soles. He pivoted in the tunnel and gestured that there was a drop. He jumped down onto hot sand then put his back against the rock to his left. Each of them made the slight jump and spread out into a large cave.

Against the wall to the left, a hot spring bubbled in a pool, heating up the rock and sand. Against the far wall, broad steps the length of the cave terminated at a stone archway. The archway stood ten feet high and five feet wide, sticking out a foot from the cave like a doorframe. A stone door with a large steel ring on its far-left side stood in the relief of the arch.

A huge arthropleuro skittered across the sand. The thing was out of Dianna's nightmares. It was fifteen feet long, and its scales were four feet wide. As it moved, the scales clicked and the feet drummed against the sand. The head quested left and right while the pincers snapped. The tail end of the arthropleuro whipped out and constricted around Big Ben before he could take a step. Big Ben's face instantly turned red, and he strained against the bonds of the arthropleuro. His glass breast plate shattered in an instant, but the axe strapped to his chest cut into the creature's shell.

The head of the arthropleuro lunged at Soles, with its mandibles snapping. Without thinking, Stephen rushed forward, and struck hard with his diamond blade, lopping off the arthropleuro's head. Big Ben's bonds instantly dissipated. He collapsed to the floor.

Dianna rushed over and asked, "Are you hurt?" She sat him up with his back against her chest and her legs flared out next to him. Both their lanterns were toppled over in the sand.

Big Ben's head dropped to his chest and he said, "The damn thing snapped a couple ribs."

"I have a healing potion," said Stephen.

Big Ben waved him away. "I took a strength potion before entering the cave." He sighed. "It saved my life." He stood up and turned to Soles. "I can walk, but I don't think I will be much good in a fight."

Soles struck his shoulder and said, "At least you're alive."

In an unconscious simultaneous effort, all four of them stared at the door at the top of the steps.

Chapter Ten

The three men added their weight and strength to opening the stone door. After a couple of moments of straining muscles, the door pivoted on a steel rod from floor to ceiling. The rod, well-worn and oiled, controlled the inertia of the stone door. No one spoke about feeling the door was only there to keep the arthropleuro out and give whatever was feeding the arthropleuro easy access to the fortress. The door was not a deterrent for intruders, only a lid for an arthropleuro cage.

A hallway made of fitted stone opened up past the door. Torches spit and sputtered in sconces every ten feet. Thirty feet down the hall, the corridor split into three different directions like a T.

"Let's try not to get lost," said Soles, holding up a stick of charcoal.

A loud bugling sound echoed off the walls of the stone corridor.

"I think something heard you," whispered Dianna.

Big Ben stoically said, "It sounds like an elk mating call for rutting females."

"Well, I don't think it's here to mate," replied Dianna, "but you're welcome to try."

Big Ben grunted and stepped on the paved stones of the corridor. The others followed, spreading out every five feet. All of them were afraid, so they took comfort in holding a weapon in their hands. Stephen and Dianna stood in the center of the group, and Soles was last, marking arrows on the stone walls at each turn. Big Ben opted to go right then left at every intersection to stay loosely going forward in as straight a line as possible. Whatever creature was bugling, the sound seemed to draw closer. Farther into the twisting corridors, a sound of meat slapping rhythmically on stone grew louder. The unfamiliar sounds grated on everyone's nerves.

Big Ben held his hand up and whispered, "I feel a draft of air."

"Follow it," whispered Stephen. The walls seemed narrower to him as time progressed. A low grade of anxiety pierced his heart.

Big Ben turned right into a long corridor. The stone walls stretched forward a hundred feet with bright light at the end. The unmistakable noise of something animalistic brayed down the hallway. Everyone gripped their weapons tightly in their hands, and their breath came in short bursts. Each member of the party slowly shrugged out of the rope harnesses. As a single mind, the group dashed down the last twenty feet of hallway.

The group burst into a round, domed, stone chamber with entrances every twenty feet. In the middle of the room stood a monstrous carnotaurus with a chain clasped to its right ankle attached to a spike driven into the earth in the center of the room. It was a fifteen-foot-long biped with a tail balancing the upper body, which stood seven feet tall. Two arms with four spikes for fingers trembled in the air, seeming to grasp at its next victim.

It rushed forward. The spiked head tried to impale the nearest invader of its domain. Everyone scrambled to get out of the way. The carnotaurus snapped at Stephen with small, jagged teeth. Stephen ducked under the tremendous head and rolled farther into the room. Soles flicked his sword, gouging a wound in the carnotaurus's rib cage. It howled in pain and swept its long tail at Soles, who managed to jump back out of range. Dianna leaped behind the carnotaurus, dragging her knife against its lower back while trying to avoid the tail. It raised its spikey head and bugled in a loud burst of sound. Big Ben, being only inches shorter than the carnotaurus, reversed his grip on his sword, with both hands reaching over the back of his head like a spike, and tried drive the glass blade down into the breast of the carnotaurus. The thing, too fast to be taken with a downward sword strike, sprang backwards. As the mighty sword drove itself into the floor, the carnotaurus butted Big Ben in the chest, flinging him against the wall. Stephen now found himself behind everyone else, including the scaled monster.

Everyone backed away from the carnotaurus, trying to gauge what to do next. The thing hissed, sweeping its horned head back and forth, searching for the next target. The tension in the room was palpable as everyone, including the carnotaurus, tried to determine their next move.

The carnotaurus decided to attack the injured Big Ben, who moved like a sick animal. Drawing upon its instinct to kill the wounded, the carnotaurus lunged at him. Dianna acted first and threw a blade at the beast's horned head. The blade nicked the eye socket of the carnotaurus, making it shake its scaly head.

Stephen sized up the carnotaurus, trying to decide where to attack. The scales protected its body. Its hands were like knives. Its tail was a formidable weapon. Its horns and teeth made the head deadly. Its haunches drew Stephen's attention to the chain around the carnotaurus' ankle. Stephen fiddled with the potions in his belt pouch. He drew out a vial that seemed to contain a grey mud and dumped the contents upon the chain holding the carnotaurus. The acid of the vial ate the iron chain. and it parted. Stephen grabbed the end, avoiding the caustic acid, and threw it upon the back of the carnotaurus. The carnotaurus whipped around, dragging the chain through the dusty floor. An intelligent spark lit in the eyes of the creature as it realized a bid for freedom. It ran down a tunnel away from the group.

Everyone dropped to the ground with their hearts racing. Dianna pulled a pouch on a string from around her neck. Dipping into it, she pushed Stem between her gum and cheek.

Stephen noticed and asked, "Why are you doing that?"

After a moment of feeling the Stem rush into her body, she replied, "Did you see that thing?" She stood up slowly. "I just needed a moment of comfort. I'm sorry, but this is just very hard for me. I've only dreamed of monsters, not fought them."

Soles replied, "Well, get comfortable, because we are killing a monster. A monster that has had a stranglehold on my kingdom for generations. A monster that others have tried to kill, but no one knows how he keeps surviving."

Chapter Eleven

Kira stood on the stone tower's terrace watching the sun rise in the east. She wore a black flowing dress to commemorate the fallen. She thought about the loyal men she had lost on the previous day to make a new kingdom. Her hand tightened into a fist while thinking about Zenith's escape. He troubled her thoughts. The man was unpredictable. He could someday return and cause havoc upon her peaceful kingdom. She sighed and turned a cheek to the rising sun. The sun warmed the side of her face. The night had been cold.

She closed her eyes and tried to imagine her worth in the scheme of history. Would she be remembered as a usurper or woman who brought prosperity to the kingdom? She decided to write her own history. She would rule as a wise patriot. She would use her very essence to shape a rich, prosperous kingdom. No mercy for the wicked. The coin hoarders, the Stem pushers, and the Potioners would suffer for a better kingdom. People would adore her lest they suffer her wrath. She felt she needed to be as hard as stone to bring the kingdom into a new age of prosperity.

First, she would dissolve the sovereignty of her royal cousins, the dukes. She would give the power to the elected mayors of her cities. The people would rejoice that one of their own would rule. She thought people would call her a visionary, one of the people who would be regarded highly. Next, she would tax the rich and educate the poor. Why should only the rich be able to read and write? She imagined a literate kingdom sharing information. Yes, she decided. *I shall be thought of as a patriot.*

"Your highness," interrupted a guard pushing a man to his knees, "we found him hiding in the stable."

Kira turned and saw a disheveled man, his fine clothes ripped and dirty. His hair was mussed, with dirt on his face. His hands were black from handling coal. A look of defeat pinching his face added to the slack shoulders of a man giving up his pride. His head hung down upon his chest.

Kira reached out and pulled the man's head up by the chin. "Master Salender," she asked, "why so glum?"

His eyes vacant, he replied, "The end is near."

She laughed and said, "Not for you. You shall be my personal valet."

Master Salender dropped his head and muttered, "I was not speaking about myself."

Kira's face flushed, and she slapped the man. "I will be the beginning!" She turned to the sun and whispered, "I will be the beginning of something new."

The old man sat on his knees, chuckling, with his lip bleeding.

Chapter Twelve

Two hours had passed since the party ran from the carnotaurus. They were foundering in the corridors under the fortress. Backtracking several times after running into dead ends, the party was becoming spiteful. After the third snide remark made by Big Ben, they agreed not to talk unless one of them came up with a brilliant plan to get them out of their predicament.

Stephen's anxiety had grown to the point that he was useless. He breathed in ragged gasps while holding onto the rope to be steered by Soles. Dianna was becoming increasingly worried about him. She believed Stephen held on to his sanity with the fierce determination of youth. But at times, he seemed to go somewhere else, with this glazed look on his face. She formulated a plan.

"Stop," said Dianna, "just stop." She leaned against a wall to catch her breath. "We can wonder around here for days unless we do something."

"What would you suggest?" asked Big Ben.

"We go back to the large chamber. You two carry a piece of coal and take a jog through the tunnels," answered Dianna. "You are bound to find a way out." She darted her eyes at Stephen and gave the two men an expectant look.

"Fine," said Soles. "I am tired of tugging junior here down the tunnels." He untied the rope around his waist. "Both of you make your way back to the chamber, and Big Ben and I will explore some more. If we don't find anything in a couple hours, we will come back to rest."

Dianna grabbed Stephen by the shoulders and turned him up the corridor then gave him a gentle push. After walking ten minutes and following Soles' dusty foot prints, they found the carnotaurus chamber. The trapped smell of the creature's feces had made the chamber almost inhospitable. The smell would only get worse the longer they stayed in the chamber.

"Stephen," said Dianna, "talk to me. Tell me about your home."

Stephen sat down against a wall well away from the stench and replied, "I cooked for everyone in my town." He turned his face to Dianna. "I guess I haven't been much help."

"No, darling," replied Dianna, "we all have our demons. I just never thought I would meet one," she said, looking around the chamber. The walls of the chamber had claw marks as if the creature had tried to escape.

Stephen laughed. The laugh became more hysterical. As he laughed, tears fell down his face. After a minute, his side started to hurt. His laugh slowed to a chuckle. He wiped the tears from his face and said, "Thank you. I think I am feeling better now."

"I hope so. You started to worry me," said Dianna, sweeping the hair from his brow. "I don't want to lose you."

Stephen gestured for a hug. They held each other for timeless moments.

Big Ben and Soles ran into the chamber, exclaiming, "We found a way out!"

"Where?" asked Dianna.

Soles strode over and sat down next to Stephen with his back against the wall "It is a ladder leading to a door in the ceiling," he said, eyeing Big Ben.

Big Ben shrugged and said, "We think it is a way out."

"Well, of course it is," said Dianna in a high voice. "We do need to go up."

Big Ben reached down and helped Stephen to his feet. "Feeling, OK?"

"Now that we have found a way out," answered Stephen, "I feel relieved."

Everyone followed Soles out of the chamber. He picked up the pace. Stopping at turns in the corridor, he read his coal marks to find his way back to the ladder. Once he stopped at a particular intersection to gaze at a coal mark for a minute. Feeling confident about the mark, he continued down the corridor to the right.

A ladder hanging unsupported filled the middle of the stone corridor. The rungs were iron bars, and the side supports were made out of stained oak. At the top, a large trap door with steel springs and a tongued catch kept the door from swinging down.

Soles did not miss a beat; he stepped down on the lowest rung and started climbing the ladder. At the top, he fiddled with the catch and pushed on the door. Straining to keep it open with one arm, he ducked his head above the surface. Sand streamed down from the hole into the corridor. He looked down between his arms and said, "It's dark. We need our lamps." He dropped the door, which automatically locked on the tongue catch.

Stephen lit the lamps from the burning torches then passed them over to the others.

Holding the lantern handle in his teeth, Soles unlocked and pushed the trap door fully open. He climbed up the ladder and held the door open. The springs on the door made the muscles in his arm tremble.

Big Ben climbed the ladder and held the door for Stephen to follow and Dianna to come last.

Stephen peered around. The feeble light from the lanterns extended out in a large circle, but the light disappeared overhead and farther into the dark. No ceiling or walls bounced the light back to them. The floor was fine white sand that reflected the light. Stephen felt he was in a cocoon of light in the pitch dark of a moonless night in the deepest cave. The shadows of the party members on the white sand seemed to be his only reference for size.

Soles barely whispered, "Don't let go of the door." He raised his lantern above his head, and the light disappeared above him. "We will fan out and look for a way out."

A blur of motion and a horrific screech passed directly between everyone. No one clearly saw the creature come from the dark and return to the dark. It startled Big Ben, who let go of the door to draw his sword. The door slammed into the ground, raising a small cloud of sand.

"Damn it, Ben," yelled Soles. "Can you open it?"

Big Ben tried to pry the door open with the tip of his sword. The door fit so well into the floor he could not stick his sword in the crack to gain leverage. Frustrated, he replied, "We are not going back that way." He sheepishly looked back at them. Another high-pitched squeal sounded in the dark, and Big Ben gripped his sword tighter in his palm.

A coughing noise came from their right, just outside of the circle of light. From behind Dianna, a loud hiss sounded.

"There is more than one of them," said Soles. "Everyone gathers in a loose circle and place the lanterns in the middle."

As everyone did as he obeyed, the circle of light became smaller, with the lanterns on the ground.

Stephen barely heard swift footsteps rasping in the sand outside of the light. The creatures were running in a tight circle barely out of sight. He thought he saw a patch of olive-green skin reflected in the light. He kept his eyes moving, trying to catch a glimpse. His mouth felt dry and parched. He kept swallowing air instead of spit.

A creature ran a few feet into the light in an upright stance with thick legs supporting it. A raptor screamed, and a purple umbrella hood lined with thick red veins shook violently behind its head. Its teeth glistened, sharp and predatory, with a rolling red tongue in its mouth as it sprayed yellow venom from gelatinous sacks anchored inside its cheeks. The venom vapor made a small, bulbous cloud. The three-foot raptor lowered its hood and twisted back into the dark.

Dianna screamed, "Do you see the claws on that thing?"

Soles growled, "I'm more worried about the yellow venom."

"The things are fast," replied Big Ben. "You must rely on your peripheral vision for movement."

One of the lanterns sputtered out, and the light became smaller. No one could see past the tip of a sword at arm's length. Dianna thought about the short range of her knives. They had always been good to her until now.

A raptor darted low out of the dark at Big Ben's shins. Claws flashing, it scored his knee. Ben swept his sword in a low arc but was too slow as the raptor snapped back into the cover of darkness. Blood flowed from the wound in his knee. He ignored the pain and concentrated on the sounds of the raptors.

One pounced Soles from the blackness. He was able to sweep his sword up from low guard to impale the raptor, which with the sword in its chest wiggled and snapped at Soles. With brute strength, he held the raptor off the ground. He placed a boot on its belly and drove it to the ground. He ripped the sword sideways, almost cutting the raptor in two. Red blood soaked the white sand. The raptor lay dead.

Two raptors sprang from the darkness at Stephen's chest level. With an underhand sweep of the diamond sword, he cut the heads off both raptors. They bounced off his thighs, and the bodies lay twitching and kicking a yard from Stephen's feet.

Two raptors rushed at Dianna from the cover of darkness from opposite sides. With one low and one high, she kept them at bay with her forearms. Each raptor bit into the leather jacket sleeves, thrashing their heads while trying to force Dianna off her feet.

As one, Big Ben and Soles turned and speared their swords into the raptors' backs. They deflated with severed spinal cords. One mewed, and the other died with its eyes open. Soles cut the living raptor's head off.

Dianna's knees buckled. She lay on her side as stiff as a board with her eyes round, breathing in a slow cadence. The poison had worked its way to the cerebellum. Voluntary muscle control stopped immediately.

"Help me," cried Stephen, turning her on her back. He put a hand on her chest and felt a slow, methodical heartbeat. He looked up at Soles and asked, "Will the poison kill her?"

"I don't know," said Soles with his voice catching. "Give her a potion."

Stephen looked into her eyes. The pupils were very large. "Poison is different from being sick or wounded. You need an antidote for the exact poison." He cradled her head in his lap and asked, "What do we do?"

Big Ben put his hand on Stephen's shoulder and said, "We wait. Maybe the poison is meant for the raptors to eat something alive."

Chapter Thirteen

Kira stood on the castle's tower watching the sun rise for the third consecutive day. It had become a daily ritual for Kira. The time was cathartic. Her mind focused on the colors of the new day on the horizon. She felt at peace during that time. After an hour of staring at the horizon, the thoughts of failure crept back into her mind. She felt like she had failed the kingdom by not being up to the task of ruling. She was locked in indecision.

Kira imagined that the ripples from a single ruling on the affairs of state could bring the kingdom to its knees. Her imagination made her stagnant. The responsibility of the kingdom weighed beyond the scope of her ability. She only wanted the best for the kingdom, but she felt lost.

Kira's lack of authority undermined her position. People were talking. In the back halls, whispers near her, all ugly half-truths that could lead to outright rebellion. Her only defense was to be merciless. Her only offense was regulating the people in her immediate sphere of influence. Lacking confidence in making a decision of state, she could not delegate decisions to capable people, so nothing was accomplished. Her personal feelings of responsibility for the kingdom made the government static. The idea of making a wrong decision frightened her because the consequences could harm a great number of people.

Kira slammed her fist on the paramount and thought, *I will be the harbinger of truth, even if it means the death of people.*

She fingered the stiletto strapped to her forearm under the white gown she wore. The knife was considered to be a punching affair. The blade, eight inches long and triangular in shape, was meant to be thrust into a kidney, liver, or heart. As she felt the leather-wrapped hilt, it comforted her.

Kira thought, *I need to shake things up. I need to keep the foes vying for the throne that owe allegiance to me off balance. I need a victim of circumstance.*

Master Salender emerged from the closed door upon the tower. He wore a white linen tunic with no sleeves, the length of the cloth falling to his upper thighs, with a belt cinched around his waist. He wore black hose on his legs with only green stockings for shoes. The man looked comical.

He bowed from the waist with his face parallel to the floor and said, "My queen, the captain of your company wishes to report."

Kira turned and said, "Send him forth."

Master Salender slowly backed up still prostrating. When his butt hit the door, he stood and motioned to someone on the stair.

The captain of her Queen's Company stood at attention in front of the queen. He wore a breastplate of glass over a fine blood-red silk shirt. His cotton pants, dyed the same color, had glass plates covering the thighs. Black boots rose to his knees. Under the crook of his arm, he held a glass, leather-padded full helmet with an open face and a nose guard. The padded leather was also dyed blood red. The only difference between his appearance and that of the regular army personnel was the helmet. The regulars wore a skull cap made of black leather.

"Do your men like the new uniforms?" asked Kira.

"Yes, your grace," answered the captain, "it adds a bit of collective to the troops." He cleared his throat and said, "A small group of soldiers and castle staff managed to escape into the mountains."

"You didn't follow them?" asked Kira.

"Yes, your grace," stammered the man, "but one of them must have been born on the mountain, because they disappeared like ghosts. We have no trail to follow."

Kira coolly walked over to stand in front of the captain with a slight smile on her face. "Incompetence will not be tolerated." With a quick motion, she drew the stiletto from its sheath and drove it to the hilt in the man's ear. She jerked it free as the man fell to the ground.

"Valet Salender," she said softly, "please pass the helmet to the next in charge and have someone clear the body."

Master Salender only nodded as he retrieved the helmet and backed to the door. He knew Kira was unraveling. She had become a wraith compared to the intelligent, gentle person he had known in the past.

Kira turned and daintily retrieved a lace kerchief from her left sleeve to wipe the blade clean. Dropping the kerchief over the side of the precipice, she thought, *I believe that should shake things up nicely.* A full smile and haunting eyes graced her countenance.

Chapter Fourteen

The four travelers lay prone upon the sandy floor. The lamps surrounding them barely flickered with life. All of them, exhausted from the previous day, had slept in the gritty sand. Big Ben and Soles slept on either side of Stephen and Dianna. Dianna's head lay peaceably on Stephen's lap. She had curled up to Stephen's body as he slept.

Big Ben woke with a dry, hacking cough. Peering into the gloom, he gently shook Stephen's outstretched leg. Stephen mumbled in his sleep, waking Soles. Soles sat upright on the dry sand and brushed the loose sand from his clothing. Dianna rolled over, and her head struck the soft sand, waking her. She smiled and flicked Stephen's nose.

"What?" said Stephen sleepily, his blurry eyes focusing on Dianna. "You're awake?"

The smile reached her eyes, and she said, "I slept like a babe. I remember waking up barely for a moment in your arms." She slapped his thigh and said, "Next time, you get bitten." She rolled on to her feet.

Soles grunted and asked, "Does anyone have any water?"

Big Ben shook a flagon of ale and said, "No, but this will parch your thirst." He gulped down a couple of swallows and then handed the flagon of ale to Soles.

Everyone took a turn and drained the flagon.

Stephen stood and asked, "Which way do we go from here?"

Soles craned his neck and rubbed the back trying to loosen the muscles. "If I had a bow, I could tell you."

"What about a sling?" asked Stephen "I use it to kill small birds, but I don't have any rocks."

"Here," said Dianna, "let me see that." She put the straps of leather in her hand and dropped a coin in the basket. Whirling the sling, she let the coin fly. No one heard a noise. Taking another coin, she hurled it in the opposite direction. She heard a small tinkle as the coin struck something. "We go that way," she said pointing into the dark.

Big Ben picked up a lantern and said, "It's as good as any direction." He lumbered into the dark, and the others followed his lead.

As the four of them walked in a straight line, Stephen's lamp blew out. Shaking the lantern, he realized it was out of oil. He tossed it into the sand. The other lamps grew dimmer as they walked. They could see barely a couple of feet in front of their noses. Stephen thought *What happens when the lights go out?*

"I found something," said Big Ben, holding his lantern high against a bricked wall. "Do we turn left or right?"

"I have always been partial to the right," answered Dianna.

Big Ben nodded and turned right, trailing his fingertips along the wall. His lantern died with a sputter. Dianna's and Soles' lanterns dimmed at the same time. They stared at the lanterns, seeing the red-hot tips die in a black, smoky haze. The darkness descended, like being completely blind.

"Keep a hand on the wall," whispered Big Ben.

"Frigging great," Dianna said loudly, "he acts like we are at a funeral."

"It wouldn't hurt to keep our voices down," replied Soles.

Stephen reached forward and put his right hand on her shoulder. She was trembling ever so lightly.

They dragged their feet in the sand, each of them worrying something could trip them in the dark. After a couple of minutes, Soles started counting his steps softly out loud. The sound comforted everyone, yet Stephen felt Dianna's shoulder tremble ever so slightly harder. Their breath sounded like trumpets wheezing. Each person felt disembodied, floating in a sea of sand with the darkness pressing hard on their senses.

"Stop," said Big Ben. "I think I found something." He felt the jamb of a door. He dragged his fingers across its width. Feeling in the dark for a latch, he found a keyhole and a handle. He pulled on the handle, but nothing gave. "The door is locked, and I am afraid to pull the handle from the door."

"Let me up front," said Dianna. She moved to the door. Feeling in the dark, she found the keyhole. She knelt down on her knees and pulled a thin, stiff wire from her boot. Her hand shaking, she inserted the bent wire into the keyhole. She closed her eyes and concentrated on her fingertips. The resistance in the lock channeled backwards into her fingers. Navigating the hole, she unlocked the door. Breathing a sigh of relief, she said, "Be prepared, I have unlocked it." She drew a dirk from a sheath strapped to her thigh and opened the door.

Light blinded all of them. Shielding their eyes, they walked briskly into the room. Cells quartered off in blocks like a maze met their focusing eyes. Once their eyes adjusted, the light was actually dim. They were in a dungeon. All the inhabitants of the cells stared at the party. Stephen noticed the inmates were running to fat. Not one person looked a bit starved. Stephen shuddered ever so slightly thinking about the implications.

"What do we do?" asked Stephen.

The tranquility was shattered; all the prisoners started screaming at once, all calling for help.

Big Ben bellowed, "Quiet." The prisoners settled down.

A man reached his fat arm through the bars of his cage and said, "Listen, you can't leave us here."

Soles slapped the arm from his path and said, "Let me think." A bleating sound reached his ears. He asked the prisoner, "What is that?"

The man answered, "They are goats. They force-feed us milk and cheese to fatten us up. Please let me out. I won't do anything, just let me out."

"I'll think about it," said Soles, following the sounds of the goats. "Ben, I think we have found some food."

They found a table laden with cheese and a bucket of goats' milk. Peeling the mold off the cheese, they ate ravenously. They stood around the table like pigs at a trough.

"What do we do about the prisoners?" asked Dianna around a mouthful of cheese.

Big Ben bit a hunk of cheese and answered, "They could be a distraction." He chewed the piece looking for his next bite.

"Distraction for us, or a distraction for the guards of the palace?" asked Dianna.

"We will use them," said Soles as he gulped down some milk from a pitcher. Wiping the milk from his upper lip, he said, "They will set the palace guards on their heels. I can find my way to the throne room during the ruckus."

"You mean lead us to the throne room," said Stephen.

"Yeah," answered Soles placing a hand on the leather mask, "it will take all of us."

Figuring a day had passed, Stephen handed out potions. Big Ben stood with his back to the entrance of the palace with sword drawn while the others opened the cell doors. Men and women milled about in the entranceway, wary of Big Ben. Soles signaled for him to let the prisoners loose. They ran past Big Ben, bare feet slapping the cobbled floor.

Chapter Fifteen

Kira sat slumped in her chair at the head of a long table with the dukes and duchess sitting along the sides. For the past hour, they had been lamenting about the shortage of food due to the drought. They were working Kira's last nerve. Duchess Fiona, of the Iron Province, kept scooping mouthfuls of cake to her fat face from the table. Duke Henley, of the Meadow Province, waved his red-stained hands in everyone's faces trying to make a point. Duke Siegel, of the Forest Province, sat with his eyes closed, just nodding his head agreeing with every point. The loudest poser of all self-righteous power was Duke Quinton of the Silver Province. He waved his beefy hand, embellishing the slightest point raised by his numbskull brain.

"Everyone be quiet," said Kira. No one listened. She slammed her hand down on the table, rocking the crockery, and said, "I said be quiet, dolts."

Everyone stopped talking and turned their attention to Kira with surprise written on their faces. The entrenched pompous power of the individuals had never been questioned by anyone with authority.

Kira turned her gaze on Duke Quinton and said, "The ruling class has always traded in silver. Why not issue a new coin of silver to stave off inflation caused by the lack of food?"

Duke Quinton gulped like a fish and then said, "We cannot issue such a coin because it would drive down the monetary trade value between the ruling provinces."

Duchess Fiona said, "We must protect our investments."

Kira said slowly, "You mean, we must protect our wealth."

Duke Quinton said, "Well, yeah."

"At the cost of people starving by the end of this winter?" asked Kira.

"I am just saying, there has to be another way," said Duke Quinton, folding his arms across his chest. The white silk shirt with silver piping in Kira's mind seemed tasteless.

"What about capping the price of food?" admonished Kira

"Then other supplies will inflate," said Duke Quinton. "Listen, these childlike answers are not going to solve anything. Since King Zenith's disappearance, I motion we vote in a new king. One more experienced than who sits on the throne. Doesn't everyone agree?"

Kira stood up from her chair and walked slowly around the table. "I take it you would like to rule."

Duke Quinton leaned back in his chair, following Kira's progress with his gaze. "If you would like to nominate me, then yes, I would like to rule for the people." He turned his eyes forward and asked, "Could I have a motion?"

Kira struck in a fluid motion with her stiletto. The triangular blade pierced the skin at the back of his neck between the first and second cervical vertebrae. The glass blade severed the medulla oblongata, where the nerves of the autonomic nervous system dwelt. He fell over immediately into his porcelain plate. His heart, lungs, and brain functions stopped abruptly.

Kira wiped the spinal fluid and blood on the back of the white silk shirt with silver piping and asked, "Would anyone like to enter a motion on the table?"

Everyone at the table shook their heads. The color had drained from their faces.

"Then we shall put a price cap on food, and then a week after the order, introduce silver currency into the market," said Kira. "Agreed?"

"Yes, Your Highness," parroted the assembled royalty.

"I will expect results within the week," said Kira. "And someone give my regards to Duke Fulton. The young boy has been promoted." She sat back down at the head of the table and said, "You are dismissed."

Not one person made a verbal sound as the chairs scraped from their resting positions. All three royal cousins exited the room rather quickly.

Queen Kira sighed and propped her feet on the edge of the table. The black dress slipped down to her knees. She had worn black for the mourning of the kingdom as a rule, but the black dress had become known by the servants of the castle as death incarnate. She felt that her royal cousins were fools, easy pickings if Stephen failed in his mission over the mountains. She was too tired to plan a defense of the kingdom. She would do it tomorrow. Her power was firmly entrenched in the ruling class. She would prepare the kingdom. She had no illusions that Stephen would prevail.

Her earlier thought of imprisoning the dukes and duchess abandoned, she now realized she could control them. Their pompous aristocratic nature made them fodder for Kira's plans. Anyway, if she tired of their protests of her governance, she would just hang them in the capitol city squares of their own provinces.

Kira never realized the brutality of her actions had made her a tyrant. People slept that night dreaming of ways to kill the new Queen Kira. The kingdom boiled with revolution on the minds of the populace. The only thing standing in the way were the miserly fools who fed off Kira's mad trappings of power. Kira's rule was tenuous at best. She would come to see factions grow in her fledgling kingdom that would decide her fate.

Chapter Sixteen

Soles counted one hundred breaths before he followed the prisoners into the castle. The prisoners had been vicious to their charges. A couple of guards laid in a pool of blood, their bodies beaten and broken in an interior guard station. All the weapons had been snatched by the prisoners for their escape. The group had followed a path of destruction. Guards, prisoners, and staff lay dead on the floor. The carnage included puncture wounds, slashing wounds, and even fingernail scrapes at the eyes. The prisoners showed no mercy in trying to escape a horrible death in the dungeons.

Soles stopped in a corridor to orient himself. Big Ben turned over a guard and pulled a war hammer from underneath the fractured body. Testing the weight, Big Ben smiled and waited for Soles. Soles motioned them down a side corridor. They ran straight into an organized resistance to the prisoner's escape. The guards were cutting down the prisoners like scything wheat. Big Ben roared and ran straight for the line of defense.

Big Ben's charge broke the line. The war hammer in his hand crushed heads and broke arms as he wielded it. Short downward swings of the hammer crushed skulls. Wide sweeping swings broke men's ribs, arms, and hips. Big Ben's potion strength shattered men's lives. The frenzy of the hammer bludgeoned the guards to death. After the guards were dead, he stood with blood spattered all over him. The war hammer had meat and hair clinging to its head. He had not uttered a sound after the initial roar; he only breathed like an iron-stoking bellows.

The prisoners rushed by Big Ben. Soles motioned for them to follow him down a side corridor. The way seemed clear. After a moment, he loosened his sword in its scabbard and slowed to a rushed walk.

He turned the corner and said to the guards there, "The prisoners are escaping. Initiate an alarm." Two brawny men stood outside a double door with steam carbine rifles in their hands. One reached for a tassel that would set a bell to ring for marshaling the troops to castle defense. The other man drew a scimitar and leaned the musket against the wall in easy reach. The curved blade, weighted and wide at the end, was intended to slash an opponent in half.

Soles' sword leaped from the sheath. It flicked out, cutting the alarm man's carotid artery. With a backward swing, he severed the other man's beefy neck until the sword stuck itself into the vertebrae surrounding his spinal cord. Both men dropped, clutching their throats and kicking their feet as they died silent deaths.

"Why didn't they shout?" asked Dianna as she picked up a steam carbine rifle. She fiddled with it for a moment. *Easy enough, just pull a lever.*

Soles slung a bloody line against the wall as he shook the blood from his sword and answered, "This is the entrance to Almanon's throne room. The guard's tongues had been cut out to insure privacy." Soles stepped over the dead guards and pushed the heavy, black, silver-bound doors open.

Almanon's throne room was empty of a living soul. Thick black tapestries with embossed silver thread depicting war victories hung over the walls of the room. Each emblem in silver denoted swirls, circles, and figure eights in a weird epitaph of a mystery language. A throne of unadorned silver on a three-step dais sat empty in the middle of the room in cold relief against the drapes.

Soles shouted, "Where are you hiding, Almanon?"

"He could be somewhere else," said Stephen, trying to console Soles.

Soles shook his head no and said, "He has not left this chamber for centuries."

Dianna walked briskly into the room. "Then he must have a sleeping chamber off to one side." She walked to a side wall and lifted the heavy drape up off the ground. The others followed her example, lifting the tapestries up and looking for a door.

At the far back of the chamber, Stephen found a blue door. "Over here. I found something," he whispered. The door felt warm against the palm of his hand. He waited for the others to join him.

Big Ben shouldered his way past everyone and pushed on the door. He ducked his head and stepped past the threshold. Everyone nervously followed Big Ben.

The chamber was brightly lit by a glass dome that fed sunlight onto a black basalt surface. The round room felt as hot as a midsummer day. The walls leading to the glass dome were white, which added glare to the chamber. Nothing else was in the room except a man lying on his back in the middle of the smooth, black surface of the floor as if sunning himself. Almanon was naked.

Almanon sat upright and swiveled his torso to stare at the intruders. He looked shorter than average. His pale skin belied no real muscle tone. The absence of hair looked eerie. Not one hair on his head or his naked, grotesquely large genitals. His eyes were steel blue. He stood from his seated position.

"Has it already been a century?" his raspy voice asked.

Big Ben raised the war hammer and ran straight towards the meek-looking pale man.

Soles screamed, "No!"

Almanon also screamed; blue lightning escaped his maw, ensconcing Big Ben. Big Ben stopped in his tracks with the war hammer over his head and howled before bursting into flame. Almanon stopped, and Big Ben fell over onto his side, with flames rapidly consuming his body.

Almanon sat down cross-legged as if he were going to teach the young the importance of life. "Every century assassins think they will slay me. The human race has such a short memory. Your race lived in mud huts when my brothers and I found you. We treated you like cattle, eating our fill whenever the slightest bit hungry. When the urge to mate overcame us, we fought for weeks. Being young, we knew no economy of power. We tried to destroy ourselves." Almanon smiled and said, "But then, I used you. The human race fought my battles. To this day, we use you as pawns."

"What are you?" asked Dianna. Her voice shook with fear.

Almanon clenched his fist and shook it in her direction. "A mighty race banished to the north. We flew over the mountains to escape persecution. We are the last surviving members of our race. We use the humans as a distraction. We dare not think of ourselves as being the last."

Dianna asked, "But why fight each other? Why not let us rule ourselves and have peace for yours?"

Almanon laughed, but it sounded hollow in the echoing room. His eyes bright, he responded, "Animals cannot govern themselves." He uncurled from the floor and stood tall and lean, as if growing. "Animals are only good for eating."

Dianna sprayed red flames at Almanon. He jumped backwards, and tucked and rolled to the side avoiding the flames. He had not expected the attack. Firing a shot at Almanon, Soles let loose flames from his hand. Almanon backed up against the curve of the wall. Then, he ran into the center of the room. He dropped to the floor; his body started flailing about while he howled. The move surprised them.

Almanon raised himself on all fours. His back arching, the skin split from his spine. His neck elongated, with horns sprouting from his head, and the skin peeled off his body.

The three of them surrounded Almanon and shot flames at his disintegrating form. A mighty head rose from the flames. Green scales on an elongated, reptilian form with horns and mighty teeth gnashing emerged from the flames, ten feet tall. The face was a horrendous mask of inhuman contours, his cheeks protruding, bony ridges for his eye sockets, his lips plump with fangs for teeth—Almanon's caricature of a human face was a nightmare. His body was a grotesque testament of human form, muscles bulging and limbs as thick as trees, and his entire inhuman skin was covered in green diamond-like scales. His feet and hands had claws extending from the digits. He laughed as he unfurled reptilian wings made of scales and fibrous membrane.

The creature's wings beat and sent a sweeping gale into the room. Soles tumbled to the side. The ineffectual flames died from Dianna's hands as the monster swung his reptilian head to bite her. She floundered flat on her stomach to dodge the bite. Stephen shot flames at the reptile's eyes. The thing pulled its head back out of the way, and Soles drove the point of his sword into the side of the green scales. Bright red sparks burst from the spot that Soles hit. The sword buckled and snapped in half against the magically armored scales. The thing backed out of the flames' range to keep his eyes free from being cooked.

"The flames can only keep him at bay," yelled Soles. The nightmare's tail unfurled, whipped out, and flung Soles against the wall. The tail, a living snake with barbs extruding from the tip, whipped in the air around the creature. With his back against the wall and his chin on his chest, Soles sat unconscious, blood seeping from a wound in his shoulder.

Dianna used the steam carbine rifle to take a shot at the green monster. The lead ball bounced off the magically armored scales and struck the wall. She flung the rifle at the reptile in defeat.

Stephen yelled, "Flame his eyes out."

Dianna ran closer to the thing and sent a burst of flame at its head. The nightmare, trapped against the wall, covered its lidless eyes with its claws. The great reptilian wings formed a protective cloak around the entire form of the creature.

Stephen ran in and swung the diamond sword at the protective shell made by the creature's wings. The blade floundered on the magical scales. Stephen struck again, and a burst of orange engulfed the blade, shattering the glass sword. The broken glass made a bloody mess of Stephen's hands and face. He backed away with only superficial wounds.

He looked at Dianna, and she looked hysterical. Both of them realized their weapons were useless against the creature. Any blades seemed not to affect the creature. The fire only perturbed the monster, because the soft eyes had no lids in the bony orifice. Stephen gestured at Dianna to back away.

The wings swept behind the creature's form. The reptile's claws clenched, the sound clicking like a beetle. It ran at Dianna.

Stephen had only a moment to think. Reaching into his potion box strapped to his belt, he pulled out a vial with a blue, viscous liquid. The creature seemed to be concentrating on Dianna as it swept by Stephen, so he tossed the vial directly into its face.

He had been mistaken about the creature only concentrating on Dianna. The reptilian tail hammered into Stephen's chest. The blow flung him to the ground.

The creature screamed, clawing at its face. Lightning erupted from its maw. Its wings beating furiously as it flew higher. Crashing against the glass dome, it fell back to the ground. The dome shattered, raining glass down into the chamber. The thing howled in pain, thrashing its head. It lay on its back, floundering its limbs. A piece of shrapnel from the glass dome struck the creature's head. The mighty horns, face, fangs, and bony eye sockets burst into colorful pieces of ice. Decapitated, the monster's screams abruptly ended. The green reptilian ancient monster lay still.

"Is it dead?" screamed Dianna. She still felt the fear in her breast.

"I think so," replied Stephen quietly.

"What was the potion?" asked Dianna, as she slowly relaxed.

Stephen laughed and said, "A potion to make water into ice."

"Why would you have that?" wondered Dianna.

Stephen grinned and replied, "I made the potion because I like ice in my tea."

The statement seemed so outlandish that Dianna started chortling, then hiccupping, and finally just smiling at Stephen.

Stephen, drunk from emotion, steered his feet over the broken glass to stop at Soles battered body. Nudging Soles with his booted toe, he kicked his boot to wake him up.

Soles inhaled sharply and coughed, waving Stephen away. Stephen obliged and checked on Dianna. She had small cuts all over her face. Tears from laughing smeared the blood on her cheeks. Her leg bled from several cuts from the glass. Overall, she seemed physically sound.

"What do we do now?" asked Stephen disheartened.

"You act like you killed your mother," replied Soles.

"No," said Stephen, "but I feel like I killed a creature of grace."

"Grace," sputtered Soles. "That thing killed with no remorse. It has choked the life out of Viridian for generations, maybe for a thousand years."

"What do we do now?" asked Dianna. She felt just as lost as Stephen. The deed was done, but what next?

"The plan was for Big Ben to take its place," said Soles. "Now I don't know what to do."

"How were you planning on Big Ben to lead?" asked Stephen. "I mean, why would anybody follow him?"

"Zenith had a plan," growled Soles. "We replace Almanon with a sorcerer. There are still two tyrants bleeding the people that have to be dealt with. Either of them could turn their attention to Erimos. More than likely, they will attack Viridian. The loss of life will be horrendous, unless someone looked powerful enough to hold them off."

"The potions," realized Stephen.

"Yeah, the potions," said Soles. "It would seem like magic."

"Well," replied Dianna, "why don't you take control, Soles?"

"It wouldn't work," answered Soles. "I am too well known. I was supposed to be Big Ben's chancellor, his military leader or whatever."

"Dianna could lead," said Stephen. "I mean, she could rule Viridian."

"It's a thought," replied Soles. "It may even be a better idea; someone to nurture the people."

"I don't know. I am not exactly the nurturing type," said Dianna. "I can barely rule myself, much less a kingdom."

"It's settled," said Stephen with finality. "The best ruler will be Dianna; she doesn't crave power. Soles, you will help her."

"What about you?" asked Dianna, clasping Stephen's hand. "What will you do?"

"I'm going back over the mountain after winter, and I am taking anyone who wishes to be free," answered Stephen. "The people will bring a new age of technology and new ideas for Erimos. After what I have seen here in Viridian, we will need to develop. As your prince, the decision is final." Stephen's stomach churned from giving the order.

"Long live Queen Dianna Harken," shouted Soles, coming to stand at attention. "May she rule with justice!"

The Viridian tyrant dead. The Viridian people would see a new champion rise to the occasion of protecting the kingdom from the atrocities of war. The three adventurers' fates would not only decide who would rule Viridian—they could also create an entirely new world.